KIDNEY

KIDNEY

R K RAJ

PARTRIDGE

A Penguin Random House Company

To order additional copies of this book, contact
Partridge India
000 800 10062 62
www.partridgepublishing.com/india
orders.india@partridgepublishing.com

**One half of the world does not
know how the other half lives.**

Oxford Dictionary of proverbs

All socialism involves slavery.

Herbert Spencer

This work
is dedicated
to the person
wrapped in rags
as many
whom
I
saw picking his food from
the   garbage of a
dumping   yard in a good
colony at   eleven pm in
the night.   Being passed
by that night easily. But that
night is still   passing through
me. It is   passing through
my   self
my   area
my   city
my   state
my   nation
my   planet

Rue Summerlea in Lachine was quiet in the morning. So was Rue Sherbrooke. The streets were revealing the shiny grey of the concrete after peeling off the white of the snow for months. A cab ran off the street of Rue Sherbrooke towards Rue Victoria. Roaming roaring and ruing clouds were warning the warm weather of Montreal. The cab turned right to Autoroute du Souvenir and moved toward Montréal-Pierre Elliott Trudeau International Airport, Dorval, QC, Canada. Silence was kept awaken in the Quebec woods. Silence in the maples. Silence on the track along with Autoroute du Souvenir. Silence on the Rue. And, silence in the cab.

"Excuse me sir!" the silence vapored out with voice from the driving seat. The driver of the cab initiated the conversation with very formal and humble-fumble tone.

"Are you from Bangladesh?" the driver enquired with the passenger giving a deep V gaze on the face of the man sitting in the cab using the rear view mirror conveying his doubts. He kept looking ahead on the Rue Sherbrooke as well as at the passenger's face alternately.

"No" the passenger replied in firm formal tone and tilted his neck to look at the face of the person in driving seat.

"Pakistan?" he continued the daring doubting with consistent deepening V reflecting piercing searching sight on the passenger's face using the rear view mirror.

"No" replied the passenger, toggling his looking at the dash board and at the driver's face in the rear view mirror in the cab.

Feared frozen passenger doubting but somehow maintained magnificence of tone while really wanted to murmur in the ears of the policing person in the driving seat. The passenger started looking at clean shaven long oval face of the driver who searched for some label on passenger's forehead.

"India" clarified the passenger anticipating driver's further inspection about his label. He wanted to avoid further scrutiny.

Why the driver was asking so many questions? Why did he identify my looks with so many other places than India? Who was he? Where was he from? Why didn't he ask his friend who hired him to drop me at the Montreal Airport? Many more questions came to the passenger's mind.

Perhaps the passenger did not bother as his friend paid the driver in advance. Dollar mattered. He thought. What was the real matter then? That should not matter. He convinced himself.

"I am also from India" voice came from the driving seat hearing 'India' from the rear. The driver surprised the passenger engrossed in his own thoughts with beaming gleaming face of the driver who wanted to ensure a pleasant drop at the airport.

"Ok" replied the passenger. He concealed all the queries and thoughts running through body and mind after similar declaration came from the driving seat.

The passenger was not sure whether he was happy to know that the driver was also Indian. The driver's enquiries worried him about his own identity. His subconscious mind was not allowing him to express his happiness to meet another Indian in land farther from his place.

"Great!" the wowed voice came from driving seat.

"It is great to hear that you are also from India" he greeted the passenger.

Looked at driver's face the passenger smiled and got engrossed in his own thoughts. When the person in driving seat was also from India why was he looking for some Bangladeshi or Pakistani smell from him?

"Oh no!" the passenger could not see full face of the person in driving seat. Rear view mirror was showing the face slightly more than his eyes. Why he could not notice that *Indianity* when he boarded the cab for airport." he didn't realize it even when the person in driving seat was asking so many questions. He learned that some laureate has written one of his books on argumentative nature of Indians. He had seen the cover of the book on the book stalls at railway stations. He did not realize that the driver was sharing doubts with so certain labels. Oh, why it was only after the declaration from the seat in front. He looked at the driver who kept an eye on the road ahead and another on the maple trees and the train track running by side. With all those assets he could have really assessed the *Indianity* of the driver. So efficiently he was driving the cab. So efficiently he was doing multiprocessing.

"Madam is great" the driver discovered for the passenger who was still engrossed in his own thoughts.

"Whenever she had her Asian friends for short stay she calls me to give a drop at the departure from Montreal" the driver presented his profile how trustworthy he was for Ms. Veronique.

The passenger again smiled.

"So sir, I am here to make your travel and shopping comfortable and finally to drop you at the airport" the driver assured the passenger.

"Madam told me that you are very shy" he shared his knowledge about the passenger.

The passenger nodded.

"You speak very less. I am surprised to see that" said the person in driving seat.

The passenger again nodded. He was not sure whether it was driver's opinion or information from Ms. Veronique. He looked outside on the road.

"Sir, what for have you been here in this city?" the driver placed another query.

That time he asked the passenger with new zeal of *indi-bhai* delving interest in the purpose of the passenger's stay in the land of his opportunity. His daring dashing Indian confidence was noticeable in the mind-your-business land. That might be owed to the bond of the land they shared in the concepts that gave him that-much-openness to a closed person in that closely open culture. Light on the face and delight in the voice just took away the plight of people like him in the land of Richie rich but not so rich in that recession in the industry.

"Some conference work" the passenger answered.

"Sir, I am Amreek from Hoshiyarpur" the person in driving seat slowed the speed of the cab to introduce himself. He assumed that person in rear seat to be an IT guy from India coming for some conference.

The person in the rear seat nodded.

"You may be surprised to know that I was an IT guy before switching to this job six months ago" widening space for his neck in the collar with his left fingers he opened himself. He was impatient to share himself with someone from the land of his roots.

"Ok" the passenger agreed. He thought a lot about Amreek's sharing.

Amreek might know why he was sharing that all but the passenger in the rear didn't have any idea. "May be no Indian during past few weeks had hired him. May be the IT spark in his eyes was fading in that recession. May be he had hope from the passenger for some new avenues. May be this, may be that" similar thoughts engrossed the passenger's mind.

"Sir, you must be thinking that I am joking" Amreek looked into passenger's eyes in the rear view mirror to ensure his words were believed in the rear. "Sir, believe me, I could survive the first recession" he turned right to look at the passenger's face. He kept the passenger informed about him.

"Sir, you know it very well that almost every company has opened its facility, concern, or sister concern in India or china" looking ahead on the road Amreek continued his narration on the recession prevailing in the industry.

"Now, no plenty of software jobs in US for Americans and other immigrants" Amreek appraised the passenger about the job scenario in the land of opportunities. "American capitalists and industrialists fully exploit the dollar rupee ratio in their balance sheets" he continued turning his head time and again to look at the passenger. He opened his heart to pour the sour experience in the passenger's ears as if he further educated the passenger.

The passenger felt forced to nod. He again looked on the maple trees to avoid yawning.

"Sir, may I know your good name?" Amreek asked the passenger. "I started telling you my own story" he pretended to regret for that.

"No problem, I am listening your story" the passenger, an Indian gave space to another Indian. "Inder" he continued to answer.

"Sir, you must be working in Delhi" Amreek asked the passenger, He was not happy with that short answer. He doubted the Indian traits and found himself failing to make Inder open up with him.

"Hm . . . yes" Inder replied.

"Otherwise Indians from some small Indian city cannot afford to be here in Canada or US" Amreek explained Inder how he could guess right. Inder's short answers frustrated him. He bit his nail.

"One easiest way to attend conference is through lucrative jobs" Amreek came with new thesis.

Inder maintain his spell of silence in the cab.

"Indians in lucrative jobs make it possible in many ways to attend international conferences" Amreek continued on educating Inder on macroeconomics of the multinational companies and microeconomics of Indians. He also talked on principles of strategic economy, human selection of choices in general and Indian selection of nations in particular. Sensing longer spell of silence in the rear he realized that he might have hurt Inder on the account of being on visit with expenses by companies in India. He kept quiet and looked ahead on the road.

"Which place we are passing through?" Inder broke silence. He looked around the scene outside on the road.

"Rue Victoria" Amreek replied. He kept his answer short in apprehension that Inder might have felt hurt of his comments on visits of Indians in lucrative jobs.

"Sir, do you want something?" Amreek attempted to control possible damage.

"I want to buy some food items" said Inder feeling friendly with Amreek who was talking like master of IT economics and Indian political sociology. Amreek smiled as Inder was opening up.

"You told me your name. I forgot" Inder showed some interest.

"No problem sir" Amreek ignored Inder's ignorance. "I can tell my name as many times as you want" he said managing his feeling out of insignificance despite of being a green card holder. He moved in the safety belt to change the position in the limited space of the driving seat.

Amreek's cell phone rang up. He took the cab on the road side to stop and picked up the call. He pushed speaker part of the phone to his ears.

"Sir, it is Ms. Veronique telling me about the status of your flight" Amreek updated Inder. He felt jealous of Inder who got well-wisher in the no-one's-familiar-land.

"Your flight is delayed by six hours" said Amreek sharing information on flight to New Delhi.

"Oh no! What happened?" Inder looked at the clock in the cab.

"Most of the flights from other airports are diverted to Montreal because of smoke" Amreek said.

"Sir, why are you so sad after this news?" Amreek asked.

"I want to reach India as early as possible" Inder replied.

"I have seen most of the Indians are happy to see that they have maximum possible time when in the States or Canada for some conference" Amreek surprised Inder with his observation.

"May be" Inder shrugged.

"Yes" Amreek replied as if he could bet.

"Why?" novice Inder voiced with squinted brows.

"Inder sir" wise Amreek solaced Inder with his tips. He wanted to educate Inder on how Indians in most of the conferences were from big companies and how they kept an eye on their perks, allowances, hotel bills, etc. and the other on pink dual core two of snow-whites.

"For example" Amreek started to continue on educating Inder.

"You can call me Inder" Inder waved his hand to interrupt Amreek. He found Amreek wise. No one had talked to him for so long since he was in Montreal. Most of the information that Amreek shared was not available to Inder when he was in India.

"Ok sir, I mean Ok Inder" Amreek accepted the liberty.

"Yes, they utilize their time in window shopping in the nearby markets" Amreek pointed out at the buildings outside. "Most of men enjoy different type of window shopping. Do you know that?" he posed a funny query to Inder which Inder could not take as fun. He couldn't understand that.

"When great ladies are in the mall for shopping they blush with high rise milky base in the top" said Amreek seeing Inder in blank on dual core and window shopping. "These two high rise milky bases make the earth flourish with human population in the Milky Way and provide gazing and grazing grounds for men and his generations to come" he continued without noticing whether Inder was listening or not. He chose different words as he thought Inder was simple man and might not be comfortable with abstract symbolization. "Remember that grazing habits of the man when he was animal had enabled him to search grazing grounds as human race evolved" he poured in Inder's ears whatever came to his mind. "The two ridge contours make high rise plateau in a tight or regular top" he went with all sensuality which he could raise in himself and Inder to make Inder feel warmth of his company on the last day of his stay.

Inder was blank. He could neither understand nor appreciate that.

"Oh no, I have complicated the beautiful anatomy. What shall I call it?" said Amreek as if he was talking to himself.

"Let me call the dairy tops if milky base is not working for you" that time he did not look at Inder for approval.

Inder kept quiet. He was not sure why Amreek was amusing him up to that extent. "Was there any sensuality to be awakened to bring out the closeness?" the question puzzled him.

"Yes it is better, dairy tops in the top. Dairy tops create a window top upfront of the dress" he explained how they definitely created a window on low cut where tailors might have been more than generous. He continued educating Inder. He himself might be having all horny thorny feeling. "Tailors are also men most of the time. What they think is also around the dairy tops in the theory" he even thought for them to make topping slopes or topping high to make it understandable to novice Inder who was sitting untouched by the story.

Inder kept silent. He could not decide whether he should encourage Amreek who was determined on explaining every inch of woman. Once he thought he should appreciate Amreek's skills but he controlled himself. Amreek was unstoppable even without encouragement. If he had encouraged then Amreek might go lower in the waist, below the waist, in groin . . . in loin . . . then Amreek would have gone mad with bad. He stopped on his thoughts and forced himself to keep silent.

"These gazing grounds provide operating system for windows' shopping to men." Amreek explained it with computer technology.

"These are the windows which all men want to touch and feel as gazing creates hunger for grazing on the dairy tops in the top." Amreek turned back and looked at Inder's chest to continue. "Here most Indians get stuck while they are doing window shopping in the big mall." with body knowledge evolved under anthropological psychology he wanted to add to Inder's body of knowledge.

"And you know Inder, this is the basic reason that many of the travel guides written here guide these great ladies not to wear low cut dresses being in India." Amreek explained it with social responsibility when he found Inder was not in the participating shoes.

Though Inder would have been amazed by Amreek's talk on bodily knowledge but he could not think of encouraging Amreek. He thought, during his stay, he also could have kept his eyes wide open in order to get amazed and amused. But he didn't. He couldn't rather.

"So it is all window-shopping that they enjoy in extra innings" Amreek reached close to conclusion.

Inder stared at Amreek.

"You are not happy that means you are not in lucrative job" Amreek wanted to conclude on Inder's working identity.

Inder kept quiet. What kind of job he was in was haunting him when Amreek anticipated. That engrossed his attention for a while.

"Am I right?" Amreek's confidence demanded Inder's attention.

Inder nodded.

"So, now you have two choices either to go back to Ms. Veronique's place and have lunch or stay here in Montreal till evening. If you choose to be at her place then I will pick you up from there in the evening to give you drop to the airport. Other way is to have a look around the area and have lunch in this area itself and spend your time with me." Amreek became generous to present those two choices.

"Let me tell you Ms. Veronique is leaving for Ottawa for follow up work of the conference." Amreek told Inder about risky and unpleasant factors of the first choice.

"Is going back to her place a good option?" Inder asked himself.

"Has she left the key or not? If I go back and stay there for few hours then how will I come back to the airport? Amreek will leave me there. What if he didn't come back to pick me up?" many questions occupied Inder's mind.

Amreek looked here and there on road and park nearby. He didn't bother Inder.

"I am suggesting you to be here in the places near airport" Amreek interrupted Inder's chain of thoughts. Inder was silent with brows narrowed to meet each other on his forehead. Amreek found it simple but what was puzzling Inder was not in his imagination.

"But it is still not advisable to go back as here in the States and Canada people love their space and they take it as aggression if someone enters their space. She has already asked me to be with you till you board the aircraft. So, I am at your service till you get your seat" Amreek interrupted with another spell of education then on people and culture in America.

"Ok" scared Inder surrendered.

"So where were we? What we were talking about?" said Amreek looking thinking, posing thinking and digging into thoughts to educate Inder. Perhaps he didn't have any Indian in his cab for many days.

"Yes, you asked my name" Amreek reminded Inder.

"Yes" Inder voiced his nod.

"Let me tell you the story why my name is Amreek" Amreek wanted to write a book on Inder's mind. "The story is so interesting that you will always remember my name" he continued with new zeal.

Inder compromised on the other option.

"Sir, when I was born in a village of Hoshiyarpur in Punjab where America and England enjoyed the status of dreamland among the people who love English even if they don't speak. Even when they don't know" Amreek opened his arms as if he started unwrapping his story.

Inder looked around. He didn't find a suitable place to spend the remaining time.

"What to do sir, the magic of English had worked in our life that way only." Amreek resumed storytelling.

Inder looked at him. He validated people like Amreek in his mind.

"You like it even when you don't know. You love it even when you don't have any idea how to understand the language." Amreek said.

Inder nodded neither in 'yes', nor in 'no', but he nodded. Amreek took that a nod to begin the story on the same note.

Amreek's voice became heavier and made Inder to worry. Inder didn't imagine that such a smart IT professional turned driver had so deep wounds.

Amreek illustrated how people in Hoshiyarpur nourished that affection of liking and loving English. After all they all were *Hoshiyarpur ke hoshiyar* or intelligent people of land of intelligence.

"I am not sure whether that affection was for their English language or English pound or American dollars. That also he came to know later why that love was there at first place." Amreek with grim on his face informed Inder.

Inder's nod affirmed to Amreek as he could relate to the subject in that state.

"Educated *hoshiyars* kept their love alive for visits to this land. Undereducated or illiterate *hoshiyars* also made their way to these lands through their relatives or other labor contractors" Amreek fixed right fingers with his left ones.

Inder moved from the place he was standing on the roadside.

"Uneducated *hoshiyars* named their sons on English rank of the Raj. They used to name them as *Jarnail Singh, Brigadier Singh, Karnail Singh, Kaptan Singh, Collector Singh, Tehsildar Singh* etc. on the line of army and administrative ranks." Amreek gave an idea how he would go on storytelling.

Inder looked at him thought that interrupting Amreek on any matter might lengthen the story.

"My grandfather wished his son had gone to America to earn money. But somehow his son or my father could not get educated properly and didn't fulfill my grandfather's dream." Amreek said to set the sad note of the story.

Worried Inder looked around and vehicles passing fast on the road.

Inder could not get the time to think on his own education and comparison with that great grandson of Hoshiyarpur as Amreek didn't let him speak few words in continuity.

"Then my grandfather and father soon realized that neither of them could go to America." Amreek looked in sky as if he was talking to his forefathers. Whether that was a complaint or appreciation about his grantparents Inder was not sure. He wondered why Amreek looked up in the sky in Canada when he knew that his parents and fore fathers lived in India the opposite side of the planet. He thought it to be human habit to look upon not down.

"Then my birth got to happen" Amreek pointed at his chest and broke Inder's engrossment.

Inder smiled to amuse Amreek who struck a sad note of his life.

"I was new hope for them that one day I would be going to America." Amreek took a long breath before he continued.

"They named me as Amreek Singh to keep it on the top of their mind that one day I have to go to America." Amreek's voice got feeble before throat got dried but his eyes didn't remain dry after that.

Inder raised his hand to stop but Amreek shook head to say everything was ok.

"This is how I got my name as Amreek Singh" Amreek said.

"So they named me Amreek Singh as if the name itself would land me in America." Amreek sighed. He again looked up in the sky.

"Hm" Inder said. He could see all-knowing Amreek was in tears.

Amreek told how he got his name. He looked at his wrist watch and preferred standing on the roadside as there was no hurry to catch flight. There was no hurry even for roaming around as no shop, no mall, or no office was open to take Inder around.

"They brought me up with the hope that one day I would go to America." Amreek started again.

Inder looked at Amreek. He looked at cab and nodded.

"Later in my life I came to know how name may be playing a vital role in shaping the fate of the person." Amreek revealed from experience. "Sir, you can see how close my name is with America" he illustrated. He moved towards the cab. Inder followed him. He opened the door to get into the driving seat. The cab ran the road.

Supporting his chin on left palm with elbow resting on the other seat in the front leaning towards the driving seat Inder showed interest in Amreek's story.

Amreek was happy to see that kind of interest paid by a passenger. The cab was passing by Parc Lassale. Seeing Inder's interest Amreek suggested to stop at Parc Lassale and spend some time.

Again Inder didn't show any agreement or disagreement with Amreek. Taking Inder's silence as agreement Amreek took right turn to enter the parking of the park.

"Let us spend some time here in this park" said beaming Amreek.

"Why Amreek is taking me to the park?" Inder asked himself. He did not find any logic other than passing the time.

"Inder sir, let's spend some time here in the park" Amreek again asked. "Still we have lot of time" he added in clarification as Inder did not move from his seat. He looked at Amreek with tinges of suspicion.

"Don't worry, the park is open for everyone and it is morning only" Amreek said to assure Inder.

Inder shook his head.

"This is a safe place, why are you so scared?" asked Amreek scratching his head. Perhaps he wanted to understand Inder's dilemma.

"Even evenings and nights are very safe in Canada" Amreek attempted another round of assurance.

"Hm" Inder said without moving from the seat.

"There are two reasons for me to take you in the park" Amreek took notice of Inder's reluctance. "Sir, your body will have cramps after sitting in the cab for long. And driving and talking can't go together for a longer period" he explained. "Sir, we are not in India where you can keep talking along with your drive through cities and suburbs" he showed his helplessness.

Scared Inder clenched on the back of the front seat. He felt unsafe with the idea of looking for safe place.

"Inder sir, you need to pass this waiting time" Amreek got Inder's unease. "May be on the road, may be in the park like this, may be in the bar or mall if we have money." Amreek intended to clarify his intentions. He wanted to say that gas in the cab was not free and he could not roam around endlessly. He could have dropped Inder at airport in the morning itself. It was Ms. Veronique who required him to be there with Inder.

Inder did not object then.

"Inder sir" Amreek again requested Inder to come out of the cab.

Sir Inder had to surrender as there were few options with many doubts. Inder stepped out from the cab and took few steps to pace with Amreek. Round the arch on the ground they took many steps together to reach the gate of the park. People smiled at both of them when they entered the gate. Inder had been to such places closed to Ms. Veronique's house during conference. When Canadian or other people greeted Inder with smile he also exchanged the greetings with equally beaming smile. He found that smile to be different.

Amreek pointed out at a corner of the park. Inder followed him. He moved farther in the corner. He saw a bench in the other half of the park.

Following Amreek in baseball field, Inder noticed unusual attraction among men watching match between local baseball teams. Many of them were sitting as if they were in man-woman kind of relationship. They were making couple like relationship with rubbing each other's back. Few of them were touching, stroking, cuddling, caressing and kissing the other person. Few other couples were just leaving the baseball field and started moving towards benches in the tree. In those lonely trees many of them are busy attempting to hug each other as if they were going to make love like that between male female. In India that kind of relationship he heard was very bad. That was not fitting in his value system. He was not aware of gayism getting its acceptance in the land of free.

Being normal thing gayism might not have left impact on Inder. What disturbed him was that a comment one of the young boys gave with mysterious smile when he was following Amreek. A tall boy rubbed his chest with his friend's hand. His eyes followed Inder. "Well, Indians are also progressing" Inder heard him whispering in his friend's ear.

"People in Mumbai are far ahead in this game" his friend corrected him on Indian advancement in that new kind of relationship between man and man.

All the hair or to be hair in the pores of Inder's skin got straightened. Inder found himself in Amreek's trap. Had Amreek also progressed up to that level to embrace the culture of free? Why Amreek had invited him to follow in corner and that too remote part of the park? Why Amreek had that kind of intentions? Those ideas scared him a lot.

Afraid Inder collected his manly strength to face the situation. He planned to revolt and prepared himself to make his journey to airport on his own. What would he do if Amreek touched his hand? He might call the cop for help. Thoughtful Inder reminded himself that he had to leave for India. The cop coming to rescue might detain him for hours. He might miss his flight in that case. That might be one possibility. So he didn't find that idea to work. Then he found it would be better to run away from the scene. Preparing to manage to reach the airport on his own he stopped following Amreek.

Amreek looked to find Inder stopped following him. He came back and gave a big smile to Inder.

"I also would have thought the same thing that you are thinking" Amreek said. Inder was standing on the road in middle of the park and pretended to wait for traffic to pass.

"These things are normal here" Amreek came closer to Inder and requested to follow him.

Inder did not object at that moment. Perhaps he prepared to face the situation that was still in future but present in Inder's mind.

They both crossed Tenth Avenue and moved under the trees in the park. Inder was already puzzled with many thoughts. Might be he was puzzled with notions of fear and uncertainties. Close to the park boundary Amreek moved towards the bench and asked Inder to settle on the bench.

Inder noticed that Amreek had located a bench in quite lonely place in the park. Inder looked around the park could not find other bench in surrounding area of the park. So he reached the bench.

"What have you made so slow?" Amreek attempted to understand Inder suspicions. He could not understand Inder's reactions. He thought Inder might have heard about that.

"Nothing" Inder pulled out his hanky to wipe his sweating face. Inder attempted to hide what was running though him.

"Inder, you might have got disturbed seeing the display of these kinds of relationships here." Amreek said as if he was Inder's tourist guide. He wanted to comfort puzzled Inder.

Inder just stared at Amreek and did not say anything. Though he planned to run away from the scene but he couldn't.

"These relationships might be unusual in India" Amreek said.

"I have heard and read many times some news and statements from Mumbai on these relationships. Awareness of rights of the people in such relationships is emerging in India also." Amreek again started to enlighten Inder but on another area. He wanted Inder not to lose anything.

Inder looked up in the sky and looked around in the park as if he wanted some miraculous escape.

"You may get surprised as it is not so open in New Delhi. Emotional and physical relationship between two men or two women may be in practice in India also. You can look at great houses of fashion industry and even Bollywood for that matter" Amreek opened his palms as if he wanted to open Inder's eyes. "Bollywood and fashion industry are commanding lifestyles of eight hundred million Indians. Much water has flown from Bombay to Banaras. It is still peaceful as it has not caught fire. Man likes man, man loves man, man lives with man, etc. Woman likes woman, woman loves woman, woman lives with woman. This may be a far possibility in India. But here it is normal in the land of free." Amreek said as if he forgot to breathe in between in a hurry to enlighten Inder.

"In the land of free" Inder repeated.

"Yep" Amreek quipped.

"Yes, in the land of free" Amreek also repeated to speak further.

Inder looked away from the places in the park to avoid the topic.

"You may be thinking you are free in free India. You may be right in your world. Let me tell you one thing that usually an Indian's world is complex structure of pride of history, selective passion and selective aversion of history, parsing and recursion of history, overflowing contents of *samskar*, inhibitions of *samskar*, segregation of *samskar*, classification of *samskar*, division of *samskar*, religion of *samskar*, etc. etc." Amreek transferred his experience gained in the dollar-land to Inder from the motherland. "I partially may agree with you that India is free" Amreek said giving a bit of solace to Inder who still appeared uncomfortable.

Inder neither agreed with Amreek not disagreed. He thought what kind of knowledge Amreek possessed.

"Indians are free under some authority or other and that too person specific and person dependent." Amreek shared his views as if he was talking as socio legal expert. "Here that authority is rule of law" he immediately completed. "Indians are free in one sense. They are free to imagine, they still may not be free to think." American Amreek opined on India.

Inder did not object on what Amreek opined. Perhaps he found Amreek right. He found Amreek was right in the current context too as he did not find himself free to express his reservations over issue of coming to that park itself. He didn't have confidence in Amreek's intentions. Otherwise Amreek would not have been passing through baseball field where many of the locals were enjoying that they were free. A man was free to like another man, to love another man, to live with another man. That was why Amreek explained that freedom in details to keep the topic live. He could not even imagine. Means he was not free. He was not free even to imagine.

"What are you thinking Inder?" Amreek asked putting his hand on Inder's shoulder.

Inder moved out instantly. He jettisoned Amreek's hand and stood up.

"What happened?" Amreek raised his brows.

"Nothing" Inder said.

"Why are you standing away then? Just relax on this bench" Amreek urged. "Just relax" he rubbed his hands to convince Inder.

"I will relax in the plane" Inder said. He still hid his doubts about Amreek's intentions.

"Inder just don't doubt my intentions" Amreek shared what he noticed. Inder was not comfortable since they decided to spend some time in that park. He was surprised why Inder agreed to come there. He found it right that Indians were not free to think. Inder was not free to think. Inder might have imagined something fearful and fed with assumed bad intentions. He could have dropped him as early as possible. He could have taken another passenger.

"You are cool, just relax. Come on Inder" Amreek pacified Inder. He maintained distance. Inder's snapping his hand gave him alert.

Inder kept quiet. He didn't move to sit down on the bench.

"I don't know what has gone into you? We can discuss the matter friendly" Amreek wanted to maintain friendliness. He found himself on receiving end. He feared the situation and looked around. He got scared as if Inder might call cop.

Inder still didn't say anything.

"Are you having any problem? Tell me Inder sir, we are more like friends now" Amreek wanted to win Inder's confidence.

"You are not having good intensions" Inder collected courage to express himself.

"What?" Amreek almost shouted as if he got a shock. "This is shocking! It's shocking to me Inder" he came with his open palms.

15

He also stood up. He posed like he surrendered. Perhaps he wanted to surrender to Inder's imagination.

"What's that? That I am not having good intentions for you?" Amreek vexed. Still he wanted to talk and clear the misunderstanding. "What happened? How do you conclude so badly on my intentions for you?" he could not be comfortable. He spoke out of frustration.

Inder did not react.

"I am with you since morning, I want you comfortably spend last hours of your stay in Montreal. I don't want you to remember me with bad experience. Speak out what is there in your mind. I am your friend" Amreek repeatedly explained. He pleaded rather.

"But I don't want to be your girlfriend or boyfriend" suddenly Inder got strength.

"Oh no, is this in your mind?" Amreek held head with both his hands.

Silence prevailed around the bench.

"What makes you conclude so? May I know with your kindheartedness?" Amreek found it pathetic at least for himself.

Inder kept quiet.

Amreek could not understand why Inder had concluded so badly on his intentions. How part of the story he might have some idea. He realized the triggers in the park and baseball field to make Inder conclude like that. "It is very unfortunate. I don't understand what has been wrong on my part?" he wanted to clarify.

Inder didn't say anything. He took a big maple leaf to extend the length of silence.

"I am sorry, I just thought this park is on the way and we can talk here comfortably." Amreek regretted. "I still have powerful and good intentions for you." Amreek wanted to open his heart to show the niceties of his intentions for Inder.

But Inder didn't move by revelations.

"I didn't have any idea that we were passing through baseball and other triggers had so deep impact on your sense of anticipation." Amreek kept on lamenting over the situations. "Forgive me for that all" he again regretted.

"Ok" Inder said.

"I thought I would tell you why I was named as Amreek and how I happened to be in this land. But I caused you land up to have great setback first and then misunderstanding." Amreek shook his head in regret. He shook his head in disgust too.

"Now, h . . . h . . . how can I make you believe that my intentions for you are to help you in this strange city?" Amreek stammered. He put his hand on right cheek to support his tilted head after that plea.

"It is Ok" Inder said and sat down on the other end of the bench.

Silence filled the space.

Amreek kept quiet. He didn't dare to speak then. He found that Inder was really free to imagine anything. Minutes passed in that silence. Silence set both of them free to imagine.

"You told that your grandfather and father named you Amreek and brought you up hoping that you would be in America someday." Inder made it normal to begin again.

"Great! People who think a lot have good memory." Amreek admired Inder.

"I was not a good student in my school days" Amreek resumed. "But I had to fulfill my parents' dream to go to US, the land of dollars. I could not get admission to graduation in engineering discipline." Amreek's voice got dryness from his past.

"In the beginning I did not have much interest in studying engineering. This disappointed my parents" explained Amreek to continue "What was making it interesting to me was only one thing. My parents when my grandfather passed away reminded me daily that my grandfather's dream was to be fulfilled. 'Amreek has to go to *Amreeka*,' they used to remind me every day" Amreek opened up the memory lanes so concealed so far.

Inder nodded to let Amreek know that he was listening.

"One day my father's friend had shown him one advertisement in newspaper showing a course in Computers. He told my father that after completing that course there were good chances for me to get a job in the States. My father showed that newspaper to me. That day I had to develop my interest in computers to keep my father's hope alive. My father arranged fee to get me admitted to that course. I completed the course at slow pace. Faculty and friends at the institute helped me in placement also" thus Amreek re-created his past for Inder.

"After difficulties in the beginning I started liking my work" he said. "The sense of responsibility went deep into me when I found my father running in debt for my education." Amreek continued on revelations. "I joined a company where I got to work in account section. There I used to work using 'tally'. Then I realized working in 'tally' and in keeping accounts of the firm as routine won't help me getting good salary." he looked at Inder to find whether Inder was taking interests in his life or not.

Inder nodded in agreement. He could identify some similarities with his own past.

"I started looking for other opportunities. Java was hot cake during those days. I had to have hands-on on Java. That too was too challenging for me. Perhaps by attitude I was not a programmer otherwise today's children in school days have good Java skills." Amreek continued as Inder signaled intense listening. "I used to worry a lot about my future" he said creating those worries on his face. "I started to study to develop skills in Java. That took me few months as I had to do that all in evening or night in different set up. I got that hands-on and comfortable level of programming in Java. Then switched to an IT based company" he took a break. He breathed a long.

"Around a year of job in the new company gave me strength and confidence to apply for the jobs abroad. Meanwhile I got married. So having a job in hand became another necessity. Risk taking capability of mine got dim after marriage. So it took one more year to have a job in the States. Thus, I came here in America. Everything was going well and then came the slowdown that somehow I survived." Amreek revealed further.

Inder looked for his enlightenment in Amreek's story. He was surprised that people like Amreek could make it to be in the land of dollars and opportunities. He also could have made it true for himself.

"Next slowdown brought me tough times. My wife could not do much to help ourselves. She has been house wife for many years. My parents have visited me twice since I left for the States. They liked to be with us but could not keep themselves in good health." Amreek paused after long narration. "I could not understand why they could not keep good health neither in the States nor even in Canada which is considered a good place to live in from the health perspectives. That was a setback to me" he gasped a lot in narrating uncomfortable incidents of his past.

"Health is the function of happiness and experience of love and affinity" came to Inder's mind but he didn't express that in reacting to Amreek's story.

"Now they keep in good health in India amidst of pollution and traffic chaos." Amreek shared the mystery with surprise. "I am happy for them but surprised to see that they are happy in country where every year as many as 370 thousand people die of disease such as tuberculosis alone. Half a million die of asthma. More than a million get malaria and hundreds of millions get dengue every year. When life is not easy over there my parents keep healthy. Isn't that strange? Isn't that miraculous? Isn't that magical?" he poured down all the knowledge to show how well he was connected to India.

"Let them be happy there" Inder opined.

"If they had been living with me it would have been helpful for me in many ways." Amreek revealed. They named their son Amreek so that he would be in America to make fortunes and they themselves are not happy in America. This is still a riddle to me. Is it not a paradox?" he spread his arms. He wanted to know from Inder. He didn't know Inder's limitations. He didn't have any idea.

Inder tightened his lips then he protruded them. He wanted to hold his thoughts undisclosed.

"Why don't you go back to India?" Inder suggested spontaneously.

"Good question!" Amreek bounced with new energy level as if he was expecting that question from Inder. "I can get a good job in an IT company over there. I won't need to drive a cab like this. My parents can live with me. I can look after them in a better way. I will enjoy good friend circle and society in India. These ideas must have been mending your question" mind reader Amreek verified with Inder.

Inder nodded.

"I am here for many reasons" Amreek came with heavy heart.

Inder looked at Amreek.

"I will get a good job in an IT company in India" Amreek started. "True! Then salary?" his analytic mind came with question. "Frequent recession or slowdowns have already sent thousands of engineers and non-graduate developers back to India. Most of the giant MNCs have opened up their centers in India to keep their stock rising in America. Reason is obvious. Dollar rupee ratio! Thousands of engineers have already moved to these branches in India to save their jobs. Not only Indians many Americans or Europeans also have opted out to work in India" he paused. "So my dear sir, getting a good job in an IT company in India is quite challenging now. Basically, I am not a graduate engineer so good salary in the beginning may not ensure growth" he presented his analysis.

Inder listened Amreek. He thought what kind of person Amreek was. So what if Amreek would not get that much money in India but he would be with his parents.

"Moreover, this US returned technical person working in an MNC or Indian company cannot drive a cab in India to maintain his social prestige or US returned image." Amreek pointed with fingers on his chest. "Here, many Indians drive cab in part time at present which has become full time job for me. You see that nobody bothers here. We Indians don't have society as such" he opened his box on experience of sociology. "Neither friend circles nor social circles. Even if we have then most of the time they all are Indians and understand each other. When I get a job again here, I can continue driving this cab as part time job for four hour. That can bring dollars sufficient to take care of my parents" his hand goes tightly rubbing on his pocket. "I don't have to save money or cut from my family budget. Income from driving here is sufficient for my parents' wellbeing in India because of dollar-rupee difference. Here no work is small but in India that is the main thing. The work menial to mental brings in a scale for prestige to an Indian in the society" intelligent analyses came from Amreek.

"Coming to the other aspect like my parents can live with me when I am in India. Right" Amreek sought Inder's agreement.

Inder nodded. He thought that Amreek might not have experienced that Indians in India were also divided in many groups. There were more than three thousand groups or castes where people seek their affinity. He found that even in India we have neither friend circles nor society but *panchayats* and *mahasabhas*.

"See the ground realities of relatonomics" Amreek shared his intellectuality with Inder.

"Relatonomics!" Inder shared his surprise with the word.

"Inder, you may be surprised with relatonomics. Let me tell you my dear that this theory is an outcome of intellectual exercise on my own" he bragged upholding his collar.

Inder smiled.

"Relatonomics is a social phenomenon which displays synonymous behavior on relationship under anticipated futuristic economy in which the economy of a relation is under a cohesive hemosphere. Hemosphere is significant" professor Amreek bragged to drag Inder deep into the discussion. He forgot that Inder was already stuffed to the extreme. "This hemosphere may have adhesive compulsions as constraints" he added to complete the statement for his theory.

"Hemosphere!" puzzled Inder repeated. He was already puzzled with relatonomics.

"Yes hemosphere. I will explain it later" spreading arms and then holding the back of the neck Amreek assured Inder on hemosphere.

Inder pressed his head with both of his palms as another Intellectual endeavor from Amreek had come on it. He could not free himself from earlier riddle.

"I know what your confusion is" professor Amreek accepted Inder's confusion with his all-knowing attitude.

"Hemosphere is not a familiar term for you in the sense it should be." Amreek said. "It is a social term rather" he deduced to explain the term.

Inder kept pressing his forehead. He was left with single choice.

Listen. Listen. And only listen.

"Well this is a hypothesis on social phenomenon in which impact of economy on blood relationships is considered as major factor to influence behavior while relatonomics covers all possible kind of relationships that person happens to enter." Amreek drew difference in similarities of his theories like a perfect intellectual. "The economy of relations leaves dynamic impact on the economy of another relation of hemosphere" he continued.

Inder held his cranial sphere to hold his brain intact.

Inder watched Amreek's narration. He listened too. He could not make what he would get out of Amreek's theory of relatonomics based hemosphere.

"Hemosphere is like our biosphere and consists of blood relations created with blood related socioeconomic entities in politico legal framework." Amreek articulated his hemosphere as if he was a domain expert of the field. He assumed a wide projector and white screen in the air where he was free to write anything which Inder could listen but he only could read.

Inder started taking interest in Amreek's intellectual capabilities. Baseball field impact got wiped away from his mind.

Maples breezed between ecosphere and relatonomics if not hemosphere.

"Coming to the point" Amreek played responsible to bring Inder and himself where Inder was not writing on any note book but on his *tabula rasa.* "My wife is enjoying the degree of freedom that is not possible for her being in India" he attempted to illustrate his theory.

Inder listened as the only choice. He did not dare to make session interactive.

"Whenever parents were here with us in US and Canada they depended on both of us for everything they needed. Wife enjoyed complete freedom. She was happy to teach her mother-in-law on the traits and culture and rights and wrongs of this land. My parents thought it to be the culture of the land that may require this kind of freedom for ladies." Amreek presented one more aspects of his intellectual capabilities.

Inder found a continuous stream of teaching from Amreek. He got convinced that Amreek's wife also might have been great teacher to Amreek's parents.

"This is one big reason that my wife doesn't want to go back to India." Amreek confessed. "When my parents were here they also gave full freedom to my wife as there was no body to make them feel that they were parents-in-laws and my wife should obey them. My mother learnt from my wife on how to behave in the malls, on the road crossings, or being at public places" he revealed what was a tick for his wife being in America. "This gave her upper hand over my mother or her mother-in-law. Such things you can't imagine for her being in India" he came with his expertise on household matters.

Inder looked at Amreek's face with no words in his mouth to agree or disagree.

"So Inder, taking care of parents is close to a fantasy for a parent-caring-wife-loving-social-Indian husband." Amreek explained sociological hinds of his theory. "Economic dependence of these socioeconomic legal entities which we call relations at this stage is so socioeconophysiofeeble in the high of DNA extension. At the DNA level we have not been aware of it till recently. These blood driven entities of which one subject molecule can drag the object molecule closure may be explained as hemosphere." he proudly propounded his theory.

"You must be eager to know, Why hemosphere?" Amreek asked Inder to ask.

Inder got mesmerized. He looked at Amreek who took that as approval to explain further.

"I'll tell you why hemosphere" Amreek took lead. "Because the blood carries one 'iron' or 'hemo' atom to carry oxygen as oxides to the entire body, similarly, money also is required to carry oxygen to maintain relations to keep alive in the social body. Men live in groups" he left Inder mesmerized.

"Relatonomics is an art that can be used in predicting these scientific aspects of money to get shared among the relations to have them cared, nurtured, cultured, nourished, flourished mostly within the boundary of hemosphere." Amreek described the subject and phenomena of relatonomics using the concept of hemosphere.

"Relatonomics makes you wise to keep balance of your relations with money supply to compensate the blood supply. Money supply is proportional to relative intensity of hemosphere. Other parameters like space, time, comfort, pain, etc. make the complex of hemosphere." Amreek explained the theory with its components and possibilities of further corollaries.

"So when I am in the other part of the globe I find myself more closely related to my parents than being in India. In India I would have been struggling for maintaining bare minimum kind of relationship with my parents in dearth of money supply. Even if I could have spared some money to be remitted to my parents than that would have been at the cost of happiness in molecular hematite or you call my nuclear family." Amreek explained the application of relatonomics in his own case to make Inder understand it better.

"They are happy in India as I am able to manage for their expenses. My wife is happy as she is enjoying freedom of being head mistress of the family." Amreek said. He didn't dare to reveal his wife's stand that she could think of taking up the job even as nanny but is not prepared to go back to India. "My kid is happy with small dreams at young age. I am happy as I find myself being able to manage happiness of all these members of my hemosphere." he was sure that his speech made sense to Inder who was looking at the watch on Amreek's left wrist.

"We have enough time to discuss about our relations, conditions, and passions." Amreek said. He wanted Inder to forget looking at his watch. Listener like Inder was rare for Amreek in the land of mind-your-own-business.

"Moreover, the impact of conversion ratio is commanding the economics on health beyond geographical and politico legal boundaries. I am also driven by this" Amreek said to begin another analysis perhaps. "There in India I would be earning rupees 100,000 out of which around

25,000 I would be paying tax. 20,000 I need spare for my parents, out of 55,000 left I would have to manage a good house by paying 20,000 as rent and minimum 15,000 on kid's schooling, then where is money if you discount these 20,000 that I am left with. With this I have to manage a car, entertaining social circle to maintain social prestige to enjoy the US returned status" he detailed out his probable pie in India.

"Can you manage all those things with merely rupees 20,000?" Amreek asked Inder to participate in the explanation of his theory.

Inder kept quiet. He did not decide what to speak. Figure of 20000 appeared before his eyes with big four zeros with meager two.

"Even by earning 100,000 per month I would be living like pauper. I would have been dying to spend lavishly among all my social conduces to show an imitable social status." Amreek lamented on the economic components of the scenarios created around the world after saturation in almost all high tech industries. He knew that inflation had marred all lucrativeness of luxurious IT jobs in India.

Inder looked around at empty part of the park. He thought Amreek preferred to live like a pauper there but not in a city of his own country. Might be altogether new society, new culture, and new opportunities were to make that magic to happen.

Amreek started to speak as soon as he could catch Inder eyes which were panning around in the park, "And, I can't drive over there in part time. Disclosing that may take away my IT job so I may again be left only with driving the cab. While taking care of my parents in better way. I am sparing dollar 400 per months for my parents and managing my homely affairs very well even with meager amount of dollar 2,500 per month. Here nobody bothers whether I am a part-time cab driver or pizza boy and working in IT company or hardware giant or not. I can still manage to send more dollars to my parents."

Inder could listen some dollars, some counts, and some figures that were entire he could focus after being defocused with figure of 20,000 rupees.

"Here living is not that costly that it is in India. I can still manage some surplus dollars every month. While living like pauper here wouldn't be hurting anyone as everybody knows that Indian have come here to earn money so they can't burn money on pomp and show. Look at other side, in India we need to burn more and more money on transport then only we can move from one place to another. In India a State returned has to maintain balance of earn/burn ratio" unstoppable Amreek kept imparting financial wisdom to Inder. He wanted Inder to listen his theories and his wisdom so that he can get benefit in the future if it was not available in the present.

Inder was also getting impressed with Amreek's financial wisdom. He could get some sense from Amreek's stay in the states.

"Enjoyment of social circle comes with huge cost at any place. Here in America whether the States or Canada we Indians meet with Indians after weighing all the financial considerations. Conversion rate is the central theme for consolidation, conciliation of all our actions and ideas. An 'Up' with conversion rate increases the level of our living and lavishing not only here but our relations in India also. But a 'down' in the conversion also creates more pauper behavior sometimes which is contrary to American culture of spending and relishing on what you have in the present. It is against what we believe and love exponentiation of our savings." Amreek spread his hands as if he was writing an article on social Wall Street which Inder might think was in the air.

Inder looked at Amreek with awe.

"These are few of the many reasons that make me 'not' back to India." Amreek concluded closing his hands first in the air to expect some query from Inder. He then closed his arms on his chest as Inder didn't have any query but awe created by Amreek's theories and corollaries.

Inder looked at the watch on left wrist open on the closed arms on Amreek's chest. Then he looked at Amreek's face.

"That's all for a while" Amreek gestured as if he was done on his part. He also looked at the watch to find that around four hours were spent since they moved from Ms. Veronique's place.

"Tell me something about yourself, your native place . . ." Amreek invited Inder to share.

Inder still kept quiet. What he should share he was not sure. Perhaps he was sure for what he was already doing, listening to Amreek.

"Don't worry sir, Indians have similar problems" he asked Inder again to share his experience in Montreal, Canada, etc.

"*Kya bataoon*" Inder thought. "Is there anything that I can share with Amreek whom I meet today only? How can I share myself with him?" Inder went into his own mind but didn't tell Amreek.

"OK, if you don't want to share, it is OK for me" Amreek freed Inder to confine. "What about lunch?" he asked.

"Aur kitni der lagegi flight mein?" Inder talked to himself. He was planning to have his lunch during the flight only.

"There is enough time to eat. You can do some shopping also" replied Amreek anticipating Inder's self-talk.

Inder didn't ask anything. He thought it would be dinner time in the flight.

"We will go to some small place to eat. We will not shop" he got an idea about what was going on in Inder's world.

Inder agreed.

"Let's move" Amreek pressed his knees with both hands and jumped to move out of the bench.

Inder followed Amreek. He chose a restaurant of his liking. Inder would like that. He thought.

James reclined in the seat placed by the window in the room. Service boy knocked the door.

James opened the door to find a service boy with morning tea.

"Bonjour Monsieur" said the service boy with morning warmth in his voice and beaming face.

"Good morning" James smiled at the service boy.

"Sir, your tea" service boy requested to come in the room to serve the tea.

"Thanks" James replied. He looked at the golden handle of the service table in boy's grip. The service boy came into the room. The boy started to prepare a cup of tea for James. Handset of the intercom in the room started ringing. He took the handset to attend the call.

"Bonjour Monsieur" James received morning greetings from the receptionist of the hotel.

"Good morning" James replied. He looked at the service boy who was preparing morning tea for him.

"Mr. Hwaib of Planet Health Organization wants to meet you" receptionist requested James.

"Please send him to the room" said James.

"Merci Monsieur" the receptionist wanted to end the call. James waved his hand to the service boy to stop preparing the tea.

"Please prepare one more tea" James asked the service boy. He showed his five to signal the service boy to delay tea.

"Yes sir" said the service boy.

"*Thuk, thuk . . .*" knock at the door.

Service boy opened the door.

"Thanks Jacob" Hwaib said reading the name plate of boy who escorted from the reception. Hwaib turned to enter the room.

"Good morning James" Hwaib greeted James.

"Good morning" James' voice warmed up the room. He stood from the chair to greet Asia head of PHO.

"Let's have our tea. By the way I called you up for morning tea." James signaled the boy to serve the tea. He looked at the clock in the room. "Please feel comfortable" he said. He pointed at the other chair in the room.

"Thanks" Hwaib settled in the chair. "I couldn't locate your room, so I went to the receptionist to get me here" he replied.

"Veronique introduced me to a boy from India." James informed Hwaib.

"She once talked to me also about that" Hwaib confirmed the information.

"The lady is mad to improve the lot of such people from the third world. She has managed to bring the boy to this conference also." James updated Hwaib on further developments. "Most of the times like other participants of his country he kept quiet in the conference. But that was quite obvious from this boy" he shared few of his observations during a Planet Development Programme conference on health, wellbeing and environmental issues.

"Hats off to her commitment" said Hwaib. "Thanks" he took the tea from the service boy.

"Welcome" said the service boy and left the room.

"My goodness, I wonder how she managed to bring him from there?" Hwaib said in appreciation for Ms. Veronique.

"That's long story" James said.

"I would like to know what that story is" Hwaib became eager. He looked at the tea level in the cup.

"It is better to hear in detail from Veronique only" James said. "I can tell you the gist as she told me few years back" he continued attempting to remember.

"Three years back Veronique visited India. She had her project on environmental studies on south Asia which involved meetings with professors in a university of Delhi. Veronique was equally passionate in improving life of the people at the bottom of the pyramid." James started telling Hwaib remembering the story as he heard from Veronique. "She got to work jointly with one of the professor in a university in New Delhi. One day she took a printout of the document and searched for stapler. In searching for the stapler what she could see was amazing" he paused to catch the rhythm of the story that heard from Veronique.

"Stapler!" surprised Hwaib rubbed his right ear lobe.

"According to her, she bent down to pick up the stapler lying under the table. But what she could see was an article written for some awareness programme on World Kidney Day thrown in the dust bin under the table of the professor. Before she picked up the stapler she just read 'Orphan Nephron's Observation: Red kidneys are blue to green the environment'." James paused to take a sip from the cup in his hand.

"Paper prepared for World Kidney Day?" Hwaib's brows tried to meet each other. "Do you mean it was written for World Kidney Day? I mean 14 March?" he asked.

"Yes, it must be Feb or March three year back." James answered. He again took a sip from the cup.

"Then what happened?" Hwaib became more curious.

"Luckily the professor went out for some work with the director of the institute. She kept bent down to read the interesting article and forgot to pick the stapler. She then realized where she was, so she picked up the article and slipped that in her bag. She then picked up the stapler and stapled the paper she had in her hand. At the end of the day she went to the place of her stay and read the article in full." James looked at Hwaib to ensure his curiosity. "She was very much impressed with the work" he took a long sip from the cup.

"Article! Do you mean some paper?" Hwaib asked. He looked out from the window of the room. His gaze came back to get stuck at James face for further narration. He also took sip from his cup.

"Yes, that's also a sort of paper but unpublished paper. I don't know the context in detail but I could guess that some organization might have conducted awareness programme among its students on kidney ailments for community involvement." James said to Hwaib.

"Then what happened?" Hwaib asked. He left the cup on the table as if he wanted to focus on the story rather than finishing the tea.

"She then searched the original author of the article." James said. He told that Ms. Veronique put lot of effort to find out the author of the paper.

"Awesome! She dedicates to the cause she takes up" Hwaib gave his reflection on Veronique's effort.

James took a clue from Hwaib to speak "Really awesome lady! Before her, the biggest challenge was searching the author and his address. The address mentioned in the article was not the address of the author. She then took lot of pain to search out address and the author. She is a bold lady with unmatched commitment".

"Great! She is great!" Hwaib came ready with admiration due for the lady.

"And you know she had ultimately located the author of the work." James also looked at the cityscape from the window of the room.

"She must have had unique experience during the search of the original author." Hwaib said.

"Yes she had a mix of experiences." James added.

"Mix of experiences?" Hwaib repeated as question. His brows squinted while eyes met with James'.

"She is so well versed in north India now she can write a travel guide for us." James said as if he was dictating Hwaib to note down. He laughed before he sipped his tea.

"Many of us don't know about the boy that he was there in the conference." James said.

"He had written good analogical account. But in the conference he kept quiet most of the time" he took the cup to the level of his eyes as if wanted to search out something valuable in the bottom of the cup.

"I have not met him, not even seen him if I remember" Hwaib disclosed his unfamiliarity with the boy.

"Veronique gave me that article. I also got impressed with analogy the boy has drawn in the paper. I am equally impressed with the facts he has presented on conditions of his lot. The episode that Veronique has undergone is great example of suppressed expression of such people." James opined on the issues in the entire story and the article written by the boy in the topic of their discussion.

"An episode or the entire story" Hwaib behaved naïve and avoided being judgmental. He did not see the article.

"That she picked up the paper from the dust bin" James recollected.

"Oh! Definitely it is" Hwaib got in synch with James.

"Veronique sent me a scanned copy of that paper" James added. He finished his tea and left the chair to open the cabinet. He pulled out a bag to pick the paper from the folder and handed over to Hwaib.

"Thanks James, let me read it first" Hwaib took the paper from James' hand. In the paper he reads.

Orphan Nephron's Observation: Red kidneys are blue to green the environment

A presentation of the nephrons of the nation going unnoticed
On their contribution to keep the safe and green health
By recycling the reusable wastes

Author: Inder Jeet
c/o Sh. Bheem Sen Byas,
Lecturer @ Dayalu College, Daryaganj, ND, India.

Abstract:

India is a fast developing nation with its ever enlarging middle classes in race to reach the heights of the moon with speed of light. At similar pace they produce about 20000 tons of waste every day which is left to be managed by municipalities and about 1.7 million unnoticed environmentalists who are engaged in managing this huge volume of waste. Unrecognized environmentalists or re-cyclists work as nephrons do to manage recycling 20-25 times some 5-6 liters of blood in human body. They sort out numerous reusable materials including semi-precious metals, plastic, polymers, liquids, etc. They contribute to keep the environment by managing waste by recycling reusable materials back into the national body to enable its middle classes to enjoy recycled bloody money at throw away price. They don't get any aid, support, grants, funds, to improve their working conditions and their lot. They are mostly homeless and generally work in inhuman conditions without any hope for improvement of their lot and living conditions. This paper presents the plight of these unnoticed, undisclosed, unclaimed, undeclared, environmentalists or intellectually called garbologists goes unheard, unheeded for decades whom the middle classes sidelining them as waste pickers. However, these kidney-like functionaries work like missionaries to keep blind race of middle classes on track to keep the environment healthy. On this 14th Match, the World Kidney Day, the author also sketches out how these red kidneys with about 1.7 million nephrons are turning blue with many diseases in the dearth of any aid or support from the other walks of life. Govt. funds and grants, that too, too little to protect them from turning blue like oxygen deficient blood but they are committed to green the environment and keeping the cities of the nation in good health.

Keywords: *Kidney, invisible environmentalists, unnoticed environmentalists, bloody money, bloody oxygen, money oxygen*

Introduction:

When someone happens to visit a theme marriage with its lavish party with all Indian cuisines where invitees relish on food rich in cholesterols and fat what generally they don't prefer to have at home. The time people leave the venue for home after the party is over, real work for us starts. The heart of the nation, the Delhi alone generally has peak of the order of 26000 to 35000 marriages on a particular day in a season. Lavish food and decoration is a must to generate the solid waste of the 10000 tons of waste on a particular day. People may not wonder to see young rag pickers at the remote corner of the marriage venue or on outside of it are busy entire night under the supervision of their elders because of the very nature of Indian society.

These young children with the elders keep collecting and sorting out the food waste and other disposable waste created during the marriage night and following day with dismantling the superstructures, facades, stages, lawns, parking. People may be happy to generate employment for these young nephrons of kidney of the nation out of what people enjoy fatty cholesterol diners on happy or not-so-happy hours. Nephron is technical term to symbolize each boy or girl engaged in this waste sorting and is more used in this paper. Kidney is the collective form of these nephrons, for the purpose of simplicity, is used in the paper. For simplicity, kidney may collectively represent their lot.

These young environmentalists are providing function, like kidney does in human or animal body, in the process of recycling the waste to push back into the main stream to generate bloody money for neither so open nor so closed nation nor its societies. These kids are really Ney like brave as they work in pathetic conditions to face the chemicals, rotten smell, radiation etc., etc.

Most of these KidNeys are homeless children who are doomed to live in the filth near dumping houses small, big or huge in size and area. They generate the bloody money in which they don't have any share as the money is obtained at much later stage of the finished recycled product. What they or their elders get for the things they sell to the intermediaries in the production chain is very very meager amount of the bloody money. Government or other such bodies are not having ear to listen to their working conditions.

KidNey Functions:

Kids of the homeless or poorest of the poor involved in the collection of wastes to pick the reusable materials can be seen with the elders managing them into rags with sacks or bags. They pick the food wastes, polyethene bags, chemicals, plastic items, metal items, metals scraps, from the heap of the solid waste. They also pick up the chemicals, containers, tins, etc. from the semi-solid wastes.

This work requires involvement of elder people also as there are health hazards at every step of the processes involved in this recycle industry. These steps are collection, filtering or sorting out, pouring or repacking, grouping, regrouping etc. They also leave the biodegradable or food waste which they don't consume to the ground where it can be reabsorbed in the soil of the land. Rest of the stuff they leave in the landfill areas where they work or move it to the areas of landfills through organized or unorganized network of waste transporters.

The functions are very similar to that of the kidney in the human body which with its nephrons filters and get 20 percent of the blood supplies from the heart through renal artery and filters, reabsorbs, secretes to complete its function to discard the body wastes of the bloods into the urine. Similarly, with municipal bodies of about 500 Indian cities and towns these waste pickers sort out or filter the 20000 tons of solid and semi-liquid wastes every day. Thus every day they save around 2000000 rupees to these municipal bodies of the nation.

They also make biodegradable wastes to be reabsorbed through natural process of diffusion that they leave the stuff in the ground. Reabsorption usually depends upon the nature of the solid waste and vicinity of landfill like grounds. This is the process that is least beneficiary at present in absence of application of technologies implied in recycling process elsewhere in the world. When kidneys secrete substances like Ammonia, Hydrogen and Potassium ions, these nephrons like KidNeys also most of the time secrete Sodium ions in their sweat, sometimes they secrete blood when they get cuts or wounds, and then their infected cells in the pus of their wounds as they don't have any primary or secondary aid available. They keep on functioning till the body gets them enabled to perform their work which people of the classes don't even recognize as such.

KidNey Conditions:

The work of these KidNeys is not even imaginable to the people of the classes who are not ready to accept them as victim of the circumstances. They don't have any protection from weather. During wet weather conditions fecal material is washed into the domestic waste from houses in the streets. The environment is adversely impacted as the air, water, and soil get contaminated on the account of fecal materials are now part of it. Hazardous chemicals too are dangerous but that get mixed during all the weathers.

These KidNeys get wounds in handling chemical waste often mixed in solid waste which is not sorted at the source. Thin skin of these KidNeys gets damaged or burnt and by the virtues of ageing and seasoning process becomes hard to protect itself. This may be one reason that people of the classes may think that these KidNeys are very thick skin people and don't listen to their call and are ruthless. This paper is not to decide who is ruthless but sometimes young ones suffer from skeletal diseases which make their life as burden when they grow up. Elders or adults are not spared by scourge of chemicals in handling chemical intensive solid wastes.

Health risks for both children and adults are rampant. Most of the times children are exposed to more risks as well more risky risks as they don't have the sense of judgment which matures with experience, knowledge and of course age in general. Weather conditions near industrial wastes are much harsh in wet weather. Heavy metals and materials are very much capable of chemical reactions in chain or radiation effect which generate cancerous growth in their body.

Conditions of their lot

In India the job of picking reusable materials from the waste considered the most menial work. No one wants to do this job out of choice. Most of the people who are in this type of job start as the last resort in the endeavors towards employment bearing heavy pressure to survive under the abject level of poverty. This abject level of poverty is created either by natural calamity like flood, earthquake or landslide which leave few hundred hundreds of people homeless in its every occurrence.

These marginalized or left with nothing kind of people have to shift to the nearby or distant towns or cities where they find no food no shelter but piles of wastes at every 100 or 200 meters to make their staple food under the dark of evening or dawn in initial stage of their function, say, career for understanding of the people of the classes. The dark of the evening or dawn gives them a blanket to hide so that their identity does not haunt them doing this menial job to keep away the stigma that it brings with. When the displaced uprooted body accepts the food from heaps and piles near food or vegetables markets then this becomes the job of the family. Thus new identity for them emerges.

Kids growing up under this new identity of the family get the tough of the life in the early stage. When the going gets tough the tough gets going gives them Ney like capability to fight with surroundings and ruthless open environment to pick the possible valuables out of the wastes in the early stage of their career. At this stage KidNeys function of picking the reusable stuff and make their livelihood by supplying them in recycling industry. The recycling industry magnates like *kawariwalas*, *raddiwalas*, up to great scrap controllers give the family a meager amount for reusable items they pick from the filth.

The amount which a recycling industry magnate offers is meager as poorest of the poor is not having any choice to live but to survive as the body does not want to die. From the business perspective these last mile workers of recycling industry do not have any bargaining power against the hunger out of the profit maximization motive of the magnates of industry. Their integration in the local social fabric is an imaginary thing as people, families or kids engaged in this job are taken to the abysmally low on the social scale. Many a times they meet middle and lower middle class wrath due on the account of theft, burglary, etc. etc.

Conditions of their health

The manifold exposure to health risks they live with as they live near the places like landfills or municipal dumping sites or any garbage dumping spot. Even other places they live are not the places where services by any municipality are available. So double exposure in-sourced in the environment is contaminated with stink and rotten smell, poisonous chemicals, sharp edge objects of metals or flint glass in the area where they work in the same environment they live in. In wet weather it is worse than normal weather when fecal material containing parasites and bacteria of middle class gastro-intestinal tract to contaminate the air to cause garbologists to activate the dormant tuberculosis and other diseases to develop. d

Lack of education and their lifestyle further worsens their health as the diseases among these people spread from hands to mouth and communicability in the air. Edible wastes most of the time cause all the disease to severity when these poorest of the poor eat them in dearth of ready cash to buy fresh food. Hospitals' wastes that contain syringes, dressings, discarded medicines, or even body parts to contaminate the air with viruses and bacteria to cause the invisible environmentalists to develop similar diseases.

Sharp edges of the objects made of metallic or glass hidden in the heap are ready to cut their skin with only two possible outcomes i.e. either make them tetanus proof or die of tetanus. Toxic wastes from the mills, factories or tanneries reward these kidneys with asthma, bronchitis and other lung diseases.

It is interesting to notice that these unnoticed environmentalists people who take up this work when they get displaced from their roots or villages under calamities are red like kidney are red in the healthy body. Luckily human body when either of the kidneys is not well then responds with unhealthy signals to indicate the disease resulting in difficulty, deficiency, or dysfunction of one or the other part of the body. However, amidst and amongst the west imitating waste generating best classes of India, these healthy red KidNeys are bleeding in sharing with municipalities' burden of 20000 tons of waste in 500 hundred Indian cities to save the 20 lakhs of rupees every day.

These bleeding red KidNeys are turning blue as the bloody money that they get for the materials they collect and supply does not have oxygen of money in return path. They keep filtering the waste and return the valuable material back into the bloody money to keep filtering air and materials to keep the environment healthy and green. They are the ones who segregate the waste materials as most of the time it is not separated at the source. In the dearth of any bargaining power they don't get the bloody money in return to develop themselves and remain with blue vein in absence of money oxygen in their blood.

Thus, nephrons or KidNeys together generate money ion of metals out of the waste to benefit the society and environment to keep it rich in mineral and metals in circulation so that environment remains green. We know that red color gets noticed fast. Nobody notices red turned blue KidNeys as that reflects emptiness of sky. Alas! These red KidNeys are turning blue to green the environment. May be they go unnoticed because these are no more red but blue in the drought of bloody oxygen. May be it is still true that red color gets noticed as these still alive KidNeys are still red. This paper may be an attempt to enable cone and rods of the eyes of waste generating west loving best classes of India to notice their plight if the cilia in their nose go insensitive towards their lots that are stinking as bad waste stinks to pollute in the open environment in a closed society.

References:

Medical Physiology
Principles of Renal Physiology
Challenge to the environment: Annual report
Waste management in India: semi-urban perspective

"Hm, if we ignore few things in technical criteria then this paper is quite impressive" Hwaib said. He focused on the title of the paper and found it interesting.

"There is lot of sense in the title itself" reflected James putting his glasses on.

"It is unfortunate that it could not be encouraged as it was written on world kidney day but belong to the field of environment." Hwaib opined on paper and its desired outcome. "May be this paper would have been chosen it could be meant for the world environment day in June. June 5 precisely" he went deep in his analytical thoughts to look into nuances of the selection criteria for competition organizing authorities.

"It is in our hands that this orphan nephron observation should not remain orphan, might have been the theme for Veronique." James heading the organization speculated as if he did not have any influence on Veronique's search and research.

"Can you manage some work for this boy?" James pointed at the paper. "He is good in statistics and drawing analogies" he said waving his hand to the paper.

"I think he'll be good for collecting data on parametric aspects in health survey and Asia report." Hwaib verbalized what was going on in his mind after he heard from James. "I wonder how he could be present in the conference. I believe he must be amongst those poor families only who celebrate in the evening if they survive for the day" Hwaib exhaled for longer period as if he had taken that deep breath and forgot to exhale.

"Again there is a long story and heroic effort on the part of Veronique with one of her contacts. Veronique had managed one of her Indian contact over whom she enjoyed good amount of influence." James started revealing how Veronique managed to bring the boy to the erstwhile concluded and completed Montreal Conference.

"Oh! h . . . h . . . how did she manage her Indian contact to finance his travel?" Hwaib went impatient to know further as if he wanted to verify his own anticipation of the story.

"No, she has done something very great rather" James clarified and continued "She rather financed the travel and stay for the boy who authored the paper."

"She could have managed him sort of scholarship for the boy from some university." Hwaib was thoughtful on improving Veronique's style of functioning.

"No, that could not be done as the boy is not studying anywhere at present. And now the boy does not have any plan to study further so that it could be provided on that ground." James updated Hwaib about the development after Veronique's efforts.

"What has she done?" Hwaib asked.

"She enjoys great influence on some of her Indian friends." James replied. "The boy was not having passport. Visa was not even an imaginable thing for him" he recalled the story on how Veronique managed Inder's journey to Montreal. "When she happened to read that paper she searched out the boy. It was a tough job as the boy was not having any residential address" he paused.

"Is the boy homeless?" Hwaib asked impatiently.

"You cannot say now as the boy has reached here on tourist visa which must have got only after possessing a valid passport which must have an address which is to be located with certainty." James judged stretching both the hands clasping his fingers. "But when you ask this question I must say, yes, he is homeless" he completed the information.

"How come he has got the passport and visa?" curious Hwaib asked. "May be possible in such countries" he joked.

"It is not like that. You also know that it is not an impossibile thing in any country for that matter." James recreated with different connotation.

"Jokes apart, I want to know what had happened after that. How did the boy get his passport? How did Veronique manage him to have the passport?" Hwaib had many questions for James.

"If you want to know the entire story then you need to hear it from Veronique." James replied. He had answered all the questions from Hwaib. "What I can tell you is that Ms. Veronique had good rapport with many of her friends from Asia" he further added to the simplification. "She asked one of her friends from some place in Delhi whom she was confident that he would be ready to show that boy as his tenant. After a year or so boy got his passport having his residence at that address. Meanwhile boy continued to stay around her friend's house. Whenever some enquiry from police for physical verification or other purpose was there then boy managed his presence at the address" he explained taking the paper to his bag.

"Who has arranged for his travel and stay?" Hwaib continued on investigating queries.

"Veronique herself has arranged for travel and stay for the boy" James informed. "She sent tickets and a thousand US dollars through the same friend who had shown the boy as tenant" he added.

"When can I meet Veronique? She must be appreciated for the effort she put in" Hwaib said as if he wanted to honor Veronique for the commitment to the cause.

"You can meet her tomorrow, she will be here with us" James informed Hwaib.

"Tomorrow, it is difficult for me. I have other commitments before I leave for Asia." Hwaib updated about his routine.

"Oh yes, it just slipped from my mind" James agreed with Hwaib. "I will ask Veronique to ring you up and make you familiar with the boy" he added.

"I'll take your leave then" Hwaib left the chair.

"We have nice discussion and updates. Have a good day!" James came to the door for sendoff.

The cab was moving on Rue Victoria. Amreek turned the cab and stopped at Sangh Leela restaurant at crossing of the Rue Notre Dame. Amreek opened his door and came out of the cab to open the door for Inder to come out. They both entered into the restaurant. Paintings in the lobby depicting Indian mythology and history were the first to welcome them to the restaurant. Inder halted to look at them while Amreek passed them to locate a table. Amreek chose a table in the corner and indicated Inder to join him. Waiter came to the table. Amreek looked at the menu and gave that to Inder. Inder also looked at that and handed it back to Amreek.

"I take everything! I mean I am non-veg, you must be a veg?" Amreek said visualizing possible orders on the table.

"Non-veg" Inder jolted Amreek's imagination on his food choice.

"Good! You can survive anywhere" Amreek predicted. "So tell me what you would like to have?" he asked.

Inder hesitated.

"Don't worry, treat this as a treat from me" Amreek invited him to speak out his choice.

"Whatever you choose I'll have that" Inder said though he again took the menu to look at. He then looked around at surrounding tables in the restaurant.

"Shall we go for buffet?" Amreek asked. He could understand Inder's dilemma with the menu card in his hand.

Inder nodded.

They moved to pick the plate to fill at the buffet counter. Amreek started filling his plate with Indian foods. Inder followed him. They came back to the table. Food started filling stomach. Silence filled the corner.

"What do you do for your living?" Amreek broke the silence.

"I am statistician" Inder replied.

"You must be working with some big company." Amreek spoke out his imagination.

"No" Inder answered licking his fingers.

"Sangh Leela food is creating real Indian taste." Amreek changed the topic as Inder was not keen to open up on the profession.

Inder smiled.

Amreek reciprocated.

In the corner silence again propagated.

Inder looked around in the restaurant and people started coming to have lunch. Among them Indians were in greater number. Few Indians came with their American friends. Other Indians were with their spouses.

"When in Delhi, who does cooking for you" Amreek again attempted to push away the silence from the corner.

Inder pretended as if he did not listen.

Amreek thought Inder might have some hearing problem. However, he changed the topic again. Why he kept asking, why Inder did not reply, why he changed topic every time. He looked back on the past 5-6 hours and found that Inder had spoken very little. What was wrong with him? Why he was not speaking out. Was Inder a right person to be here or not? No Inder had been staying with Veronique. So, Inder was not from the group of wrong people. Having his food Amreek kept thinking a lot and long with the silence in the corner.

"I am a statistician working for my landlord in New Delhi." Inder broke the silence. "My job is to keep track on the items as they are sorted, collected, bought, and sold in the store. My sister-in-law cooks for me when I'm in Delhi" he further added to reply.

"That's what I say. Thinking people have very good memory." Amreek reacted to Inder's answers in the exact order that he asked. "Means you are inventory manager? Right?" he wanted to give a new word to Inder's profession.

"Yes" Inder agreed.

"Thanks Inder" Amreek acknowledged. He took his wallet out.

"Not you, I must say thank you Amreek, and thank you for the treat." Inder showed his gratitude. He leaned towards the lunch table.

"You're welcome, let's move now" Amreek said as both had finished their meal.

They left their table to move towards the counter. After paying the bill they came out of the restaurant. Inder felt indebted to Amreek. He had felt more gentled humbled in his experience.

"Don't worry Inder! You just meet my parents if it is possible for you to go to Hoshiyarpur." Amreek said. He experienced Inder's transformation. Now Amreek emerged as great intellectual and economic guru propounding great financial concepts with deep understanding on geopolitical economics and sociobiology.

"What is the address of your parents?" Inder asked Amreek.

Amreek took out a paper and bent over the bonnet of his cab to write down the contact and address of his parents.

"Keep this paper in your wallet. I have written down my parents' contact number and address." Amreek handed over the piece of paper to Inder.

"Can I have your number and address" Amreek asked Inder.

"I will write you email. Give me your email address" Inder requested Amreek in reply. He kept the piece of paper in his wallet.

Amreek looked at Inder's face for a while. He managed another setback. "Ok, please give me that paper. I'll write down my email address on the same" Amreek pointed at Inder's pocket the same piece of paper. Inder took out wallet to give the paper. Amreek wrote down email address on that.

"Now, is it OK?" Amreek gave back that to Inder.

"Thanks" Inder said. He again kept the paper in his wallet.

"Let's move to the airport now?" Amreek said.

"Yes" Inder replied. He looked at the watch on Amreek's wrist.

"Please" Amreek opened the rear door for Inder.

"Thanks Amreek, now I want to sit in the front seat" Inder opened the front door of the cab on other side.

Amreek got surprised. "No problem" he smiled. He closed the rear door which he opened for Inder and settled in the driving seat.

"You have got good financial wisdom Amreek." Inder said.

"Thanks Inder, you have got great listening skills." Amreek reciprocated on Inder's listening capabilities.

Silence replaced their voices in the cab. The cab moved fast towards the airport. In that silence Inder got deep churning within since morning. Inder managed many shocks he got during his stay in Canada. He thought about his stay in the land far from his own place, his past that got buried in the dust and dirt for those eight days. Only future was visible.

But Inder experienced that his past chased him since morning when he happened to have conversation with Amreek. He didn't tell about his parents, address, relatives etc. to Amreek. Nor he gave his contact number or address to Amreek. He didn't have the clarity to share his details with anyone in a foreign land. Finally, on the turn, he saw a flyover. Amreek took right turn to drop Inder at International Airport of Montreal. The cab was running on Boulevard Bouchard and moved a left round heading to avenue Dorval. Amreek stopped the cab siding on the Rue Romeo Vachon. Inder also opened the door on the other side. Inder came out of the cab and breathed deep.

"Thanks Amreek! Thanks for being with me" Inder said.

"I must thank you for listening for long, your listening made me forget that I am driving your cab, and that's it, nothing more than that." Amreek regretted.

"No problem, don't worry I am also a down-to-earth person, a man of ground. Grounded in the ground" Inder said. Amreek came to the back of the cab. He took out his luggage from the cab.

"Again great thanks to you and to Ms. Veronique. I'll write to you after I reach India" Inder bent down to show his gratitude toward Ms. Veronique.

"I'll convey to Ms. Veronique. She is a great lady indeed" Amreek shook hand with Inder to move into the cab.

"Bye Amreek" Inder waved his hand bending down so that Amreek could see him waving hand. Amreek also waved his hand. He kept looking at Amreek who had settled in the driving seat to move out from the airport.

Inder turned back to enter the airport premises. Inder showed his ticket at the security at the entrance. Security officer scanned Inder and waved in a direction. Inder put off the luggage on the security scanner. He put his luggage under x-ray and got that tagged 'security checked'.

He moved to emigration counter and got his passport and visa checked. Now he appended himself to the queue for boarding pass. Reflections visited Inder's mind on the delight and plight that Amreek had shared half an hour ago. Inching with pace of queue to the counter was also helpful for him being in the world of thoughts. Amreek's bursts haunted him. Amreek talked too much but didn't lose any moment to demonstrate intellectual prowess. He might have lost his job even on that account. To have a look at the people of different lands cultures and faiths, beliefs and thoughts were in the queue. Every other thing might be different but concern at that moment was the same for all, the boarding pass.

"*Pardonnez moi, monsieur*" voice from the counter disrupted Inder's engrossment.

A beautiful combination of square and triangular face draped in red with golden puffy hair with few curls here and there resting on torso with great contours through medulla and cervical spine clad in Airline's red requested Inder to show his ticket as he was then first in queue. That beautiful integration of prominent nose, petalic lips, wide opened bluish inviting eyes commanding beautiful figure was plenty to kindle Inder's masculine reflexes so far deep dormant in reflection about delight and plight of his own lot or about Indian Amreek of America.

Inder didn't get French she spoke. First he thought he would apologize then he made out why he was standing in the queue. So, without asking what she said what he heard or didn't listen he gave his ticket to the beautiful lady at the counter.

"Your luggage please" reading name on the ticket she smiled and asked in English. She waved her hand to bring luggage on weighing machine.

"Yes madam" Inder placed his suitcase on the weighing machine.

"What about that one?" she hinted at bag still on the airport trolley.

"This I will carry with myself" Inder said.

"Cabin luggage?" her eyes measured the dimensions of the bag to qualify to be cabin luggage. She murmured French words, may be numbers and sides. May be length, width and height may be the problem.

"Is there any problem?" worried Inder asked her as her eyes were still measuring the dimensions as well as attempting weighing the bag.

"Ok" she said. Her murmur stopped.

She weighed the suitcase. She pushed the suitcase forward and pressed the control of conveyer belt. The man behind tagged that with 'security checked'.

"Sir, what is your preference for seat?" looking again Inder's ticket she asked. Inder did not respond in word. He wanted to tell something which he couldn't explain. She couldn't get anything.

"Window or aisle?" she probed Inder to speak out his choice.

"Aisle on the window side" he said. He wanted flexibility to move off the seat in need without seeking any excuse from the fellow passengers. He learnt many things thing about the flight during his outward journey.

"Is 14 B Ok" she asked.

"Yes" Inder said.

She snapped Inder's boarding pass and handed a tag for his bag. Inder slipped the boarding pass in the pocket of his shirt and tag the bag. He headed to the waiting lounge.

He came to the entry gate. Most of the people around in airport looked happy. They smiled at him. Indians were even more than happy as they greet and intend to talk. It might be that people in Canada were generally happy. He noticed during his short stay that people were free in exchanging smiles. That was something that he could never get in India. He was sure that he would never get that kind of smile reciprocated in India. But they also smile at him in the land of free.

Hwaib reached at the airport. He took out his mobile phone and dialed Veronique's number.

"Bonjour Monsieur" said Veronique at the other end when call got through.

"Ca ba bien, Veronique" Hwaib reciprocated in French. *"Hwaib ici"* he added.

"Oui, je suis bien, merci" said Veronique on other side to ensure everything was fine.

"Comment allez-vous?" Hwaib asked her about her wellbeing.

"For you, I have learnt French this much only" Hwaib laughed and switched to English in the conversations with Veronique. "I don't know French beyond this" he added.

"No problem" Veronique extended English comfort to Hwaib's laughter.

"I couldn't know much about that boy" Veronique said.

"Personally I met him in the conference. Before that I had met the boy once when I searched him out. In the conference we both have been in the same working group. That boy can work with you in the survey team. This might better his life. I asked him to stay at my place to know a little more about him" Veronique detailed out in single conversation.

"He had just stayed here for few days. He has good observing skills. He concludes on things in a balanced way" Veronique said. "Working with him may work for us. I am not sure about how you will establish rapport with him. He will be in the economy while you will be in the executive class" her voice posed a dilemma to Hwaib.

"Hmm" Hwaib hummed.

"The boy does not have any clue about you and the work. You don't have any idea about him. And also remember that you don't recognize him. You won't be able to initiate" Veronique further shared her confusions with Hwaib on how he would establish familiarity with the boy. "Would it be comfortable to you?" Veronique asked Hwaib before he could speak out his mind.

Hwaib just listened.

"It's not big a deal" Hwaib said. "I will exchange seat with the person sitting next to that boy. Veronique, please don't scare me as if that person won't be ready to exchange seat. I believe anyone would happily be in the executive class for an economy ticket" he added with confidence.

"If it is comfortable for you then it's a great idea, the person sitting next to that boy would be more than happy if he or she is alone." Veronique acknowledged the idea of exchanging seat Inder's neighbor in the flight.

"How will you recognize him?" she asked. "The boy is in his late twenties" she informed about the boy.

"Then how can he be a boy? He is a man" Hwaib commented and laughed.

"Ok" she appreciated the joke. "The boy is a man in his late twenties" she corrected on joking line. "A man with pale brown in skin with medium face. His height may be about 5'6". He is from India. I contacted him after having seen some of his writing through a paper. He works in recycling industry" she added.

"James told me about that" Hwaib updated Veronique.

"Even than for your convenience. He is wearing indigo shirt and navy trousers" she said.

"When he left your house?" Hwaib interrupted. "Recognizing him is not a big deal" he added and laughed.

"Exactly" she also laughed. "No, not like most of the Indians on the way back to India" she shared her observation. "He is not having loads of luggage" she added carefully.

"Even then it is not big deal to recognize him. I will ask the crew member about the boy by name. That's all" Hwaib shared his action plan.

"His name is Inder Jeet. He is from New Delhi" she introduced Inder without having Inder in front.

"James told me his name. Can you please share some description about him? How he looks like?" Hwaib said and kept looking at the entrance. He wanted to know the description of Inder Jeet if name and seat did not work.

"Ok" said Hwaib to listen. "Is that?" Hwaib raised eyebrows.

"I see a person with similar looks at the entrance and is showing the ticket at the security. Let me follow if he is the person." Hwaib shared his anticipation about what he saw at the entrance.

"Ok, thanks a lot. *Merci*" Hwaib quipped in French too.

"He has already left for airport. This is what I feel worth sharing that I have at the moment" she wanted to conclude the call. "I will tell the entire story when we meet next" she added.

"Thanks Veronique, you have put effort in good work. *Merci*" Hwaib acknowledged.

"*Je t'en prie*" she shared her pleasure doing all that.

"Is that your luggage?" security personnel asked Hwaib as soon as he slipped his mobile in his pocket.

"Yep" Hwaib nodded.

"Are you waiting for someone?" security personnel asked.

"Yep" Hwaib nodded.

"Ya, that's what is worrying me" Hwaib said. "How will I recognize Inder Jeet?" he rubbed his forehead.

After completing formalities Hwaib again came back to the place where he saw a person with similar description. He followed the person. Hwaib also came and appended himself to the queue for boarding pass. To feel at leisure he took an issue of Global Health. He flapped pages of the magazine and slipped that back in pocket of his bag. He smiled at the person just ahead in the queue. The other person also exchanged smile with him.

Hwaib didn't have doubt about Inder like description and similar person just ahead in the queue. How to make sure without having any conversations he thought. He didn't get any clue from smile. He got impatient to make sure. He moved around. He found a name tag. Hwaib's eyes got new spark as the name tag read as "Inder Jeet, Address . . . . New Delhi, India."

Hwaib expanded his shoulders. Inder looked in some other direction.

The lady at the counter asked Inder in French. Looking at Inder's ticket she switched to English. Hwaib was interested to know the seat number Inder would choose. She gave 14 B as a choice for which Inder agreed.

Hwaib placed his luggage for cargo and security check tag for his cabin luggage on his turn. He urged the lady to offer his executive class seat to the person on seat 14A. He explained some story in brief to convince the lady. He got his seat as 14A and collected the boarding pass and walked to the lounge. He glanced in the outlets on the way to the lounge. World class whiskies and wines beautifully wrapped to win the wealthy hearts as ready gifts. Dummy demo woman jeweled tangled danglers to tangle brave hearts handsome wealth some wholesome to lure their friends. Hwaib moved further to look no further on being amidst fumes of perfumes. He found Inder sitting in corner seat. He chose to settle in a seat distant in the other corner to keep a watch on Inder.

Airline announced for the flight to New Delhi. Inder walked out of the seat to board the aircraft. Hwaib also made the same move. Their destinations might be the same. Who knew their work also might be going to be same. Might be same for a while. Might be same for a mile. Might be same beyond Atlantic. Might be same beyond Nile.

Hwaib reached his seat in the aircraft. He pushed his bag in the cabin and fitted himself in 14A. He straightened and closed his eyes.

Inder moved to the entry gate to board the aircraft. Security officer checked Inder's bag and seal on the tag. He moved ahead heading in the aerobridge to the aircraft. Aircrafts of the airlines were parked in line along with lines on the ground to leave the ground on schedule that smoke determined. He entered aircraft. "Namaste" lady hosting at the entrance of the craft welcomed him with Hindi utterance and appearance. He beamed and gave a look at her *saree*. Her controlled smiling eyes were in synch with her hand to show him the way to his economy. He turned right to drag his bag and reached 14B. He saw a person was already seated in his economy. He kept his bag in cabin sparing few items handy.

Aircraft got populated. Africans, Algerians, Americans, Asians, Caribbeans, Chinese, Chi niece, Danish, Egyptians, English, Europeans, French, Gaul ones, Paul ones, Germans, Haitians, hate ones, hate once, hated ones, Indians, Indonesians, Italians, Japanese, Kenyan, non-Arabians, Arabians, Palestinians, Russians, rush ones, rush once, Slovaks, slow walks all have contributed to populate the aircraft.

"Excuse me" Inder first hesitated then requested the person in his seat. "This is for me" he pointed at the seat.

"I hope I am in the right seat now" he laughed shifting to the next seat.

"Welcome, and happy journey" he waved his hand for the seat he just left. "By the way I am Hwaib. Your neighbor during this journey" he offered a warm handshake.

"Thanks" said humbled Inder occupying the space of 14B. "I am Inder from India" reciprocated with handshake. He was surprised to see Hwaib as he could make out that Hwaib was the same person who stood next in the queue to the boarding pass.

Announcements were in progress with instructions on safety. English. French. Hindi too.

"You said, neighbor in this journey" said Inder.

"Yeah" Hwaib confirmed in cheering voice acknowledging Inder for making sense of his presence. "Where are you heading to?" he asked.

"I am going to New Delhi" Inder answered.

"Me too" he confirmed neighborhood till the destination.

"You are really my neighbor then" Inder said. He took candies and eye caps from the lady distributing them.

"My pleasure" Hwaib said. He also picked up eye caps, a bottle of wine from the tray in her hands. "Two quick nights in the journey on this side" he informed Inder about flight to Delhi.

"Is that?" Inder asked. "When I was coming from Delhi that time there was one long night" he added.

"To make you comfortable to work here" Hwaib quipped.

"That way" Inder shared his ignorance.

"And two quick nights from this side as you should roam around in your city and relax in the evening." Hwaib shared his wit.

"How come?" Inder's brows squinted.

"When you go back in India generally few days at home and offices are passed without much load of work with impression that you are returned from the states. So days in the office and evenings at home are relaxed till deadlines are not making their pressures." Hwaib joked on jetlag.

"May be" Inder shrugged.

"I am with Planet Health Organization" Hwaib said. "Was it your vacation here or work?" he asked.

Inder looked at his own dress. "Work" he answered.

"Only work?" Hwaib teased Inder.

"Ya, I have been here for a conference" Inder said.

"Great! Otherwise most of you are more on vacation during their foreign assignments." Hwaib commented. He shared his evaluation to provoke Inder to speak.

"Is that? Are you sure?" Inder inquired in defense. As an Indian he wanted to defend. It was his social responsibility in national interest. He looked at Hwaib hiding the remote possibility of what Hwaib said might be true.

"Look at your leaders. It is hardly something that hides the phenomenon. They make their family enjoy during their official visits. Also true about employees who travel on frequent cards. Foreign travels are the greatest push in the career rather than growth in the career." Hwaib provoked.

"About leaders or officials I would rather say they are efficient and effective time managers as they are busy all the year working throughout the year. So they optimize their personal and professional responsibilities." Inder was also equipped with reply though he was not sure.

"Then my dear Inder" Hwaib confided Inder leaning towards window stretching and putting left hand on Inder's right shoulder. That means India is on the right track for progress. Hwaib surprised Inder showing so deep interest in the Indians' life, culture, and country. "However, that's not the case. India is still a country where poor men die 20 years earlier than a rich man and 30 years earlier than an elite Indian. Seventy percent Indian defecate in the open areas polluting the environment slapping the cities with shining cars and glazing windows on high. 60 million people die every year because of chronic diseases. There are 13 deaths every minute because of road accidents" he stated. He posed his hands open on the video as if he was reading data on the screen though it was off.

Inder got shocked to see that an alien was not so alien with facts on India. An external, no, not an external as most of the world economies had opened their branches, then who, someone concerned with Indians' lot pointed out on the aspects that were generally taken for granted for making Indian progress euphoric and that too so confidently.

"We are the land where civilization visited first. We are the land of culture" Inder didn't have any other thing to boast the most.

"Rightly you said Inder you are the land where civilization visited" Analytic Hwaib confirmed Inder's righteousness on culture in congratulatory tone and continued "You are right when you are the land where civilization visited first. You are the land of culture. Then what is happening to the people is that more women die due to maternal mortality than any other country. Women are not safe when they are out on the roads for work or amusement. Not only is that India becoming AIDS capital of the world" he restrained his opinion but could not restrain to share few observations. "You are right when you claim that civilization visited first. You are still there where civilization met you first" he asked Inder to speak more on civilization and culture.

"H . . .h . . .how do you know this all? Sir?" Inder got surprised.

"I told you that I am working with PHO" Hwaib answered.

"I forgot" Inder regretted.

"Is health anyway a matter of concern among Indian people? Or you always want to keep singing the civilization song and being busy in keeping the civilization as it was when it first came to the land?" Hwaib's knowledge on India turned into great enquiry and account.

Now Inder was looking at the hostess who was serving meal at distance. He pretended to wait for her to serve him. As Indian he didn't like the food for thought so he looked for food for his body. "Sir, are you doing some research on India and Indian people?" he asked Hwaib when he found hostess won't come to serve him so soon.

"I am Asia head for my organization which monitors health aspects in the different regions of the planet." Hwaib then explained what he was up to.

"Hwaib is right" Inder thought. "Why we are still not the nation, no we are the nation also when we talk about our neighbors. We are the nation when we are in cricket" Inder got engrossed with his own questions and probable answers and left Hwaib to be busy with magazines. "Why are we busy in tracing that we were the first to invent this or that? Why we are busy in tracing today's science to be mentioned in our scriptures? Why are we busy in? . . ."

"Sir, what kind of food would you like to have in your meal?" the hostess inquired with Inder. He couldn't know when she came to his seat. Her voice broke the continuity of Inder's thoughts.

"Vegetarian" he replied. He suddenly woke up and made out what she might have asked him. She unlocked the table and gave him a 'veg' meal packet. He thought he had compromised with his choice as he couldn't hear her properly. Otherwise also he was not sure what kind of non-veg he may have in that flight. That gave him satisfaction on his choice.

Inder looked around and found most of the passengers were enjoying the meal. Neighbor Hwaib too. He looked at Hwaib. Hwaib looked up. They exchanged smile. He opened up the meal packet and started eating.

"I have seen Indian people get shocked when they see some urban lady smokes cigarette. They fan out whatever hate or despair and sulk on 'deteriorating culture'." Hwaib again initiated as he completed his meal.

Inder didn't reply in 'yes' or 'no'." Hwaib waited till Inder finished his meal.

Hwaib continued from where he started, "By the way Inder do you know how many women in India smoke in one form or other?"

Inder shook his head in negation.

"16 percent of Indian women smoke in one form or other. This doesn't include the smoke of fire to cook food. Women in rural India and urban poor classes are heavily exposed to this smoke." Hwaib updated Inder on Indian facts.

"Sir what do you want from me? What shall I do for that?" puzzled Inder asked. He surrendered and didn't want any discussion with Hwaib.

"I am looking for few people who are committed for health and break the pattern of culture that arrests progress of the Indian people." Hwaib disclosed his purpose.

"Hwaib is not an Indian but he is taking lot of interest in Indian people. Now I understand why he is taking interest to this extent." was the thought that came to Inder's mind.

"In what way it is benefiting you Mr. Hwaib?" Inder inquired.

"That's a good question?" Hwaib said. "Why I am doing all this is for two reasons. As I told you I am working with a health organization. Second is my interest in my own health. My health could be ensured only when everywhere I walk on this planet is being taken care of. Indian subcontinent is quite significant part of the planet. Unfortunately Indians have resistance in some form of other when it comes to hygiene. What I want can happen only when Indian people also focus on health aspects. So far it is government that bears the burden of public health. But its performance is challenged on many accounts" he paused to breathe in.

Inder was mixed of surprise, loss of confidence, shame, guilt etc. etc. on various fronts which he was not sure of being as such.

"Thus government appears to be failing in every measure every time. One of your ministers claims that people in rural India are having mobile phones in hand while defecating in open areas or in their crops' fields. They still have resistance to have toilet in house or closer to it. It is not true that they don't have land because of scarcity like people in the slum areas in your cities have limitation of space. But still they don't have any interest in aspects of health." Hwaib continued to complete his long explanation.

Inder was overwhelmed by the interest and concerns that Hwaib had for Indian people though it was in his own interest in long term. Why that long term interest was not present among our own rich and elite classes. Wondered Inder got impressed with Hwaib. "What can I do in this?" he asked Hwaib as if he wanted do his own bit in that effort. He leaned towards Hwaib.

"Other than my routine work for PHO I want to have peculiar kind of understanding about Indian people. Other than poverty what makes them insensitive to health or wellbeing is my subject. That understanding will help all of us to focus on the weaknesses rather than managing damages in reactive manner." Hwaib again explained his purpose.

"How can I alone do this work?" Inder apprehended. He shrank himself in the seat to accommodate Hwaib who expanded his arms on the seat.

"You can build up a team of people dedicated to work" Hwaib wanted to instill confidence in Inder who had many doubts. He turned a bit towards window to create space for Inder so that he can expand. "I know one more person who may join you in India. He may be traveling with us from Paris." Hwaib gave a hope to Inder.

"Are you sure about that person will join us?" Inder shared his next part of doubt.

"Are you sure about yourself?" Hwaib answered in question and smiled as the doubts that Indians have first than anything else appeared as a live example to Hwaib.

Inder got that sense and agreed and put no questions further. Silence filled space. Inder focused on the sound that aircraft generated out. Hwaib put eye caps on and straightened in his seat. Night arrived early at a kilometer high in the sky. Inder also put eye caps on. With that his thoughts were on . . . thoughts on strangers were taking interests in Indian people . . . thoughts on Indians who were taking care of their deposits in the banks . . . thoughts were on and on . . .

When something seems difficult,
dare to do it anyway.

Unknown

ðIs si:z

This seize

"**I** need to halt for few hours in Paris" Hwaib said when he found Inder also woken with morning sunlight in the flight.

"OK" said Inder. Inder sat upright. He didn't sleep as night was too short.

"You can enjoy the transition at Paris if you have gotten your Schengen visa. There are many things other than Eiffel tower in Paris to see in limited time." Hwaib guided Inder like his team member.

"I would like to stay here only as I don't have that visa" Inder limited himself. He heard the announcement to land at Paris Airport. All the passengers needed to leave the craft.

"Most of the smart guys generally get that Visa for their visit to European countries." Hwaib quipped again on Indian hobbies. He patted on Inder's shoulder with witty smile. Hwaib made a move to leave the airport.

Inder looked around the airport. He looked for Indian faces. None of the people around Inder were having Indian looks. He moved away and came downstairs to have a look at the outlets. Inder picked up a Croque Monsier. He doubted his tasting buds. He had heard much about that sandwich. Inder got high cognitive dissonance from that exercise. He then reached at wine shops. Evan Williams, Jameson, Jim Beam Black, Maker's Mark, De Venoge, Bollinger, Jacquart, Henriot, Jean Pearnet, Krug, Mercier, Tsarine, Oudinot, why not? Inder thought why not he bought one for his landlord. But landlord didn't drink. Seeing foreign label the landlord might like it . . . a remote possibility. Inder didn't want to take chance.

Virtual tour on wines got over as limits of wallet shrank his hands in the pocket. Might be the pocket itself. He felt miserable standing over there. How miserable was the situation of people like him. He left the outlet before his miserable condition haunted him to the extreme. He moved to see different 3D replicas of Eiffel Tower. Replicas were made of brass, steel, polymer, or of material that he didn't know. He compared that with the 3D replica of the Taj from Agra. Inder came back to the waiting area. Reflections began to overwhelm him . . .

"All the time you have been here only? Did not you go down?" suddenly Hwaib put his hand on Inder's shoulder entering waiting area at the airport.

Inder nodded. He lied for various reasons.

"Ok, if you had been downstairs you could have found this place quite expensive" Hwaib commented after understanding what might be going on in Inder's mind and pocket.

Hwaib cheered quickly and waved his hand to welcome a gentleman coming from the entrance. "You will get good company" he informed describing the person coming towards them to involve Inder.

Inder looked at the person appearing from the entrance.

"He is also from India. You two may be a good team on the work and company in the flight." Hwaib made Inder comfortable.

"Hello Vilas! How are you?" Hwaib greeted Vilas.

"I am fine, thanks Mr. Hwaib" he said. "How are you, sir?" he reciprocated to Hwaib.

"I am also fine, thanks. Meet your friend from India, Mr. Inder Jeet." Hwaib introduced Inder to him. "Inder, he is Kul Vilas. He is going to travel with us." he said.

Inder greeted Kul Vilas. Inder's face lit up as he saw a companion in Kul Vilas. They got to know each other, discussed formalities, commonalities, similarities, differences, indifferences, clarities, confusions, fusions, diffusions . . .

And . . . and . . . arrival to New Delhi was announced.

Hwaib, Kul Vilas and Inder stood up in their seats along with other passengers. They lined up to move out of the aircraft. Inder exchanged smile with the air hostess at the exit of the aircraft. Kul Vilas and Hwaib also came out to reach the exit of the airport. Hwaib talked to them to further the work. Inder was still in dilemma. However, he nodded in agreement as Hwaib explained their possible course of action in coming future.

"So, Kul Vilas, you will be in touch with Inder" Hwaib instructed. "We will work out a plan as soon as we have estimates" he added.

"Yes, Mr. Hwaib" Kul Vilas agreed.

"What about your contact information Inder?" Hwaib asked Inder.

"You can contact me on this number" Inder wrote a number on a piece of paper. He showed the piece of paper to Kul Vilas and gave it to Hwaib.

"Bye then" Hwaib said. "Kul Vilas you please note down Inder's number" he instructed Kul Vilas.

"Bye, bye" Kul Vilas said. Inder echoed.

They both watched Hwaib moving out to the exit. Driver was waiting for him. Inder watched Hwaib till the driver opened the door and Hwaib settled in the car.

"I'll contact you on phone" Kul Vilas shook hand to move out.

"I will write you email" Inder replied.

"Don't you have the number that you have just noted me down?" Kul Vilas asked Inder.

"That's a PP number, I can't give that number for routine interactions" Inder showed his helplessness.

"Ok, bye then" Kul Vilas moved to the exit. Inder had to withdraw his hand extended for handshake. Inder also moved out of the airport at slow pace.

Inder came out. People with rich skin and clothes coming with heavy baggage from the States were busy locating their sons or daughters who came to receive them. Old aged couples coming back from the States or Canada where they were united with their sons for a month or two. Few of them might had been united in the states for longer as they might have been a great help during expecting months of their daughter's or daughter-in-laws. After all their grandchildren were going to be a born citizen of the States.

No one was waiting for Inder. He moved towards bus stop. He crossed taxi lane and came on the road. He stopped there. How to reach home was his challenge. Suddenly he heard shouting. Someone was shouting as he started moving towards bus stop. He stopped and looked in the direction. He found no one. Or no one was visible. He again moved towards the bus stop. Again he heard same shouting. That time he could hear someone was shouting his name. He stopped before he reached to the bus stop. Far on the crossroads, his friend Jhihari was calling. His face lit up seeing someone was waiting for him.

Jhihari came to Inder. Inder hugged him. They hugged held each other tightly.

"*Kitni awaj lagayin, tumne suna hi nahin*" Jhihari complained that Inder didn't listen his shouting.

"*Gate par kyon nahin aaye? Sab to gate par aa rahe the*" Inder also replied with complaint Jhihari did not come to the gate. He still held Jhihari's hand.

"I came to the exit door to receive you. Security people didn't allow me to stand there for longer." Jhihari clarified looking at his clothes. Inder looked at his clothes they were slightly better than rag.

"I am not sure if they really are there to receive" Inder opined. "Main interests were in the gifts and valuables" he protruded his lips.

"I got that only good looking people can be there to look good to these security people. This is the best dress that I had saved for this occasion to receive you." Jhihari lamented. He tightened his belt in loose loops of trousers. "Then I found that place safe for me to stand beyond the taxi stand" blooming Jhihari's face turned into longer to lose the light of it. He tightened his lips while his tongue wanted to vibrate had his mouth let that come out, shout and complain.

"Jhihari, I can get that, we need to carve out our place under the sun." Inder comforted Jhihari. "Our night is getting longer and longer" he looked at the stars twinkling in the night sky. *"Chalo yahan se chalte hein . . ."* Inder looked around and moved. "Let's move to the bus stop" he lifted his suitcase.

"I got my rickshaw tied over there" Jhihari raised his hand to point at remote place in the dark of the night.

"Rickshaw? Here!" Inder got puzzled.

"Remember? Ranchit *bhaiya's* rickshaw. I got it fitted with scooter engine. We will go by that" Jhihari took suitcase from Inder's hand.

"No, Jhihari, why did you take that to the airport? We could have gone by bus." Inder attempted to hide guilt being in such a poor company. "That may not be safe in this night" Inder found that risky.

"Inder *babu*! *Ae babu sahab*! I have driven it all the way from Ghazipur through this thick of traffic. That is just for you. This might have burnt 2-3 liters of petrol one side and same it will take on the way back." Jhihari's eyes got wet in a dry night of April.

"Jhihari! I did not mean that" Inder put his hand on Jhihari's shoulder.

"I just could not understand why this is not acceptable to you or the people at the airport." Jhihari took Inder's hand from his shoulder. "Security also objected so I had to park that a kilometer away from the airport. So that no one can make out that Inder *babu* is going in this grade of vehicle" he continued with tears rolled down on his cheeks to the neck.

"No, Jhihari. That may be because foreigners also pass through the same way" Inder explained. "Abject poverty of the people should not be the one to welcome them" he added reason behind it.

Jhihari was not convinced.

Inder then realized what had gone in Jhihari's head and heart. Inder also realized, no one was watching and hearing the discussion. Then why he was worrying about that all. How did it matter to anyone in the Airport? He also thought that Jhihari had already come driving the vehicle. He found no other way to go back to Ghazipur by then.

"Ok Jhihari, we'll go by that rickshaw" Inder again put his hand on Jhihari's shoulder to pacify.

They both started walking together.

"How others are doing?" Inder asked Jhihari who kept Inder's suitcase on his head.

"They all talk many things about you." Jhihari updated Inder about people in Ghazipur in context of his visit to Canada.

"What do they talk about me?" curious Inder asked. He came to other side of Jhihari to make it safe to walk on a pavement of the wide road where vehicles were moving with rocketing speed in top gears.

"They talk like you must be enjoying everything over there." Jhihari said. He changed his hand to hold the suitcase on his head.

"Everything means?" Inder asked.

"*Sab kuchh*, their food, malls, madam's house stay, wines, ladies, girls, etc., etc." Jhihari numbered the topics.

"What rubbish they were talking about me" Inder objected.

"Were you not enjoying these things over there?" Jhihari asked Inder. He stopped and turned towards Inder to emphasize.

"Had I not taken food over there? Had I not stayed in some place over there?" Inder feigned fury.

"*Bhale aadmi bigad kyon rahe ho?*" Jhihari asked. "They are just thinking that you must be enjoying burgers, pizzas, sizzlers, pies, ties, suits, whisky, white girls, etc. etc. Were you not enjoying all those things over there?" he again stopped and to complete what was in his mind.

"What would I have eaten over there if I had not eaten burgers?" Inder again objected. "You know it very well I don't drink. Suits and tie I hardly have any" Inder continued with same anger.

"What about white mams and girls?" Jhihari tried to make Inder feel shy.

"What?" Inder whined, "Come again"

"*Gori mam, gori chhori*" Jhihari grinned.

"What do you think of madam? You guys are just too much" Inder rebuffed Jhihari.

"Ok, leave your mam, what about other English mams?" Jhihari kept teasing Inder to ease out himself. He wanted to forget the burden of Inder's suitcase on his head. He then kept that on one of his shoulder.

"What these white women are I don't know, they don't look at people like us at all" shy Inder explained. "It is just here we don't have any attractive value in our personality. Neither someone value any attraction that we may have." Inder shuddered with the pain that he had accumulated in his entire life so far.

"There is one in this world for you" Jhihari updated.

Inder didn't listen. Rather he didn't want to listen. Might be he knew what Jhihari was talking about.

"I have heard that they like Indian men" Jhihari wanted to stick to the topic as Inder ignored.

"May be rich or international Indians, not the destitute like us" Inder modified Jhihari's knowledge if he didn't refute.

They talked and walked. Jhihari kept turning and stopping to talk to Inder as if he wanted to have a face-to-face discussion. They walked a kilometer or so. Beyond the pavement in an open area, a rickshaw with scooter handle and bike's wheels was standing on the side. Jhihari got instilled with new strength when he saw his rickshaw was intact. He walked fast with full strength and kept Inder's suitcase on the wooden flat of the rickshaw. His shoulders might be tired. Inder also kept the bag on rickshaw. It was already eleven O' clock in the night.

Jhihari started the rickshaw and asked Inder to sit on the wooden platform. He rode it to bring it on road. Then his rickshaw was running on the outer ring road. Big trucks which were at halt during day time were running on the road. Jhihari managed his rickshaw moving amidst of these trucks. That made the ride so adventurous that Inder's body got shaken time and again when heavy trucks passed by. Jhihari had learnt the art of surviving between such big trucks. He was enjoying the ride.

Inder found that Jhihari had taken him for ride. After returned from a rich land he was in no mood to take cheap risks for precious life. He got to know the value of life. Sometimes he got that so scaring that he thought of jumping out of the rickshaw to save his life when big trucks ran fast close to Jhihari's rickshaw.

Jhihari experienced that engine of the rickshaw was not able to pull it properly when came to the flight of the flyover and stopped running. Jhihari pulled it to the roadside manually. Inder jumped out of the rickshaw and started walking on the busy road. Jhihari dragged the rickshaw. They crossed the flight of flyover. Jhihari asked Inder to sit down in the rickshaw.

"Don't worry Inder, next flyover I will avoid coming over that." Jhihari comforted Inder.

Inder kept quiet. He didn't have any choice by that time.

Jhihari passed through the same level road using crossing under the flyovers. Then came before Ashram over a flyover where no crossing road was there below the level of the flyover. Actually it was bridge over railways. Again the rickshaw had tough time and Jhihari pulled that manually. Inder walked. Jhihari came down under the flyover at Ashram to cross Mathura Road.

Inder saw some headlights and zzzzzzoooooooooooooooooooooooo mmmmmmmmmm . . . Inder saw those lights crossing them with speed of sound if it was not of light. Inder fell on the Jhihari's back. He caught hold on the riding seat. There was no other way than applying break with all possible force which Jhihari could he did. A long sports car might be a Lamborghini passed them to let escape themselves on their own. That went like Haley comet and left the spark in the dark of the night at Mathura Road. Inder found India much more advanced than the land he visited. The speed of the car was very high as if people in that wanted to fly on their night out.

Inder jumped out of the rickshaw. He looked at Jhihari's face, drown in the sorrow that Jhihari had invited. Jhihari would have rested that night what was the point in going to receive him at the Airport. Inder kept looking at Jhihari's face.

"Sorry" Jhihari regretted.

Inder did not speak and kept looking at Jhihari's face.

"*Maaf kar do* Inder, I'll be extra careful" Jhihari touched his ears to regret.

Inder moved his tongue in lip tight closed mouth.

Jhihari folded his both hands before Inder and requested him to sit on the rickshaw.

Inder watched here and there. He looked at his wrist as if he was wearing a watch. He looked at the sky and took back his seat on the rickshaw. It was around 12 O' clock.

Jhihari started his rickshaw and moved towards Sarai Kale Khan.

Road jam was there because of flyover construction. Big trucks were lined up in many lines in parallel. Rickshaw was not moving in the jam. Inder again jumped out of the rickshaw and walked along with rickshaw. Both reached at the police barriers. To save petrol in road jam Jhihari pulled the rickshaw.

"*Thuk thuk thuk* . . ." Jhihari looked up and found a policeman knocked at the handle.

"Yes sir" Jhihari spoke in submissive voice.

"What's there?" a policeman asked pointing at the baggage in the rickshaw.

"This is my friend's baggage?" Jhihari spoke with proud.

"Are you fooling me? See this tag of Air France airline?" the policeman turned the security tag on suitcase. "Since when are you doing this all?" he shouted at Jhihari.

"What sir?" Jhihari mumbled.

"That you pick the luggage of foreigners at the airport" the policeman said with confidence.

Inder reached with fast steps and joined Jhihari in that hassle.

"This luggage is mine" Inder claimed with confidence.

"Who are you? I am talking to this man" the policeman asked Inder.

"I am his friend" Inder spoke before Jhihari could speak something.

"Yes sir, he is Inder, my friend, he is coming back from foreign country." Jhihari's voice gained confidence.

"Again you are fooling me" the policeman refuted confident Jhihari and called his fellow policeman. "You will not speak the truth until this '*aan milo sajna*' is printed on your back" he beat Jhihari with his baton. On the baton, *aan milo sajna* was written in Devnagri Hindi. Jhihari cried in pain. Another policeman joined.

"He is telling the truth" Inder interrupted again. He took out his air ticket and passport from his pocket and showed to the policeman. The other policeman took his air ticket and passport and looked at Inder from head to toe and again from toe to head.

"What is your name?" he asked Inder.

"Inder Jeet" said Inder. His tone was not submissive as Jhihari's was.

"Even if we agree that you are the same man. That doesn't mean that baggage is also yours" the first policeman said. He took Inder's passport and air ticket from other policeman's hands to look at. "This had only one visa stamp" he added flapping all the pages of Inder's passport.

"Yes, this is my first visit" Inder answered.

"Where have you gone?" the second policeman asked.

"I am coming back from Canada" Inder replied.

"*Wahan kya karne gaye the?*" both the policemen asked Inder almost simultaneously.

"I went to attend an international conference" he replied.

"What I was asking" first policeman recalled and came back immediately. "Yes I agree that you are Inder that doesn't mean that these bags are yours. This *rickshawwala* might have stolen these bags from airport" the first policeman showed his investigation skills.

"What can I do to make you trust me that these bags are mine?" Inder asked the policeman. He found himself helpless.

"Nothing, you need to come to the police station" the policeman said. "I'll put this *rickshawwala* in our custody till we enquire at the airport about some theft report" his baton pointed out at Jhihari.

"I am innocent. Sir! I am innocent. *Maine kuchh nahin kiya*" Jhihari begged the policeman for mercy.

"It is already midnight, I am getting late" Inder showed his helplessness. "I can show you that these bags are mine" he opened up his suitcase to show some file and other document in his name. "You can read my name on both items, see here on suitcase itself, this name slip" he opened up his bag and showed one by one all the items. Idea of showing name tag on the suitcase came late to his mind.

"What do you do?" asked the second policeman.

"I am environmentalist. I am in recycling of waste for green engineering." Inder gave long answer for short profession.

"I could not understand what you said" the second policeman said. "How do you know this rickshaw puller? How come you are friends" he further wanted to know.

"We work together he picks the waste and I manage that for recycling it" Inder said.

"Oh ho!" both the policemen shared their surprise.

"How come you gone to a conference in Canada?" the first policeman asked in exclamatory tone.

"The international conference was on health, wellbeing and environmental issues. I have attended that because I am one among them, sir, anything else you want." Inder replied.

"Are to pehle hi bata dete ye sab" the second policeman scolded them why Jhihari din't tell that all earlier.

First policeman now realized the baselessness of his doubts. He could see the link between bag on Jhihari's rickshaw showing airline tag and Inder friendship.

"What shall we do now?" the first policeman asked the other one.

"We have been solving this problem for hour or half. What will our senior think?" other policeman told the first policeman pointing towards a police Sub Inspector busy surrounded by few policemen and truck drivers.

"You please come to our senior" they took Inder to their Sub Inspector and showed Inder's air ticket and passport. They became like gentlemen.

Sub Inspector asked the policemen to let them go.

"Bravo! Good work, you people also should get your identity" the first policeman said. He patted at Inder's back.

"Thanks" Inder said in reply and moved further with Jhihari. "Let's move now" Inder asked Jhihari to ride his rickshaw.

"I have caused you to land up in many problems. That all happened because of me. *Bahut abhaga hoon*" Jhihari cried on his illfatedness. He could understand that worst would have happened if both the policemen were not convinced with Inder and his documents.

"Chalo" Inder asked Jhihari to ride the rickshaw. He was in a hurry to reach Ghazipur.

"It is good that everyone is getting chance to represent his group or community" the policemen talked among themselves. Inder and Jhihari heard them talking nice things about the destiny of destitute.

They left them talking to reach Ghazipur.

"Are! Jhihari had brought two new bags!" shouted a rickshaw peddler looking at Jhihari's rickshaw. Jhihari was sleeping in his rickshaw taking support on Inder's suitcase.

"Yes, Jhihari must have got these bags from big people to dump their sins, on their behalf." anticipating the story behind the baggage in the rickshaw another person commented. He had to bend to adjust with burden of semi-empty big sack on his back when he passed by Jhihari's rickshaw.

"When a person gets baggage like this then he sleeps like this." commented a rag picker when he passed by Jhihari sleeping in his rickshaw. *"Kya maje hein"* he added sensing the fun of luxuries contained in the bags.

"Who is the other person?" one of the rag pickers surrounding Jhihari's rickshaw attempted to identify Inder who was also sleeping next to Jhihari in the rickshaw.

"Look at this, who is he?" the rickshaw peddler also looked at Inder's face.

A group of children with their bags out for work huddled Jhihari's rickshaw. "He is Inder" a boy shouted as he had identified Inder. *"Inder bhaiya London se laut aaya, Inder London se laut aaya"* he shouted and went back running into slums of landfill area of Ghazipur.

"What has he brought for us from foreign country?" zealous children huddled Inder in Jhihari's rickshaw talked among them. They were waiting for Inder to wake up. *"Inder bhaiya aaye, hamare liye kya laye"* a new group of children joined them within ten minutes.

"Ye sab kya hei?" Inder opened his eyes. He wanted to know what was happening. He found a crowd of odd 20-30 children and elder people huddled him.

"Why didn't you come to the house?" a lady asked Inder coming close to the rickshaw. She took the bag from the rickshaw.

"Nahin bhabhi, we came very late in the night" Jhihari replied to Sachi, his elder brother Ranchit's wife.

"Whatever was the time, you should have come home, *tumhein ghar aana tha"* she complained. She cuddled her neighbor's son who informed her when he identified Inder. She asked the boy to take the bag from Inder's hand. *"Koi chaku dikha ke chheen leta to"* she dreaded on potential risk of Inder being looted. She didn't have any idea about the risk that Inder managed during truck jam and police enquiry in the night.

Children who were out to work in the colonies could not afford to stop and have a look at the things that Inder came with. They started moving out from the Ghazipur slum of the rag pickers. Jhihari and Inder walked home in her company.

Many boys and young girls had huddled them when they reached home in the slum. News of Inder's comeback had spread in whole of the slum of landfill area in Ghazipur. Every boy just looked upon Inder's face. Every girl's eyes were admiring Inder's pace. Pace with which Inder has just covered the world that no one in the slum could think. No one could dare to dream.

"*Inder bhaiya aaye hein, hamare liye kya laye hein*" they were just making it slogan hoping Inder would have brought something for them.

"*Namaste bhaiya!*" Inder greeted Jhihari's elder brother Ranchit. He bent down to enter into the jhuggi, an igloo like hut made of bamboos and thatches in semi-circular arch.

"*Ab is Jhuggi mein ghusne mein dikkat hogi*" Ranchit replied Inder's greetings. He saw Inder bent down to enter the jhuggi.

"No, not at all" Inder replied with ease of bending again. "*Yahin aapki chhaya mein pale badhe hein. Kaisi dikkat*" he added to show his gratitude as he was brought up in the same jhuggi with Ranchit's blessings.

"We have heard that there are big houses, big malls, and big fields. *Koi slum jaisi jagah nahin hei wahan*" Ranchit asked to confirm what he knew. He shrank to give space to Inder for sitting on the same cot. But Inder sat on the stool lying nearby.

"*Haan bhaiya*" Inder agreed. "Yes there is no slum in Canada. This is what they claim." Inder added as if he shared amazing thing.

"*Inder ku pani la ri*" Ranchit asked his wife Sachi to bring glass of water for Inder. "*Wahan kya kiya?*" he turned to ask Inder.

"I attended a conference over there." Inder replied.

"What conference? Meeting?" Ranchit asked. He gave a probable answer on his own.

"Yes" Inder replied.

"*Phir kya hua?*" Ranchit asked again.

"I went for the first time" Inder clarified his position. "I was called by Madam Veronique. She only spent on my journey and stay" he continued.

"*Bharat se koi aur bhi raha hoga*" Ranchit asked.

"*Haan*, few members" Inder answered.

"What did they do for us? Did they talk about the abysmal conditions we are living here in these slums?" Ranchit wanted to know what happened in the conference. "*Tumne kya kiya?*" he added to know if Inder had achieved anything.

"*Main wahan kisi ginti mein nahin tha*" Inder said in sad tone on his unnoticeable presence in the conference. "I am not very sure about others whether they had achieved big things for them or for us. But they have talked on our conditions" he said recalling experience from the conference.

"Then what happened?" Ranchit asked. "*Hamare kabhi din badlenge*? Will someone do something to improve our lot? Will those rich people in conference ever talk about our lot in our own words?" Ranchit wanted to know from Inder whether conditions of his lot would ever change as if he was asking the conference leaders.

"*Bhaiya*, only we have to improve our lot, no one else will improve out conditions, leaders and people in such conference can only improve us as person not our conditions, conditions will improve only when we ourselves will improve our conditions." Inder explained as if he wanted to educate Jhihari's elder brother, his mentor, who brought him up to Ghazipur as kid of four years. "That may be a reason this time in India they ensured that someone from amongst us should participate. That's what I think" he added.

"What have you learnt? How will this improve your future? How will that improve our lot?" Ranchit asked the bottom line.

"*Dada* again my answer is same. I have to improve my conditions. People in the conference were eager to improve me as a person. How I should behave in the conference, how should I behave during the flight, how I should behave being at the airport, how I should behave in some rich person's drawing room, but if I want to improve my condition then I have to do something for myself in that direction. If I learn to behave in improved conditions then I will improve my conditions of living. This is what leader and delegates in the conference believed. That's what I think." Inder shared the entire learning at the conference in a nutshell.

"*Achchha*!" Ranchit shared his surprise.

"Yes, in a way it will impact my future if I use this experience in improving my living conditions then my future will also improve." Inder presented a different perspective so that Ranchit must get crux of his story of the conference.

"*Bhabhi* has prepared breakfast to keep your present intact as you both are busy in thinking about improving our future." Jhihari interrupted.

"What is for us? What is for us?" few children shouted if Inder had brought something for them.

"Jhihari, just distribute these chocolates among the children" Inder opened up the bag to take out a packet of chocolates. "Don't forget *bhabhi*" he cautioned Jhihari handing over the packet.

"Children, come and have chocolates, Inder has brought from Amreeka!" Jhihari came out of the jhuggi and called up other children.

Only few children came out to take the chocolates as most of them were out for the work. It was already eleven O' clock.

"Take this packet Inder, most of our children have gone out for work. They must be picking the useful stuff from the waste by now." Jhihari came back.

"Ok, you distribute it in the evening" Inder asked Jhihari.

"Do you have any dollars Inder?" Ranchit asked. He scratched his waist under the pocket of his shirt.

"*Ye kya baat hui*? Why are you asking this question?" Inder answered in question.

"I haven't seen a dollar note in my life." Ranchit said in a tone full of unfulfilled desires. Disappointments of his past life appeared on his face. His mouth was opened till Inder reacted.

"This is five dollar note" Inder showed a note from his wallet.

Ranchit's face lit up as he saw the five dollar note. He took the note in his hands and came out in the sun to see that note in the daylight. He folded that and unfolded again. He kept looking at the photo in the dollar. "*Ye wahan ke Mahatma Gandhi hein kya*?" he asked looking at the photo in the five dollar note.

"*Nahin bhaiya,* he is not Mahatma Gandhi of that country." Inder clarified. "But he had fought against slavery." Inder said. He told Ranchit about Lincoln's photo on five dollar note. He thought his lot was also not better than slaves. 'Volunteered slavery' out of no choice, not options to live but to survive.

"What are you looking for in this five dollar note so carefully?" Inder wanted to know.

"Paper of our Indian note is thicker than this, and quality of our note is also good one." Ranchit shared his observation.

"Then also there may be risk of fake notes in our country than there." Inder again pointed out. "The photo in the note keeps changing from time to time to avoid the risk of chances of making it fake." Inder informed. "Most of the presidents get their photo in the dollar notes" he added. "Here we have only one figure to be figured out on every kind of Indian note" he further said

"How many dollars have you saved there?" Ranchit asked.

"Not many, only few" Inder answered. "I was at the mercy of that great lady" he further clarified. He got imbalanced on the stool he was sitting on. He would have fallen from the unstable stool if he had not taken care in time.

"Ok leave it, if you don't want to tell us, it is fine" Ranchit said.

"No, it is not like that *bhaiya*. Believe me they are not in thousands but only few." Inder defended.

"Let's have tea" Jhihari asked his *bhabhi* to prepare tea for them. "Today we will sweeten your tea with what you might have been sweetening in Canada." Jhihari disclosed.

"Sugar cubes" Inder anticipated.

"*Wo to pata nahin*" Jhihari shared ignorance.

"Where from you get these cubes? These are expensive" Inder said.

"Niranjan worked in housekeeping for few months in a company in Noida. He used to bring these cubes" Jhihari informed.

"Used to bring these cubes, means what happened then? Is he not working there now?" Inder asked many questions about Jhihari's cross cousin who was also living with them in the same jhuggi.

"One day he was caught red handed" Jhihari said in sad tone.

"This is what we people do when we get some work in good place." Inder lamented. "This is what happens to people like us because of diehard habits" he worried about Niranjan's future.

Bhabhi had poured the tea in three cups. Inder took his cup of tea to feel he, his lot and conditions were still the matter of his cup of tea. Foreign trip didn't fade it away. Jhihari and his brother also picked their cups from the plate in her hand.

"I want to make a move" Inder asked Ranchit for permission to go when he finished his tea.

"*Sachi, Inder ko bahar tak chhod ke aao*" Ranchit asked his wife for sendoff. "Jhihari, go with Inder. Help him he is having dollars, so he should not be in any trouble" he asked Jhihari to be with Inder till he was settled in Jain's house.

"Thanks *bhaiya*, I will manage" Inder assured.

"You have grown up with us from that little to this height" Ranchit said. "Let Jhihari give you company" he continued.

They both came out.

"Movie dekhne chalein" Jhihari desired to go for movie. He held Inder's suitcase.

"You can think of movies, now I am at fire since the conference got over. I don't want to go for movie." Inder rebuffed.

"Ok, then we will first go to Ishwar Jain's house and keep baggage there. Then we will move for movie" Jhihari wanted to force Inder.

Inder kept quiet with grim at his face.

Jhihari and Inder kept suitcase and bag in his rickshaw.

"Can we go by something else, Jhihari?" Inder wanted to avoid the rickshaw to Jain's House.

"No, we will go by this. What is wrong in this? Indian *jugaad* is now very popular" Jhihari started the engine. He asked Inder to sit on the bench of the rickshaw.

Inder kept whined but sat down on the seat.

They came out of the slums in the landfill area of Ghazipur and moved towards Jain's house in the neighboring area across NH24. Jhihari stopped at NH24 and chained the rickshaw with electric pole. He took baggage in both of his hands. Inder jumped out of the rickshaw to take bag from Jhihari hand. They came down from the highway and walked to the colony where Ishwar Jain lived with his family. Ishwar had his concern to do with recyclable waste including chemicals and other metal scraps as raw material to other factories. They kept moving straight on the way till they reached Jain House.

"Inder had come back" Jain's daughter Bhumi went inside to inform when she saw Inder at the gate, opened at that time. She came back immediately.

"Hello Inder, *Namaste* Jhihari *bhaiya.*" Bhumi greeted Inder and Jhihari.

Ishwar Jain came out at the gate. Inder went inside and touched Ishwar Jain's feet.

"Be happy, keep happy, how was the tour?" Ishwar Jain blessed Inder.

"Thank you uncle" Inder replied.

"I thought now you won't work for me, now you are foreign returned and having an address of a posh colony in New Delhi mentioned on your passport." Ishwar was sarcastic or not Inder couldn't know. "You still come with your baggage! I am happy. I have not asked anyone else to replace you. Same thing I did with the room" he complimented Inder. He came two steps forward in the verandah as if he came to welcome Inder.

"No, sir, I have been working for you for last five years, how come I go just like that, If you don't want me anymore then tell me, I'll take away my belongings immediately." Inder replied sensing Ishwar Jain's perspective. "I am still your statistician cum manager and I am working for you. If you want I will join tomorrow" he wanted to assure his employer for immediate availability.

"I don't know much, generally foreign returned persons get to leave the old job immediately or after sometime they come back." Ishwar explained.

"I am here till you kick me out for others' job" Inder said out of loyalty to his master.

"Ok, be here as long as you like" Ishwar showed his generosity. "Bhumi!" he turned to call his daughter. "*Beta kamre ki chabi to lana*" Ishwar Jain asked his daughter and went inside. Bhumi also went to bring the room key for Inder.

"Come with me" key in her hand Bhumi took command from his father. Both Inder and Jhihari followed Bhumi to Inder's room which was outer part of Jain's house.

"I am just coming with the key of your room" Bhumi looked in Inder's eyes with smile.

"Ok" Inder nodded and exchanged smile with her.

Bhumi went inside the house hiding in her fist the key that she brought in single command from her father. She pretended to forget to bring the key. She wanted Inder to wait for the key. Not sure she was. She had tough time with her study without him. She also had tough time as she kept waiting for him to come back. For the same thing? Studies? Not sure she was. Perhaps she wanted Jhihari to go back. Was she eager to show that she was eagerly waiting for Inder to come back from Canada? Not sure she was.

"Boss, once you are foreign returned then you find everyone likes you." Jhihari propounded his theory. "Same is here, this girl, Bhumi also likes you very much" Jhihari said. He wanted to show application of the theory on Bhumi.

"No, it is not like that, don't cook up any story out of her joyful nature" Inder warned Jhihari. "Moreover, she took help from me many a times in her statistical topics in the past" he reminded Jhihari.

"Sir, here is the key, the key for your happy home." Bhumi interrupted. She looked at Inder's chest. She looked at her own breasts. "Welcome back" she said.

"Ok, Inder boss, I'll watch the movie sometime later. I am taking your leave" Jhihari said. He saw Bhumi touched Inder's hand during handover of the key. "*Mere apne to sare kaam adhoore rah gaye hein*" he reminded himself about the pending tasks.

"You please stay with me *yaar*. I will be alone. You can complete those tasks later" Inder requested. He tried to catch hold on Jhihari.

"Please Inder now let me go as I have to work a lot to transport what those kids in the field might have sorted some useful items out of the waste." Jhihari reminded Inder about his responsibilities which he was ignoring in Inder's company. Foreign returned company. "Moreover, I am leaving you in good company." Jhihari whispered, winked at Inder and then looked at Bhumi who got busy in looking into the account books in Inder's room. "*Koi achchha sa hath pakdo mere hath mein kuchh nahin rakha hei*" he kept away his hand from Inder's catch so that Inder could hold Bhumi's hand. A beautiful hand.

"Ok Inder, bye, see you soon, I may come again." Jhihari moved out of the room very fast.

"Ok Jhihari, I am coming" Inder also came out to sendoff Jhihari.

"Why are you coming with me?" Jhihari asked with surprise. "*Kab kya karna chahiye ye to dekh liya karo*" he reminded Inder to make priorities and looked at Bhumi.

"I have come for sendoff" Inder replied.

"I will go my dear. She may feel bad as you are giving more and more time to me." Jhihari smiled at Inder. "*Kahin main dobara nahin aa jaoon? Chaloo*" he complimented if Inder was smart enough to make sure that he had not come back.

"No, nothing, there is nothing like she can feel bad. She is my employer's daughter, that's it." Inder clarified. He wanted to talk more and more with Jhihari at the gate to prove him wrong in his observation.

"But she thinks she is also your employer." Jhihari winked. "A beautiful employer" he again winked.

"Do you know her mind?" Inder asked.

"I have read her mind for a while." Jhihari spoke by his own theory.

"You and your mind reading, both are just like that" Inder rebuffed Jhihari. "You want to make some stories that please you and with which you want to please me. That's all" he reasoned to disagree.

"Ok time will tell my dear" Jhihari predicted Inder's future.

"Ok let's see, I know what I am up to" Inder was confident that he would not let Jhihari's prediction go true.

"Bye" Inder shouted. He saw Bhumi had come out to see what was going on. "Thanks" he whispered as if he also was waiting for Jhihary to push off.

Inder came back to his room. He found no one in the room. He got little worried.

Room was open, neat and clean. Inder got surprised. Who cleaned the room in his absence? First he got puzzled. Then he left worrying about that all. He opened the suitcase, took out the documents in a rack in the room. Next he took out clothes and set them in the cupboard. One by one he had set all the items in the room at appropriate place. At last he kept suitcase and bag also to their respective places in the room.

"Now what should I do next?" Inder asked himself.

"Shall I tell you, what you should do next" a voice from bathroom.

"Oh no! Are you hiding in the bathroom?" Inder asked Bhumi.

"Now it is bathroom only where I can hide myself. You are very busy with your friend" Bhumi complained when she came out.

"Bathroom is not the right place, what people will think when they come to know?" Inder worried about her.

She stepped towards Inder.

"This is not fair Bhumi." Inder warned.

"What is not fair? I am not fair. Then suggest me some skin therapy. I will also become fair." Bhumi wanted to take away Inder's seriousness or drama for seriousness, either or both. Moreover, she was having in her mind that Inder had been seeing white girls and women in Canada during the conference. So whiteness might be overwhelming her mind. "Give me a fair chance to be fair" she added.

"No, I didn't mean that" Inder clarified.

"Then, what did you mean?" Bhumi's eyes were impatient to create space in Inder's.

"I say, it is not fair that you are in my bathroom" Inder shared his morality. He avoided eye contact with her.

"Is it your bathroom?" Bhumi questioned Inder's logic.

"No, that's your bathroom Bhumi, but right now it is with me, for me" Inder gave other logic as he realized that the house belonged to her through her father.

"Oh, Mr. Inder, foreign returned, you have just come, just before an hour or so, and this bathroom is with you, then with the same logic you will claim that this girl is also yours since I have been keeping this room neat and clean these days." Bhumi took her right hand on her face and moved down her beautiful fingers on her cheeks, then neck, to down on the bosom she waggled ridged contour of her left breast, then her hand traveled down the waist and moved on the girdle to the thighs to the toes via knees. Inder's eyes got stuck in her bosoms when her hand was on her knees. His eyes again got stuck when she rose up touching her toes slowly having her hand moving on her knees. Inder moved her eyes away to the account books of his works and avoided getting stuck again.

"Inder sir, you are having jetlag, if you keep working in your jetlagged conditions then my father may go bankrupt." Bhumi intended to create fun to relax Inder. That might be the reason her hand's journey over her beautiful figure was very slow to make Inder notice at her details. Inder also could free himself from his eyes massaging her soft skin of toping bosom rocks.

"Tomorrow or other day I have to take the work" Inder said innocently.

"O Mr. workaholic I would not let you work to make my father bankrupt." Bhumi stood before the account books to hide them from Inder's eyes after she took a book from Inder hand. Now contours were again before his eyes. Her well contoured ridges went up and down with her breathing rhythm. Rhythm on which Inder's eyes could have danced. Rhythm on which his thought could have danced. Rhythm on which his rhythm wanted to dance. Rhythm on which his waist could have danced over her. But he couldn't.

"How was your trip by the way? How is your madam Veronique?" Bhumi changed the topic. She honored Inder's limitations.

"It was fine." Inder answered.

"Veronique?" Bhumi raised her eyebrows in question.

"She was also fine, do you still remember her?" Inder answered with question.

"Who can forget Ms. Veronique? She is the one who made it a possibility for you." Bhumi came closer to Inder. She didn't want any other name, thing or person to so close to Inder. Her eyes were talking more than her tongue.

"Yes, indeed, she only has made this all to happen." Inder confirmed.

"Are white women more beautiful than Indians?" Bhumi's insecurity vented out.

"No, it is not like that, Indian beauty is Indian beauty. Indian women are the most beautiful in the world." Inder eyes met Bhumi's to reply.

"Did you miss me during your trip?" her eyes had conversation with Inder's. Her index finger moved around the button in his shirt on the chest.

"No" Inder saw her finger in his chest. Answering the question with that style was very difficult for Inder.

Bhumi did not remove her finger from his chest, pierced with her nail deep into his chest just above the heart and kept pressing it mildly. Inder understood the game but he didn't want to play.

"Yes, I missed you a lot" Inder confessed. Inder remembered Jhihari's prediction. It was live for him.

"Thank you . . . sir" Bhumi released the pressure of her finger and kept her head on his chest. In Inder absence, she missed him a lot. Her studies? Not.

"Your father is calling you" Inder said. He heard father's voice from inside the house.

"Ok" Bhumi got shocked, and was not prepared for that. She moved out of the room unwillingly.

"Thanks Bhumi" Inder said.

"Thanks for what? Leaving you alone?" she busted in fury.

She found her father busy in his own work. She went inside the bathroom of her room in the house. She stood in front of mirror above the wash basin, laughed at her in the mirror. She kept laughing at herself till her laughter brought tears in her eyes. Seeing tears in her eyes, she cried. She cried a lot. She kept crying till Ishwar Jain knocked at the door to know what happened to her. She came out from bathroom.

"*Sab theek to hei?*" Ishwar Jain wanted to know whether her daughter was alright.

"Yes, it happens, sometimes your laughter echoed in the room and then your cries filled the room, what's happening. I have not seen some one so impacted by his foreign trip." Inder asked himself as he heard Bhumi's laughter and cries from her room, adjacent to outer room inside the house.

"I have lot of things to do." Inder reprogrammed himself. His real programme wanted to hear more laughter and cries.

"I understand you have been chosen by Ms. Veronique, she may have given you some assignment for her team's work." Ishwar shared his own interpretation when he entered Inder's room. He came to confirm whether everything was alright when Bhumi was in Inder's room. He got worried about his daughter.

"What kind of assignments have they asked you to take up?" Ishwar enquired.

"Some survey kind of work" Inder said. He thought that keeping it secret might have confused Ishwar with some illegal kind of assignments under religious ideologies as if Inder was influenced by some religion. The conference might be a farce to cover these activities. These kind of thoughts terrorized Inder.

"That needs a big team, are you alone in India for them to take this work?" Ishwar enquired. He looked at Inder suitcase and bag.

"No" Inder replied.

"Then why are you worrying, as the team gets formed, the clarity will be brought forth by team leaders." Ishwar encouraged Inder to take up the work.

"Don't worry, be happy" Ishwar went back to his room inside the house. He was able to find that nothing happened to Bhumi in Inder's room. He could not get why she was laughing and crying in her room. He again went to Bhumi's room. He could not find her in the room. He saw her in the kitchen with her mother. He went back in the drawing room. It was difficult for him to spend time on Sunday.

Inder was alone. Rather he was again alone. He threw himself on the folding bed. He fell asleep very fast, very deep.

Bhumi again came to the room. She watched sleeping Inder and closed the door of the room. She locked the gate.

If you desire ease, forsake learning.

Nagarjuna

ðIs i:z

This ease

'**A**mar Exports' was at first floor of a house on interior road in Amar colony in New Delhi. The ebony finished door of the premise housing 'Amar Exports' was known for its rare designer collections. Mirror finished shining coming from Italian marble of the office floor created envy definitely not a competition in the export industry. Glass finishing top of lion footed higher the lion leg table was mirroring a crystal astray from Belgium. Go *fida* like painting from Fida on texture of the side walls placing the customized designer tube light to tune the light to the tone containing the body of the lady lying like dying on the horse back sets conducive stimulus to the moods of international clients to the 'buying attitude'. Texture matching velvet wall paper replicating Michelangelo depictions to indicate the intricacies of garments through significantly striking balance between open and covered areas of human body were another instrument to provide hue of the business of the fashion industry. Kul Vilas was sitting in the matching ebony chair with high back designed to provide best ergonomics. On the other side of the table his three friends were sitting in the other identical chairs.

"Our Kul is cool *yaar*" one friend Vaibhav declared. He lit up a Dunhill International Lights lying on the table as a ready reception for the close friends or clients.

"During his trip, Kul was hot for the girls in Paris. No dobut" another friend Manoj in second chair speculated about Kul Vilas. "How was your trip? You didn't tell us much about it" he asked further adjusting his chair to make space.

"Which trip?" Vaibhav asked Manoj. "Our Kul had many trips in the Parisian nights" his quipped compliment triggered Kul Vilas to pretend shy then to collar up to trim the hair from the right in single stroke.

"You must have brought things other than this cigarette, whisky, and wine *yaar*" his friend Anang in third chair asked. He giggled rubbing his goggles on his designer Armani.

"I swear my friends! Every girl over there was a fashion icon, *Kya cheej hei yaar*. You can't compare any one from our Bollywood. You can always learn some etiquettes of the fashion from her. I swear" Kul Vilas gave description of firsthand experience about lick loving girls he enjoyed in Paris. "I swear" he regenerated his surprise.

"What about penetration? How many have you penetrated over there?" All three friends Vaibhav Khanna, Manoj Umang, and Anang

Sexaria asked in an almost synchronized and orchestrated chorus thumping on the table.

"I was running out of cash, so, very few" Kul didn't boast.

"You had so many cards *yaar*. I heard that they accept all types of cards." Vaibhav suggested Kul about transactions in Parisian nights.

"Parisian transactions will perish your pocket very soon." Kul cautioned all his friends. "You have to be rich enough to throw money like anything. Without that no girl would ever let you touch her" he added.

"So, our friend has come bare-handed! Dry!" Manoj sniggered.

"I don't believe this, how come?" Anang asked Kul Vilas.

"Bare-handed?" Vaibhav commented. "You call his bar a hand?" his laughter was louder. Then all friends laughed. Their laughter triggered envious slurping for the flesh from Parisian nights.

"See, everywhere you can see the impact of recession" Kul explained. He also lit up another Dunhill Lights. "Keshav, Keshav *beta*" he called up his servant in the office.

"Yes sir" Keshav came from the other part of the office leaving everything in between.

"All of you will take coffee or tea? I will take coffee." Kul asked his friends. "*Beta*, make a strong coffee for all of us" he asked. He didn't wait for their choosy responses.

"Coffee!" Anang vented his surprise.

"Wait for evening" Kul assured Anang on expecting much more than coffee. "Not in the afternoon" he cautioned.

"So it will be happy hours, to all my dears" Manoj commented. His index finger knocked his hundred mm Dunhill Lights between his middle finger and thumb.

"Don't be so sarcastic Manoj. It is office. I must always be ready to welcome my clients with my sober impressions." Kul imposed cautions over friends' emotions.

"Then what? We are going to get a French evening today?" Vaibhav also vented his expectations.

"I have brought good things for you from Paris." Kul Vilas assured them about an evening in Delhi with Parisian flavors.

"Have you brought any penetration hardware also?" Manoj raised the level of his expectation in demanding tone.

"*Sale*! Penetration hardware from Paris! Have you gone mad?" Kul rebuffed Manoj. "Without consent you can't even look at them for few seconds, more than few second means you are staring at them. They don't like that. It is not like Indian cities where you can drag any girl walking on the road in your fabulous Audi or Bayerische Motoren Werke that you are driving. You will be put behind the bars" he cautioned them on French culture. "Here if you can't dream to drag her then your eyes can happily pierce every pore of her body to feel every other experience than your bar in her" he was relentless to point out the penetration luxury of the Delhi in contrast with Paris.

"Delhi?" Anang questioned the validity.

"Any city or town for that sake" Manoj came forward to correct the data.

"Other cities are safer as media may not reach there." Anang Sexaria came with his strategies on forced penetration in towns and countryside. "May be consent is essential in Parisian nights." he switched to Paris as he didn't want to divert from the topic.

"But your bar will be liked, licked, sucked, like the best lollypop in the world, if consent is there." Kul Vilas assured. Their faces got disappointed by apparent absence of muscled 'macho freedom' in Paris contrast to Delhi. He also switched to the topic which got dried in the debate on cultural contrasts.

"Drugs would do half of the work if you want." Vaibhav shared his part of probable knowledge about Parisian nights.

"No, it is not like that, drugs and all are required in Indian milieu to prepare for penetration in a rave or hen gathering. I am not sure about that all over there" Kul educated his friends on luxuries of the rich in Delhi.

"So you have not penetrated any one?" Vaibhav and Anang asked out of surprise. They were not ready to accept that.

"It is not like that" Kul came straight.

"Then what! I was guessing that our friend is smart enough to manage few penetration hardware units." Anang expressed.

"*Sale human trafficking mein under chala jayega*" Kul snubbed. He warned his friend for being trapped in human trafficking.

"*Andar chala jayega! Is se badhiya kya baat hei.*" Manoj drew his convenience. "Not me but mine will be in her, more than fine!" he specified immediately.

"Not your bar only but you entirely will go behind the bar." Vaibhav assisted Kul in explaining the phenomenon. *"Andar chala jayega!"* he repeated in sarcasm.

All were silent in Kul Vilas' office. Room temperature was moving high in the dry of the topic again. That might also be so in the smoke from cinders of Dunhill Lights one after the other in hand by one or the other among them.

"At ChatNorde Au Noirre and Push Push Inn I had good experience." Kul Vilas smiled.

"How long did you stay?" Anang asked relocating his belt over trousers.

"Look at him, *sala*, as if getting prepared!" Vaibhav pointed out at Anang.

"Look at him or look at his" Manoj wanted to correct Vaibhav.

They all again laughed. Room temperature came down.

"Anang, no one is there right now. You will have to pick up from the road" Manoj just cautioned Anang. "Or you have to finish it by your hand" he suggested quickly.

"I will not pick up from the road, if my bar is too high in tension. To fulfill my intentions I will choose from the domestic help at home." Anang coached them based on his experience. "You cannot be lucky every time you pick up from the road. Sometimes your date may bitter your fate. There are many risks picking up a penetration hardware from the road" thus spake his intelligence. "Domestic help is ninety nine point nine nine percent safe" he was ready to bet. He stroked his right thigh as if he invited them to challenge his knowledge. Knowledge from experience was like listening from horse' mouth.

"How come? You are having this accurate statistics?" Kul Vilas cajoled with Anang.

"Simple, as a rich man you are always a prince charming who is an 'impossible' to be with them in life. They work as a tired person thoughout their life. It is when the prince charming shows little interest in them then they are with you under your control." Anang explained the push and pull of socio-psychological phenomenon of lucrative libidinal satisfaction available from domestic which had its genesis in economic disparity. "With you' means 'under you' and 'under your control.' Try to understood *yaar*" he continued educating on penetration with domestic help. His smile was victorious. His laughter was celebrating one.

"*Yaar*, you are so confident on this then why are so many shining cases there in the courts?" Kul Vilas enquired with Anang with a bit of challenging sprit driven from his knowledge. He dropped flakes of the Dunhill Lights between his fingers.

"I am not so shining *yaar*. I am a common man. So far not a big name, so safe in this game. *Sala* no press, no *tamasha*, but only fun, and pure fun" Anang came with ready answer. "That's why I say it is ninety nine point nine nine percent safe" he added more light on specific advantage of being from middle class businessman's son.

"You are just great boss, I surrender" Kul stood for salutation. "The rascal has applied all his management theories in the matters below the belt" he added to improve salutation.

"Cheers! Be happy *yaar*! *Apna Kul kisi dost ko itne achchhe aur itne compliments deta nahin hei*" Vaibhav said to Anang in congratulatory tone.

Keshav came with tray decorated with four designer coffee mugs with human faces embossed, cookies, and roasted cashews in matching plates.

"Excuse me, friends, just coming" Kul Vilas left his chair.

Kul Vilas phone rang up. It kept ringing.

"Calling number begins with thirty three! Must be from Paris" Vaibhav crooned looking at the number in Kul Vilas' mobile phone.

"Just come back to your sweetheart, as you have taken her heart. This is call from your sweetheart." Anang uttered as Kul came back in the chair. He guessed that some girl was calling from Paris.

"No my dear, it is not from a sweetheart. It is from a sweat hard who wants me to sweat hard." Kul Vilas clarified as he looked at the number in the list 'missed calls.'

"You just call her back" all three spoke simultaneously as if Kul Vilas was fooling them.

"Let us also hear how sweet her voice is after Indian penetration" Manoj cajoled. They laughed.

"That's what, I just said he is sweat hard boss, and I will call him later" Kul Vilas said relaxing in his chair.

"Who makes you sweat hard?" Manoj became curious.

"*Yaar*, one of my relative is working in Indian office of a global health institute. He has suggested my name to an international organization engaged in health, wellness, and environmental business." Kul Vilas updated his friends recalling the episode from his France visit.

"What are you supposed to do in this business?" Manoj took interest in the story.

"I am supposed to lead a survey on health parameters and the status in different communities in India vis-à-vis urban and semi-urban phenomena capable of demonstrating health keeping patterns of individuals and communities." Kul Vilas briefed them on the supposed assignment.

"Why are you saying it is sweat hard? It is really a sweet opportunity Kul, *sale*, you already have a team. You don't see that we are your team. We exhaust our hard earned money when we go abroad every time. Let us also see the world on others' expenses." Vaibhav shared his wisdom of the business. *"Business ki business, survey ka survey aur tour hi tour"* he wanted to greet the opportunity with greed indeed.

"Aish ki aish" Anang put toppings on the platter that Vaibhav prepared.

"Sala, France mein to sabhi tarah ki aish hein. Koi kisi se kam nahin hei. Sali sab ek se badkar ek hein" Anang said on availability of all kind of luxuries in France. He mildly chewed his lower lip.

"Yes man, just reply you sweat hard back and tell him that you are forming a team. You lead the team we will work together." Manoj strengthened the idea. Room was running on the standard temperature that air-conditioner controlled.

"Are you guys serious in taking up this business?" Kul Vilas asked them.

"Yes man, when funds are there to flow for our travel and other expenses it will be really interesting to do this business." Manoj quipped.

"It is not that easy my dear all. We have to have data from survey and have to prepare a report. First condition is data should be really collected." Kul Vilas emphasized on really and warned his friends on the sweat part of the work. He thought they were cooking up some stories to write in the report.

"So what? We will engage some NGO, engaged in this kind of work, and get the data from them. So simple!" Anang prepared a strategy. *"Sab real hi hei"* he added to point out that NGO work would also be real.

"That may be one lookout" Vaibhav added to the shared idea. "In that case we need to share handsome part with the concerned NGOs in this kind of business." he also showed the cost aspects of the idea.

"You just ask more expenses accommodating the cost on NGOs." Anang wanted to mitigate the risks that Vaibhav pointed out. "What is there? Nothing new?" he didn't want them to worry.

"In that case we need to accommodate for travel of NGO people with us in the same slot." Kul Vilas pointed out secondary risk of the solution. "*Phir aish kab karoge?*" he pointed out in difficulties for his leisure in that case.

"We will fix the package for them and they need to manage their travels within that limit of expenses." Manoj wanted to mitigate the identified secondary risk. "We'll keep them on different schedule to have our plans separate" he prepared alternate plan.

"We'll outsource that all. First you call him back *yaar*" Vaibhav lost his patience. He picked another hundred mm from the Dunhill Lights. He held Kul Vilas' hand and took the cigarette in the fingers to light up the one between his lips. He took a deep breath to light up. Cinders like flakes flied on to the collar of Kul's designer shirt.

"Hey . . . hey, *maa ke . . . behen ke . . .* look at what you are doing" Kul Vilas shouted on Vaibhav. He got busy in cleaning the dust and black of the flakes left on the shirt. "Keshav, O Keshav, come here." Kul called up. He controlled himself, being at the brink of anger.

"Yes sir" Keshav gasped. He came running from the other part of the office.

"*Dekh is shirt ka kuchh ho sakta hei?*" he asked Keshav to come close to do something to save the shirt.

Keshav came close to Kul Vilas to look at black on the collar of his shirt, "*dry clean karna hoga*" he concluded.

"*Chal meri doosri shirt rakh de*" Kul Vilas asked him to bring another shirt.

Keshav went to Kul's customized designer wardrobe in the office made for those kinds of emergencies. Also for other emergencies that generally were on the account of penetration stuff and penetration exercise. He picked another designer shirt of purple shade with golden random spreads to make some abstract painting like impressions with golden collar and cuffs with matching trousers.

"Sir, I have kept other shirt for you" Keshav peeped.

Kul Vilas stood up and moved to the washroom in the office. He looked at Vaibhav with burning eyes. He came out from washroom after he got dressed to match the tone of the office. He forgot to settle in his chair when he kept looking at Vaibhav. He wanted to vent out his anger.

"*Kya baat hei yaar*, looking so dashing in the new dress! Vaibhav! Why didn't you do this earlier?" Anang scolded Vaibhav to complement Kul Vilas' dressing sense. He wanted to bring his friend back to normal.

Kul Vilas had to forget his anger through smile in responding to Anang's compliment.

"Much time has been over, you should now call your sweetheart or sweat hard whatever it is." Manoj reminded him to call back to the missed call.

"I am busy in this meeting right now, so how can I call him back? I will call back after finishing my meeting." Kul Vilas demonstrated business sense to his friends. He came back to normal glad state. Vaibhav also smiled. He overcame his guilt to make Kul Vilas' previous shirt black from cinders and tobacco.

"That way" Manoj and Anang commented simultaneously on demonstration of the business sense in their friendly gossip.

"So where were we?" Kul Vilas asked his friends.

"Your sweetheart was calling" Vaibhav reminded Kul Vilas.

"Guilt has clouded your fantastically working mind." Kul Vilas scolded Vaibhav. Actually he got the chance to vent out his anger that was accumulating after flakes on the collar of his shirt which was running at the back of his mind. "I was asking where we were in the discussion. It was other than this. This topic was already done in the continuity. How anyone can forget the current topic?" he completed his scaffold scolding spell on Vaibhav.

"That was the same call. You can't remember any things other than sweethearts." Manoj also used his skills on Vaibhav to show that he was on Kul Vilas' side.

"Paris was the background, no penetration was theme, and perhaps penetration hardware was the topic of our discussion." Anang kept back the coffee mug.

Again Kul Vilas' phone rang up. He looked at the number, kept his index on lips to ask his friends to keep quiet.

"Hello, good morning Mr. Hwaib, Kul Vilas here." Kul Vilas picked the call. "I have just come out of a business meeting" he said.

"I am fine. How are you?" Kul Vilas asked. "It seems you are in Paris. How is Paris?" he modified his greeting.

"Inder? Who Inder? Whom you are talking about?" Kul Vilas was clueless for the moment. He was not sure what Hwaib on other side asked. "Yes, now I recall, he was there in the same flight" he didn't expect Hwaib would talk about Inder. "I don't have his number but email Id. I have not scheduled any meeting with him" he added.

"He is a third-rated man from the slum area or even worse. He is from landfill area in Ghazipur. He is not having any sense of personality or integrity." Kul Vilas shared his opinion about Inder when Hwaib started talking to take action with Inder on project. "I stayed for around fifteen minutes with him at the airport after you left" he explained to Hwaib in a single breathe.

"He is not fit for this work and I have to build new team. I need funds and resources for that. When are you planning your next visit in India? We can discuss it out on team formation." Kul Vilas showed urgency to the work.

"Estimates? Do we really require estimates to start the work?" Kul Vilas attempted to understand Hwaib on the other end. "Oh! Oh No! *Yaar* this fellow is asking estimates for the work" he whispered putting his palm on the microphone.

"I will attempt on estimates for entire work. Shall I send you the details on mail? Give me some time for estimates." Kul Vilas said. He didn't tell Hwaib that he didn't think of estimates. He ended the call. "What we have to do now is to prepare estimates. I don't have any idea about this work. What to do, this is not our domain" he shared his worries.

"Leave it for today. It's already evening. Let's move out and have fun." Manoj suggested to spend the evening in place grandeur like Emporio.

Kul Vilas instructed Keshav in detail before he left the office.

"Wake up Inder" Bhumi opened the door.

Inder didn't respond. Bhumi entered the room. She shook Inder's left shoulder.

"Your sleep is not complete. Better you sleep for some more time" she suggested when she found him struggling in opening his eyes.

"Why . . . are . . . you waking me up then?" Inder asked in sleep.

"Your friend is knocking at the gate" she informed Inder. "I will ask him to come tomorrow" she added and turned to the door.

"Let him come" Inder said. He was ready to leave his sleep. He opened his eyes as if he was ready to run a marathon with Jhihari.

Bhumi didn't like the idea. "But you need to sleep" she again moved to the door.

"No, let him come, I am Ok" he caught her hand to convince.

"Ok, I am calling him" she smiled. Lightening ran through her body.

"Please go and call him" he requested again.

"First you leave my hand, else how can I go?" Bhumi asked.

"Where are you? I caught your hand and left at the same time. What happened?" Inder got puzzled. He rose to leave his folding bed. He looked at her.

"Oh, I thought you are still holding my hand" she slapped in her cheek mildly. She smiled at Inder and moved out of the room.

Inder smiled.

"Come" Bhumi opened the gate of the house.

"Ok madam" Jhihari entered the house and turned towards the room where Inder stayed in Jain's House.

"Come" said Inder stood at the door. He waved his hand for Jhihari to settle in the chair.

"No, I will sit here" Jhihari sat on other end of the folding bed.

"I have come with food" he opened his bag and took out a polyethene packet.

"You keep this inside the bag. Right now I don't feel hungry" Inder asked him to wait for a while. He just woke up so he was not feeling hungry.

"Why do you feel hungry now? Jhihari taunted. You are getting your food through your eyes. When your eyes meet with beautiful eyes then hunger goes off" he commented.

"Jhihari! Nothing is like that" Inder scolded.

"Then have food my dear" Jhihari offered food again. He waved his hand in the air to take the bag.

"I will have it after some time" Inder said. "I have just got up" he rubbed his eyes.

"Ok" Jhihari agreed.

"Now, tell me boss what you are going to do now? Ranchit *bhaiya* explained me how big things you have taken for our future." Jhihari saluted Inder. "I want to do my bit in your great work" he became emotional. His eyes were on the brink of having tears.

Inder got impressed with Jhihari's commitment.

"First I need to contact the person whom I met in the flight. I want to plan for further actions then I have to write to Mr. Hwaib." Inder counted few of the tasks at the top of his mind.

"Ask me at any hour of the day or night. I am there with you at your service." Jhihari forwarded his hand.

"I am sure for this commitment from you. You will be doing great job in this all. First let me know what is the plan, accordingly we will do our part as required." Inder held Jhihari's hand in his hand. "I may require one mobile phone" he started counting what was required.

"You can use the mobile phone which Jain *Sahab* has given to you." Jhihari reminded Inder.

"No, that will not work as I have that for few hours and that too not regularly. Same number Jain *sahab* also uses for factory matters." Inder pointed out difficulty.

"Then, you ask Jain *sahab's* daughter to arrange some mobile for you." Jhihari smiled at Inder.

"Have you gone mad?" Inder shouted. "I can't do that. Jhihari what you see is not what you want, and what you want is not what can really happen, we should not forget our conditions, who we are, what we are, people like Jain *sahab* and his daughter may like us out of pity. They may like us for their own needs. They may like us because we can meet those needs at lesser costs" he did not take breath in between to explain the intricacies of the business needs and flexibility of social constraints.

"I didn't understand" Jhihari showed his ignorance.

"Ok, you want me to explain this" Inder asked Jhihari.

Jhihari didn't say anything. Had he understood then he also could have gone to some conference or other.

"Look at Jain *sahab's* case. I am working here for last five years. You know it very well that Jain *Sahab* supported me at the age of 18-19 years when I completed my twelfth standard with science from a government school. In those days I used to sort out his scrap materials for recycling setup in the court yard of this house. I used to stay with you and Ranchit *bhaiya*. For years Jain *sahab* used to give me six hundreds rupees per month. He continued it for years. In those days, during the day time his daughter used to come for problems in her studies of tenth standard. Then she kept coming regularly and along with that job I became her tutor also. That I continued to be even when recycling work was shifted to the present settlement. Now I have two jobs in same salary and second job not like Jain *Sahab* had asked for. It is Bhumi who convinced her father for me to come regularly to take care of her studies. Her father never engaged me for tuition so that I could get some increase in the salary I used to get. I got admission to the college with the grace of one teacher's support." Inder went on longer narration of the economy that social structure provided its flexibility for.

Jhihari understood some part of it. Other either he didn't understand or he didn't appreciate.

"Jain *sahab* then realized that I was getting graduated and that I was good in studies. He offered me account keeping for his scrap business with around thousand and two hundred rupees. I accepted the offer as nobody was offering me even that amount on the background of being a rag picker. Then, one challenge was before Jain *Sahab* that work load got doubled and I had only 8-10 hours of productivity. Out of these 8-10 hours 2-4 hours used to be a loss when we were staying together. Time of few roundtrips to landfill area used to take out working time. Jain *sahab* saw that as wastage of time. Seeing my honesty, discipline, character strength, last year he offered me to stay here in the outer room of his house. This has ensured him my availability for 24 hours." Inder paused for breathing.

Jhihari listened carefully. He forced himself to understand what Inder was explaining as he reminded himself the cause of his lot and readiness to be one with Inder.

"One more reason was there that indirectly I came to know that a worker in chemical part used to avoid me on the account being rag picker. He used to pretend as if I got stinking smell. So, he offered me this room to stay and to make him happy. This I could not realize when I used to provide tuition classes to his daughter. I could have made out if she tolerated my clothes if they really used to stink. I am not sure what the reality was. After having shifted here in the house I got another unassigned function of guard as responsibility. After I shifted here then Jain *sahab* shifted his watchman to his scrap settlement. That too, I am still not on his regular employee like list. I am not his employee in any way" Inder wanted Jhihari to understand every bit and pieces of destiny and wellbeing of people like him. He developed capability to explain uninterrupted as he did not take any pause or break in between. Perhaps the responsibility had become his willingness rather than a burden.

"Why?" Jhihari wanted to know.

"Because Jain *sahab* has to provide other benefits to me as he may be giving his other employees who are very few." Inder explained.

"It is not necessary that someone in such role would be as honest as I am. He relies when his daughter is with me to solve her study problems. She is now in graduation, she is grown up and he relied on her and my character as well." Inder looked at his bathroom where Bhumi was hiding when he came back. That reminded him the strength of his character.

"But she has developed liking for you." Jhihari wanted to make it a point.

"May be but that does not ensure any threat to Jain *sahab*, I know my limits. I can never think of crossing them." Inder showed his firmness. His eyes were still on the door of the bathroom to draw the same strength to speak.

"Even if she pressurizes you for what she wants or you being under pressure for physical needs?" Jhihari asked Inder. He was also undergoing the age pressures as Inder was passing through.

"Yes even she pressurizes me to cross the limits. I have to make it clear to her that I am not the right choice nor she is for me." Inder again said it with confidence. "I have many things to do. I have to go long distance in my life." Inder refreshed his dreams got fueled by conference.

"Then one day she will complain her father about you and make him throw you out of this house." Jhihari again predicted a fear. Rather he posed a fear before Inder.

"How can you say that? That too with so much confidence" Inder asked. He didn't think in that direction. He was not sure of any possibility of that too.

"She cannot tolerate your ignorance for longer time. Now you are with foreign returned tag also secured a place in her heart deeper and deeper." Jhihari explained.

"You keep this story with you. I am his father's employee" Inder reacted. He didn't want to believe Jhihari's story.

"You can't forget that Jain *sahab* had denied when I needed an address on the passport." Inder reminded. "He was not ready to provide even rental agreement to show me as his tenant." Inder showed how much he was carrying from the past to fuel his dream to come out of the filth and waste.

Jhihari nodded. He remembered most of the problems Inder faced.

"Then, madam Veronique used her influence over an NRI owning a house in Mayur Vihar and arranged to show me as his servant staying there for a year. So, on the record as per my passport I am staying in Mayur Vihar in New Delhi. If her liking or affection is expressed then I will be nowhere." Inder explained that Ishwar Jain could any time show him as intruder in his house.

"Hmm" Jhihari said. He looked at Inder.

"So, I have to limit myself to work" Inder said. "Things like liking, loving are not for people like us" he added to caution Jhihari not to joke on these lines. "*Ye pyar muhabbat hamare liye nahin hein*" he reemphasized on his eligibility for love or romance kind of thing. He again looked at bathroom where Bhumi hid that day. That time he did not drive the strength of his character but limitation and his helplessness of being in the filth and waste, and that of his lot.

"Ok baba, now what to do, tell me, I am feeling hungry" Jhihari looked at the polybag. He wanted Inder to eat as he felt hungry.

"Ok, now I also want to eat" Inder also looked at food.

"Friend, the food may not be that good that you had enjoyed during your foreign trip." Jhihari opened the food packet.

Inder pretended to slap Jhihari, "Before that also I used to eat the same food my dear." "For years" he reminded.

"Generally, a person stops using substandard things after using good things." Jhihari didn't want to lose his point on ongoing discussion. He took out chapatis from polybag.

"Let me be grounded, grounded on the earth" Inder claimed to be little and humble.

"What you said? Grounded on the earth" Jhihari asked.

"Yes, grounded on the earth" Inder repeated.

"What this earth means?" Jhihari asked.

"Earth means earth, land" Inder said.

"Means Bhumi" Jhihari said. He pretended to be in jesting mood.

Inder again pretended to slap Jhihari. "How dare you are relating like that, where did you learn this English?" Inder screamed at Jhihari.

"Many movements like save earth, save environment, etc. enabled me to make this meaning." Jhihari disclosed his secret of learning English word.

"So, you want to be grounded in Bhumi or with Bhumi." Jhihari ragged Inder. "Grounded with Bhumi" he laughed. "Grounded in Bhumi" he kept laughing.

"You are extra-intelligent, that is dangerous" Inder warned Jhihari on making new meanings on and on.

"Bhumi is in your desires. Bhumi is in your dreams. Bhumi is in your grounds" Jhihari laughed. Jhihari again wanted to make Inder laugh.

"Jhihari! How come?" Inder shouted.

"You said ground, grounded, grounded . . . then what does that mean?" Jhihari showed his palm to Inder to stop shouting.

Inder held his hand tightly on food, and started eating chapatis. He understood that Jhihari wanted him to be on lighter notes. Not to feel the burden of responsibilities which were much bigger than his shoulders.

Jhihari laughed. He kept laughing.

Inder organized papers, contact numbers, people's names. He planned to go to cyber café. He made a bunch of those pieces of paper with contact numbers and email addresses. He was waiting for Jhihari. In the morning Jhihari was generally free as he transported recyclables the children picked from the heap of the wastes, and at waste bins at the corners of the colonies. Bhumi came with a coffee mug in her hand. She had just poured tea in that coffee mug and came out to share it with Inder.

"Hi Inder" Bhumi greeted. "Must be waiting for your great friend" she commented.

"Exactly, how do you know?" Inder confused her comment with compliment.

"Just like that" she said. "Busy man" she added. She was not sure if she was teasing him or herself.

"No I am waiting for him as he would take me to the cyber café. Bhumi I am a selfish man. I think about myself first" Inder disclosed his ugly side. "I am waiting for Jhihari for me, myself" he added to convince her.

"No, I didn't mean anything. I always find you busy after you have come back from Canada. You spend hours or days with your friend I don't have any problem. After all he is your friend since childhood. You have lived a longer life with him there in Ghazipur." Bhumi gave long justification for her short comment. Perhaps she got bored witnessing Jhihari's importance to Inder's life. She bit the nail of her left middle finger.

"What I doubt is you may not get time to justify your job with my father now. You won't be able to spare some time for difficult topics in my subjects. Now you have got new assignments from Ms. Veronique. What I have also found is that you may not like working with your hands that you were used to do before your foreign trip. How would you keep this room clean?" Bhumi listed many doubts.

"No, Bhumi, why do you think that I would not like any more doing things which I used to do?" Inder asked.

"I heard that In US, Canada or Europe for that matter daily work is also done by machines." Bhumi shared her bit of knowledge from classmates and Google. "You don't need to clean your utensils as your dish washer does that. You slip some dollar coins in washing machines in your apartment. Take your washing powder and your clothes are washed. Most of the people wear wrinkle free clothes, so they don't need to iron them. What else do you want? Yes, even your shoes you just put your foot after wearing shoes under shoe polishing machine, your shoes are clean and polished" she explained. She told Inder many things that he would not require to know.

"Being everything automatic or by machine does not make somebody to stop doing things by hands." Inder accepted her knowledge with keeping space for his own logic. "Complimenting me for being too busy, Bhumi, tell me how many days have been over since I have come back?" he asked looking into her eyes. He wanted to tell her what she was complaining was of no use. "Is a week or two are over? You tell me" he insisted.

Bhumi looked at him. She didn't expect him to retaliate as if he was prepared. She didn't think what to answer.

"No, then how do you find me busy, or how busy I am, it is Jhihari only with whom I had been whole day yesterday." Inder countered her logic. Why he was giving such clarifications he didn't know. She was not related the way females, so far, related to him in his life. One was Sachi *bhabhi*. Perhaps submissiveness in the relationship demanded to clarify. He found that submissiveness was shaping his response not only in the relationship with Bhumi in which he might have reasons to be submissive but it was everywhere else also.

"But you didn't come to your room directly. You first went to Ghazipur area. You could have directly come here from the Airport to reach your room early. You could have gone to landfill area later." Bhumi opened her complaint box. She was not sure why she was complaining. She was not sure what she wanted from Inder. She was not sure why she wanted to show Inder what she could see in the relation which Inder could not see. She wanted to know why Inder could not see what she could. "By the way you certainly have not brought anything special for me. How about chocolates?" she changed the topic as she saw Inder was puzzled with her nagging questions. That was not her purpose. Hers was to instill a new wave of confidence in him.

"I forgot" Inder attempted to recall.

"You didn't bring even chocolates for me" she asked with big face. She wanted to scream but she realized the space she was in didn't allow her to scream.

"I forgot to tell you about chocolates. They are here in the bag, you just open" Inder indicated to a bag.

"No, I will not, your Veronique might have kept something special in the bag for you, I won't open it" she smiled. She came to know she didn't want anything from Inder but she wanted to have Inder has everything for her.

"Ok you leave it, let me open it" Inder opened the bag and took out chocolate packet for her.

Bhumi held Inder's hand first and the packet later. She went inside the house to keep the packet in the fridge. Call bell rang up.

"*Kaun hei?*" Bhumi asked and came out to open the gate. Inder also could have opened the gate as he came out of the room. But she wanted to know if it was Jhihari. Why it was Jhihari every time she couldn't understand. She thought she could nourish dislike for Jhihari. She got to know that she couldn't be demanding but she could still be complaining. She could think of complaints but not to complain. She got to know that she could imagine complaints if she could not even think of. She could feel jealous. That's what she was doing. She got jealous with Jhihari. She knew that it was very poor competition. But she felt jealous.

"*Namaste Bhumi ji*" beaming Jhihari greeted her.

"Come inside" she opened the gate. She forced herself to smile.

"Please go inside side, Inder is waiting for you for hours. Better you start sharing this room with him." she could not control herself. After commenting she realized what could be its meaning in the landfill area of Ghazipur. She ran to her room. She came back to Inder's room.

"Why are you talking like this? How can I stay with him?" Jhihari asked Bhumi when he saw her again. He sat on folding bed as Inder was in bathroom.

"Because he misses you a lot" she took some time to reply to Jhihari. She pointed at bathroom door.

Inder came out when he heard their voices. He didn't have anything to do with the discussion between Bhumi and Jhihari. He became busy in collecting the pieces of papers.

"Why are you joking mam?" Jhihari asked Bhumi reading such a long face of her. He got scared. His fears were more for Inder than himself.

"Because he likes you more than his work, more than his assignments, and whenever I come out to the gate, he asks only one question? Bhumi have you seen Jhihari? Has Jhihari come? Today I want to go to this place with Jhihari. Tomorrow I will go to that place to meet that person with Jhihari, blah blah blah . . ." Bhumi's tone was getting shrill as pitch matched with her gloomy face. Soon she realized that she can't scream as her mother might come out to check what was going on.

"Ok Bhumi, if you don't like me to come here then I won't come again." Jhihari wanted to surrender. "Many times it is disturbance for you to open the gate, I understand" he added to justify her anger.

"I don't have any problem in opening the gate for you" she got melted as she failed in teasing Inder who kept busy in reading, investigating and sorting all those pieces of papers which he wanted to prepare for his next move.

"I will come to open the gate, no problem" Inder interrupted between complains and clarifications. He looked at Jhihari and Bhumi.

"How many days can you open the gate? The day you are on the work with my father then you won't be here to open the gate" she again reminded Inder who kept quiet.

"Inder, what's this? Why Bhumi ji is so angry with you? You are not focusing on your job with her father. Why is she showering all the anger on me?" Jhihari asked Inder keeping the lunch packet aside.

"Now, I understand why he misses you so much." Bhumi whispered. She looked at the lunch packet Jhihari came with.

"Bhumi ji, if you really don't like me to be here then I won't come to meet Inder." Jhihari wanted to know from Bhumi. He didn't know many forms of communication other than straight communication. He was not sure whether submissiveness was also a form of communication.

"No, no, Jhihari *bhaiya*, it is not like that" Bhumi's tone got mild. "You keep coming here I was just joking. My father doesn't have any plan to make food free for Inder" she joked. She again looked at the lunch packet kept on the folding bed. "You two have your lunch or brunch and let me go off" she stood up in the chair and moved towards the door.

"Thank you Bhumi" Inder said. "You are already off" he murmured.

"Thank you for what?" Bhumi came back. She didn't hear Inder's murmur.

"Opening the gate, allowing Jhihari to be here, taking so much care, many things, thanks for everything" Inder said.

"Why are you so generous in thanking me for these things?" Bhumi went sarcastic. "Just thank me to leave this place" she added. She pretended to maintain her anger.

"Thank you" Inder murmured as she reached to the door.

"Hoooonnn" she turned around and stared at Inder. She heard his murmur.

"Oh no, not again" Inder folded his hands.

They laughed.

Jhihari looked at both of them.

She again looked at lunch packet on the bed. She smiled at Inder and left the room.

"Now we are already late. Let us move" Inder looked at the door.

"You please just have this lunch, *bhabhi* has prepared for you." Jhihari pointed at the lunch wrapped in a polyethene bag. Many wrinkles and holes here and there were capable to demonstrate it was over reused.

"It will also make us late" Inder showed impatience.

"Why don't you say that this very old lunch box which has irritated Bhumi is disturbing you now?" Jhihari scoffed. He thought that *bhabhi* could have packed it in a nice polyethene bag to make it more graceful. His *bhabhi* should know that Inder was a foreign returned person by then. Bhumi or Inder were disturbed by the packet or not but Jhihari himself thought a lot looking at wrinkles and hole in the polyethene.

"No Jhihari, it is not like that" Inder consoled Jhihari.

"See, Inder, since you went to the cause of our lot, *bhaiya* and *bhabhi* are very happy about that. They have lot of expectations from you to come out to improve conditions of our lot. They will even replace this old and junk lunch box in this lunch packet. They right now don't spare money to buy new lunch box, moreover our work has to do with lot of old things so they might not have noticed that this lunch box may irritate rich people like Bhumi or foreign-returned Inder." Jhihari lamented. He could not do anything to replace the lunch box as soon as Inder came back to Ghazipur.

Inder kept quiet. "Ok we will have lunch first and then we will think to move" he said after sometime. He was learning to keep patience. He chewed many spells of anger. "Open the box" he asked Jhihari. "Arrange the food on the table" he pointed at the table. Jhihari was still in lamenting state. He didn't listen.

"Come and have your lunch" Inder himself opened the lunch box and asked Jhihari to have his lunch.

"No, I have already had, you have it" Jhihari replied.

"Why would you have your lunch carried in this junk box? Now you are friend with the daughter of a rich man" Inder took his turn to taunt at Jhihari.

"What do you mean?" Jhihari showed his ignorance. He really didn't understand. He was not convinced of existence of friendliness with Bhumi. He didn't even imagine. He didn't know that his persona was not designed to imagine such friendship. He only knew scolding, scoffing, beating, shouting, sulking, sniffing, rebuffs, etc., etc.

"Now, Bhumi is very friendly with you." Inder complimented Jhihari.

"Oh, that is because of you are here in her father's settlement, not that it is my own." Jhihari returned the compliment. He could see that Inder to be credited if he knew at all, a girl like Bhumi.

"But when she is with you, she goes very sarcastic on me." Inder took on Jhihari again. "*Tumse ladne mein meri halat kharab kar deti hei*" he quipped further that she targeted him while she fought with Jhihari.

"I don't know what happens to her, what I could understand is that she likes you very much." Jhihari shared his understanding of the matter going between an employee and the employer's daughter.

"She pulls my leg when she is around with us." Inder said with pretense of envy.

"Which leg?" Jhihari asked. Jhihari laughed.

Inder looked at him. He smiled. He also laughed. They laughed.

Despair often breeds dis|ease.

Sophocles

∂Is i:z

Dis-ease

Jhihari came to the electric pole where he chained his rickshaw. He didn't have that rickshaw six months ago. That was new achievement for him so he didn't have any hesitation in claiming the ownership of the rickshaw.

Inder passed Jhihari and walked further as if he didn't have any relationship with the rickshaw that Jhihari was unchaining. He also didn't have such complex before his visit to Montreal. The visit had introduced a complex to him. He might be confused with shifted sense of personality. Though he was very much down-to-earth-kind-of-person, but he couldn't avoid the feeling or craving to look like people where he went for the conference. That part of the world was altogether different from the one he had to be destined with. There was no slum in that part of the world. The world Inder was living in was having slum at every nook and corner, every two hundred meters in a posh residential area. Before the visit Inder's world was full of dust, rust, junk, punk, sunk, etc. etc.

Now, Inder had different notions of cleanliness and closeness. He started believing in reserve nature of people. When he was in Montreal he was surprised to see many things different in the land of the materially advanced people. He found many things different from the land of the ancient civilization. The restlessness and chaos in the land of ancient civilization was contrast matched by orderliness of the things in the land of new civilizations. Silence came as the result of his shyness in the land of surprises. His confidence earned so far in the land where old civilization got frozen in the cool of museum for showcasing material progress in the land of orderliness under snow cover. So he was standing far from Jhihari's rickshaw.

"*Kahan jana hei?*" Jhihari asked where they were heading. Jhihari came to Inder standing under Ghazipur flyover.

"Laxmi Nagar" Inder kept his answer short.

"Which place in Laxmi Nagar?" Jhihari asked again.

"I am not sure about that right now. I want to go to some money exchanger, nearest I can get that is in Laxmi Nagar." Inder shared his intentions.

"Money exchanger?" Jhihari repeated in question.

"Yes, I got some dollars to spend over there during the conference. I have saved most of them as I stayed in Ms. Veronique's house. I want some rupees out of it." Inder explained.

"*Videshi paisa*? You did not tell me about that" Jhihari got hurt. "Why didn't you tell me about that? OK I got that. You don't trust me." Jhihari concluded. He experienced the distance between him and Inder that was visible when Inder stood far from the place where he unchained the rickshaw.

Inder didn't listen. He thought Jhihari was joking.

"Inder, I didn't know that you don't trust me now. You thought you should not tell me because I would have stolen your dollars. That's why you didn't tell me about that. *Chura leta kya main unko*? No, Inder, no, I am not that mean that you think. You have taken me for granted." Jhihari's pitch got high. His voice got blocked as air might have got stuffed in his throat because he gasped a lot. His eyes drew a thick waterline. But he managed himself to stop from crying.

"What rubbish you are talking about? Had I not any trust in you, why would I have come with you even right now? This is the trust in you that makes me say that I want to exchange the dollars in rupees." Inder held shoulders and vibrated them to wake up Jhihari to a level of consciousness. The consciousness that was required for Jhihari to look up at the world that was ready to take people like him as part of the whole. "If you keep sulking on petty things then how can we progress?" Inder busted out with his anger. He didn't imagine that Jhihari would think of triviality at that level.

"Why didn't you tell me earlier?" Jhihari got stuck.

"Jhihari, it hardly matters it is only second day since I have come back." Inder emphasized.

"You thought. I might have stolen your dollars" Jhihari got stuck with same emotions and perhaps same question rather. "*Jhuggiyon mein chhoti cheejon ki chori hoti hei. Lekin biswas bhi koi cheej hoti hei*" Jhihari wanted Inder to understand that petty thefts were routine in the slums but trustworthiness in the relationship was still valued.

"Jhihari, I don't think so" Inder clarified. He thought something else. "Look, I would have gone alone to get the dollar exchanged for rupees if I had not trusted you" he added to explain.

"I don't know that, you would have told me earlier, this has shaken our relationship since childhood." Jhihari didn't soften his attack with trivial arguments.

"Ok, I am sorry" Inder surrendered. He held his ears to start sit-ups. He understood that no other method would work.

"Ok, I didn't mean that. Please sit down on the seat" Jhihari pointed at the bench like upper fixture of the rickshaw to sit down.

Inder looked around and then looked at the ground and sat down on the bench part of the rickshaw. Jhihari bent down under the rickshaw and put his foot on the kick to start the engine. Jhihari took right turn for Laxmi Nagar.

"Yes, who will give you the change for your dollars?" Jhihari asked taking left on Kadkadi Mode flyover.

"Let's see I have to keep looking on the roadside for people who change the currency." Inder answered. "It is bubbling on the road. Please ride carefully. Better you slow down on this slope" he requested when Jhihari had no mood to control the rickshaw speed on slope towards Preet Vihar.

"So, I must keep riding?" Jhihari asked.

"There may be some places in Preet Vihar. I will tell you when I see the one" Inder replied.

"So, I need to focus on riding or waiting for you to notice and speak about the place." Jhihari said with sarcasm.

"May be both" Inder replied.

"Yes boss, you are my master" Jhihari improved sarcasm.

"You just stop Jhihari" Inder asked Jhihari to stop the rickshaw when he saw one money exchanger outlet.

Jhihari stopped the rickshaw on side of the road.

Kiiiiiiiiiiiiiiiiiiiiiii kiiiiiiiiiiiiiiiiiiiiii and krrrrchh, a vehicle just collided with the rickshaw and some other vehicles immediately started screaming with their horns even when Jhihari stopped in left side on the road. Vehicles behind rickshaw were stuck in the road down because of blockages as the metro construction was on.

"Jhihari, what have you done? You could have taken to the service lane." Inder pointed out at the parallel road opening in the market.

"I'll tell" a fat man came out of his car which got stuck with the rickshaw. He came close to Jhihari and started slapping Jhihari left and right. Before Jhihari could understand what was happening he started beating him in stomach and back till Inder jumped from the rickshaw for rescue.

"Bastards, don't have any sense to ride on the road." the fat man slapped Inder also. Inder kept quiet as that would have given break to Jhihari who was beaten up heavily by that fat man.

"I am sorry for his mistake. Forgive him" Inder begged before that man.

"Sorry and all doesn't work with me. Pay for the scratch on my car" the fat man showed his muscles pointing at a scratch on the bumper of his car.

"I just stopped my rickshaw, and you could not stop your car in time, it is not my mistake." Jhihari cried in tears to make his point. He did not want to pay for damage which was not even damage from his perspective.

"Bastard, *madar- . . ., maa ke . . . behen ke . . .* if you stop on the road then where will I drive my car?" that man again slapped Jhihari to start second round of beating.

"Where should I go on the road even when I am in the left most of the lanes?" Jhihari sulked.

"Go to hell, why did you stop on the road?" that fat man lifted Jhihari by holding his collar. Jhihari was hanging as if his shirt was weighing scale with spring and he was an object to be weighed.

"Sir, I am sorry, I am sorry for him." Inder interrupted again. *"Ise chhod dijiye chahe mujhe mar lijiye"* he again begged for Jhihari's life even if the fat man would be happy to beat him.

"Ok, let him pay for repair" the fat man dictated.

"Sir, he is very poor man, he is a rag picker, and he won't be able to pay you the damage in his entire life" Inder still pleaded.

"I don't know anything, whether he is rag picker or king, I want my car repaired. Better you pay for repair then" looking at the rickshaw that fat man asked Inder.

"I am also like him only. We are poor people, somehow managing our life." Inder begged to be free from that fat man's visible and invisible clutch. Visible clutch was on Jhihari's collar and invisible with his voice that possess coercive power that he might even call the cop. The fat man commanded the clutch of wealth and opulence that might have enabled him to keep police in his pocket to make both of the poorest of the poor behind the bars.

"You are poor to screw up my car, why have you come on the road?" then that fat man again slapped Inder. Inder tolerated the slaps. He cursed himself for being on the road.

Kiiii, kiii, teeeiiiiiiiiiinnnnn, kiii, kii, ki, Kiiiiiiiiiii, kkkkkkkiiiiiiiiii iiiiiiiiiiiiiiL, teeeiiiiiiiiiiiii

"Oh *bhai*! Why are you all together screwing up our day?" Inder heard shouting voices of many people who came out from their cars as road got blocked. Trucks for metro construction were moving inside the barricaded area of the construction.

"Leave them, they are poor people. You are fighting for a scratch on your car in a city where almost every car gets little or even big scratches every now and then" some people came out of their vehicles to counsel that fat man. "You have already beaten them much more than that. *Ab to tujhe unhein hospital ka kharcha dena chahiye*" a person shouted at the fat man in anger. "*Sale ne car ke ek scratch ke liye ladke ke itne scratch mar diye thappad mar mar ke*" he shouted from his car on how that fat man brought wounds on Jhihari's body to revenge for a small scratch on bumper of his car.

"You have scratched their cheeks and arms, you have already equalized." other person also said to improve the same logic. He looked at fat man's car in front, "*Sale scratch car par dikh bhi nahin raha aur paise mang raha hei*, that too from poor people" he screamed when he turned back to be in his car.

"*Sale*, these bastards, collecting the wastes and wasting the country" the fat man screamed. "Bastards have come out to make all the smoke to pollute the road and surrounding. Neither rickshaw nor scooter" he was not ready to lose arguments when he looked at Jhihari *jugaad* rickshaw. He filled all the abusive filth in his mouth. "*Sale sab kachre walon ko dilli ke bahar khaded dena chahiye*" he kept screaming at them as he wanted to chuck them out of Delhi as if it was his private property. He then went back in the driving seat of his car.

"Let's move" Inder took sigh of relief and put his hand to solace anguished Jhihari.

"That fat man was rascal. He wanted to loot anyone on the road." Jhihari opined about the person. "It is good that you didn't disclose under pressure that you have some money with you" he added. "Otherwise the moment he knew that you had dollar to convert he would have looted you" he added to his murmurs.

Jhihari pulled the rickshaw by hands to the parking area of the complex. Inder followed him.

"A money exchanger's office is upstairs, let's go there" Inder said to Jhihari. He saw a board on the window at first floor of the complex.

"Inder you go, todays' is a bad day for me" Jhihari declined to go to money exchanger with Inder.

"Come, nothing is like that" Inder pressed Jhihari's hand in insistence.

"Let's see what else we have to face today" Jhihari came along with Inder to move up on the stairs. They were standing in front of the glass door of the money changer's office.

"May I come in sir?" pushing the glass door a little Inder requested the person to get into the office.

"Yes" the money exchanger allowed them to come in. He kept counting notes of Indian currency for another person sitting in the chair in front.

"Sir, this is your 144700/- rupees, for your 3500 dollars" money exchanger said handing over rupees of different denominations in packs tied with rubber band.

"How will you carry this big amount? You better be careful for its safety" the money changer cautioned him of the pickpockets. "Nowadays most of the people like you prefer to cash them through account" he added.

"Don't worry. I handle much more money than this. You know everything cannot be done through account. You have to do like this also" the customer of money changer took his goggles out from the pocket of his safari shirt. The money changer smiled. He left the office.

"Tell me, what do you want?" the money changer turned to Inder. He looked at Inder and Jhihari alternately from top to bottom. He looked at them with suspicion. He didn't notice whom he had allowed in during counting of notes for his client.

"I want to exchange my dollars for rupees" Inder asked.

"Dollars? Do you have dollars?" the money changer now looked at Inder with inspecting eyes. "How many dollars have you got?" he further asked.

"Around eight hundred" Inder replied.

"Where from did you get these dollars?" the money changer asked Inder in scolding voice.

"Sir, I had been in Canada for six day visit" Inder replied. He didn't like suspicion shown by money changer. But he didn't have any choice.

"How dare you fool me? You bloody thief I have been watching your drama on the road with traffic jam for hour." money changer pointed out at roadside seen visible through his office window glass. He related the matter the traffic jam on the road with scratch drama of that fat man. He turned to watch to the traffic jam from his window when honking noise fell in his ears which were deaf for Inder's voice.

"No, no, no sir, I am not a thief, I have been in Montreal for a week" Inder clarified.

"Shut up, you bloody liar, *sale ne Canada Montreal ka naam sun liya aur kar di thugi shuru.* This person was there with you on road when you were haggling with that car owner" money changer pointed at Jhihari as his witness rather a companion who came with Inder. He treated as if Inder was a big thug.

"Is that your cart in the parking?" money changer didn't spare Jhihari also.

Jhihari nodded.

"I know people like you come in the traffic with such kind of intentions. They engage the rich people to steal their money, their gold, their dollars" money changer busted with anger. He pretended to stand up to push them away from his office.

"Sir, listen to me, listen to me first, before you issue a character certificate" Inder moved to anger.

"This is my passport with visa stamp from Canada" Inder showed his passport to the money changer, and opened the page with visa stamp from Canada High Commission.

"Oh, my god, you are having fake passport also, you cheat, heading a fraud gang, I will give you to the police" money changer was not ready to believe them and shouted at Inder.

"Sir, now you have crossed every limit of decency and civic sense." Inder said. "Call police" he asked.

"Don't shout at me, I will call people around here. Then I will call the police to hand you over for lockup" money changer warned Inder.

"*Sahab,* leave it, we are at mistake, we are poor people, leave us on our own if you cannot change his dollars." Jhihari interrupted to beg the mercy from the money changer.

"Take him out, get lost" money changer ordered Jhihari. "I am sparing because you have pleaded for mercy" he showed some kindheartedness to Jhihari when he asked Jhihari to push off. "Had you not interrupted I would have handed over this fellow to the cop" he said. He again waved his hand to show them push off. His neck got damp with perspiration. He changed temperature display of the AC to 18 with remote in his hand.

"Ok, sir" Jhihari dragged Inder out of money changer's office.

"Get lost from my office, make sure you are not seen in the complex" money changer warned closing the glass door of his office.

"Why did you stop me Jhihari? Why did you drag me out? How can that money changer talk like this?" Inder screamed at Jhihari coming out of money changer's office.

"Don't you know Inder, he is a big man. If he calls policemen then they would listen to him only, not you" Jhihari explained. He pushed Inder off on the staircases to move away. "You didn't hear what he said. He would have called his friendly people from neighboring shops to prepare them as witness.

"Police would have taken us to the police station. There I would have explained every reality." Inder insisted on his point of view. He believed fairness of the system.

"You have been there in Canada only for six days, this is India, have you forgotten?" Jhihari scoffed Inder to show ground realities of the land and its people. "This money changer would have proven that you have stolen the dollars from his drawer and you would have been in the jail for years" he was in a hurry to add to his explanation.

Inder kept quiet. He sat down on the stairs of the building. Jhihari followed him. He looked highly upset. How to get his dollars converted in rupees was a big question. He put on the clothes that he bought for Montreal visit. Why that money changer was adamant not to listen to him. If Inder had shown or given his dollars to the money changer then he would have kept them in his safe and would not have given rupees in return. Why money changer was prejudiced and didn't see his passport. Why he was not looking into details to ensure fraudulence or originality of the passport. For him there was no end to unnecessary problems.

"Why this happens to me? What wrong is there with me? What kind of life I am living if I am denied like this at every step? What wrong I have done? What else is to happen to me? Why no one answers my questions?" Inder was having lot of questions in his mind. Inder was churning out with these questions after being out of money changer's office. After coming back to India he thought things would have been better for him at least, if not for his lot living in the landfill area in Ghazipur. The first day was better when Ishwar Jain showed some respect to his existence or capabilities. Things appeared better even when Bhumi took lot of interest in taking care of him after he was back. Water started dropping from the tip of his nose. Tears rolled down on his cheeks. Belief in his being human was shaken. Being human was elitist concept perhaps. Being human was limited to television screen and reality shows. For him being human was reduced to being sub-human. Being human was mirage if it was denied even to be sub-human. Being human was denied existence. Even being sub-human was denied existence. His existence was not his own. He was not responsible for his existence but his parents.

Idea of his parents haunted him a lot. Had his parents been in the world? Had they been touchable in the physical world of objects? Had they been palpable then perhaps the chain of denials in his life would have ended somewhere. Why had they left him alone? Why had they disappeared? Why was he so discarded? Why was he still in life? Why he had not been disappeared with them from the world.

His queries became endless. When it became endless then it ended there itself to leave the invisible endless trail with the visible end. Continued. He could not control himself.

"*O mere baap, O maai baap,* where have you gone leaving me alone" he cried. He cried like a kid at ten. He cried like a kid at eight. He cried like a kid at five. He cried like a kid at three. He cried like a kid at two. He cried like an infant. He cried. His existence cried.

"They had already done their part to bring you in this world. Inder, they could not live longer in this world full of people filled with scorn, filled with filth, and to fill this world with filth. And, we are left here to clean their filth, fecal filth" Jhihari held Inder with shoulders firmly and wiped his tears.

"Don't lose heart my brother, you are a brave man, you have studied being submerged in this filth, cleaning this filth, collecting reusables from this filth, making them ready for reuse, amidst this you studied. You have got high education, one day this education will free you from these miseries." Jhihari consoled Inder. "May be it will free few more of us." Jhihari still held Inder's shoulders with both of his hands.

"Hm, this will not let me lose heart" Inder stood up. "Ability to learn had moved me ahead in life" he also counseled himself.

They came out in the parking area where Jhihari's rickshaw was chained with an electric pole. Jhihari got busy in unlocking the rickshaw. Inder looked upward. Inder looked at the complex building. His eyes were panning the building. Education Board hoarding haunted him a lot. To Inder that education was farce if it was not relieving the people from the scales of the millennial sufferings, centuries of darkness, decades of turmoil, even after centuries of renaissance, even after decades of planning, even after decades and decades of green revolution, even after decades of white revolution, even after decades of liberalization, even after decades of globalization, even after decades of human investments given in improvement of living, even after decade of India shining, even after decade of innovation, but might that liberation come in decades of booming, decades of . . . decades of . . . Inder's eyes again brought their waterline along with anguish. But anguish also flew down on his cheeks only nowhere else.

"Seeing this board, what comes to my mind is that I should collect my certificates and come here to throw them on the face of the head of the Education Board." Inder busted his anger. He pointed at the building and its hoarding.

"What will you get out of this?" Jhihari asked Inder. "You have got degree too" he reminded him. "Will you go to the university to throw your degree on someone's face?" he asked. He wanted to question the idea of showing anger like that. He again held Inder's hand to sit on the bench of his rickshaw, "Come and sit on the seat, let us move from here" he started the engine of his rickshaw to go out of the parking area.

But Inder did not buzz.

Jhihari put the engine off. "Anger will not get you anything Inder, it will not get you anywhere, but I can, I can take to your place, Bhumi's place" Jhihari attempted to amuse Inder. *"Gusse se kuchh nahin milega"* he reemphasized.

"Come and sit down in the cart, I am starting it again" Jhihari again asked Inder to leave the space.

Inder looked at Jhihari who had already started the engine. He stepped up to settled on the bench of the rickshaw.

In her room Bhumi looked at her books. Sometimes she looked at the wall clock. She looked into her course books. She was a bit restless. Her mother, Mahima entered her room and sat on the chair nearby. Her mother closed her eyes. Bhumi looked at her mother's face. She then looked at the wall clock then into the book in her hand.

"Bhumi, my daughter, can we discuss something?" she asked. "I want to discuss with you about what I have observed in few days" her mother pulled the chair close to her.

"Tell me" Bhumi said. She anticipated how discussion was going to be. Still she said "*batao maa kya pareshani hei?*"

"For last few days, you are having lot of restlessness" Bhumi's mother bent down towards Bhumi who was sitting on her bed.

"No *maa*, nothing is like that" Bhumi differed. She differed to defer the talks.

"*Beti*, I am your mother, I know you better" Bhumi's mother insisted to discuss. She pruned Bhumi's hair with her fingers.

"Why are you asking all this?" Bhumi wanted to know the reason. She knew the reason rather. Still she wanted to know what her mother had observed.

"You are taking lot of interest in Inder since he is back" Bhumi's mother looked into Bhumi's eyes.

Bhumi looked back into her mother's eyes. She didn't say anything. She kept looking into mother's eyes.

"Why are you saying like that?" Bhumi broke silence.

"You move here and there around Inder's room when he is in the house. You kept an eye on the gate when he is out for some work. You take interest in keeping his room and surrounding clean. You look into kitchen even when each of us is done with meal but Inder is around and not taken his meal. More frequently than before, you visit outer room since he is back from Canada. Before that you limited yourself to your coaching from him. Even right now your eyes are looking for Inder when he is out for his work. Your ears are waiting for his knock at the gate. Why are you doing that? He is not from our community. He is not your match for sure" she wanted to educate her daughter on limitation of her family and community norms.

"*Maa*, that all I used to do even before. Nothing is like that, that I am interested in him. I have not done anything extra which I had not done before his visit to Canada. Why do you doubt so much? I don't understand." Bhumi wanted her mother to believe in her.

"But your attention towards him has increased, it has increased a lot" Bhumi's mother held up Bhumi's face by chin. She looked into Bhumi's eyes. "This is not me only who have observed that all. Even your father also has noticed that. Inder is just our servant nothing more than that. He cannot be more than that as he is amongst poorest of the poor. It is your father who wanted to help people like him by giving them employment so that person like Inder should come up in life. That's it. Your father is aware of his duty towards society and other people. But he never forgets the belongingness to our community" she spoke continuously as she wanted to erase every liking bit from Bhumi's mind. She thought continuous speaking might clear Bhumi's mind fast.

"What's going on between mother and daughter? Let me hear" Ishwar Jain entered the room. He was sitting in the hall. He heard bits and pieces of long going discussion between mother and daughter.

"So, Mahima you are counseling Bhumi. Counseling her for what? What has our daughter done so she needs counseling?" Ishwar took another chair to settle.

"I don't understand anything. You just fix some good match for Bhumi" Ishwar's wife Mahima wanted to dictate him. She thought Bhumi should be given to a suitable boy in marriage as she was hiding her intentions for Inder.

"What happens, are you OK? She wants to do CA first" Ishwar was sure about his daughter's intentions. He looked at Mahima's face with surprise.

"I am saying after considering many things. Why don't you understand?" Mahima exhaled all of her breathe. Her nostrils swelled in anger.

"Let her complete her CA" Ishwar wanted to pacify the matter between mother and daughter.

"She can do CA after marriage also" Mahima didn't want any respite to Bhumi. She also wanted her husband endorse her decision.

"Let me know what has happened that made you reach at this" he said. He could not understand Mahima's hurry for Bhumi's marriage.

"She does not take interest in her study" Mahima pointed at Bhumi.

"How can you be so sure? *Kya hua?*" he asked his wife. He looked at Bhumi on the bed sitting with her head down.

If she does not take interest in her study then how can she complete her CA?" Ishwar wanted to divert Mahima's attention.

"Then you just give her to a suitable boy in marriage. She can't complete her studies anyway." Mahima disapproved Ishwar's logic to complete her study.

"Do you want to say something" he asked Bhumi. He wanted Bhumi to pacify. *"Koi galti hui ho to maafi mang lo maa se"* he added.

"Papa, just ask mom, what makes her to be so sure that I am not taking any interest in my studies." Bhumi broke her silence. She forgot to say sorry to keep her father's word. Might be she wanted to discuss her stand then say sorry.

"Haan, I am just a fool, I don't know anything" Mahima used her parental authority in cursing Bhumi. Then she cursed in general and fanned out her anger in the room.

"Cool, have patience let me understand what has happened? What makes you so sure about her?" Ishwar made it a point of discussion. He wanted to know everything before any other thing to happen.

"She keeps roaming around the outer room where Inder is living in our house. This tendency is on the rise since he has come back from Canada." Mahima described her immediate problem. She scornfully looked at Bhumi as if she hated her daughter since birth.

"Since Inder is back from Canada? Does this have any connection? Inder is our servant nothing more than that" Ishwar said in simple terms. He didn't accept her daughter had any liking for Inder. *"Hamari beti Inder ko kaise pasand kar sakti hei apne liye?"* Ishwar Jain wanted to make her mother believe that Bhumi can't choose Inder as her fate. He looked at Bhumi in question. At the same time he wanted Bhumi to comply with his words. Though he maintained his cool but his eyes got red as if blood vessels poured more supply to energize his communication to his daughter.

"It is good that Inder is nothing but servant, but he may not remain merely servant if your daughter keeps her focus on his presence, whether he has taken food or not, where he is going, what he has to do, when he is waking, when he is sleeping etc. etc." Mahima counted on evidences against Bhumi in single breathe. Against her daughter.

"Oh my goodness, I don't believe this, our Bhumi is not like that." Ishwar looked at Bhumi. "How can you believe that all?" he attempted counseling Mahima. *"Tumhein jaroor koi galatfahmi hui hei"* he wanted to pacify with Mahima.

"Ye sab chinta karne jaise kaam to use bhai samajh ke bhi kiye ja sakte hein" Ishwar counseled his wife that Bhumi might have taken

brotherly care for Inder. At the same time he gave her daughter hidden instructions to mold her attraction towards Inder.

"Aajkal koi saga bhai saga nahin hota" Mahima still warned her husband about shifted sense of trust in Inder on brotherly relationship.

"Like an elder brother Inder took care of Bhumi's studies, in this sense Inder is more than our servant." Ishwar added to shape her opinion. He wanted Bhumi to look ahead for studies. Chartered accountancy was his passion that he thought her daughter would fulfill during his life.

"Sorry *Maa*, I am sorry, why are you making it unnecessarily some important subject to discuss at this point." Bhumi reacted. She got what their parents wanted. She had to reshape the entire design of her thought and future as well. "There is nothing like that to worry about me or my future or for fixing the match" she added before she left the room to let her father handle the situation. Her mother was still not convinced with the decision to defer the idea of marriage. Or not taking any decision regarding Bhumi's marriage first of all. Mahima felt helpless.

"Brother and like brother in this case are conceptual things in today's time, don't you read newspaper?" Mahima dug into Ishwar's eyes. "I hear much news on the television or from the neighborhood" she put her logic from daily experience.

"What do you want to say?" Ishwar asked.

"I don't know. You only gave him a job five year ago. Now gave him a place to live. Tomorrow you will give your dau . . ." Ishwar kept his hand on Mahima's mouth to stop her saying which he could not even imagine so he didn't want to hear. Mahima wanted to blame it on her husband Shri Ishwar Jain.

"I gave him a job five year back because I found him sharp in keeping things in order. I remember he used to come with very useful things which he collected from the wastes in the streets. This *kawad* business is with us for generations and I find him useful for our business and gave him a job." Ishwar wanted to explain his business sense. He looked around in the house know about Bhumi who could not hear them talking. "That's it nothing more than that" he emphasized.

She did not show any signs that she got convinced.

"Inder started collecting useful things from household. He used to be very good in keeping things in order. He had been good with his studies and passed his Intermediate with science. He developed very good understanding in commerce subjects also. Seeing this all I gave him book keeping for our work. He has mastered the art of book keeping even being science student. Many of us may not have that kind of capability that he has got. If you look at this from business point of view, keeping him for so many jobs is very cost effective. Cheap labor you don't get easily, that too an honest one. Though Inder is poorest of the poor but he is an honest person. His honesty is rare being among such kind of people who collect petty valuables from the waste. His honesty is beyond doubt" Ishwar whispered to Mahima. Ishwar did his part in counseling Mahima to have some considerations for business sense over emotions of relationship stuck in trivial matters. "To get our own work easily done I had asked him to stay in the outer room of our house for many things, such as, his availability, saving traveling time and security" he wanted Mahima to understand his viewpoint.

"*Is se hamari insecurity badh gayi*" Mahima wanted to come back in discussion with pointing out increased insecurity on account of Inder's presence in the house. She didn't want to lose just like that.

"*Ab main tumhein kaise samjhaoon*" Ishwar got puzzled with Mahima's stand. He felt helpless as he wanted to convince her on Inder's honesty and truthfulness would reduce the risk of insecurity rather than increasing risk of that.

"If you have seen so many good points in Inder then you won't listen to my point of view. You do whatever you want to do. Tomorrow you just don't come to me with complaints that our daughter has lot of interest in Inder." Mahima clarified. She wanted to leave the room before Ishwar Jain said something more to counsel her. Ishwar held her hand to stay.

"Bhumi may be having interest in him just because Inder is intelligent, we will make sure that Bhumi is always aware of the fact that Inder is a waste picker from landfill area of Ghazipur which is full of filth and fecal stuff. His all wealth is up to survival of his life, no comfort, no quality, no good future, no life style, etc." Ishwar attempted to convince his wife.

"That means we keep our eyes closed when she is around Inder." Mahima asked in blaming tone. She was worried why Ishwar was not thinking and deciding as Bhumi's father rather than an intelligent and wise person engaged in business out of the waste items collected by *kawadis* and people like Inder.

"No, what I have said doesn't mean this." Ishwar clarified.

"Then what?" Mahima had big query with confused mind. Her husband did not seem to clarify her confusion.

"Look, Bhumi is now in college and studying commerce. Among new friends from rich families with good background she will automatically discard Inder's poverty." Ishwar wanted to assure Mahima on the basis of peer pressure the most effective tool in the college life which can improve or deteriorate life. "She will not give weightage to Inder's foreign visits etc. as there may be many more boys in the college having opportunities to settle abroad. Meanwhile Inder may settle somewhere in career and life as we are not his permanent employment and stay" he added to counsel and convince the lady hard to buzz to new perspectives to look at thing in modern times.

"So, you are in favor of Inder's stay here, and Bhumi may meet him as she meets." Mahima said with worrying long face. She found her husband didn't buzz idea of marriage.

"No, I didn't mean that, you can always warn Bhumi about limits she has to maintain while talking or behaving on any matter with Inder." Ishwar gave space to Mahima for being a responsible mother. "Not even this, you can claim sanction from my side to keep extra care and scolding to make her behave responsibly" he wanted Mahima to enjoy her liberty in that regard.

"That's what I was doing when you interfered" Mahima took on Ishwar. She gave such big face at him as if he had wasted two hours of his valuable time. She thought where the business sense was.

"Choose the way that doesn't hurt or humiliate her." Ishwar pointed out that she needed to improve in dealing with young generation.

"You run your business and deal with people so sophisticatedly while we deal with the fire in the kitchen, pressure of *belan* roller on chapatti, clamping hot chapatti with tongs, so ladies know these ways to deal with people and children as well." Mahima justified her ways of managing the kitchen and kids in similar manner.

"Ok, I agree, now you know few more ways to deal with, in relationships." Ishwar gave counseling tips to his wife on dealing with people in relation and otherwise.

Silence filled the space that discussions and argumentations had left. Silence stayed for longer. Bhumi entered the room.

"Bhumi, your mother may be right in her place, you just listen to your mother. She has lot of experience of life and cares for you and your wellbeing and safety." Ishwar left a cue for discussion between mother and daughter before he left the room.

"So, you have convinced papa also regarding your view point of life." Bhumi said to her mother with bit of acerbity. She looked at other side on the wall to avoid eye contact with her mother. Then she took a book from the rack in the bed to read.

"*Beti*, I don't know much about you and Inder, but I know for sure that nowadays we cannot trust anybody. You must have read news like driver for ten years has abducted the daughter of the house. Servant for fifteen year in a house has allured the daughter of the house with all the money available and left her after few months of abuse. Not only that so many events in which the girl gets raped if such people could not allure or trap the girl in their tricks." Mahima wanted to cite examples from the endless list of the cases. Being mother she explained to show care for her daughter.

"*Maa*, I know this all and I know my responsibilities. Believe me I will never deviate from my responsibilities." Bhumi assured her mother on righteous behavior. Mahima pruned Bhumi's hair with her fingers and left the room.

Bhumi was alone in the room giving a thought to the parental hold on her emotions. She looked in the mirror of her bathroom.

"You look pretty and beautiful. You want to become bold and beautiful." Bhumi said to herself in the mirror assessing her assets. "A shift is required to be like that" she advised the girl in the mirror. She looked into her big eyes blackened at the edges of eyelid and tear duct. She liked beauty of her eyes. She found her eyes were inviting ones. Her close lips loving each other to compete with each other. Cupid bow, white roll with pinky vermilion all were enough to make someone think love and only love. She could understand that day why pink was for love. Pink was from lips ever competitive to love each other.

She then looked in the totality of the face for what she was known as Bhumi among the people around her. Her forehead, temple, cheek bone, cheeks, hanging lobules of the finely curved out ears, slim and sharp nose balanced with triangularity of the face, philtral dimple shaping the cupid bow of competing lips, slim chin to match prominent long neck to give the space to high bosoms of the breasts were more than enough to make her eager to look for someone who looks madly at her looks and only her looks.

"It is sure that Inder is a good person and has good place in her life" then she assessed Inder who was living in herself. She searched him with herself in the mirror. "He is so irresistible after he is back from Canada. When he became so irresistible she could not know. May be he was called by people abroad so she could see his future." She could see her future in his future. "Was he not merely her tutor before he went to Canada? Am I so weak to him to be her future?" Bhumi asked herself in the mirror.

"You had not felt this attraction any time before this." Bhumi complained the girl in the mirror. "You had been taking guidance on many subjects from Inder. Most of the people in neighborhood hold very good opinion about you" Bhumi assured herself about reputation that Jain family commanded in the neighborhood.

"You just could not love a lot. You feel jealous of mine being mine" then it was the turn of the mirror to warn Bhumi who was complaining. "You have been watching me for years. You could not realize how beautiful I was. You just focused on your beauty" mirror remained to be mirror as Bhumi again wanted to be cautious about her. "You could not realize how beautiful I am but Inder's eyes seem to realize if not his lips." Bhumi came back into her and wanted to play the blame game with the mirror.

"Man's eyes can realize anything love worthiness in a woman. Every inch of a girl in her youth for that matter" the mirror wanted to say something different at that time.

"I didn't know the knot between you and me as you never said what was in your heart. I thought it is Inder that I could fell for. I didn't know what was between you and the behind wall. I was waiting for Adam's fall. Inder didn't fall so I fell, so that people can make my life hell. Had you fallen in love with me would have made me not to fall till you are on the wall. Till you are on the wall" she cried after her painful complaints to the mirror.

Her body was paining her. She could not make out before she cried out. She cried out but not clear and loud. Then she sobbed, and she sobbed a lot.

"If you keep allowing Inder to be so tempting that one day you would be covered under his aura. What are you doing is not right thing for you" she wanted to discover her own aura outside Inder's.

"You want to grow along with the tree that you are budding from. Inder may be a tree that coming leaning towards her to have a graft of its own kind. Graft would be painful act. Graft would be a joint adventure of existence of equality. Graft would take a unique space to grow in a unique way. A Graft would be a graft. Its fruits would neither of the original ones nor having any new identity" Bhumi seemed to emerge out of Inder's aura.

"So, Inder is not my cup of tea. He had been my tutor. He had been my teacher in many aspects. He had been my mentor. He is definitely not a match. If you force it to be a match then it will be a painful match. He is certainly not her future" she evaluated Inder's influence in past, present and for future. Garnering closeness with Inder was to be avoided. It should be visible also, so that parents should not feel hurt. Bhumi was submerged in thoughts to come out of her old thoughts.

Success without honor is an unseasoned dish. It will satisfy your hunger, but it won't taste good.
Joe Paterno

∂IS i:z

Dish ease

Inder took fast pace when he came down from the rickshaw. He was more cautious than he was in the morning. He took pace as if the money exchanger was still watching him. He was behaving as if everyone in the street led to the Jain house in the colony was a money changer. He forgot that Jhihari was still with him. He almost ran towards his room. Jhihari chained the rickshaw with pole on the road. Jhihari understood Inder's difficulty. It was around three O' clock in the afternoon.

"Jhihari have not come yet" Inder asked himself. Inder took out his passport from the pocket after he entered the room. He looked at the father name written in the father's name column of the passport. It read as 'Jamb Deep'. His fingers touched the letters in his father's name. Perhaps nothing else remained as palpable as the letters in his passport and certificates. They were to make him feel his father's presence. His fingers were open like he wanted to hold his father's hand to move in the direction where his father would have taken him. Inder closed his eyes as if his father had come and said, "My son, open your eyes and see how beautiful this world is."

No picture was formed in his imagination for his father. Why no picture was forming in his imagination. When did he see his father last time? How old he was at that time? Memory was not responding. What he could remember was that he was sitting in his father's lap in the fields after harvest season of the crop. Some people came with big sticks in their hands. They were taking the harvest. Inder's father resisted. No memory being in father's lap or its warmth after that. Inder opened his eyes and closed his passport to keep it in the almirah.

"Jhihari has not come yet" Inder asked himself. He came out to the gate to see whether Jhihari was stuck with some new problem. He came back in the room and lied down on the folding bed. He changed side on the bed. He heard some sound on the gate. Inder left the folding to come to the gate thinking it must be Jhihari. He saw Bhumi when he opened the gate to come inside the house. It was hard for Inder to smile at Bhumi but he smiled. She also smiled and went inside the house. Inder turned back again when he heard knocking sound from the gate.

"Where you got stuck up?" Inder asked when he saw Jhihari at the gate.

"I stopped to buy some food." Jhihari came inside and moved towards the room.

"Good" Inder followed Jhihari after latching the gate inside.

Jhihari opened the packet of chapatis on the table, removed the rubber band from the polyethene containing curry. Inder picked a plate and bowl from the window sill and kept them on the table.

"Your Bhumi is not around." Jhihari wanted to make it lighter space for Inder to forget money changer's attitude.

"Must be in her room, she is just back from the college." Inder informed chewing piece of chapatti he took.

"Let us finish fast before she may come to meet you." Jhihari ate his chapati in bigger lobes. He ate fast to finish fast.

"May be, and may not be" Inder replied late to Bhumi's entry predicted by Jhihari. He was stuck in the idea of his father.

"I didn't get you" Jhihari was confused.

"She was tensed when she exchanged smile on the gate, and went inside as soon as she could after she saw me at the gate." Inder said. He told what happened when he went to open the gate anticipating Jhihari.

"Now, what is to be done?" Jhihari asked Inder.

"First I need to contact Mr. Kul Vilas to know action planning. Hwaib assumed Mr. Kul Vilas is coordinating the team." Inder explained background of the action needed.

"Do you have his number?" Jhihari enquired.

"Yes, I have" Inder replied. He also finished his meal fast.

"How would you contact? You don't have mobile phone." Jhihari asked.

"That is why I had gone to exchange the rupees, so that I can buy a mobile phone." Inder answered.

"Will some old mobile phone do?" Jhihari asked.

"How will you get that" Inder asked.

"I will ask Niranjan to arrange a phone." Jhihari replied. He didn't want to tell many details about Niranjan.

"Niranjan? How come?" Inder wanted to know.

"Nowadays, he is in the network of the boys who pick mobile handsets from the car on the road crossings." Jhihari did not want to tell Inder anything more about his cousin.

"Nowadays? I don't understand?" Inder got puzzled with Jhihari's reply.

"He keeps changing the job as he finds it to be risky and to avoid any face-to-face confrontation with the police. He is still not in the knowledge of police." Jhihari updated about Niranjan.

"This is the only work left for him? *Kuchh aur nahin mila karne ko?*" Inder put his palm on his forehead.

"That all I don't know, do you want mobile?" Jhihari's question was simple.

"Now where from will I get a SIM card?" Inder answered with question. "If everybody starts behaving the way money exchanger behaved in the morning, it will be difficult to get a SIM card" he added.

"He will arrange you a SIM card also. Do you want a mobile phone?" Jhihari asked Inder. He knew Inder would not accept a stolen mobile.

"No" Inder denied.

"*Sach mein?*" Jhihari asked. He looked into Inder's eyes.

"No means no" Inder replied.

"Why are you biting your nail? You just ate your food. Are your nails sweet dish?" Jhihari asked. He wanted Inder to win over his disappointment.

"Now I have doubt about myself, my existence, and my possibilities" Inder went cynical.

"Then what will you do?" Jhihari asked. "Such kinds of humiliation I face every day" he added with grim on his face.

"You are educated, intelligent and hardworking. Why do you have doubt about yourself? I don't understand this riddle" Jhihari questioned Inder's cynicism which didn't have utility for his lot.

"I don't know" Inder answered.

"He denied my passport" Inder complained about money changer.

"And you are finished after that" Jhihari didn't want to entertain Inder's cynicism. "I used to remind you to get a ration card then it would have been easier" he nagged Inder.

"Even ration card I cannot get easily" Inder said.

"Are you a terrorist?" Jhihari questioned Inder's identity in sarcasm.

"Even a terrorist can get mobile phone and SIM number, an intruder can get ration card, but a poor Indian may have to struggle to get that also. Even if he gets then also he does not enjoy the power to convince that he is an Indian." Inder opined. He revealed with utter helplessness and hopelessness that was covering his aura unto his core.

"You have got passport, haven't you?" Jhihari asked.

"That is another thing" Inder answered.

"Yes or no" Jhihari stopped Inder for justifying with long cynical answer. "*Uljhao mat*" he insisted.

"Yes" Inder said.

"How?" Jhihari asked.

"That is because Ms. Veronique arranged some rich nonresident Indian having his house vacant in Mayur Vihar to show me as his tenant." Inder reminded.

"But you got it" Jhihari said. "Some similar way must be there to get you a mobile phone" he assured Inder. "Forget about Niranjan and his network of mobile pickers" he added.

"If I don't get mobile phone than I need to communicate with Mr. Kul Vilas and Mr. Hwaib through email." Inder said. He cleared the food remains on the table with the polyethene bag used for packing.

"You are a good boy" Jhihari amused.

"I have to" Inder said.

"I thought Bhumi will come to clean it" Jhihari cracked a joke. "She claimed so" he reminded Inder.

"In my absence" Inder reminded the remaining part of the claim. He smiled with Jhihari as he could see Jhihari also had very strong commitment to the cause that Inder had embraced.

"You can use my brother's number temporarily" Jhihari suggested another solution.

"Yes that may be done, in that case how will he do without mobile?" Inder pointed out.

"He will get another mobile" Jhihari said. "he doesn't need it as badly as you" he added.

"No, no, I remember he had faced lot of difficulties in getting that number also" Inder recalled.

"He can take that much pain for you. You are the only hope of ours" Jhihari assured Inder. He took the debris of food items and the packet with plates and bowl to wash.

"What else you are supposed to do with Kul Vilas or Hwaib?" Jhihari enquired with Inder.

"First I have to contact Mr. Kul Vilas. I'll ask what my role in the work is. Then I'll collect information on ailments of our people that they suffer due to the very dirty nature of our work. Same things I need to discuss with Mr. Hwaib when Kul Vilas send him the compiled information. Most probably I will be involved in preparing a final report which Hwaib needs." Inder counted one by one.

"Did you take photographs over there?" Jhihari asked.

"No I didn't have camera" Inder replied.

"Oh, I may require camera also to take photographs of our people who are suffering from different ailments. It needs to be a good camera." Inder reminded himself. He cursed himself for morning situation which delayed the availability of mobile and camera, "*sala sab chaupat ho gaya subhah.*"

"*Jane do*" Jhihari asked to forget the morning failure.

"We will buy a mobile phone with camera" Jhihari suggested.

"That will not work as photos taken with such camera will not serve the purpose" Inder cautioned.

"Then we will hire a good photographer for one day" Jhihari counted on other solution.

"That may be done" Inder agreed.

"By the way, I don't have any clue about your new assignments, what will be the result? How we are going to get benefit?" Jhihari enquired with Inder.

"Right now, I am also not very clear about that. I think these survey and report by international bodies are instrumental in good planning. In this case government can use the report in planning health facilities and services." Inder gave one probable answer. "Many studies don't focus alarming situations we are facing because of habits. This survey has consideration for waste management and our role that may be meaningful for us. In many of the countries they produce electricity from the waste" he updated Jhihari with possibilities.

"Will our conditions really improve by doing this?" Jhihari asked.

"I hope so" Inder replied.

"People like me will get a job in that power house?" Jhihari asked about himself. He chose to support Inder in that effort with nothing in his mind other than friendship and brother like relationship since childhood. But some interest for himself was making him strongly committed.

"Many of us think that it will leave us without waste and useful materials out of it. They all are opposing that machinery to process wastes. But I don't think so." Inder opined.

"I am sure you will get a job in that power house." Jhihari shared a hope for Inder.

"Who knows?" Inder said. "Most of our people should get a job in that power house according to the capabilities. Waste collection will undergo structural change in that case." Inder put forward a point for discussion.

"I could not understand anything, but you may get a job in that." Jhihari concluded.

"Let us hope" Inder agreed.

"By the way how much did you pay to buy our food?" Inder asked Jhihari. "I must think some other option to earn money" he added.

"I am your friend *yaar*, and I also earn money that may be little but it will do." Jhihari replied.

"No, I must restore to the routine work now. I spent the savings from my salary on preparation for the visit like buying shoes, clothes, bag, suitcase, etc." Inder explained his situation.

"I know that. You don't worry. I couldn't study but when I see you I find great satisfaction for myself that at least someone of us has got educated in college also. I am with you with everything I have." Jhihari opened his heart to support the cause.

"I know this all" Inder sighed.

"Let's have tea outside" Jhihari asked. "We can go to some PCO also where you can make call to your Kul Vilas and Hwaib" he suggested Inder to come out for a walk.

They left the room to have a round around.

Inder and Jhihari reached at a tea stall in Ghazipur area. They sat down on the bench along with the wall of the stall. Jhihari had left his rickshaw open. There was lesser risk of theft. Everyone in the landfill area knew them.

"How are you Babu *bhai*? Make two glasses of tea for us." Jhihari asked the person sitting on a stool behind platform housing big stoves. He ran the tea stall.

"How are you Inder ji? You have gone foreign. *Kaisa hei wahan*?" Babu asked Inder pouring water in the tea pan. "When you were in foreign Jhihari used to talk about you daily" he added.

"*Main achchha hoon Babu bhai*. Now I have come back. Foreign is also fine." Inder replied. He wanted to match Babu's tone.

"*Tum kaise ho?*" Inder asked to know how Babu was.

"What is there with people like us to tell you?" Babu said. "Whole life I have to spend sitting behind the fire of stove, rotten smell of this waste hill of Ghazipur" he described how his life was going on. "You have been lucky that you have got Jain *sahab's* job and got some distance from this filthy hell" he added. "*Hamare pass batane ke liye kya hei, kuchh nahin*" he reemphasized the meaninglessness and futility of his life in despair.

"*Nahin Babu bhai aise himmat nahin harte*" Inder sugested not to loose heart. Yes, you are right that I have been lucky to get a chance to distance myself from the filth" he agreed with Babu. He could see how last 10 years has put all the ageing marks on Babu's body, face, hair, and might be on his self or soul of religious notion.

"Had I tolerated the beating of the teacher in my primary school?" droplets dropped from each of Babu's eyes. "I also could have thought to come out of this hell. What to do I got very bad teacher in the beginning of my life, in class one I got beaten. I ran out of school in our village" he lamented on his conditions in Ghazipur. He was aware of the significance of education.

"Why don't you go back to your village? *Wahan ki aavo-hawa is Ghazipur ke waste se to achchhi hogi.* You can live a good and healthy life over there." Inder wanted to show him a way. He knew that foreign tag make people like *Babu* to listen. He looked at Babu's bony rib cage. Flesh got disappeared from that.

"No, no, Inder no, life for poor man in our village is also very bad, day-night labor work for rich landlord is your fate if you don't have land to plough." Babu said. "*Hamare hi gaon ka kya, ye to bahuton ka haal hei, yahan jara panch sau meter ke area mein dekh lo. Beesiyon gaon ke logon ka dera yahan gande teele ke aas paas hei*" he also wanted to educate Inder on rural conditions where earning two meals had been a great challenge. Rather that waste hill was capable to ensure some earning out of selling useful items collected from the waste that came from rich people who worked in offices.

"For weeks you don't get food and find yourself at the mercy of your rich landlord in the village if you are not having land to plough" he could not stop himself to explain conditions of a rural poor man in most of the Indian villages.

"Hm" Inder could not say anything further on going back to his village. He found his logic very weak as he himself had been brought up by Ranchit who had come thirty years ago and didn't go back to his village. How could Inder teach anyone what he or people in his life could not do so" he kept quiet.

"Here you get menial work and get few rupees to fill your stomach. Or, even you don't get anything then you collect some useful material in the waste around in the city and can get some rupees." Babu added looking at the clouds. After scorching heat for past few days it was cloudy evening. Black clouds worried him.

"You can call up your Kul Vilas first" Jhihari reminded Inder.

"Are! wahi hua jiska dar tha. It has started raining now" Babu made a big face looking at waste hill of the landfill area. "Now, you will have to tolerate worst kind of smell from this waste hill. When wastes get wet its smell becomes worst in world" he cringed and touched his nose.

"Now, you can't go to the public calling office at *paanwala* shop, so let us finish tea first" Jhihari said.

"Take your tea Inder" Babu poured tea in two glasses.

"In the rainy season, Babu *bhai* you can always shift your stall to some high place where this kind of water logging is not there. So that, waste is not mixed with water and fecal stuff" Inder suggested. He took his tumbler full of tea and looked at the rain water outside the stall.

"I also suggested him the same thing in the past" Jhihari said to Inder taking his tea.

"Are, what is this? Babu *bhai* Thatching roof of your stall is leaking in this normal rain what will happen if it rains heavily in the rainy season." Jhihari asked Babu as few drops from thatching of stall dripped into his tea. He moved to other bench.

"What to do in today's tough time I am not able to save enough money to get it repaired." Babu showed how helpless he was.

"But, this way your health will be affected worst." Inder cautioned Babu.

"Kya, Inder it is not only our health but our lives are affected worst, see that side, our houses are also having this mix of waste and water creeping and seeping in to our jhuggies." Babu said. *"Mujhe khushi hei ki tumhari zindagi to ban gayi"* he expressed his happiness for Inder who got freedom from the filthy fecal feigning waste getting fecal disposal mixed in the water down in the feet. He looked at Inder who got worried about making phone call from PCO.

"I have shifted eight months back only. Till then I had been one among you only" Inder reminded Babu. Now Inder realized the value of staying in Jain's house. However, that smell and polluted air covered much larger area than that colony where Jain's house was situated. *"Ye badboo to wahan bhi aati hei, haan is se thodi kam aati hei"* Inder equalized the impact to lessen Babu's pain.

"Look at Jhihari and Ranchit. They also suffer from diseases for ten months in a year." Babu pointed out Inder's support family in which Ranchit was suffering from many ailments. He pointed out decades old problem of the poorest of the poor. Waste filled. Land filled. Land hilled. Wind milled. Wind smelled. Nostrilled. Nose filled. Throat gilled. Voice shrilled. Lungs filled. Lungs stilled. Slowly . . . slowly . . . Poor gets killed. Slowly . . . slowly . . . To be fossiled . . . Will be fossiled . . .

"Jhihari is fine. Jhihari doesn't have any disease." Inder looked at Jhihari. Inder didn't want to weaken Jhihari morally to live in the area as there was no other option.

"No, Inder, you may not have noticed because Jhihari is still young. But look at his brother his lungs are having problem." Babu's eyes diagnosed Jhihari.

"Not only is he young but also because he is still away from liquor" Inder counted on another reason for Jhihari's good health in bad area.

"Theek kehte ho Inder" Babu nodded in agreement with Inder. *"Jhihari ne abhi peena shuru nahin kiya na isliye theek hei"* he came with available health consciousness. *"Jab peena shuru karega tab shuru ke do ek saal theek rahega phir daru aur waste air donon mil ke usko khayenge . . ."* he looked at Jhihari. His envious eyes appreciated Jhihari's health because of being away from liquor.

"Hm, that is there" Inder agreed.

"Rain doesn't seem to stop, what shall I do now?" Inder asked Jhihari.

"Babu *bhai, chhata hoga?*" Jhihari asked.

"It is there. Will that serve your purpose? It has broken spokes" Babu said.

Inder and Jhihari just kept their glasses as they had finished their tea. Babu took them in his left hand and poured water with other hand to wash.

"Give us for a while, Inder will go to the PCO" Jhihari requested Babu to bring the umbrella out for Inder.

"*Dekhta hoon*" Babu left the seat. He bent down on his knees to look under a bench and dragged out an old umbrella. "This will not be sufficient for you two in this rain" he gave that to Inder.

"I will go to the PCO and Jhihari will stay here in the stall" Inder said. "*Abhi aata hoon*" he looked at Jhihari assuring to come back soon. He himself was not sure if he could reach to the PCO in that rain. But he assured Jhihari because he had to assure.

Jhihari nodded.

Inder opened the umbrella and moved towards PCO.

Babu looked at Inder's feet when he stepped out of the stall.

"I want to make a call" Inder requested the boy at the counter. He reached a roadside *paanwala* who kept a phone for PCO also.

"*Lo kar lo*" *paanwala* boy pushed the telephone set towards Inder. Inder took out a piece of paper to dial a number.

"O *bhaiya*, mind your umbrella, it is piercing and disturbing my Gutkha chain" *paanwala* reminded Inder to mind the umbrella in his hand. Inder took a step back and bent down to pick the chain of fallen Gutkha pouches with receiver on his ear. As he bent down telephone set sided with dragging force to fall down from the counter.

"*Are bhai, kya kar raha hei? Call karne aaya hei ya mere khoke par bulldozer chalane aaya hei?*" *paanwala* looked at bunches of pouches and chains of Gutkhas hanging on the wire tied at the ends of opposite walls of the counter. "*Aisi barish mein phone pani mein gir gaya to band ho jayega*" *paanwala* warned Inder if phone set fell then that might go faulty in the rain.

"What is there now?" Inder got puzzled. In the rain like that perhaps mind also got wet and didn't work." Inder laughed at himself when he saw that *paanwala* had just stopped the phone set from falling.

"*Aise mein humein to apni cheej ki chinta karni padti hei*" *paanwala* still held the phone set by his left hand on the counter as if he didn't let it fall in the rainy water on the ground.

"Thank you boss" Inder added.

"*Theek hei*, you should be sorry rather" *paanwala* corrected Inder.

"Hello" Inder said as the call got through. He looked at *paanwala*.

"May I talk to Mr. Kul Vilas?" Inder said. "I am Inder" he introduced himself. "Inder, I met you at Paris airport during flight on the way back to India. Mr. Hwaib introduced me to you" he further reminded Kul Vilas about himself by various means.

"Yes. Mr. Hwaib" he said with shining face. Finally he succeeded in reminding Kul Vilas about himself.

"I have called you up to know what I am supposed to do in this survey work. How will we do our assignment?" Inder put up his queries to Kul Vilas.

"I mean I . . . me . . ., myself . . ., in this team" Inder attempted to clear confusion as Kul Vilas told him that team was already there and he need not worry about that.

"I was talking about you and me. Mr. Hwaib said we will be working in a team." Inder still reminded Kul Vilas to know what was assigned to him by Mr. Hwaib. "I don't have a separate team as such" he added.

"Don't worry sir, I am enjoying my life" Inder managed himself as Kul Vilas said something which went uncomfortable to Inder.

"Let me know your email Id" Inder asked Kul Vilas. Inder noted down Kul Vilas' email Id.

"OK sir, thanks for your time, I will write to you" Inder completed the call.

"Can I make an ISD call?" Inder asked *paanwala*.

"There is no demand, sir, here people don't demand for ISD, and having ISD on this number scares me. Misuse might be there so I may lose much more than what I earn from this business" *paanwala* described situation rather than answered. "*Itne ghaple karte hein log ki bill bahut aata hei aur apni aisi taisi ho jati hei*" he emphasized.

"Sir, if you will be regular than I would arrange ISD on this phone." *paanwala* wanted to assure on the condition of regular revenue. His mannerism got a shift hearing Inder had been on foreign visit recently.

"I am not sure" Inder didn't assure him.

Inder paid the bill for the local call to Kul Vilas and moved for Babu's stall. Meanwhile, it stopped raining. Inder packed the umbrella. But Inder got wet due to dripping the water from broken and piercing spokes which left many small holes in the umbrella. Inder's trousers also were wet due to water logging. Shoes had been the first casualty to make Inder sad that evening. Kul Vilas' attitude was another reason to make him sad.

"Thanks Babu *bhai*, thanks for umbrella" Inder said when came back.

Babu grinned. He felt happy as that broken umbrella also brought him significance in that rain. Inder smiled at him.

"Let's move Jhihari, let us finish some other work. Today entire day went like waste only." Inder cursed himself. He also thought waste picking people had their days gone waste was not unusual. During the conference he got to learn the significance of time as urgency and priority.

"What happened? Didn't you talk to them?" Jhihari enquired.

"I got Kul Vilas to talk but he was talking very casually. He is not willing to have me as team member." Inder said in sad tone. He turned to look at waste hill of the landfill area of Ghazipur. He interpreted Kul Vilas' behavior as if Kul Vilas got the stinking smell through the fiber and wireless mix of mobile technologies that got Kul Vilas off to him. Poor innocence matched rich ignorance.

"What was he talking to you then? How was he talking?" Jhihari asked.

"He said, 'enjoy your life'." Inder repeated what he heard from Kul Vilas.

"You must have told him that you are enjoying life." Jhihari suggested.

"No, that rich fellow didn't want to listen anything from me." Inder said. He bit nail of his right index.

"How come he talks like that?" Jhihari said with bit of surprise. "Kul Vilas also must have been impressed by your Hwaib and the work" he added.

"I don't know whether he is impressed or not, but he said '*aish karo aur is kaam ko bhool jao*'." Inder updated Jhihari with the bottom line of the call to Kul Vilas. His grim face witnessed anger and tension in his body.

"Oh" Jhihari said. "Then leave him. You directly contact your Hwaib" immediate suggestion was available from the friend who was committed to the cause.

"Then Mr. Hwaib will get wrong impression about us as Indians" Inder talked with misplaced sense of national responsibility. The responsibility that became burden on Inder's shoulders.

"You are thinking that way. Kul Vilas might have even written to Hwaib about you that you are not sincere in taking up the work or even trustworthy for this work." Jhihari cautioned Inder.

"Let me give one more attempt to contact." Inder replied. "Or I will write to Kul Vilas first then I will follow your advice" he added to agree with Jhihari.

"Ok" Jhihari said.

They left the tea stall. The day for Inder had been in dismay.

Society is not a disease, it is a disaster. What a stupid miracle that one can live in it.

Emile M Cioran

∂Izi:z

Disease

Inder sat in the chair with both hands on his forehead and his elbows basing on the table. His immediate worries were to have a mobile handset or cheap and easy access to Internet. He thought of buying mobile set when he would get rupees for his dollars. Computer he didn't think was required at that time as that would block all of his money. He discarded the idea of buying computer for himself. In that case he needed to write some communications to Hwaib so that it could be converted on email to be sent through cyber café.

He took out one register pad and started writing on it. When he was with Jhihari he thought he would write to Hwaib about what he required to start the work. However, the day when he faced dollar-rupees conversion failure and money exchanger behavior, he wanted to communicate on many other aspects which were responsible for that all. With passing hours he managed over his emotions and reactions. He chose to communicate on the aspects which he thought would impact health in totality.

How to begin communication with Hwaib was a puzzle for Inder. Whole night he kept writing. It was ten O' clock when Bhumi came to check whether Inder had come back or not. She found Inder was sitting in the chair and writing on the pad she went back to lock the gate. Inder kept writing and improving the communication. It was morning when he found birds started flying. He thought they flew in search of food. He had written few pages since evening. He read them for himself to check if any improvement was needed.

Dear Mr. Hwaib,
Greetings,

This communication must find you in good health with healthy weather in the States. I am writing you first time after your India visit which followed my visit to your country. I am not clear what way your unique survey, search, research that you want to have done in India would benefit us, Indians. You may be right that your team from the States or any other foreign land may not get the results that you want or the way you want them to have sanctity and sensitivity of data collected. However, you may not be right when thinking that any Indian would correctly present cultural traits or other aspects of Indians in comparison to others but many of the foreigners have observed, captured, and recorded better than many of the intelligent but biased Indians. Though mirrors have been part of our technology and culture since ancient times, Indians don't have time to look into mirror as we are busy mirroring you and your culture. Ever increasing sale of whiteness creams for women and now for men may suffice to what I want to explain when I am mirroring you. Similarly, backless backs of our elitist princesses to salaried and hairless chests of elitist princes to driving riding machos all are in the race to be at the helm of affairs either on the big or small screen or on the ramps from Durban to Daurala and Montreal to Malkaganj titles for both the genders to regenerate the whitenized culture of yours. You may congratulate us for culturally going global. I mean the culture of the erstwhile new world. You can boast the whole new world is modernized. You can boast that the whole today is Europeanized to maintain the originality of the concept.

Moreover, we the Indians don't love mirror as it demands us to look deep into our personality. Personality for us has been physique till recently, like spiritualism in India means religion, that too basically religion of the majority. One more thing to be mentioned here is our *Yog* which is also considered as spiritual in nature. Spiritual in the sense that I just have explained, means religious in nature. I used to think that *Yog* is like basmati rice or *neem* products that are geographical innovations of ours. I may be wrong as I heard that many variants being practiced in the states or elsewhere are claimed or patented over there. Anyway that is not our cup of tea in this context.

Coming to the context, as I had agreed earlier when we happened to meet and discussed, I again agree with your point that you need Indian people to do this job. That is why we are on the same job. Right! However, job that I have taken up now is very tough one. It may not be tough for experts like you. But it is appearing to me to be so. Not only hard, tough, difficult, and toilsome it is also appearing huge, ginormous, and humongous to me. Reason you may know. I am not an expert in your field. I am not an expert in understanding people. My communication skills also may not be sufficient for the job. Nowadays experts don't limit to communication skills. They have added many other things to that and call them soft skills, interpersonal skills, personality traits, life management skills, etc., etc. Ok let me limit to communication skills as I am lacking even this fundamental need and so not to let these skills confuse me.

Then why I should be on this job. Because you say you don't require an expert for this job. Because you say experts hinder the objective of the work. They have their own descriptions, interpretations, explanations, judgments, conclusions, justifications, a justification over what they want to see is what they watch and call them their observations. You say they have predilections to theorize and publicize before they submit, before they submit the main report to the main. And you say they come clear after meshing up things by clearing that they have been misquoted or quoted out of proportion. I was not having any imagination on this deep thought that you have put in the process. Shall I call the process of resource selection? Selection based on choosing few amongst the collected many. Have I understood correct? Shall I feel lucky on being among the chosen ones but what I feel now is confusing me.

Let me accept why this work is appearing huge to me. Frankly speaking we Indians are averse to planning. We love to hate planning. Planning kind of work we do only once in millennia. Now we are forced to do so under some compulsion or the other. However, this is today's phenomenon. In the ancient times, we were not like what we are today. Once upon a time few thousand years ago we had loved planning the work. That's what I just said we do once in millennia. That too we liked it too much. That planning had been very effective in assigning the task. Who will do what? Till when who will do what? Who will do it permanent? Who may have to do it as exception? Who are to do it throughout the generation? Who are to do it generation after generation? Who have to do it forever till dooms day reach? Who have to do it till the

Saturn cuts the sun completely on no moon days? I am telling you planning you do in the world that you are living in, had been in our best practice in our ancient times. You all may not be doing that much planning even today when you have developed many planning tools. The blueprint of the whole society was registered with a society for its protection like trade secret that in your land like a cola company keeps for protecting the chemistry of its drinks. I have heard this about the cola on few of the IP presentations during my education times, you may know it better. I also heard that company also going to open its trade secret.

So, I will communicate with you on the work as the work progresses. In the finalization we together and other team members may be preparing a report on this. The executive summary of the work may likely to include the introduction that is obvious, objective of the work, executive summary, search research survey contents. I would not be including any conclusion to avoid the expert flavor to top up the report at the bottom. I just don't want to do that.

Sincerely yours,
Inder Jeet
Landfill Area, Ghazipur

After reading and improving here and there Inder folded register pad. He prepared to take bath as he had to resume his work, Jain's disposal business. He had to manage the accounts of Jain disposals where reusable items were bought from the waste collectors and sorted out to supply in recycling industry. Other part of the business of Jain Disposals was chemicals for recycling industry were produced from both fresh and recyclable chemical wastes. When he was brushing his teeth his sight got stuck with a red dot on the mirror which was not there before he left for Canada. He could not get it in the beginning. Then he could make out that Bhumi maintained the room in his absence. That dot didn't give him any excitement. He came out of the bathroom and dressed up for the work.

Half of the Jain Disposals was a shaded area where pyramid like heap of materials collected from the waste was lying at center. Other half was the chemical part to process chemicals to produce raw materials for recycling in the industry. Factory like shaded area with eight feet high wall between pillars was open for heat generated by processing of the materials to vent out. Inder did not have to go inside the part for the chemical recycling other than taking readings for different parameters of processes. The shaded area where all the waste material was dumped by the collectors engaged with Jain Disposals was a work place for Inder.

Waste lying in the center in the shape of big pyramid was to be sorted in groups of reusable and recyclable bags, plastic toys, steel scrap, rods, nuts and bolt, screws and fixtures, cans, chemical containing cans, etc. At periphery there were open wooden racks aligned with the six feet high walls under the shade fixed in bricks coarsely masoned to support these boards on both ends. There was big space for reusable and recyclable bags of paper and plastic as they could not fit in the wooden racks.

Maithili, Mahabi, and Uttar of the landfill area came to the center to dump their collection after measuring done by Inder. After measuring all the material, Inder was assisted in the sorting work by Maithili, Mahabi and Uttar also who collected waste materials from different places in the residential colonies and Ghazipur wastes as time and season forced them to do so. Maithili, Mahabi and Uttar were working in the Jain Disposals for six months. Maithili and Uttar were about twelve and eight years old boys. Mahabi was a ten years old girl. Inder guided them to sort the reusable items from heap lying in the center and keep them in the wooden rack marked for each item along the walled periphery of the area under the shade.

"So Inder you have joined the work today" Ishwar Jain appeared from gate of the settlement.

"Yes sir" Inder came pushing the polybag chunk to the central heap.

"These children have been doing that work for six months or so." Ishwar said. "*Kaisa kaam kar rahe hein ye log*?" he enquired with Inder about their performance.

"They have understood the work very well." Inder replied.

"What is there in this work, they need to sort out the items and keep them in the wooden rack. That's all" Ishwar made that easy for them and for him to justify low payment like throw away money for the work.

"Sir many times small things are heavier for them, to lift and carry that to the marked rack." Inder pointed out difficult part for the kids.

"How much is that work?" Ishwar Jain asked. "For that they have rickshaw. I have seen them playing around and sitting on bench of the rickshaw then I feel they are enjoying their work which is good for their health. It is good that they got the work they enjoy otherwise they would have had tough time looking into the books to dig out the knowledge" he explained ease of waste picking vis-à-vis difficulties and challenges of studying in the school.

"Sir, it is their time to be in school but they are here as they don't have any support system from their parents. May be there is no support system for their parents." Inder replied with a bit of surprise as Ishwar Jain didn't talk on that line in the past.

"Inder, you must have enjoyed studying that's why you have been through in every class you studied but everyone of your lot is not having interest in digging the books." Ishwar justified what he said. "Now you are educated and foreign returned so chances are there for you to lose interest in doing this all. You have got foreign assignments also." Ishwar communicated to the point indirectly.

"What has made you think that way?" Inder asked. "I am very much here in this work" he declared his stand.

"Nothing like that I am saying what generally happens." Ishwar didn't want to answer Inder's question. He moved to the chemical area.

"Why Jain *sahab* was so changed now?" Inder got puzzled. "He had never talked to me like that. What could be the reason behind this?" he enquired with himself first. What wrong he might have done? What could have been his mistake? Inder was still investigating with himself. He heard Uttar's bellowing with pain. He rushed to the place where Uttar was working close to the rack. He took front wheel of tri-cycle for kids with pedal from the scrap to keep that in the marked rack for heavy iron items.

Before Uttar could place it on the rack properly he rushed to Mahabi who shouted as a reptile from the rags of polyethene and rubbish came out on her foot. Uttar could not move further to remove the reptile from Mahabi's foot as he got hurt by the pointed pedal fell on his right foot. A pedal without rubber pad and covering bowl on the pivotal point was a bit sharp to hurt the boy of eight. Weight of wheel housing the pedal caused aggravation.

"What happened?" Inder rushed to Uttar.

"*Pahiya paon par gira hei aur pedal ki naunk se chot lagi hei*" Mahabi replied in place of Uttar who kept wincing. She also winced with pain seeing the reptile left mark on her foot.

"You should be careful enough while working with heavy items." Inder said. He lifted his hand as if he would scold Uttar but took down in the next moment. He controlled himself and avoided chiding the child.

"*Wo Mahabi chillayi thi to main uski madad ke liye bhaga tha to pahiya mere hath se rack mein rakhne se pehle gir pada paon par.*" Uttar wiped his tears and explained what happened. He could not control the crying. He got scared when he saw Inder's hand up in air to beat him. Eight year kid maintained the mantle which many boys fail to maintain at eighteen.

"*Ek kantar sa keeda mere pair par tha. Main dar gayi thi*" Mahabi reasoned why she cried when a raptile was on her foot. "I had asked Uttar not to take that wheel. I would have kept that in the rack." Mahabi said. "*Par wo mana hi nahin, us se khelne laga*" she added. She complained that Uttar took that wheel for playing before he went to the wooden rack.

Uttar kept crying as his foot got swollen fast. Inder looked around and found one long rob like rag in the waste. He pulled it from the heap. He went to the water tap and washed it in the scrap tub to remove the dirt and dust. He then squeezed the wet rag to wrap it around Uttar's swollen foot.

"Now you just sit down and don't' jump here and there" Inder instructed Uttar. His hand went up in the air. Perhaps he wanted to scold Uttar so that he should be careful in future. He knew that physical violence on the kids was prohibited where he visited. He again brought his hand down. He was inspired to bring the same flavor in the culture here.

"Jain *sahab* talked about the simplicity of the work. He forgot the risks involved in that work." Inder murmured. He lifted Uttar's foot to look around if the rag was properly wrapped.

"*Kya hua Inder bhaiya?*" Mahabi asked Inder. She heard his murmurs.

"*Kuchh nahin*" Inder said.

"Why I have not learnt to tolerate the reptiles and insects. They are important part of our life in this work full of dust, dirt, damp, and stinking smell. Why girls are so weak in tolerating reptiles and insects. Why I am girl" Mahabi lamented as Inder's fury didn't come down. "*Bahut dard ho raha hei?*" she asked as if she experienced Uttar's wincing.

Inder started helping Maithili and Mahabi in sorting out the reusable items from the scrap and wastes collected by these kids and others.

"Inder *bhaiya* you just do your work. We will pick right items" said Maithili and Mahabi who collected their energy to resume.

Inder went to the chemical processing area where Ishwar Jain himself supervised the workers.

"Sir, Uttar has got hurt in his foot, he needs dressing" Inder informed Ishwar Jain.

"What have they done now?" Jain asked. "First aid box must be here. You do the dressing" he instructed Inder.

"There is nothing in the first aid box other than Burnol." Inder said as he already checked the First Aid box. He looked for something to relieve the swollen foot.

"Many times I told them to mind their work when at work. They should not play with the items they find in scraps. This kind of injuries happen because they want to play when they need to work" Ishwar Jain started cursing the kids.

"Sir, they are just kids of eight or ten years. They would have been playing and studying if they were not from the families where they have nothing but shortage of food, shelter, and education." Inder described their situation. *"Kahin amiri mein pale hote to khel hi rahe hote"* he added to emphasize the need to play and study. He told Ishwar if Uttar were from rich family then Uttar would have been playing rather than putting himself in the heap of scraps.

"In that case I am giving them employment otherwise they would have been starving. I am helping them in their survival" Jain declared. He wanted to pat on his shoulders in acknowledging himself for bailing out the families of these children from miseries.

"Thank you sir, right now Uttar needs some other medicines." Inder requested his boss to have mercy on the kid.

"Munim ji! Give him some rupees to take the kid to the doctor for dressing" Ishwar Jain understood the situation. Cashier opened the drawer and took out a hundred rupees note for Inder. After all he knew that Inder had come back from Canada where living and wellbeing were well taken care.

Ishwar Jain looked at the Cashier.

"Pachaas ka note nahin hein Sahab" cashier showed his helplessness in giving hundred rupees note to Inder as he could not find lesser

denomination like fifty. Cashier took the message from Ishwar Jain's eyes and replied, *"Aajkal doctor pachaas rupaye mein hath nahin lagate"* to justify the scale of costliness of medical treatment. He grinned to hide his folly.

Inder took hundred rupees note from the cashier and held Uttar's hand to support him to reach the rickshaw. Uttar had difficulty to walk. He took both of Uttar's arms over his shoulders and lifted Uttar to the rickshaw in which these kids came for their work from Ghazipur. He released the break as he slid the steel wire band wrapped over handle and break lever of the rickshaw. The kids also tightened that steel ring to park the rickshaw after they reached with the burden of the wastes collected from the landfill area. On weekly basis these kids collected waste from the households also. Inder took that rickshaw which he was feeling shy when he came back from Canada. That day Inder had got back to be a waste picker. He started pushing it manually. Uttar sat in the rectangular depression mend for waste. He pedaled it to the doctor.

"What happened to this boy?" doctor enquired seeing the rag wrapped around Uttar's right foot.

"Nothing doctor, he got hurt by wheel fallen on his foot. The wheel is from a junk rickshaw for small kids. He took that wheel to the rack but got that fallen on his foot." Inder explained to the doctor at once.

Doctor looked at him and smiled at Inder's hastened narration. He bent down to examine the foot. "Why you people bring kids like him to work?" doctor asked unwrapping Uttar's swollen foot.

"Foot is intact, nothing much serious has happened. It needs edema treatment" doctor applied a gel and gave the tube to Inder. "Keep this with you and apply it two times till the foot gets ok" he advised Inder.

"Doctor *Sahab*, how much shall I pay?" Inder asked.

"Nothing, this gel is from samples. I also have not paid for this" doctor said.

"Sir your fee" Inder said.

"No, you just take care of this kid" doctor said.

"Thank you sir, otherwise also this kid doesn't have any money to spare for you" Inder showed his gratitude to the doctor's generosity. With Uttar he left the clinic.

"Uttar, out of mercy doctor didn't charge. But that doesn't mean you keep hurting yourself while you are at work." Inder scolded Uttar on the way back to Jain Disposals.

"*Uttar aa gaya!*" Mahabi shouted as Uttar was back to the scrap shade. Maithili lifted Uttar in his arms to get down from the rickshaw. Uttar moved towards the place where polyethene bags, rags were lying in the layer above layers to make it like cushion. Maithili took Uttar to lie down on that cushion like pile for a while.

"Lucky boy, you have got this dressing when you got hurt so little." Maithili murmured.

"How come I am so lucky, I am also poor like you." Uttar asked with his little analytic mind as he heard Maithili's murmur. Maithili told a story to Uttar from his childhood when he was seven years old boy.

"I was younger than you when I was picking rags from the waste heap higher than myself. One good poly bag attracted me so much that I wanted to pull that bag which was packed little deeper in sedimenting layers of the waste in a big hill-like heap. I put all my strength at that time to pull that bag with the force that I could and fell down on a plastic can filled with acid. The acid got spilled over under my back. I was not having shirt or vest on my body and my skin got burning heat of the acid. I couldn't get any help I was running like bee. I wasn't getting any cool from that burning heat in my back. I ran to a pit big on the ground filled with dirty water. I lied down in the dirty water and remain lied in that water till I had burning heat in my back. That day I got some cool by wallowing in that punk pool but I could realize that my back got charred badly." Maithili unbuttoned the few buttons remaining on his shirt to show his charred back to Uttar. Uttar cried seeing Maithili's charred back. He kept crying. There was labyrinthine mess of burns and scars and flash altogether on a single back. Maithili's back.

"*Are beta chup ho ja*" Maithili asked Uttar to stop crying.

"*Bhaiya*, why do we suffer like this every day in our life?" Uttar asked Maithili. He didn't feel pain. He thought he had just piercing pinching hurt in the foot while Maithili had got his entire back charred with acid.

"May be because we are poor and we have to earn our food with or without help from our parents." Maithili said what he knew.

Inder who went to chemical area to take some measures from the process units came back to the shade area and asked the kids to leave for day. He had updated Ishwar Jain on dressing. The kids left the place. Inder came to the office. He took the account books of Jain Disposals. He took receipt books of different heads and started entering details in the relevant account books.

Everyone had gone but Inder was still in the office to update the account books. It was nine O' clock. He also closed the books and moved out of the chair. He splashed his face as he wanted to work for longer period. He took a break to think about his other tasks. He wanted to focus on what was to be done to contact Hwaib. Kul Vilas appeared to be callous but it was Kul Vilas only who would decide his participation in the work. He was worried about how to contact and communicate directly to Hwaib. He recalled whole journey and he found Hwaib supportive.

Inder decided to post the letter to Hwaib at office address as he didn't have Hwaib's personal address. Moreover, Hwaib might be expecting email or phone call from him. What he was dealing with was not so obvious to Hwaib that he could not write even an email just because he didn't have access to computer or internet.

Cyber café was one good choice for internet access. But that can be done only on coming weekend. By the way if he posted the letter that might reach Hwaib by the weekend only. No, it might take longer time. Email would be faster even if he would be able to have access to cyber café on weekend. What happened if he didn't get to be at cyber café even on Sunday then everything would get delayed. What about going to cyber café after the office time? In that case the letter had to be written on the computer in parts and then on the last day only it could be emailed to Hwaib. Inder was busy in solving his riddle. He felt presence of some one. He looked up. He saw Jhihari was watching him for a long.

"Jhihari!" Inder cheered.

"Yes" Jhihari said.

"How did you know that I am here?" Inder asked.

"I went to the room" Jhihari replied.

"You didn't find me there so you have come" Inder asked again.

"Have you had some fight with your Bhumi?" Jhihari asked

"What happened?" Inder said. "My Bhumi?" he squinted eyebrows.

"Have you really fought with her?" Jhihari asked.

"No" Inder said.

"She says you are not speaking to her" Jhihari disclosed.

"Tell me what do you want?" Inder smiled.

"Nothing, my friend, why are you making things complicated?" Jhihari poured his irritations in Inder's ears.

"Have you gone mad?" Inder asked. "What do you think is there to make things complicated?" he waved his hand in the air.

"My great concern, my dear, is that if she is not happy with you then you cannot stay in that room." Jhihari shared his wisdom over the matter.

"So what shall I do?" Inder asked. He looked puzzled as he was not sure what Bhumi had complained about.

"Do what she wants you to do?" Jhihari came with one point solution.

"She thinks that you have changed since you are back." Jhihari said. He inferred from the discussion he had with Bhumi.

"Did she tell you like that?" Inder enquired. He took one of the account books. He wanted to work for some more time. But this puzzle made him tired to work on the account book. He kept it back on the table.

"No, not like that, but she came to open the gate." Jhihari updated Inder. "She saw tiffin in my hand and said so much you care for your friend but your friend may not even bother where you are, whether you have taken food or not" he repeated what he got from Bhumi. "She also hinted that it may be possible that you like someone else and are ignoring her" he added.

"You please just stop making stories. I haven't seen her since I called up Kul Vilas." Inder said.

"That's why she says you are not speaking to her" Jhihari said.

"She herself didn't come out for days then how can I be responsible for any problem?" Inder analyzed. "Don't dig more meanings in it" he added. He pushed the account books to the other end of the table.

"I don't want to dig anything. She wants to meet you where she can talk to you freely." Jhihari disclosed. "What would you do if she wants you to dig her?" Jhihari couldn't control his digging into the matter.

"Jhihari! Mind what you are saying" he shouted.

"Sorry" Jhihari surrendered.

"Did she tell you anything like that?" he felt shy on the idea though he might like to dream such things.

"That mean you want her to beg you for affection, beg you for love, my dear not everything is communicated by words in this game." Jhihari educated Inder. "Do you think any girl can say what you are expecting?" Jhihari shared as if he was surprised.

"I don't want anything from anyone." Inder busted.

"But she wants, she wants something from you." Jhihari mystified Inder's little understanding on law of attraction.

"Do you know what she wants?" Inder asked.

"How do I know? Ask her" Jhihari simplified.

"Jhihari, you only told me that she wants something. You just leave me alone" puzzled Inder revealed his vexations.

"Means you also have that 'something' for her?" Jhihari claimed some discovery.

"Go to hell, let me do my work" Inder grinded his teeth.

"No, I will tell you what she wants from you" Jhihari pretended.

"Don't disturb me" Inder kept his anger live. He put head down to dig into the account books.

"She wants you to want something from her" Jhihari revealed another discovery.

"Jhihari you are meshing it again" Inder grinded his teeth.

"*Chhodo jane do*, now I want you do something for the kids of our landfill area." Jhihari asked what he wanted from Inder. "*Wo to bataye na bataye par mein bata raha hoon mujhe tumse kya chahiye*" he added what he wants from if Bhumi did not. "On weekend I will come there. Kids want to send money to their relatives." Inder replied.

"Inder you are great, you never take time to understand what is to be done when you are called upon." Jhihari extolled Inder.

"That's what I see there right now. Their grandparents might be starving in their villages. I will collect their money on weekend to go to post office on Monday." said Inder sensing his responsibility.

"That's what many of us expect from you" Jhihari continued exaltation. "She also will come to the post office to meet you" he surprised Inder.

"Who?" Inder squinted his brows.

"Whom we have been talking about. Few days ago. A week ago" Jhihari hinted at Bhumi.

"Then I won't go on Monday" Inder made it clear.

"Why are you telling a lie my dear? See the shine on your face. Even the idea of her brings this shine on your face. How long will you hide that?" Jhihari became a psychologist.

"What I will get in hiding and what will I gain out at disclosure?" Inder posed his confusion.

"That means you have some beats in your heart" Jhihari smiled.

"You must meet her and explain things at the end. Not every boy among us is that bright and lucky that you are. Not every day a girl like her has some space in her heart for people like us." Jhihari explained all the permutations.

"I don't know much about your philosophy. I know only one thing she has not come out to the room in past few days." Inder again reminded Jhihari.

"She went inside after her father came." Jhihari summarized.

"May be her parents have talked to her after she took lot of interest in me. I think we must mind our business, that is, we must mind our status that we work for Mr. Jain." Inder wanted to conclude on the truth of economies not the volume of emotions. He took tiffin box from Jhihari's hand.

Gates on both the sides of the double road entering to landfill area of Ghazipur were still capable enough to remind Inder many of the stories from his past. Eight months period in the outer room of Jain's house was still weak to erase years of his past living with Ranchit, Sachi, Jhihari and Niranjan. For more than twenty years Inder had been a part of the never ending filth of Ghazipur. Sedimentation of the wastes had been taking place under the weight of house making and house running garbage into layers for years and years. The sedimentation was visible in different forms at different places in the landfill area. Close to transformers networks of the electricity distribution it had filth of chemicals and animal wastes.

Other side around the access road sedimentation showed infinite rags hanging on with mix of polyethene waste along the vertical of the mount at the landfill area. Down the mount shaping the slope, deposited were the fecal and animal wastes from *murga mandi*, egg *mandi*, storage area, etc. endless sources. Mainly filling the landfill area was done with the semi-solid wastes transported with municipal trucks from most of the east and central Delhi. The mound waste of landfill area on the dairy farm side was most of the time looked as if the waste was just-poured-onto-the mount to topple in the ground.

Inder since his nourishing and formative years had witnessed sedimentation of the layers. He had also been part of the environment which had set the sedimentation formed by layers of the waste dumped on weekly and monthly basis. Layers formed monthly basis were the layers that had been forming themselves under the weight of their own. Inder didn't know the natural process of sedimentation that was taking place even in that manmade hill. "People in coming time would love to call that hill as Mount Waste" Inder thought when he looked at extent of the hill.

Standing at the gateway to the Mount Waste where corporation municipal people were keeping the record of the dumping by the municipal trucks, Inder walked on the road to enter the settlements down the hill. Newness of the area, the gate and the beyond, the access road leading to the Mount Waste haunted him to the tune of tearing his eyes which were attempting on tearing apart the then and the past.

Entering the gate Inder walked on the road to the Mount Waste of the landfill area. He stood around the scales being used to weigh the corporation trucks full of semi-solid filth from nooks and corners of east Delhi. He watched the trucks unloading the filth into the landfill area. Most of the rag pickers were coming closer to the trucks getting unloaded. Many of the people have covered nose as the stinking garbage was getting unloaded.

Maithili, Madan, Kaalandi, Jagdish, all were working at the middle of the Mount Waste. They were busy picking something which must be more valuable than what they would have gotten in the filth on the slopping side. Inder was standing amidst of the garbage bed at the height sloping and stepping down towards the entrance. Some waste pickers were busy in picking their valuables from the filth on top and others in lower slope. Maithili and Madan were atop at the middle mound while Kaalandi was at mid height of the Mount Waste collecting bricks from the waste.

Suddenly Kaalandi jumped from middle height of the slope to another layer step like plain of the garbage but fell on all his fours. He quickly stood up to balance his body to run towards the entrance. Two new trucks had entered the landfill area were new hopes for him and other waste pickers to get more valuables. These trucks coming from the Tahirpur and Jhilmil were laden with waste might have contained waste of building material, iron waste from the debris out of the factories. The boys in their teens were not able to keep patience till the trucks got settled properly to dispose the debris. The drivers opened the panes to unload the trucks. The rolling broken and full bricks, concrete mixed with sand in the house material. Rolling broken bricks were coming close to the boys enthusiastic to collect pieces of reinforced iron rods which might have lost their strength after supporting the house lintel for decades. The boys wanted to collect these valuables before anyone else, much more than anyone else, jeopardized their lives under rolling bricks and pieces of iron rods on the sloping panes of the trucks. Maithili and Madan also came down to collect their fortunes.

"Jhihari, O Jhihari" Maithili shouted to call up Jhihari who was at the remote end on the ground of the landfill area.

"Yes" Jhihari shouted back a loud from the remote end of the mound.

"*Rickshaw ke sath taiyar rehna*, we have to rush to the factory after this." Maithili spoke to Jhihari instructed to be ready.

"You won't be here by this time if it is not Sunday." Jhihari reminded them when he came closer.

"Oh we have just forgotten that" Madan said.

They started picking small items of metal from the debris poured down from the trucks.

Niranjan started picking the broken bricks, half bricks, full bricks which were rare in the debris, and nothing he was leaving unturned. He needed to build a new shelter for himself. He had been sharing the same jhuggi where Ranchit and family stayed as shelter since his childhood. He did not have much interest in that work of waste picking. He was interested in notorious activities which brought him petty money immediately. He escaped the police many a times in the past. He didn't have interest in any activity more than three-four months. He continued an activity till the police got clue about his whereabouts. The kind of activities he was engaged were demanding independence of stay. So he determined to build his own space for living in. To start with small jhuggi without any money in hand, the bricks he was picking from the debris were bricks of gold for him. He wanted to save money for thatched structure. The pieces of old rusted weaken iron rods out from the lintel debris were also valuable for him. He was so focused on collecting those items. He couldn't see Inder who was standing ten feet away from him.

"*Are*! *Inder tum, yahan kab aaye?*" Jhihari shouted in excitement. He left picking up valuables from the debris.

"*Are bhai* Inder! You have been standing here for long and I couldn't notice. It is Jhihari who called you up then only I could see you are standing here with us." Niranjan exclaimed at Inder's presence.

"Just remembering my days like this and school in the second shift." Inder said. He saw them expressing their concern. He watched them and remembering the moments in the past.

"*Chalo*, let's move home. Inder has come to collect money for your money orders." Jhihari called up all the kids and teeming teens.

"If we leave this incomplete then some other people would collect the rest of iron." Maithili and Madan replied. They looked at Inder for permission to pick up some more valuables.

"*Inder padha likha hei, hamari tarah nahin.*" Jhihari reminded Inder was educated person and about what was more important in that moment.

"Your time is much more valuable than this rusted iron in the debris. Why do you want to waste your time in standing here?" Jhihari asked Inder. "See the power of education with which Inder has come up in his life. Now he is free from this dirt, fecal, and filthy waste." Jhihari wanted to inspire all of them to grow like Inder. He was particular about the kids if not the teeming teens to fulfill his expectations to take education. "Come soon" he added to hurry up.

"You have been part of us, now education has made you different from us." Niranjan expressed his jealousy over Inder's freedom from the fecal wastes and filth.

"You also can come up like him Niranjan. You are busy fulfilling your stomach and head with liquor and Gutkha." Jhihari attempted to inspire Niranjan before Inder could speak something to explain him.

"Don't you have been part of us? Inder?" Niranjan asked. "You know it very well that most of us have liking for these things as we don't get enough time to develop love to live. Country liquor, Gutkha, etc. are our love of life and good past times for most of us." Niranjan justified his habits and character. "*Kya karna hei, yahin jina hei yahin mar jana hei*" he added as if he did not have anything to do further but to die at the end.

"Do you want to send money?" Jhihari asked Niranjan.

"I don't have any money to send" Niranjan replied. "I have to build a shelter for me first so I don't want to send the money" he justified.

"If you stop drinking liquor and eating Gutkha then you would make your jhuggi fast." Jhihari counseled Niranjan.

"Why everyone is after my drinking and Gutkha, it doesn't take much. It does not take anything from your pocket." Niranjan yelled.

"*Jane do*" Inder wanted Jhihari to leave the topic.

"You also say something. You have your life. You have been that lucky. You are gifted with intelligence" Niranjan invited them to debate.

"I said leave it, I asked Jhihari to leave this matter. Perhaps you don't want to leave this topic. You want us to scold you to stop all these. You want us to beg you to shun the fun of insanity." Inder said.

"A lot more time we have already spent in discussing this all. Let's move" Jhihari dragged Inder by pulling his hand. Other kids and teeming teens followed them. Niranjan also stepped down to follow them towards their jhuggies.

Maithili and Madan brought some money, they saved. Jagdish and Kaalandi also came with rupees in their hands. They all handed over the money to Inder for money order to be sent to their relatives in villages.

"You note down their addresses" Jhihari suggested.

"I have addresses in one of my note book" Inder replied.

"Let's move to work" Niranjan hurried up. "Inder one day I will also send money to my village." he predicted.

"Ok, I am waiting for that day" Inder said. He moved to the gate of the landfill area.

Kids and teeming teens also went back to work. Work in the mud. Work to dig their fortunes in the broken bricks with muddy paste not accepting any adhesive of cement but its Niranjan's hope that he would be able to make a shelter. Perhaps he also knew the futility of that all. But he also knew that tough time was for him without any education, no liberation.

And soon, too soon, we part with
pain, to sail o'er silent seas again.
Thomas Moore

ðɪ siːz

The seas

The money order counter in the post office adjacent to the boundary wall of the fruit market got populated in the morning. On the counter of the just opened post office people queued up. People wanted to send money to their relatives in the remote villages. Staffing clerks were yet to come.

"*Das baje to bahut der ho gayi abhi koi nahin aaya*" a woman asked other people why nobody was there after ten O' clock. The woman clad in green *saree* held a knotted hanky. The dust got coated to level of shining on craggy nooks of swollen knot of the rag that were sufficiently telling the story of piecemeal collection of her small money.

"*Sahab* must have been busy in dropping his children to the school." Sachi, standing in the queue replied. She wore pink *salwar* suit bigger than her physique which was ready to slip down from her shoulders. Her slippers with contoured impression of her feet were barely providing cushion between the soles of her feet and the floor. *Salwar* longer than her legs covered not only the contoured impression of the slippers but the entire foot. Her breasts covered by the pink colored scarf of which covering capacity got challenged by bigger open fashioned neck of the top of her *salwar* suit.

"How do you know so much about him?" lady clad in green *saree* turned to Sachi. She pulled up the suit on Sachi's shoulders with its sewing line.

"Nowadays, wives of most of the *babu Sahab's* work in offices. So may be the case with this *sahab* also." Sachi pointed out at the counter. "I keep pulling up the shoulder of this suit but with no result" she added. She pruned her scarf again.

"Then you must have put on some other clothes" the lady clad in green advised Sachi.

"Where shall I wear such clothes?" Sachi asked. "I am scared to wear this when I work in houses of the *babu sahabs*. Their eyes dare to bare the body. So wearing these loose clothes is safe in public places at day time where many people are around. That too, I don't wear bra when I wear this to avoid staring of people. Their eyes get stuck on the strip itself" she described her routine and context for wearing that loose suit in the post office.

"But I don't wear these suits at all. Take some other ones from your mam *sahiba*" the lady clad in green suggested Sachi.

"What shall I tell you? Sister, there are many reasons. This is not the only suit that I have. My mam has given me many like this. On every Diwali she used to give me a new suit of my size. She used to buy that suit from the weekly bazar on the pavement. Once she went to her mother's place for few days. I also went to my village for a month two days before she left for her mother's place." Sachi was eager to explain. "As I was going for a month so she fixed another girl for household cleaning. After she left for her mother's place her husband started screwing up the girl that mam fixed for household cleaning. Not only this, her husband brought another lady who was working in his office. The day my mam wanted to come back from her mother's place cancelled her scheduled flight and booked a day before. She came one day earlier and caught her husband red handed" she completed the longer story in sort as people in the queue started paying attention.

"Sachi, how do you know all this?" lady clad in green asked. "Did your mam told you about this" she speculated.

"No, one day they both had big fight when I was working in the house. They both were slinging mud on each other. The husband was blaming wife for not caring. The husband blamed her for fat figure that she looked like buffalo as if there was nothing in her to attract him. She took the blame to her heart and lost interest in life. She started taking leaves from her office as she lost confidence in her personality and figure. She started eating more and she gained more weight." Sachi narrated uninterrupted.

"So she gave you all of her suits which got her tight" the lady clad in green anticipated.

"No, one day she was on leave and watching a TV programme where a film actress gave tips how she got her zero size. I was working in the house" Sachi said.

"But she has fixed another girl for all the work. How did you get that same house again?" the lady clad in green asked.

"My mam goes to the office early at eight O'clock in the morning and husband goes to the office after nine. On working days I used to go and finish the work before she left for office. For me that house was the first house. But the girl she got fixed never came before mam left office. She tolerated that girl till I came back." Sachi explained how she got back the same house for work.

Lady clad in green *saree* listened to Sachi but she got worried about some clattering in the post office.

"Once she caught her husband red handed with that girl." Sachi said. "Then mam called me back" she added.

"How she caught her husband red handed" the lady clad in green got interested to know more.

"One day she pretended to go to office but she came back home after half an hour. What she saw from a window slit was shameful for her. She saw her husband had lifted the girl in his arms. He slowly brought her down on his body. They both had put off clothes. Husband started licking the girl. She unlocked the main door with her copy of the house keys and entered the room when her husband started penetrating that girl." Sachi completed the story.

Lady clad in green *saree* wanted to provide pin drop silence to listen more.

"She only told me all this, when she fired that girl and did all the work till I came back from my village. That too, she told as if that girl was big crook and her husband was innocent like a saint. I reminded her about the last fight then she started crying on her conditions. Again she got to watch the programme on size zero. She went to the mirror to look at her body and along with a parallel watch on TV. She switched to a news channel where a breaking news on how a handsome man had lost his weight from 150 to 80 kilograms. The size zero and that breaking news got to be turning point in her life." Sachi explained.

"How long these *sahabs* take preparing for office?" the lady clad in green then got impatient for clerk. She lost interest in the story as she didn't find any part as if she listened to hear Sachi's seduction or exploitation.

"I don't know why he had not come. By this time even my *sahab* also reached after dropping his kids at school. If we demand the babu to come early then he would have kilos of denials to send our money order to our relatives. Sometimes they fill our money order forms also. We should understand our helplessness also" Sachi spoke like a wise.

"Let us take help from someone else. So that, we can ask why money order babu is late." lady clad in green suggested.

"Generally educated people are in a hurry to push off" Sachi said.

"This time some good person will be there. I am sure" lady clad in green predicted. "You were telling how you got so many suits so loose on your body" she reminded. She wanted to switch back to story as there was no chance that the clerk would come in coming minutes.

"That day when my mam, was watching TV programme on how that man lost to half of his weight, decided to reduce her weight. She noted down a number written on the back of auto rickshaws on the way to her office. She rang up and got tips on how to lose weight. Two weeks she followed the tips she got more fat on her body rather than losing it. Her husband started staying away in the office in late hours as if he had lost interest in her" she resumed. "Then she joined weight loss clinic. In the clinic she got some results as they controlled her food and all. With six months rigorous workout and diet control she is quite slim and has joined a gym to maintain it. Her clothes got loosened. She realized that they can be given to someone else and has given all her loose clothes to me. This is one of them" she completed the story.

"Why don't you get them fit by some tailor? Some learning tailor may take very less" the lady clad in green suggested.

"No, tailor asked for twenty rupees per suit" Sachi said. "I would have gone for getting fit but I need to send money as my mother-in-law is not keeping well in the village. I saved some money and my husband is not keeping well here. These people living in old colonies don't leave any usable items in the rag. They sell it to the *kawadi* and *raddiwala*. He cannot pull a rickshaw in the sun after picking scraps in the morning. Some other work he is still searching for himself" she shared her worries.

"Sell them to some fat women" lady clad in green suggested a solution to Sachi's genuine problem.

"Woman engaged in household cannot get that fat on her body to become stout or plump. So it is very difficult to get such women engaged in waste picking or domestic help. So no one was ready to take these clothes" she again pulled the top on her shoulders.

"Then what will you do? Someday you will go in this suit in the same house he will confuse you for his wife." lady clad in green apprehended.

"That is the first house that I start my work and he does not get up in the morning before I leave the house. On weekend her husband sleeps like till ten O' clock" Sachi explained.

"Good morning sir!" one middle aged man entered the post office and greeted the in-charge of the post office.

"Good morning, Mani Ram, *daridra narayanis* are waiting for you" the in-charge replied with a smile.

"Oh, today they are really many more than usual." Mani Ram looked at the crowd in the open space of the post office.

"Yes, there must be some special day" the in-charge agreed.

"Alas! I may also have to fill their money order forms and write letters for them. Oh god, give me strength" Mani Ram prayed before he proceeded towards the counter.

Mani Ram distributed money order forms.

"Mani Ram *ji*, please take these fourteen hundred rupees to send to my mother-in-law at this address in Singbhum." Sachi who was second in the queue gave her form first and took out a wallet from her waist lining rag under her top which she unzipped. She took out seven one hundred, a five hundred, and five fifty rupee notes. She gave all the money and a piece of paper with name and address written. Sachi pushed off the post office to catch hold on next household for her work.

"Who is here on this counter? I need two stamps of ordinary envelope, registry envelop, speed post envelop, and an aerogram" asked a young girl at the stamp counter. She looked at faces of all the people in the post office.

"The babu is just reaching here. Wait for a few minutes" someone voiced in the corner.

"Please send these seven hundred rupees to my father in Samastipur. Name and address are written on this piece of paper" lady clad in green requested Mani Ram.

"*Beti*, you please write a letter to my father at this address." she then requested to the girl waiting on the stamp counter.

The girl looked at the lady clad in green. She wanted to decline the request. The lady clad in green begged for help with her folded hands. Mani Ram called her to the counter for confirming the name and address of money order recipient.

"Aunt I don't have pen to write" the girl checked in her bag.

Lady clad in green begged people around for pen and then she begged Mani Ram also. Mani Ram was busy in entering money order details. Finally she got a pen from an old man among the people waiting to cash their saving certificates.

"Take this pen *beti* and write down the letter to my father." lady clad in green requested. The girl took the pen to write down letter for her.

Inder entered the post office for sending money for Maithili, Madan, Jagdish, and Kaalandi to their relatives. Seeing the crowd he decided to come later.

"Inder, Inder, O Inder" a voice chased him. He turned back to see. He couldn't make out who was calling. He again turned to the gate of the post office.

"Inder, O Inder, just listen to me" the voice again chased him. He turned back and found a face smiled at him.

"How are you *chacha*?" Inder went to the person. He reciprocated the smile.

"You have just forgotten us *beta*, after you shifted to new place" *chacha's* smiling face turned into big gloomy and complaining face.

"No, it is not like that. I came over there yesterday." Inder said. He recognized the person from jhuggies of landfill area.

"You didn't meet me before you leave. I couldn't see you there" *chacha* carped to show his importance in Inder's life.

"May be you have gone for some work. I came to collect money orders." Inder reasoned.

"*Hamara* Bikaru treats us very bad. He always spends all the money he earns. He spends on being drunk all the times" *chacha* shared complaints about his son.

"*Chacha*, he is gone case, I have had many discussion with him. Now I don't find him when I come over there." Inder explained his stand for *chacha's* son.

"I have to send two thousand rupees to my wife. You just fill in this form" *chacha* gave money order form to Inder. "I have been saving for a year" he added.

Inder filled name and address of *chacha's* wife on the form as *chacha* dictated him.

Inder gave up the idea of going back and asked Mani Ram to give ten money order forms. He filled the money order forms with names and addresses which *chacha* gave him.

"Inder *beta*, you just fill this form also, my husband had gone to settle land issue in our village. He has stayed for long and still the issue is not resolved so he needs more money" another lady who has been watching Inder for long.

Inder stopped filling forms in his hands and started filling the money order form for that lady. After that he filled the details in the form for each kid and teen he took money from. He was waiting in the queue for his turn.

"Sir, these are four forms and money to send." Inder hurried up with Mani Ram on his turn. Mani Ram looked at Inder and smiled.

"Two thousand rupees you want to send to Chandra Narayan in Samastipur for Maithili, right?" Mani Ram asked Inder to confirm after taking all the forms and money. He checked the notes and counted the money.

"Yes" Inder confirmed.

"Three thousand to Bulajit in Midnapur for Madan?" Mani Ram asked Inder to confirm.

"Yes" Inder confirmed.

"And, two thousand seven hundred rupees to Biju in Sirubal, Kalahandi for Kaalandi? Right?" Mani Ram again asked Inder to confirm.

"Yes" Inder confirmed.

"And this two thousand three hundred to Digpal in Kanker for Jagdish? Ok?" Mani Ram entered into his log and kept the money in the drawer and money order forms in the corner of the table.

"Thank you sir" Inder just moved further and took few steps looking at the floor. He had to stop when passing by stamp counter as he was just to bang into the forehead of the person standing at the stamps counter.

"In few days you got so tired of life that you don't want to look up in the life and people around. Then at least look at me" the girl whispered holding Inder's shoulder with one hand to stop him banging into her.

"Bhumi, when did you come? What are you doing here?" Inder asked. He asked Bhumi who was waiting for stamps counter to be manned by the clerk. He didn't react to Bhumi's comment.

"Well I came here when you were busy in writing on money order forms for an elderly uncle or even before that I am not sure. Then you got busy in filling the money order forms for that lady and for four of your team." Bhumi detailed Inder what she witnessed since his entry in the post office. "I am waiting for some person to be here on this stamp counter. The *babu* generally is not there as nobody buys stamps nowadays. They might have merged two three functions of early days in the post office" she added her observation on the changing scenario of post offices.

"And you! Now you have so many questions. Otherwise you don't have time to talk to me" she whined. She wanted to tell Inder how her life was going without having any motive.

"I am very much there in the room outside. You just call my name I will be there." Inder declared his readiness.

"Why should I call you up? Why should you not call me up? Why should you not fill me up?" she fretted on Inder ignorance.

"Let me tell, w . . . wait . . . let me tell you the truth" Inder wanted to resolve. He spoke as if Bhumi would stop him in between. "When I couldn't find you around I got disappointed. I noticed you have been in my room too frequently immediately after I came back and suddenly you were not visible in next two days. I got that you were undergoing some counseling sessions from your parents." Inder said. He reminded himself about Jhihari's prediction that Bhumi would be coming to the post office. They shifted to the gate of the post office.

"You are right! My mother thought that I am crazy for you so she made it an issue and urgency both. I could understand the mistake I had done." Bhumi accepted. "I also got emotional after your absence for a week. So I had been taking liberty to visit you every now and then. I just kept myself confined to my room for a week. I am not feeling well these days and you got busy in your work. I spoke to Jhihari on many things about me and you. Then he suggested I must meet you somewhere else so that I can speak freely. I knew that you come regularly to send money for those kids' relatives. That's why I am here" she explained at length.

"You just manage your emotions" Inder suggested Bhumi. "Otherwise without having any fault you may suffer in your life" he added looking into Bhumi's eyes. He wanted to be in the role of a coach.

"Buddha says life is full of suffering." Bhumi welcomed Inder's coaching. "I wanted to suffer in my life, just give me a chance" she went philosophical to provide the return gift to Inder for coaching.

"What do you mean? What are you going to do? Why are you saying so?" Inder wailed.

"I just don't know what I am saying. I just know what's happening to me. Today I am feeling a bit better in your presence." Bhumi whispered looking at the stamp counter where babu had come. She moved to the counter to buy the postage stamps. She asked for two stamps of one, two, and five rupees each. She also took two postcards, two inland letters, two registered letter envelopes, two aerograms, etc. She gave a hundred rupees note to the babu. The babu gave her stamps of one, two, and five rupees each kept over a pack of postcards, inland letters, registered letters envelopes, aerograms two each, few coins of rupees in change.

"What will you do with these stamps and different types of letters?" Inder asked. He also moved to the counter.

"Aunt in neighborhood asked me to bring these as her twin sons are studying in standard three. These stamps and letters are for their homework" she said.

"Now stamp sale is driven by schools in the age of emails with document attachments." the stamp clerk commented hearing Bhumi's reason to buy stamps.

"One more way can improve the sale of postcards or envelopes if they can be printed with photo of the buyer." Bhumi gave an idea on how postal sale could be improved.

"Who knows when the day would come" interrupted the in-charge when he overheard her. "For that we need to have infrastructure with camera to take stamp size photo of the buyer" he shared his vision on how postal service might get stuck in implementing the idea in the dearth of infrastructure and technical knowhow among the existing staff in the postal services.

"What will happen if someone buys for some other person but wants the stamp size photo of the person for whom he or she buys?" Inder presented a condition.

"When that system will be there then postal department would think about various options to provide personalized stamps on these postcards or envelops." the in-charge wanted to talk more and more to Bhumi and Inder as he found that was rare appreciation of the postal services and new ideas. He got busy in some other function at the call from one of his staff.

"Now, its school people who keep this sale continued and keep next generation informed on our old technologies." Inder uttered in acknowledgment touching the pack of postcards, inland letters, registered letters envelopes, aerograms. Bhumi held his hand in her hands and looked into his eyes. She did not speak. Her eyes spoke. Her eyes asked rather. He also looked into her eyes. His eyes were communicating innocence. His eyes were promising helplessness. His eyes got the questions that her eyes asked. Her eyes lost the spark as she could not see any spark in his eyes when her eyes looked for commitment. The spark had disappeared as fast as it came. It disappeared in the grounds that he did not have. It disappeared in the rings and whirls formed of the lubricating water in his eyes which moved with uncertainties lying ahead in his way. Bhumi got the significance of uncertainties in his eyes. His hand came to her shoulder to make her move out of the post office. They went out of the post office.

Babu at the stamp counter smiled. He thought they would promise each other about their children and their schooling as the topic of children was going on and would worry if the stamps would be available when their kids would be studying in school.

"Jhihari told me that you badly needed a computer and internet connection." Bhumi sympathized with his cause when they came out of the post office.

"Yes, he has seen me roaming around cyber café, PCOs, etc. and many a times with no results." Inder confirmed.

"Shall I ask my father that you need a computer for your work. He will not disappoint as it makes business sense for him" she suggested. "Otherwise you would keep roaming around cyber café" she added.

Inder kept quiet. Inder thought if she could contribute to his objective like a true friend.

"Inder, you need to learn taking help from people" she reacted. She took his silence as negation.

"No problem" Inder said.

"No problem in roaming around cyber café or no problem if I ask my father to manage a computer for you?" she asked him to come clear. She could not assess his intentions from his two word answer. She expected him to come out with plenty of reasons based on effective utilization of resources to priorities and urgencies that might trigger a demand for a computer.

"Ok, as you wish" he read her mind. "You are an intelligent girl" he added.

"What is your wish?" she delved into his intentions and ignored intelligent part of her being.

He smiled and looked into her eyes.

"Keep smiling, you look good when you smile" she demanded.

She kept pack of stamps and different types of letters and envelopes into her bag. He had to go to the scrap settlement of her father. She went to her college. She evaluated her request to neighboring aunt to let her go to buy postage stamps and find that didn't go waste. She could talk to Inder from the depth of her heart. Free from being snooped. Free from being scared of being watched and interrupted.

Non present like clear glass door of Harley Davidson showroom in the Emporio welcomed Kul Vilas and Anang. Kul Vilas looked at different types of super bikes available in the showroom. Anang looked into the details of the bikes. The manager came to attend them.

They liked to take a Harley Davidson. Kul Vilas chose to have test ride. To complete formalities before the test ride the executive took a zerox copy of their driving licenses, credit cards and damage responsibility pledge. Kul Vilas chose to ride Night Rod. Anang chose to have the test ride on Fat Boy. The executive at the showroom took a Roadster to escort them.

They reached at Priya. They took a halt. Kul Vilas and Anang exchanged their models and rode back to the showroom. The executive followed them. They handed over the bikes and helmets to the attendants.

"Sir, which model did you like?" the executive asked.

"They are costing higher side?" Kul Vilas assessed. He looked at the other bikes in the showroom.

"You may please consider another model like Super Glide" the executive suggested a lower priced model.

"Super Glide doesn't appeal me" Kul Vilas gave a mild hit on seats of the bikes with his right hand on Night Rod and left hand on Fat Boy in the showroom.

"Kul, Roadster is also good, you can have a test ride on roadster also" Anang suggested.

"No, no, Anang, that's not the thing I am looking for. You know it well" Kul Vilas winked at Anang.

"They are good bikes but Roadster also may solve the purpose" Anang said. "That may be a good alternate" he added.

"I don't know the world of alternates" Kul Vilas bragged blowing into his hair.

"Sir, what are you looking for in your bike?" the executive wanted to know.

"Dear, that's too personal. Leave it" Kul Vilas tapped executive's shoulder.

"Then you please go ahead with your choice" the executive asserted.

"You are charging too high for my choice" Kul Vilas said as if he wanted to hold him responsible for bike's price.

"Kul, for that purpose you can even go for simple one with single seat" Anang suggested.

"No, single seat is not giving me that punch. I want my space intact. That's it" Kul Vilas pronounced himself once again.

"Sir, let me know your number, I will contact you when such bike will come" the sales executive said.

"Let me tell you why he is insisting on these two bikes" Anang volunteered.

"Yes sir" the sales executive turned his attention to Anang.

"Look, when our boss wants to enjoy a ride with his date, a good date. Tall beautiful legs holding good prominent haunches narrowing towards the waist with rhythmic motion to balance the high rise bouncing pouching fronts to support ready-to-lick lips with lush tongue in blushing cheeks." Anang described the enjoyable features of a dream date. "The bouncing pouching fronts are to enjoy resting over boss' shoulders while he enjoys the ride with his date" he added immediately not to miss how to utilize the features of a good date.

"Have you gotten what my friend has explained?" Kul Vilas asked the sales executive.

"Yes sir" shy sales executive said.

"Do you know that you are liar?" Anang scoffed the executive.

"How come sir" sales executive shared his surprise.

"Boss, my friend has not understood what I have said. How would have you understood what I have said?" Anang teased the executive on the description of a good date.

"What he wants is the bike having seat high at the back for his girl so that her bouncing pouches front are not suppressed upfront rather taking rest on his friend's shoulders. Every now and then they must make him feel horny during the journey." Anang came with same terms and conditions in simplified language. "He doesn't want that they should be pressed on by his back. A woman should not be suppressed at that level, upfront in the front" he quipped further.

"Really I could not understand anything from the earlier description. Sir, you are right" the executive took pride in entertaining clients like Kul Vilas and Anang. "Nice description, sir" helpless sales executive further said to adulate Kul Vilas.

"That's good on your part you have understood me well" Kul Vilas summarized the talk.

"Let's move now" Kul Vilas asked Anang.

"Have a nice evening sir, we will call you when we have one for you" the executive vowed down his head with hand on his heart. "Good night" he added.

"Better you wish him good night ride" Anang corrected.

"Ok sir" the sales executive again humbled down. He knew they had taken him for ride but he couldn't do anything. That was his job to entertain all sorts of clients.

They came out of the showroom to enjoy the evening with the eves of the mall. Roaming around with looks and good looks was decided as activity for that evening in addition to window shopping. They entered in a watch showroom. Attendant opened the door and one tall beautiful sales executive came to attend them immediately. She took them around in the showroom to have a look at the watches and to know what they wanted. Two girls in short tops and short shorts were looking at the watches in the showcase. Kul Vilas and Anang looked at them and then at each other.

"May I request to show me that handbag for my date?" Kul Vilas requested.

"Please have a look at the watches that you were looking for" the sales executive ushered them to move to the watches where the girls were busy.

"Ok let me have a look whether you have my brand" Kul Vilas adjusted the limited edition of his wrist watch from Armand Nicolet.

"We can get you most of the limited edition watches. Almost all the international brands" she asserted the USP of the showroom with confidence that she got from her experience and training to handle window shoppers and windy stoppers.

"Ok" Kul Vilas said. He and Anang followed her to the watches.

"This is from Blancpain, this from Bvlgari, from Paul Picot, Dewitt, from Breitling, Jeanrichard and many more international brands." she showed them the limited edition watches of almost all the international brands. They took interest for a while then intended to move to the other part of the showroom. Executive at the counter requested them to wait for ladies' watches they might be interested in. She wanted to have them under libidinal pressure as the girls were around. She casually looked at the girls' hairless high thighs.

"Is any Breitling Professional model available?" Kul Vilas enquired.

"Right now it is not available. You please note down the design number with us. We will get back to you" she assured. She got that Kul Vilas had worth shopping experience with and without libidinal pressure. Her lower lip got curved when she smiled at him.

"Ladies watches? For your partner, for a friend" she pushed a design from Bulgari.

"Again single" Anang murmured. Kul Vilas was cool as if he had managed his libido by that time.

"Something like handbag you may require to gift" she prompted Kul Vilas to look at the handbags.

"For whom shall I buy?" Kul asked the lady executive. He looked at one of the girls in short tops with her curls matching the radius of her danglers.

"You can have a look at least" she requested Kul Vilas. He looked at her face. He kept looking into her eyes as if he was making a decision. That worked as magic and her curves swelled to rise high in response to his gaze. Similar responses came from the girls in short tops. Reverse swing of libidinal pressure took place in the showroom.

"For a single, no friend, no partner, does this worth investing?" Kul asked.

The executive's eyes started moving around in the showroom as if she wanted to manage a match. "A match for life? No, that's not a possibility. That's not guaranteed. Also, that's not responsibility. Then match for a month as friend, may be. A match for week. No. A match for a night. Is that tonight? May be. But it was dangerous" like many thoughts came to her mind.

"My number is with you" Kul intended to leave.

"Is there something special in Breitling?" Anang asked Kul with curiosity when they came out of the showroom.

"You know it all, all the girls, hungry for their glimpse in page three, like the limited international editions." Kul reminded Anang who wanted to decide where to go further. "Whether it is watches, goggles, shoes, perfumes, clothes, suits etc. etc. They come pulled like iron items to the magnate" he added.

"Excuse me, just help me select my design of shoes, please" a gasping whisper chased them. The girls in short tops were there when they turned to respond the whisper.

"Oh you, it's on your right side" Kul said. Anang looked at their short top and shorts then at the faces.

"If you are busy then it's fine with us, no problem" she said. Other girl just bent down to relieve her foot in the footwear.

"Let us help them selecting their brand, *yaar*" Anang asked Kul Vilas to give company to the girls. His eyes got stuck in the two soft rocks bulging out of the short tops.

"Hmm" Kul Vilas thought for a while. "Ok" he looked at Anang's eyes digging between the rocks and approved the proposal.

"First we will select her brand then she will choose the brandy" Kul whispered his prediction how that evening would go. To Kul Vilas they appeared to be great conviviality.

They turned right to enter the showroom. She went to the stand where some models of the running shoes were placed.

"This would be good for you" Kul Vilas selected a brand for her.

The boy in the showroom put her feet in the shoes and tied them properly. Then he requested her to walk. She walked few steps came back.

"When I walked in this pair. I felt like a drunkard" she complained.

"May be madam these are running shoes" the boy didn't dare to wrong Kul Vilas.

"Try that" Kul Vilas then suggest her to try on a Vomero 5.

"That seems fine" she said after trial. "Thanks" she added.

"It's Ok" Kul said. "This is also a running shoe which she finds fine" he thought when he looked at the boy who assisted her.

She asked the boy to keep them aside for her. She started flirting with Kul and the other girl still behaved shy. "Let's have something very light this evening" Kul Vilas felt hungry. He wanted to have light snacks.

"Is this the time to eat?" Anang wanted to defer.

"That's what I said, I would take something light" Kul Vilas repeated. He looked at the girls for their choice. "What about you two?" he raised his brows.

"No problem, light snacks will do" said the girl who wanted to buy shoes.

They chose a table in a restaurant on their walk.

"Yes sir" waiter stood behind Kul Vilas' chair showed his readiness to serve. Anang picked up the menu.

They ordered two large Jean Pearnet, two cokes, and two Sicilian sizzlers.

"Where do you go for work out?" the girl who showed interests in shoes asked Kul Vilas. Her eyes praised broad shoulders bulging out from Kul Vilas' designer shirt.

"No, I don't go out for workout" Kul replied.

"Then either you or your shoulders are lying" she concluded.

"I am sitting like that they appear to bulge out" he disclosed.

"But you look so stunning! The chiseled body like yours comes out only with rigorous workout" she said. "By the way I am Numi" she introduced herself.

"She is impressed by your style statements" the girl sitting left to Kul Vilas dragged her chair closer to Kul Vilas'.

"She is Nikki" Numi introduced the other girl.

Nikki looked at the waiter. Waiter got the command to take her word to fill their worlds. He knew rich people didn't come to the restaurant to fill their bellies. He thought that they come to ooze out the larva.

"What about you? You are cool Mr. Kul!" Numi surprised Kul Vilas.

"How do you know my name? We have just met in the showroom" he asked suspecting her intentions.

"Your friend called you by this name" Numi disclosed.

Kul Vilas looked at Anang. Anang looked at Nikki.

Waiter moved away to keep distance as they moved to reduce the distance. Anang noticed that Kul Vilas otherwise full of Freudian instincts was behaving cautious. His description of tall beautiful legs configuring prominent haunches to house chiseled waist rising in bouncing pouching fronts over the shoulders on the bike was almost realized within an hour or so. The girl claiming to be Numi possessed similar features and Kul Vilas was still cautious like never before. He wanted to play safe.

Waiter prepared two large Jean Pearnet and coke for ladies. Later he brought Sicilian sizzlers.

"Kul, have you seen *Chandni*?" Numi asked loosening her Nugget on right heel.

"*Chandni bar*?" Kul tried.

"*Chandni*" Numi said with mysterious smile.

"Ya, I have seen" Kul nodded.

"Do you remember the dialogue '*Cognac sharab nahin hoti*' hero claimed like that?" Numi copied Sri Devi.

"Waiter" Kul got the clue.

"You are so brilliant" Numi awarded Kul Vilas. She looked at the waiter coming to the table.

"Get us two large Cognac" Kul ordered drinks for the girls.

"You are genius, Mr. Kul!" Numi praised Kul for demonstrating powerful behavior with the lady. "You must be running and flourishing some export business." Numi added her investigation results.

"Your drink is yet to come, Numi" Kul looked at the waiter preparing Cognac large for the ladies. Waiter placed one each before Numi and Nikki.

"You will be surprised to know that I declined the offer from the leading advertising agency in the city when they approached for their ad films. I simply said I am not interested in these clippings of one minute or two." Numi claimed big on her profession. She stirred the ice with right hand while her left hand forked into a boneless sizzle. She changed her right leg towards Kul Vilas hanging its Nugget on her toes.

"Ok, then you must be doing show stoppers." Kul Vilas nodded to her brags.

"How do you know? We haven't met earlier" she was amazed with Kul's sixth sense.

Kul looked at her glass after she took a sip. The level travelled fast towards the bottom.

"You are super genius" Numi bestowed Kul with new accolades after she gulped to finish. She turned to Kul leaning with her arm flat on the table to give gorgeous looks exclusive to him. Nugget from her left heel slipped on his trouser. He looked at the footwear and then at her bulging fronts.

"Do you want to have food? We can go for food now" Anang looked at Numi and Nikki.

"She is alright. Don't worry, she will manage" Nikki assured them.

"Hey! What are you guys talking about?" Numi corrected her postures and bent down to look for her Nugget lying in Kul's feet.

"Evening at its youth and you guys are talking about food" Numi said. She sat straight and straightened her neck with snake coming out of a heart in the pedant hanging in almost invisible chain. She finished her large as she gulped the remaining Cognac in her glass. She looked at the waiter.

"Yes mam" the waiter came to the table. Numi looked at Kul.

"Make it large again. Two more sizzlers" Kul asked the waiter.

"Sir" the waiter went to the bar counter.

"You are great. Kul, you are really great!" Numi declared. "I haven't met the one till date" she decorated her lips with accolades. Kul was not willing to react on such flirts and bluffs but he got what's on her mind other than Cognac.

"He was talking about my dream date when we were in Harley Davidson." Kul pointed at Anang. He revised his intentions and started taking interest in Numi.

"Kul you are luckiest man today. Your date is here with you" Nikki looked Numi.

Numi smiled. Her top got tight. Kul started sipping from his large. Anang got close to Nikki. Anang kept his hand on Nikki's shoulder to slip down to her arm.

"I said she is the date" Nikki snubbed. Anang took back to his glass on the table. She stared at Anang. Anang looked at Kul but didn't say anything. "Hey, you got scared. Got scared of me" she laughed at Anang. Then her fingers measured his biceps. He chewed his lips.

"I think we must order for one more and that's it. I don't feel hungry anymore. What about you all?" Kul asked Anang, Numi and Nikki.

"No, it's fine with me" Numi agreed hanging designer Nugget in her heel. Anang and Nikki were also done.

Kul waved his hand to the waiter for the bill.

The waiter placed the bill. Kul Vilas took out his bulging wallet to pay the bill. Only two denominations of five hundred and thousand rupees could have impressed Numi and Nikki. The waiter tendered few hundred rupees in return with receipt. He left two hundred rupees for tip. Anang also looked up at him and nodded. He called it a day.

They all moved to the parking after spending the evening with eves in the mall. He pressed remote to open his Audi coming out of the lift to the parking. He took the steering. Anang went to the rear to be seated with Nikki. Numi came in front. He vrooooommed the Audi and came out of the mall. Anang removed clip to open Nikki's locks. His hand bent down from the locks on her back. She slowly got into his lap. Numi looked at Kul after having a look at what was happening in the rear. They got busy in caressing and massaging each other.

"Don't you think you are losing something because you are driving?" Numi discovered.

"Hmm" Kul rolled the tongue in his mouth. He also looked at the busy couple in the rear.

Numi smiled. She laughed. Amidst the smiles and laughter Audi moved ahead.

"*Yaar*, it's enough now" Anang requested Kul.

Kul smiled and stopped the car when they reached Anang's apartments on the way. He dropped them and moved ahead.

"Are we going to your office?" Numi asked.

He nodded.

"Let me tell you one thing about you. You got very charming personality" Numi opened up. She opened up wide.

He nodded again.

"You are fascinating me" she leaned on his shoulder.

"I am driving" he reminded her. He focused on the road ahead. Her fingers touched his cheeks and left hand figured out the micron thick of the dark film in the car. He kept driving undisturbed. She knew speed thrills. He knew it kills as well. The people on the pavement knew it only kills.

"Please slow down your Audi. Or park it to drive me now" she got restless and wanted her busts to be controlled before they busted out.

"Have patience. The film does not make any difference in speed but balance does" he maintained his elegance. He was more careful.

"Scared of *thullas*? They will be happy if you give them a hundred" she leaned again on the shoulder and kissed on his left cheek. He shook his head in negation.

Traffic got slowed down on the road. He was waiting on the crossing for green signal. A girl dared to came close to the car. She wanted to clean the car with a rag in her hand. He was cautious as rag in her hand would make the car dirty instead. He scolded her to keep away from the car. The girl started begging for paisa or food.

"I hate these little beggars. I hate their parents. Bastards! They leave their sperms to grow on the road like parasites" Numi commented. She also wanted to scold the girl who was begging him with one hand on forehead and other on her mouth to indicate she needed food. Window glass stopped her cries to fall in their ears.

He kept silent and looked at the girl. He looked at the watch. He looked at the phone. Perhaps that reminded him Hwaib's assignments and estimates. He moved fast when signal on the crossing turned green.

"Oh, you are cool, but your silence speaks" Numi again touched his cheeks. She licked first finger of her left hand. She kept her right index on his lips with intentions to open them. Open them to speak in her praise. Open them to make her feel lush. Open them to kiss hers. Open them to lick hers. Open them to open her. Open them to tongue in her.

He Smiled. He stopped the car at a chemist shop. He waved his hand to the man in the shop. The man came round the car to give him a packet and took hundred rupees note from Kul. The hundred rupees note in his wallet spared after giving tip to the waiter was odd one among five hundred and thousand notes. He moved towards his office. After driving for a minute he stopped the car to park in the side.

"Here you stay?" Numi asked.

"My office" he looked at the first floor of the building on the road.

They came out of the car and took lift to the first floor.

"Wow" she acclaimed entering in his office after he opened the door. "Entrance is very impressive!" she continued. "It talks to your guests" she added.

"Comfort zone will also impress you" he ushered her to the interior part. He touched her cheeks.

She blushed.

"Ease yourself" he waved at the couch full of pillows of different sizes.

"Excellent dear" she left her handbag at the table and portrayed herself on the couch as if she wanted to have a pose. She stuffed in the couch to ease out before she could tease him for long. For longer. For longer in future. For longer future.

"Just a minute" he moved towards washroom. She held his hand. Both the hands got a stretch as he still moved ahead.

"I am coming" he said.

"So soon, we have not done anything? We have not even started?" she laughed. "You must meet Dr. Prakash, one of the greatest in India. I can take you there" she cracked a joke to make him laugh. She laughed, he smiled.

"Where are you? Numi! I just said I am coming from restroom" he enjoyed her sense of humor. He also got the idea up to what extend he could go. He also got the idea what's on her mind. He took one tablet and gulped water from a bottle. His servant Keshav was on leave that day.

"Yeah Numi, let's play *bajate raho*" he switched on the TV.

"*Bajate raho?*" her brows rose. "*Bajate raho* on TV?" she craved for clue from him. "I have not heard any program on TV by this name" she added.

"Today we will create" he assured. He put a CD in his laptop that was attached to the TV. All the eroticapornamental stuff started with licking and lusting scenes on the big TV screen.

"You naughty" she aahed as she got that late. "You are too much" she took a pillow to toss on him. "You are great! You are genius! Really!" she loaded him with many accolades.

"Never mind, I am like that only" he confessed.

"You know Kul. I am not new to you, though this is our first meeting face to face" she disclosed. "I had seen you twice in the same mall" she added.

"Really?" he fitted himself in the couch completely. Few pillows fell on the carpet. She gave him space on couch then few more pillows rolled down in her feet. She caught hold a pillow with both of her legs.

"Remember that an icon singer came to rock Delhi. At that time I was sitting some ten seats away from you in the front row" she pruned his hair with her fingers.

"That was you? That day you were looking different and stunning" he pretended to recall. He was looking for an opportunity to make her faltered. "So, you knew me?" he added a query.

"Yes, I am Numi" she aahed at him to caress and finger his chest between third and second button from the top. Then she wiggled the third button. He slid up her short top. He also waggled ridging contours with both the hands one-on-one. They wiggled waggled their hands and fingers on each other's front and back, cheeks up face and down the waist.

"You know, I am Numi, you find a new me every moment. This is my promise to you in this evening" she claimed. She started licking in his chest.

"Yeah, I am finding a new you at every inch, every centimeter" he pretended to confirm her claim.

The bold and beautiful got a handsome and strong penetration.

Mobile phone rang up.

"Who is that bast . . ." he saw the number before he completed.

"Oh no! Not again" he said. He controlled over his pants as he knew that call was from Hwaib.

"I have to take the call. It's a scheduled one" he said. Not Numi but he knew that Hwaib had missed him on the calls, many times in the past.

Numi didn't say anything.

"Hello, good evening Mr. Hwaib!" he greeted after picking up the call.

"I am fine. How are you?" he replied. "Yes" Kul added. He kept the mobile on sill of the couch to keep himself free for what he was doing as if uninterrupted.

"Sir, I am working day and night on the estimates" he pretended.

"Yes, it is that huge work and it is to be determined on the basis of how deep we need to penetrate the society" he said. Thus penetration and the call went uninterrupted. She didn't imagine that level of parallel processing. That made Numi happy. Numi found a new him.

Hwaib appreciated his ongoing effort.

"Mr. Hwaib! Deeper is the penetration better would be the survey and the results" he claimed with another round of mild pushes. Hwaib on the other side of the call might be happy with his commitment to the society and the cause.

"I am working hard to work out the estimates. Within couple of days I will ring you up and update you with the details" he kept pressing hard in her to give Hwaib an impression that he was working hard. So what that was not on the estimates for the survey and project scope. But he was working hard on the penetration hardware.

"Ok I will send you the details in the document" he promised. He kept digging into the details of the population of heir in her head which might equalize target population of the survey.

"Bye then, good night" he switched off the mobile after that.

"You flirt people on the phone also" she admired.

"I was telling the truth. I was not flirting. I am working hard to work out. And deeper is the penetration, better is the survey of every inch, every centimeter" he continued the lush, licking, lusting, busting . . . She took that for loving. She was happy in confused state of being loved. They again indulged. They indulged in depth. They indulged at depth. They indulged deeper, and deeper.

The sun filtered through the glass of the windows was printing on the floor of the living room in Jain's house as curtains were tied at both the ends. Sofas embossed the impression of the window rods and partition bars presented a parallax from the floor. Shadow had its own limitation as that didn't tell about the wood of the window. However the flowery iron work in the window was leaving its impression on the newspaper that Ishwar Jain was reading. He was busy in analyzing the news of metro rail extension and its possible benefits to the people of the area. On the gas stove a pan was consuming the heat of fire to prepare the tea under Bhumi's supervision. Her mother was at Digambar Temple where *Muni's* talk was on. She was regular assistant to her mother in the kitchen. She didn't face any difficulty in locating tea bags, cardamom, sugar, homemade cookies, etc. for preparing tea for her father.

"Your tea papa" Bhumi came with tea and homemade cookies in a tray. She kept the tray on the side table aligned with the sofa where Ishwar Jain was reading newspaper.

"Where is your cup of tea?" Ishwar asked his daughter putting the newspaper back on the center table. "*Tumne bhi to chai peena shuru kar diya hei?*" he asked as if he wanted someone else also to have tea with him. Probably he was missing Mahima, her mother.

"I didn't prepare for myself" she said. She sat in the other chair of the sofa.

"Where is Inder? Nowadays Inder is not visible here" he took the cup in his hand. He chose that topic as he couldn't talk about Inder in Mahima's presence to avoid clashes. One more reason was that he himself wanted to check Mahima's claim about Bhumi's affection for Inder.

"That is my cup of tea" she thought.

"Did you say something?" he asked her.

"I was thinking to ask what Inder does during these long days and late in the evening" she pretended to be in thoughts about her studies. "I also have not gone to his room for problems of accountancy and book keeping" she turned to her father to have full discussion.

"First he guides the kids in the shade to sort out the usable items from the scraps. Then he updates the accounts of the books in the office related to the items. After that he checks stocks at chemical works and takes measures on the process units. In the first part he himself does sorting with the kids. That takes hell lot of time" he explained.

"Now he has also got other work from Hwaib" she shared her concern.

"How is he progressing in that? Any idea?" he asked. He expected that she would answer as Mahima claimed that she took lot of interest in Inder's work.

"No, no idea, I had seen him going out with Jhihari on Saturday evening or Sunday. May be he roams around the cyber café for Internet" she shared.

"Then he may not be getting time to clean the room" he said.

"Now he may ask you for computer and internet for his work. He is now foreign returned" she prepared ground around Inder needs.

"No, he has not asked me for that" Ishwar said. "That way he is very simple person he is not demanding. May be this is the reason he has been chosen by Hwaib for the assignment" he spoke about Inder's qualities. He kept looking at her face for reactions and reflections. She was looking at small figurines of Jain *thirthankars* on the platform aligned with the wall separating the lobby from her room. She fixed her eyes on the figurines to avoid eye contact to protect her reaction and reflection.

"Most of the time we Indians heed to the problems when some foreign body points out." Bhumi commented on his assignment from Hwaib. She also wanted to show the maturity on recycling and environment.

"May be, but we should not give him if he doesn't demand for a computer." Ishwar Jain wanted to deny. He didn't say a categorical 'no'. "Computer that we have at home may be shared with him" he pointed out a solution.

"*Maa* may have problem as she is not comfortable with Inder since he has shifted to room outside in our house." Bhumi pointed out one concern.

"Your mother is from a traditional family. I'll talk to her on this issue" Ishwar gave his consent for sharing computer with Inder.

"Then I don't have any problem in shifting the computer to the outer room for Inder." Bhumi didn't talk about common sharing as that might hurt her father.

"How will you manage in that case?" he wanted to know.

"You will get me a new one" she pretended to be demanding. She was thrilled with the idea of common sharing of the computer.

"Let's see, I will do that" Ishwar Jain assured for a while. He thought Inder might not stay for longer. Same computer might be shifted back to Bhumi's room if he was done with his assignments or his stay in the outer room. He had undergone such thoughts under the pressure of effective utilization of resources and his pocket as well.

"Then, buy me a new computer" she pretended to resist common sharing.

"Do you really require that computer so frequently and so urgently?" he asked. He wanted to see whether she is really interested in new computer or not.

"No, not much" Bhumi said. "But when it is required then it becomes very urgent" she added to emphasize her needs though spurious in nature.

"That means it can be shifted to the room outside" he said.

"But what about *maa*" she asked.

"I will talk to your mother" he assured. "Hmm" he thought about something. "No no, first let me talk to your mother on this topic. I will tell you" he added.

That was what Bhumi wanted from her father. She was happy she could freely move around. She felt all powerful to get things go the way she desired.

She just went back to the kitchen to prepare breakfast for her father and herself. She poured water in the cooker and added few potatoes for boiling. She then took wheat flour started kneading that in the pan. She was twisting. She was singing. She started kneading wheat flour. Venting cooker communicated that potatoes got boiled. She peeled them off to add salt, pepper, chilly, coriander, and meshed that all to prepare the stuff.

"What are you doing in the kitchen now?" Ishwar asked.

"Papa, I am preparing potato stuff *paratha* for you and myself." Bhumi replied from the kitchen. Ishwar was happy that his daughter took responsibilities in the kitchen. Whatever would be the age and times, modernity and technologies, the food would be required for human beings to feel like living things. Whatever would be the woman's position in the society, woman would be happy being in the kitchen to ensure the life was felt through the tummy.

She took the dough and rolled that spread on the platform. She filled it with stuff prepared and again made it flat in the platform to give it shape of *paratha* by pressure rolling with wooden roller. She baked it on the pan. She applied ghee to make it baked on hot *tawa* to prepare stuff *paratha*.

She came to prepare the dining table ready for breakfast. She prepared a plate for her father to have *parathas* with *dahi*, pickle, etc. to reward him for deciding on what was in her mind.

"Papa, your breakfast is ready. Please come" she called.

"What time is your mother supposed to be back?" Ishwar asked.

"She must be enjoying *Muni's* discourse on non-violence. She may take time" she replied looking at the wall clock.

"So, you have taken her job to feed your father. Good!" Ishwar acknowledged.

Ishwar and Bhumi both had breakfast. She got confident in household skills and how to influence emotions in relations. She experienced that relations were nothing but emotions. Emotions recognized. Emotions solemnized. Emotions legalized. "Isn't it?" she asked herself.

Ishwar Jain went to his friend. Bhumi started dusting in her room. She reached the gate when she heard knock. "*Maa*" she opened the gate.

"Has the maid turned up today or not?" Mahima asked before she entered the house. "But your room is very clean today. Did you clean it?" she reacted seeing Bhumi's room after she looked in the entire house.

"Yes *maa*, she rang up after you left" Bhumi replied. "Yes, I have cleaned the room" she added.

"What about breakfast? Did you prepare breakfast for your father?" Mahima asked.

"Yes, he had his breakfast and left" Bhumi answered.

"Your father must have gone to his friend Paras Nath." Mahima said. She had an idea about Ishwar Jain's Sunday routine.

"Let's clean the house" Mahima started cleaning the house from her bed room. Bhumi started with drawing room.

"Your computer is very clean today" Mahima asked.

"Yes *Maa*, but now it doesn't work as fast as it used to do" she replied.

"You have cleaned it hoping it may start working fast." Mahima smiled. "Then sell it out to some needy" she suggested. "You can ask your father. He may know someone." she added.

"May be papa needs it for some of his work" Bhumi answered. She didn't take risk to tell her mother about one needy for sure, that's Inder.

"Did he talk to you like that?" Mahima asked.

"No idea *maa*" Bhumi replied.

"He may need it for the office" Mahima inferred. She wanted to know why Bhumi had cleaned it so properly.

"He was talking about computer" Bhumi said.

"Don't you need this computer anymore?" Mahima asked.

"I need but papa may need it more than me" Bhumi replied.

"I am asking because you also may need it more than before." Mahima shared caring her daughter's needs in the modern time of electronic gadgets and technologies.

"I may get a new one" Bhumi said. She thought her mother would agree with her father when he would discuss about sharing the computer with Inder. Sense of victory regarding computer for Inder was instigating her to speak more about possible shifting of the computer to Inder's room. But she knew her mother.

Forty lives smitten in the debris and dirt were foraging in filth. It was *Modus operandi* of the group of related families in Industrial Site Four of Sahibabad. More than fifteen boys and girls age around ten were busy digging the semi-solid black debris stinking like fecal and rotten eggs. Few teens building their muscle power which also was on test to dig out the semi-solid which became hard stuff as having with bricks and pebbles stuffed with.

These boys in early teens and adults of the families were digging the debris with shovel or spade. Three brave and young ladies were also giving them tough competition. Five kids of one to two years were cheerleaders for the group. They sat in a rickshaw wearing cheering smiles or cries to keep encouraging either or both the parents who were toiling in the debris.

Powered teens forgotten their poverty were happy with barefoot as uniform for the teeming forty. They had their spade or shovels digging deep into the industrial debris to bring out some reusables like iron articles or wires or plastic items. Few boys were busy pulling deep iron wires thrown after use in packing the bundles of pipes or pulleys manufactured in the factories in vicinity. Two elders of the families had taken the responsibility to sort out the metal solid broken black bricks unearthed in rotten debris which got frozen hard.

One good thing was that all the ladies had some clothes on their body loose or too loose to hang on the shoulder or tied on the girdle if not their waists. Strips were failing to give strength to hold their busts properly. However, the dirt, dust, punk had smitten their body to protect them from vulturine eyes of the rich passing on the road and hungry and tired hands of the poor co-workers. Few kids who were not only barefoot but also bareback were challenging the weather under the scorching sun what if they didn't get their place under the sun. Perhaps there were no children around in the area whose parents could have thrown out their clothes. One more potential and logical reason for their bare back was that were no rich residents in that exclusive industrial area to throw their kids' clothes on these kids or lower middle class people nearby who could happily sell the same in disposal markets. The children around were all working in the factories themselves might be buying from traders in disposables. Few others boys managed some clothes on their body. Dirt smitten their bodies got grey dark or light was depended on when that body part got painted with that dirt and mud from the debris.

"See, what is this?" A kid of ten attempted to pull a plastic strip that probably was used to pack the wooden boxes in the factories.

"Some iron must be there in the ring" another kid of same age helped the kid in pulling out the strip. A ring of plastic strip came out of the solid dirt and filth. Both the kids were happy as there were two iron staples used in industrial packing clenched the ring. They kept that in the sack with other usable items they had found so far.

A family of four members then arrived at the drainage debris to collect their fortunes in the dirty mud and filth. Male member of the family had started digging at a corner in the filthy debris of semi-solid hard.

"O *bhai*, where from you have come here?" elder lady in the teeming forty had asked the new joining family.

"*Hum Ghazipur se aaye hein*" the lady of the new joining family replied to elder lady of the teeming forty. She got busy in preparing a bag to collect the items expected out of the dirty mud and filthy debris which appeared to be continually generated by some iron factory where draining or sewage water might have caused water logging.

"They are not from this Site Four area. How can they dig in this?" the lady in teeming forty said. "They are not from this area so they can't dig here" she whispered in the ears of other lady holding the plastic sack.

"The family is new to this area. I have not seen them anywhere nearby. They must be strangers. But why they are digging just like that. They have not talked to us. How can they dig our dirt and filth?" looking at new joinee family, another boy who dug in the filth put all these questions to the girl holding the items in her *jholi*, the folded lower part of her long top.

"You just talk to *chacha* about this" the girl holding collected items in her *jholi* asked the boy to complain. "*Chacha ko batao*" she again emphasized.

"*Chacha*, four people in that corner are not from our area. They are coming from Ghazipur" elder lady of the teeming forty and the boy complained about them to the elderly man of the group.

"*Bahu ne bataya tum Ghazipur se ho?*" the elderly man asked the new joinee going close to man of the family. He wanted confirm whether the new family was from Ghazipur as informed by his daughter-in-law.

"Yes" man of the new joined family replied.

"Why are you hitting in our belly? You go back to your Ghazipur. That has plenty of wastes and plenty of scraps" the elderly man of the teeming forty asserted their rights over the debris. "*Hamare tumhare jaison ki pidiyan pal jayengin itna hei us Ghazipur ke bade se pahad mein. Jao wahin par rehna*" he reiterated in no mood to fight, that many generations could survive on ragpicking in Ghazipur mounds. "*Hamare pet par laat mat maro*" he kept denying them as he foresaw a threat on his family fortunes.

"Why are you stopping me? I am also like you and digging to save my life" the man of the new joined family asserted in mild tone as he saw teeming forty group was very large in number. They could easily beat him down. "*Kahan jaoon?*" the man of the new joined family asked the elderly man of the teeming forty. He showed his stomach to indicate that he needed to earn for food.

"Choose another area and leave this" the elderly man of the teeming forty moved into anger.

"For that matter the truck from some factory that had dropped this debris in the night would have come to our Ghazipur in the day time" the man of the new joined family gave his logic.

"Oh, what is this rubbish? How do you know the truck dropped this debris in the night?" the elderly man of the teeming forty asked. "*Jyada chatur ban raha hei!*" he said to convince the new joined man.

"Sweeping in-charge of the factory contacted two of our men to collect the debris in the truck. They told me that for saving diesel they dropped the debris on the way. They didn't come to Ghazipur to drop the debris over there. That way this debris belongs to Ghazipur. I also will dig this debris to collect iron items" the man of the new joined family again started digging by his hand only.

"Naya path padha raha hei ye. Ye kehta hei truck to Ghazipur hi aana tha so ye malva Ghazipur ka hua. Jara ise batana ye yahan ka malva kaise hei" the elderly man of the teeming forty called up their boys who were busy in digging and collecting reusables. He guided them as if the head of the new joinee family was fooling him. They came to heed the call of their elderly man leaving their work in between.

"What's happening, who is he? Send him back. Beat him if he doesn't go on his own. Send him back to Ghazipur" many boys shouted at the man of new joined family.

"Bhaiya ji, have mercy on us, we are looking for jobs in this area" judging the situation which became so serious that the lady of the new joined group came to rescue her man with folded hands. Her two year daughter started crying amidst shouting of the large group dealing with the parents.

"We all have been sick in Ghazipur. Gas rising from the rotten swampy municipal solid waste lying for years is making us ill over there. It is for sure that we will not get gold out of this debris. Even iron wires or other scrap was not guaranteed. Have pity on us. May be with your grace and my luck we may get food this evening" the lady begged the elderly man of the teeming forty.

"Boys get back to your work. Let this man dig his luck from the debris" the elderly man then got melted down totally when he heard the lady crying for mercy on pathetic situation of the family.

"Aapki badi meherwani" the man of new joined family thanked the elderly man of the teeming forty and started digging with his hands in the debris. The lady gave him a long knife like scrap of a pipe which she just pulled out of the debris. Seeing the knife like pipe scrap the man got happy. He saw his smitten grey looking hands and found no difference with grey knife like pipe scrap in his hand. His fingers and toes got dirt filled in his nails. He then started digging his fortunes with knife like pipe scrap.

A boy of ten was busy pulling something soft and stretchable. Because it was stretchable the boy got backward to the point it got stretched. He kept stretching it with all his strength. Suddenly he fell down backward as the strip like object came out of the debris.

"Oh! It is snake" the boy shouted and threw it away on the road. The snake was not recognizable as snake by any part of it. Entire snake got stuffed with the dirt and mud. Not only could the boy who was ten, even older people couldn't recognize that. The snake was dead. It couldn't remain alive in that dirt and filth. A car passed over it. Teeming forty and the new joined family once again got busy in their work after little distraction because of snake.

"*Is kichad mein gandhak hei tera cut theek ho jayega*" a boy of twelve with small polyethene bag suggested his partner to apply mud of the debris to the fresh cut in his left foot sulpher in the punk would cure that. The debris might have had broken pieces of sharp edge items mixed.

"What is this?" the lady of the new joined family asked her man. She took out a round solid object that was heavy in weight.

"I think it is pulley" the man said after he removed the mud wrapped around it. He was happy as that was two step pulleys with toothed gear wheels which might be worth reusing in the machinery if it was cleaned properly. He didn't know that rusted part like that pulley could not be used in machinery. Man of the new joined family gave that back to his lady to keep in the bag. He started digging further with shine on his face. However, the finger marks with dirt on his shining face were more prominent than the shine on his face.

"Let's go and keep it in the jhuggi. We have collected two bags of wires and other scrap" the elder woman among the teeming forty said to the elderly man.

"It is full, weight wise we have not got anything worth more than fifty rupees. Because it is wires and other scrap that make sack look big. But you can go to keep it in the jhuggi" he accepted her suggestion.

"You have got good number of pieces. You are done with your day Shyam" the elderly man of the teeming forty extolled his nephew who pulled rickshaw and chose to collect broken bricks from the debris.

"No *chacha*, these are hardly hundred or hundred fifty pieces of bricks smitten black not worth of any brick work or masonry. They are not even good to be broken in the flooring ground" his nephew Shyam said.

"But you have been standing only. Digging work was carried by your wife. You have been holding your son in your lap. This is what you have done since morning" the elderly man of the teeming forty shared his observation. He would have scolded Shyam if his wife were not there in the team.

"This is what my wife wanted to collect as if some gold she would get from this filth. She took my time also. I would have earned forty-fifty rupees since morning by making two three trips to Vaishali or

Kaushambi." Shyam explained the economics of his time, effort and his gain.

"So you don't require these broken bricks?" the elderly man of the teeming forty asked.

"She requires them to make a wall to protect the stove from the winds." Shyam pointed out at his wife. "She wanted to open a curry shop to cater rickshaw pullers" he added.

"Ok, otherwise I would have given you some rupees for these. I also need these for similar purpose" the elderly man of the teeming forty said.

"I don't know whether she is firm on her plan. So, *chacha* you don't lose hope" Shyam assured the elderly man of the teeming forty.

"You are tired now. We are not getting anything by digging debris here" the lady of the new joined family said to her man.

"How much we have collected from this filth?" the man wanted to know. She showed him what was collected.

"Let's move if nothing is there" the men left the debris and removed the dirt and dust from his hands. He assessed the collection and looked around for a place to take shelter. "We have managed today's food" he added.

"Jhihari! You?" the man got surprised. "Who told you that I am here?" the man of new joined family was surprised when he came to the road and saw Jhihari. Jhihari had come searching for him and family.

"*Bhaiya* told me that you might have gone this side. I have just taken a chance" Jhihari said.

"How is mama now? Is he angry with me?" the man of new joined family asked Jhihari.

"He is fine. He has talked to other people. We all together will remove some waste near our place and shift your jhuggi closer to ours." Jhihari updated with the latest decision making in the landfill area regarding new joined family. So that ill effects of smell and filth on your health would be less.

"*Bhaiya* wants you come back. Here you may require many things to settle." Jhihari explained the intelligence behind his invitation to be back to the landfill area.

"If Mama wants me to come back then I am there" the man of the new joined family expressed his intention.

"Let us move then" Jhihari asked them to sit down in his rickshaw. All four members sat down in the rickshaw. Jhihari moved towards Ghazipur.

Inder changed month page of the calendar. A month back he came back from the conference and his unimagined visit. The deep impressions that visit had left on Inder's *tabula rasa* were not that bright after a month. Temporal dust attempted to dim that. Roads, security, civic conditions, and their claim that Canadians didn't have slum were still live inspirations for Inder to keep hope for India's civic conditions to accept that there was some place where slums were not there. He was thinking over the month and hurdles he faced regarding the assignment, his own limitations, constraints that he had to live with. The assignments between Inder and Kul Vilas as team were yet to be determined. Kul Vilas was not ready to accept him even as a team member. That was great constraint for Inder to work on the survey. "Should he write to Mr. Hwaib about non-acceptance on part of Mr. Kul Vilas? Should he assume some role on his own and start the work in alignment with the objective of the survey? Was it easy to conduct the work? Where from he should start the work if he had to work on assumed role?" Inder got stuck with such questions.

He thought he could start from his own area to present a case study. He had been part and parcel of people somehow surviving over there since his memory. He was aware of what was going on with more than thousand people in the area. If he had taken small sample and started looking at the details on the ailments among his people. There was absence of any care or any health maintenance system other than government funded popularity driven schemes to keep them around cities for menial work to lessen the load of municipalities.

He started thinking on names of the people of his lot. He meditated over single person with whom he was familiar with. First of all he took the person with whom he had started his juvenile time. Ranchit Chhidra, Jhihari's elder brother who was around forty five years old and suffering from ailments on the account of the very nature of the work he engaged in. He came thirty year back in search of employment opportunity. Twice he has been under direct observed treatment scheme for his lung infections. Inder remembered very well when his father figure Ranchit first came under attack of the tuberculosis. He used to chew *paan* beetle nut with tobacco 'tetra zero'. When landfill area shifted to Ghazipur then his adverse days began. He used to chew tobacco with fragrance because the rotten smell around the waste mount of Ghazipur was intolerable to him in the beginning. The fragrance and flavor of *kimaam* in the *paan* gave him instant relief from the rotten, fecal, and filthy smell of the wastes.

But that *paan* chewing played a deceiving role in his tuberculosis. When he used to spit around in the air the color of spit was always red. When infections got deeper in the lungs he couldn't know. He used to spit blood stains and sometimes blood clots. He used to convince himself that it was color of his *paan* effect of red not that he had some disease. When lung infection got too deeper and caused high fever in continuity then he became bed ridden. I and Jhihari took him to the direct observation therapy center in Ghazipur village. Doctor at health center scolded us a lot. The health worker with the center used to come regularly to ensure that Ranchit *bhaiya* had taken the medicine. The treatment was slow in curing him completely. Reasons were many in the landfill area. First of all the area was dumped every day with all filth, fecal waste, dirt waste, dust waste, waste from sewage treatment plant, poultry waste, fish market waste, chemical wastes were having their permanent stay.

After nine months of direct observation therapy he felt that he could take up some work. But doctor in-charge at the center still didn't recommend any hard work for him. Though treatment didn't cost much as medicines came from the center but the supporting cost disrupted the earning and broke the family's backbone. *Bhabhi* also fell ill during those days of *bhaiya's* treatment. Rickshaw pulling was still a good option as that brought cash in hand. One day he again took his rickshaw to the mechanic. The rickshaw was ready for use after minor repairing. It was because Jhihari kept that in function to carry reusables collected from the waste.

Many times Ranchit *bhaiya* was not available to health worker who came regularly from the center. That became fatal as the treatment had met some sort of termination before its completion. Doctor used to warn him about that. For few months he was able to earn good money by rickshaw pulling to ferry passengers between Ghazipur crossing and the UP gate. He spent some money on his diet to overcome his illness and weakness. Also some rupees flew in family matters. Rain protection of jhuggi and kerosene stove were such examples. Doctor told us that *bhabhi* was frequently falling sick because of wastes we used to burn to cook our food which was having lot of gases in the jhuggi during and after food preparation. Ranchit *bhaiya* bought one kerosene stove for cooking. Previously cooking was not that costly due to use of brick hearth where *bhabhi* used wooden waste and other wastes as fuel.

Household expenses also went high in response to ever increasing inflation of all the consumables. Need to earn more money to survive forced Ranchit *bhaiya* to make more ferries. He couldn't have proper diet to keep him in workable health as additional income was already having its outgo. He survived on rickshaw pulling strength for next few months. After certain point of time his health started deteriorating in dearth of proper food. Poor living conditions in his jhuggi and surrounding worsened it.

On the account of break in the direct observation therapy treatment he used to fall sick quite often. Again one day we had to take him to the primary health center. He started spitting blood after coughing for few weeks. He coughed blood without chewing *paan* so we all could make out that he was not keeping well. The doctor in-charge went red in fury when he examined him. The doctor told us that strict monitoring treatment was required to save his life. Ranchit *bhaiya* wouldn't have survived if treatment was not complete. The direct observation therapy went on for much longer time.

After that Jhihari sold the rickshaw that Ranchit *bhaiya* used to make ferries between Ghazipur and UP gate. The rickshaw was resold to new immigrant from Kankuri. Jhihari bought another rickshaw and contacted one of his friends to make some arrangements to carry load. Jhihari's friend prepared the rickshaw by fitting with scooter engine, wheels of motor bike, and other jigs and fixture required to run it on petrol. He also fitted a wooden bench adjacent to driving seat at the top of the wall housing the loading portion to be used as sitting place for sub-human. Jhihari customized that rickshaw as the doctor had warned all of us might be having infection from Ranchit *bhaiya*. Jhihari thought pulling rickshaw and living in the landfill area would make him meet the same fate because he had to run the family then.

Having infection from Ranchit *bhaiya*, Sachi *bhabhi* also frequently fell sick. She used to do many works in the waste collection and sorting. She also could not withstand the landfill area environment. The worst thing that happened to her was that she couldn't conceive for many years because complicacies generated in her bodies. She met the fate of miscarriage twice when she conceived. Then Ranchit *bhaiya* decided to focus on Jhihari, Niranjan and myself as their kids.

She left collecting, sorting and working with the wastes. She started doing household work like cleaning and washing in a colony in neighboring area. Then she was free from such environment at least during her working hours. She accompanied Ranchit *bhaiya* only on weekends or when her household mam gave her 'off'. Other benefits were also there as she was given the food before that might go waste. Her landladies gave her their used clothes. On one *diwali* she got new clothes also.

If survey contained facts and description then that survey would be huge story with repetition. Inder couldn't think a better way to start the survey. The story of Ranchit and his wife was the story that he also has been part of. What should be the way to be part of the intended survey? How to contribute significant data in the survey was another challenge. His dilemma was still his dilemma. No one knew that.

"When did you start talking to the walls?" Bhumi asked. She heard Inder was talking aloud to himself when she peeped in.

"How do you know?" Inder asked her.

"I heard your self-talk" she replied.

"When?" he wanted to investigate.

"I have been here for around ten minutes. You were talking to yourself about someone" she said.

"How are you? Welcome" he again greeted her.

"After we meet in the post office, I talked to my father" Bhumi took her space in the room. Now she was not as cautious as she was before post office meeting. Her face also showed some sign of victory over the environment.

"You are comfortable today. How come? Are you not scared of your mother?" Inder raised his brows.

She smiled at her victory which she was yet to disclose. "Do you need phone?" she asked. She didn't want to limit her victory to computer sharing only.

"It is fine with me to manage with PCO" he declined.

"But that's not good for you at this point of time" she wanted him to identify his needs.

"Not every day I need to communicate" Inder solaced himself. "It was urgent to call Mr. Hwaib or Kul Vilas otherwise I don't need such things" he wanted to hide his helplessness.

"One more idea" her face shined.

"If I give you my mobile phone" she showed her readiness.

"What would happen if someone steals your mobile?" Inder came with immediate analysis.

"Steal my mobile" she turned back to Inder. She lost the synch as her focus was on hearing the voice coming from outside.

"Your mobile may get stolen from my pocket or someone can snatch it from me. Or I may lose that" he said.

"So what? That may happen when I carry it" she cleared that to Inder.

"But it is dangerous for you. If someone misuses it for terrorist activities after capturing it then what will you tell to the police?" Inder replied a question.

"I will simply say that I have lost my mobile" she replied that simplified.

"It doesn't happen that way. You simply may say that Inder has stolen my mobile and supplied it to the terrorist group." Inder laughed.

"Do you think that I will do that in case of trouble? You rate me like that?" Bhumi turned furious at Inder's statement. "I am noticing that you are not interested in taking any assistance. Or any girl for that matter" she reacted to Inder's reluctance to take help from her.

"No Bhumi, it is not like that" Inder tried clarification. "I mean tha . . .that . . ."

"It is like that only" Bhumi interrupted.

"Ok baba, I will take your mobile phone." Inder accepted her helping hand. He thought boys from the middle and rich class families might be after her in the college. She still valued him so much that he could feel proud of himself. He didn't want to confuse that with love.

"No, not now, it exactly happens as you have explained it in detail. Mobile phone is passion and is dangerous to you" Bhumi repeated what she got from the talk. "Mobile's presence or its absence both will take away your sleep for a while if it misplaced, for days or week in case of loss, for a month in case of being stolen, for whole life if it is misused. There is no end to miseries and Buddha said life was full miseries" she wanted to philosophize what she had gotten in that enlightening session on attachment to the electronic gadgets from Inder baba.

"That's great! You have understood the happiness by mobile's absence in my life." Inder covered his helplessness before he complimented her.

"No Inder, it is not like that, I was just kidding" Bhumi said. "You thought it was philosophy. No, not at all" she turned back the discussion to the original direction as she wanted to help Inder in his assignments.

Inder scowled.

"You can use my mobile when you are here in this room, when you are with me. Or you are with us in this house" she still sought to extend her helping hand to Inder. She still discovered a new way. Her confidence was on ninth cloud she wanted to retain that.

"Ok" Inder grinned. He welcomed her assistance.

"You keep smiling just like this. Your Bhumi will die for the sake of this smile" she got into the pink of love. She wanted to win over Inder who was lost in wastes and managing waste items in her father scrap settlements.

"Your mother is not calling you today?" Inder initiated a new topic with flavor of surprise. He noticed that Bhumi was no longer in a hurry to avoid showing interest in Inder.

"Papa and I had a discussion about the work you do for us. He is of the opinion that you should have computer in this room. For office work" she described.

Inder got amazed with her daring dashing adventures with parents. That all was new for him as he heard cries, shouts, and vexations from the inside. He found it pleasant in a moment and painful in the other as he knew what he was and how he had to lead his life. "Bhumi, Bhumi" her mother called up.

"*Aayi maa*" Bhumi moved out of the room smiling at Inder with a tender touch on his hair. She left her words echoing in the room. She left her victorious smile and fragrance in the room.

Timepiece at the table near the folding bed buzzed to wake up Inder. He stretched his arms they touch the wall on head side. Inder picked the alarm clock in his hand and searched the 'off' button.

"Papa is calling you" Bhumi came to inform Inder.

"Yes, I am coming" Inder assured.

"Come fast" she went back.

Inder entered the passage to the living room of the house. It was first time he went up to the end of that passage. All Bhumi's coaching times also he was confined to the verandah in front of outer room when he was living with Jhihari in the landfill area. He thought Ishwar Jain was lucky as the sun blessed him sitting on sofa every day when he read newspaper and planned for his day and business. Mahavir statue on the platform fixed on the carved table aligned with the wall which showcased plasma television in the room. Small statues of Adinath, Ajithnath, Sambhavanath, Abhinandannath, Sumatinath, Padmabrabha, Suparshvnath, Chandraprabha, Suvidhinath, Shiatnath, Shreyansanath, Vasupujya, Vimalnath, Anantnath, Dharmanath, Shantinath, Kunthunath, Aranath, Malinath, Munishvrata, Nami Nath, Nemi Nath, and Parshv Nath were placed nicely on the same table of a feet and half wide with length matching to the plasma television above fixed on the wall.

Carved wooden arms of the sofa were providing fixtures after taking turn in oval shaped lower to the leg of the sofa chair. Rear legs were joined with the seating square platform of the seat of the sofa. The frame of the sofa was placed on the wooden support between front legs of the sofa. Triple seater sofas was placed aligning to the wall common to Ishwar Jain's bedroom. Another similar sofa was placed aligned to the large window giving the Sun its place in the living room every morning. Single seater sofas were placed to the opposite to the wall common to the neighbor's house. They were interleaved with glass top table. The glass top of the center tables provided elegance to the living room. Inder still stood in the passage.

"Yes Inder, come inside" Ishwar called Inder. He was seated on a triple seater sofa. The sun rays passing through his glasses in hand were focusing on a heading about green environment in the newspaper in his lap.

"Yes sir" Inder stood with both the hands holding each other in front with ready-to-serve attitude. Ready-to-serve attitude of the servitude. That kind of humbleness Inder didn't experience in his settlement or chemical unit. Perhaps Inder's subconscious mind had been waiting for that call for a long. Waiting for that honor, honor to be called, honor to be a required one if not to be a respected one.

The Veronique's house in Montreal was also highly elegant and impressive but that too didn't give him the experience of belongingness. His subconscious mind was searching for his space in his own country for years. Perhaps Inder knew that his stay in Veronique's house was mixed with the sense of mercy and charity.

Here the house where Ishwar Jain was sitting was capable of reminding him that people like him were also to get their place under the sun. Perhaps the unseen craving, ignored need, or denied requirement potentially gave him an experience of being called, desired, or required. Though that might not be similar case.

"What is happening?" Ishwar Jain asked. He waved hand for Inder to sit on the sofa.

"Thank you sir" Inder said. He took few steps to settle in the sofa.

"What's happening?" Ishwar asked.

"Sir, what shall I tell you?" Inder replied.

"How is your work going on?" Ishwar asked.

"You see it entire day sir" Inder replied. "Kids are also doing fine" he added.

"What about your conference work?" Ishwar asked. "That should not hamper your work in the office" he cautioned Inder.

"Don't worry sir" Inder assured.

"That should be the spirit" Ishwar acknowledged. "You must have started your survey work" he added. He wanted to be generous towards Inder.

"I contacted the person with whom I was introduced by Mr. Hwaib at the Paris airport during the halt in the flight back to New Delhi. When I contacted him to know what was to be done he discouraged me outright, to be part of the work. He literally said '*aish karo ho gaya survey, hum kar lenge.*' After that I just couldn't contact Mr. Hwaib to update him in this regard." Inder narrated that all in single go. He spoke as if he was telling to Hwaib and saying 'look what is happening even after you assigned and allocated to me that work?' He stopped thinking as if he realized that he was with Ishwar Jain not Hwaib. Might be because of similarities as Ishwar was his employer and Hwaib's position also was like that of an employer in the survey. Might be because Inder wanted to be heard by a person of Hwaib's position, that got to be Ishwar, his employer.

"Then?" Ishwar prompted Inder to speak further.

"Then, I thought, I should not talk to Mr. Hwaib on that line as it doesn't give good impression about Indians. Then I thought I would write an email to him regarding the team and assignments." Inder said. "I have started writing down on a note pad daily in the night. Bits and pieces of

Kidney

writing are to be compiled. I will write to Mr. Hwaib not on what is going on between me and Kul Vilas but clarification on task list and who will do what. Mr. Hwaib has assumed that Kul Vilas would lead the team in the field." he detailed out his thoughts.

"When will you write to Mr. Hwaib?" Ishwar Jain asked.

"I need to compile those bits and pieces into a well written letter to send to Mr. Hwaib." Inder answered. He leaned forward.

"How will you send that letter?" Ishwar wanted to know.

"I will go to cyber café and type that letter on a computer to send the letter on email." Inder came out on expectations from himself. He was having best intentions for writing the letter to Hwaib.

"I mean when will you be able to send that email to your Mr. Hwaib?" Ishwar reiterated his question.

"Hmm, around two weeks" Inder thought for a while to estimate. "I may take two weeks to send that letter on email" he added. He calculated on his fingers to verify the estimates that he committed to his current employer.

"Shall I get your breakfast?" Mahima asked. Her eyebrows automatically rose up and squinted when she entered the living room and saw Inder sitting in the sofa. Inder shrank in the sofa the moment he found Mahima's eyes were on him.

"Good morning aunty" Inder's meek voice greeted her.

"*Haan lagao*" Ishwar replied.

"Have you done your breakfast?" Ishwar asked Inder. Mahima again turned up to hear what her husband asked Inder. Since childhood her ears were not trained to hear so her eyes wanted to confirm that.

Mahima looked at Inder. Her burning eyes cast all the heat of her body on Inder. She then looked at Ishwar Jain who wanted to avoid eye contact with her after he had asked Inder about breakfast.

She turned back to the kitchen to prepare breakfast for Ishwar Jain. When she was passing by dining table in the lobby she stopped and called her husband before Inder would answer 'yes' or 'no'.

"I'll have it on the way to the office." Inder couldn't lie.

"*Pehle drawing room mein use sofe par bitha liya, ab use dining table par apne sath nashta bhi karaoge? Are you Ok?*" upset Mahima opposed the idea of offering breakfast to Inder. She was upset as Ishwar first allowed Inder to enter the drawing room and asked him to sit on the sofa. She talked to her husband in such a manner that it was audible to

211

Inder who was sitting in the living room so that Inder knew that she was against to feed him on the dining table.

"For *Muni* sake, please speak low." Ishwar Jain whispered. She didn't heed to his request. She was about to shout but Ishwar put his hand on her mouth. She didn't oppose. Ishwar removed his hand after a minute. She didn't say anything. Ishwar Jain thought his honor was saved. She went into the kitchen beating the floor with her steps.

Ishwar didn't say anything. He couldn't say anything rather.

Mahima's gaze was capable to shrink Inder in the sofa which was meant to sit expanding and comfortable. Hearing her conversations with her husband worried him.

She came again and called her husband, "Why you are making him so important in this house?" Mahima winced in the social pain. She was restless. "First you have brought him to the exterior room of this house. Now you have asked him to be seated on the sofa. What do you want?" she whispered her complaint. She didn't expect that from Ishwar.

"How can I explain you? How can I convince you?" Ishwar showed his helplessness. "Inder is working for us in our premises. He is no more doing any menial work in filthy heaps of waste in landfill area." he whispered to convince Mahima. She moved into the kitchen and Ishwar came back in the living room.

Ishwar looked at the Mahavir statue. Inder also looked at the statue. Silence took its due place in the room as Inder heard almost entire discussion. Ishwar took time in setting up his upsets. He was yet to discuss with Inder about computer and its shifting to outer room.

"Sir, may I go?" Inder dispelled silence settled in the room. He stood up from the sofa which he thought he should not sit in after his entitlement was questioned.

"We were discussing about your assignments. They will take hell lot of your time." Ishwar talked to Inder in totally changed tone. "When will you get time for office work?" his voice was high enough to reach into Mahima's ears in the kitchen. Ishwar continued in the same tone and volume.

"Sir, sir, you have asked me that is why I was explaining that all." Inder mumbled about what he was saying. Inder thought Ishwar named his assignments as green assignments when he began the discussion. Now he was talking on different note. He accepted his disappointments caused by Ishwar's pitch and tone. After all Ishwar was his employer.

"Papa" Bhumi called up her father as she also got wind of what was going on in the room. "Today I have to leave early for my college" she interrupted.

"Ok let me know when you are ready. I will drop you" Ishwar Jain assured his daughter.

"Sir, may I go to my room. I have to go for work" Inder repeated his request.

Ishwar looked at Inder.

"Ok sir, I am very much here" Inder mumbled again. Ishwar Jain was his boss. His work was where his employer was. He convinced himself.

"I was asking how you would do our work if you are busy in green assignments." Ishwar Jain was able to set up his upsets by then. Perhaps Bhumi's interrupt reminded him how he should tackle the topic.

"Sir, I am doing your work as per my routine" Inder answered.

"I want my work to be done first and fast." Ishwar stated. "How will you do it fast? Tell me" he added.

"I will do it. I will do it fast" Inder attempted to assure Ishwar. He knew that he couldn't quit the job as situation in the landfill area was worse. He might not get a job somewhere else. Or he might get a job somewhere else but not a place of shelter like that. His subconscious mind had said good bye to landfill area. Slums in other places in India were eventualities. They were natural for some other set of people called being human. He was sub human being.

"I will do it. I will do it fast" Ishwar imitated Inder to show his irritation. "Are you a computer?" he commented. He stood up in anger and then sat down again to show his unhappiness.

"No sir" Inder answered. He got scared. He couldn't understand. Bhumi told him that she had talked to her father about computer but he found her father's talk on different note, tone, amplitude, pitch, and attitude. He was puzzled. He couldn't know what was in store for him.

"Then how will you do my work?" Ishwar asked.

"Sir I will do it day and night" Inder came with a poor solution which appeared the only feasible solution to him.

"Do you know how to work on computer?" Ishwar asked.

"Yes sir" Inder said. He said 'yes' because he didn't want to take risk of saying 'no'.

"How good you are in working on computer? As far as I know you haven't learnt working on computer." Ishwar questioned Inder's capability again.

"Sir I know little bit. But I will manage" Inder assured. "Once I get an opportunity to work on computer then I will improve" he continued.

"Where is the computer? I have to buy a computer for you first. Then only you will work" Ishwar went berserk on the issue of computer. He soon realized that he couldn't come out of the upset that he had during discussion with Mahima in Inder's presence. Perhaps he didn't know how to manage his failure before someone who was very junior in age, that too, his employee. Employee was like a servant.

"Papa if you don't get angry let me tell you that we have a computer" Bhumi said. She entered the room catching the discussion.

"Where is it?" Ishwar asked Bhumi. He kept his anger intact.

"That's in my room" Bhumi said. "If that works for you" she added.

"That doesn't work for you now?" Ishwar asked Bhumi. He didn't want to give message to Mahima that he deprived his daughter from computer to give it to a servant under confused sense of socialism.

"It works papa. Only thing, it works slowly" Bhumi answered.

"Ok, you give that to this man. He will work on this" Ishwar Jain asked Bhumi to shift the computer to outer room of the house.

"Schedule the shifting of computer to your room. You need to finish all the work in time." Ishwar ordered. "New accounts are to be created on the computer" he dictated him. "Can you do that all?" he asked Inder.

"What will you do till computer is not there?" Ishwar asked Bhumi. "Is there any alternate for you?" he turned to Bhumi.

"I didn't use that much so it won't affect my routine as such." Bhumi assured her father fearing his anger. "I can wait till we buy a new one" she whispered.

"Bhumi just tell your father that his breakfast is ready." Mahima asked her daughter to convey.

"Have you done your breakfast? Want to have your breakfast here?" Ishwar asked Inder.

"Yes sir" Inder said. "No sir" he immediately corrected himself only to get confused with his own answers. "No" finally he said. Inder left the living room.

Ishwar sat in a dining chair with newspaper in his hand. Inder came out of the living room to go for work in the scrap settlement. He found himself puzzled with things around. "Was this what he wanted to do? Would Inder not misuse the computer? Would Inder not take liberty to use this house? Would Inder be the right one to be supported? Why Mahima was so worried about Inder's presence in the house? Why she was not taking it as an affirmation action in the States? Might be she didn't know what's happening in the States. Might be she was driven by tradition?" Ishwar had many things to occupy his mind to challenge his learning and thinking that got shaped since childhood. The peoples' traditions didn't advocate equal treatment here. For that reason she couldn't accept Inder's presence in the house. Ishwar questioned himself. Ishwar answered himself.

Bhumi also went in the kitchen to take breakfast for herself.

"*Maa*, please take your breakfast first" Bhumi said.

"Leave it there, I will have when I feel like" her mother reviled.

Bhumi took breakfast to the dining table where her father had already finished his breakfast. Her father looked at her then at the door of kitchen. There was no sign that Bhumi's mother would come to have her breakfast with them. He left the table. Bhumi finished fast her breakfast.

Books Atmajyoti, Dharmamrut Angaar, Dharma ke Das Lakshan, Gnaanu Gnaanatva, Ishtopdesh, and Indriya Gnaan . . . Gnaan Nahi Hei, Muni Gnaan Saagar, were interleaved with books of Social Awareness Foundation Course, Mathematical and Statistical Techniques, Computer Systems and Applications, Business Communication, Business Economics, Business Organization, Principles of Accounting, Financial Accounting, Accountancy and Financial Management, Banking in Financial System, Business Development Commerce, and Business Laws of the graduation course in commerce stream were in the book rack of study table in Bhumi's room. The notebooks for each subjects of her course were supported at the other end of the lower rack.

Desktop monitor on the study table was adding extra studiousness to the room. Study table having a hole for required cabling to make monitor work for personal computer with Intel Core2 duo inside. The speakers attached to the personal computer were not visible at glance as they were placed under on a wooden platform fixed in the side walls of the study table.

Bhumi touched the thin film transistor monitor of the computer. She then unplugged the power cord from the extension board connected with power supply. She finally unplugged the power extension board also. She coiled the cable of the computer.

"I have unplugged the computer. It can be shifted from my room." Bhumi informed her father who had just reached home from the factory. She looked at her face in the mirror to get surprised as her face was telling different story. She felt that she was happy that she finally could be able to help Inder in providing resources to the green cause. Handing over her computer to him was not a good idea on her face. She could not understand the secret of the dichotomy. She again and again stood in front of the mirror to check whether she was sure to spare her computer if she was not allowed to share that with Inder.

"Inder is still in the factory" Ishwar Jain informed. "Wait for some time. You can shift it to his room when he is back." Ishwar settled in the sofa after he came tired from his factory of scrap and chemical processing for recycling.

"Why are you shifting the computer to Inder's room?" Mahima entered in the living room with a glass of water in tray.

"He requires it for office work. We have to work using computer in our office." Ishwar said. He kept back the empty glass in the tray after he gulped the water.

"But, that day you were asking so much about his other assignments than office work for which he may require computer?" Mahima asked. She wanted Ishwar to recall the day when Inder came first time in the living room of the house.

"I was making him think that I have deep concern for his international assignments." Ishwar showed how smart employer he was to keep his employee happy. Bhumi caught what he meant. Mahima looked at Bhumi who pretended to be busy in reading newspaper.

"What will you get if you make him think that this computer is being shifted to his room for his conference assignments?" Bhumi's mother asked Ishwar Jain. She wanted to understand the strategy.

"So that he will work hard for the office to finish in time or even before" Ishwar replied. "*Theek hei na*?" he wanted to confirm his reason with Mahima.

Mahima was silent. She neither approved nor disapproved the idea of shifting the computer to outer room.

"You can get work done by your workers by motivating them to do your work." Ishwar explained theory of motivation to Mahima as he could see Mahima doesn't want to be part of the decision. He wanted to make her a strong stakeholder for the success. "To keep them motivated you need to provide incentives" he taught his wife about the significance of theory of expectancy to keep motivation live and its application in everyone's daily life. "Shifting this computer in outer room is incentive for Inder" he added to top up the explanation.

"This computer in that case may be shifted to office. There Inder can work for office" Mahima gave her own reason. She had an idea that Inder should not use the computer for his personal use or his conference assignments.

"Shifting it to the factory is not a good idea as Inder has many jobs in the factory." Ishwar Jain said. He wanted Mahima to understand and think like he thought. "And they are of different nature. He may not be able to spare time to work on this. Then this computer may become useless over there. This is the reason this computer should be shifted to his room." Ishwar explained his management to Mahima. "The computer in outer room is available for all of us also. This will make us use it optimally between possible users" he further explained. He didn't want to tell Mahima that Inder did many manual and menial tasks to match the aura of scrap and computer might get all the dust and dirt over there till that was not properly installed in an air conditioned environment.

"That means Inder may come and go in this interior part of the house?" Mahima wanted to know future course of action. She was apprehending problems for Bhumi. She looked at the floor as if she wanted to trace Inder's footsteps when he walked there in the morning.

Ishwar kept quiet.

"That means there will not be any restriction for Inder." Mahima apprehended.

"Where are you? He is working for us. He is no more a waste picker. I have told you earlier also." Ishwar reminded.

"No, we also can go to the outer room." Ishwar said. "We may buy a new computer for Bhumi which I also can use. So there is no question of regular interaction" he intended.

"Even now he works with scraps. Reusable items, waste items and these all are collected from the waste." Mahima put the same logic to Inder's current tasks in the scrap settlements.

"What Mahima! With that standard we all are working with scrap for generations for that matter. We are still not touched by any stigma which these people are ridden with." Ishwar wanted Mahima to understand the social changes.

"I don't work with the waste. I don't work with reusable items of scraps." Mahima declared her stand.

"Don't you sweep when your maid doesn't turn up. In that case you sort the waste of the house to the dust bin. Don't you reuse daily the same utensils after cleaning?" Ishwar wanted Mahima to understand the social dynamics of change as need. "Do you understand that? Moreover, are you not what I am?" Ishwar asked.

"Yes, I am not" Mahima shouted. She stunned Ishwar.

Ishwar keep quiet.

"Shall I call Inder to shift this computer? He might have come from the factory." Bhumi asked her father. She came for rescue as the social debate between her parents might have left emotional bruises on their ego.

"Just ask your mother. I am nobody to decide" Ishwar showed his anger. "I am nothing" he said exhaling hot for long. He wanted to use that to develop unanimity in decision making.

"You call him Bhumi, you just call him inside." Mahima shouted. "It is your father who should be listened. He is head of the family. He only can be obeyed" she competed. "Otherwise also, whether Inder came once or many times that doesn't matter now. You just call him" she added. The logic might have worked for her as self-healing. She became calm after that.

Bhumi went out to outer room to call Inder.

"Yes sir" Inder came in the living room. "Good evening mam" he greeted Mahima. He again got shrunk in humility as he remembered her whispering over his presence in the living room.

"The computer is in Bhumi's room. You can shift it to the outer room." Ishwar ordered. Inder looked at Mahima. She stood quiet.

"*Kya soch rahe ho Inder*?" Ishwar asked him to hurry up.

"Ok sir" Inder obeyed his master. He also apprehended an opposite command from Mahima. He moved to Bhumi's room. The computer was already unplugged from power supply. He held computer machine with both the hands to carry that to his room. No, it was not his room. Nobody in the house referred to the room as his room. It was outer room. Outer means outer room for outer people. These things do not bother Inder as it was Ishwar Jain who was benevolent to him. In many cases people like him engaged in menial work for the factories and household left to manage with store rooms. In store rooms of five by four feet and they sleep on slab in one wall of the store room and spread legs on the slab on adjacent wall. Things were better in that outer room which Ishwar Jain might have visualized when constructing the house that the outer room would be used for servant on duty with watch dog responsibilities.

Inder brought the computer to the outer room. He went back to Bhumi's room to take other parts of the computer. Inder had shifted all the parts of the computer. It was time to make that working. Mahima was supervising Inder's effort put in shifting the computer. Inder was scared of doing it on his own. He didn't know the basics of the computer machine. He had used computer to see files, send few emails earlier. Not more than that.

"Sir, I have shifted the computer." Inder said.

"Finally he has shifted it in his room. Now how will you do?" Ishwar asked Bhumi. He looked at Inder.

"I'll manage" she said. She avoided eye contact with Inder.

"Ok, have you placed all the parts of computer as they were set in Bhumi's room?" Ishwar enquired from Inder. He moved towards outer room.

"Can I check if all the settings are done as they were when it was in my room?" Bhumi asked her father whether she could come to the outer room. She knew that Inder was scared of power connections.

"Yes Bhumi, you can ensure that. He may make a mistake as he has not been a computer man." Ishwar gave his approval. "Do you remember all the connections?" he further wanted to confirm from her.

Ishwar and Bhumi came to the outer room where Mahima was already there looking at all the parts of the computer and their details.

"Let me see how you have set up the computer" Ishwar inquired.

"The computer may go bad sooner here without proper arrangement." Mahima vexed. She looked at Bhumi who was checking the connections.

"Nothing will happen, *Maa*" Bhumi assured her mother. She knew why her mother was worrying. Her mother's concerns were focused around her relation with Inder. "*Aap kisi bhi tarah ki chinta mat karo*" she assured emphatically with intentions to take away her mother's concerns.

"Let it be like this, he will connect power from the point just below table in the left corner of the room." Ishwar also replied to Mahima. "I have seen many of the offices have computer in the same set up in the beginning" he added. He wanted to solace himself as he knew he was not going to buy a new computer table. He knew one thing for sure that if he agreed with Mahima then she would advocate keeping it back in Bhumi's room. Entire shifting exercise would go useless in that case.

"Inder, did you connect the power cable of the computer?" Bhumi asked Inder. "Let me check all the connections once again" she bent down to look into the back of the machine for keyboard and mouse connections. She picked up the keyboard and mouse connectors to insert in the slots in the back of the computer. She then plugged interfacing nob of the lead of the speakers into their sockets in the front. She was a bit confused for computer's power connection. She took monitor cable and attempted to push the connector in the slot in the back of the computer. She pushed the connector but that didn't get into the socket. She found it difficult to fit in. She looked at Inder.

"Achchha bhala chal raha tha Bhumi ke kamre mein" Mahima commented when she saw Bhumi needed help from Inder.

No one spoke.

Inder bent down to look into the slot in the back of computer. He took the connector of the monitor cable from Bhumi's hand to understand the design of the connector. He found that pins of the monitor connector to the cable were visible in the hollow connector. He pushed that into the other slot in the back of the machine. He was happy as the connector fitted into the slot.

He picked up the other connector for power supply and pushed into the slot in the back of the computer machine. The connector fitted into the slot. He took out again and looked into the connector. He found no pins were visible but the rectangular holes in solid polymer stuff of the connector of the same size and shape. Inder smiled at his foolishness as two connectors were complementary to each other in design.

He forgot to look at both the connectors simultaneously. Bhumi also could not find the difference of the connectors.

They could make out the three pin power side of the connector to the electricity supply easily. He plugged the same into the electricity supply. He was happy as nothing happened. He was scared of wrong connection as it might have spoiled the computer. Inder was surprised to see that even by mistake he could not make a mistake. Mistake proof design of the computer was order of the day.

"It was working fine in Bhumi's room" Mahima winced again.

"Theek ho jayega, donon mehnat kar rahe hein" Ishwar assured Mahima.

Mahima found that Ishwar was also committed to get the computer to function and that too in the same room. She didn't want to stay any longer. She stared at Bhumi before she moved out.

Bhumi cheered as there was glow around the push button of the computer when she pressed that. Power supply was there in the computer.

Nothing happened on the computer. Bhumi and Inder looked the computer. They looked at each other. Bhumi started biting her nails. Inder got puzzled. He started sweating on his forehead. What might have happened? Suddenly Inder's eyes got stuck with another cable hanging with the monitor of the computer. Inder touched that cable and found nothing happened. He went back to the monitor. He again bent down to look into hanging end of the cable. He took the cable end in his hand turned up the connector.

That connector was different from the other connectors. He looked at the monitor where power was glowing on the 'on' 'off' button of the monitor. He looked in the hollow structure of the connector. There were so many pins inside the hollow cover. Two screws were also loosely fit into polymer housing. Screws were there in the connector. Inder turned the back of computer machine.

He found two different sockets of the same shape and size on the back of the machine. At first he got puzzled seeing two connectors again. Then he smiled. He touched the sockets on the back of the machine with his fingers. He could make out the difference between the two sockets then. One socket was full of pins like the connector at the end of the monitor cable.

Pins could not go in to the pins. He touched the other socket in the back of the computer. He could make out the presence of many small holes on the surface. He took connector and pushed that into the socket. The connector got into the socket.

"Shall I again switch it on?" Bhumi asked Inder who looked confident at that time.

Inder nodded.

Bhumi again switched the computer on.

The computer worked, Inder also cheered after he saw the windows on the screen of the computer. Bhumi entered password to log on to the computer. Ishwar's photo with her mother Mahima on the wall paper on the monitor screen gave lot of satisfaction to Ishwar Jain. He looked at Bhumi with lot of affection.

Ishwar was also happy to see that computer was working. He was also happy to see that his daughter had very high place for him in her heart in the times of it's-my-life kind of generation where kids demanded their own privacy and freedom from parents.

"Bahut achchha, ab ispe jaldi se kaam karna seekh lo" Ishwar appreciated Inder and instructed to gain proficiency fast.

"Thank you sir" Inder said. "Thanks for your blessings" he expressed his gratitude towards Ishwar.

He went back to the living room.

"Ok papa, I also come in five minutes. I need to tell him about files on the computer." Bhumi assured her father.

"Ishwar settled in a sofa in his living room. Mahima came fast leaving her room to enter the living room where Ishwar had just settled. "Who is there with them in the outer room?" she asked Ishwar.

"I have just come from that room only. Bhumi said she would come in five minutes." Ishwar explained. "She had to tell about files and documents on the computer" he repeated what Bhumi said to him.

Mahima ran towards the outer room. She just stopped before the room as if she wanted to catch Inder red handed to throw him out of the house. She was preconceived with idea that Inder had strong intentions to play on Bhumi. But she found Bhumi was explaining about files on the computer.

"You love your parents very much!" Inder asked. He looked at her parents smiling on the wall paper of the computer screen.

"Whatever I am today is just because of my parents." Bhumi said. She wanted to show the significance of parents' in her life.

Mahima snooped into the room to know what was going on between Bhumi and Inder. She finally entered in the room. She did not speak any word. She came back to the kitchen. She was now a bit sure that her daughter behaved responsible in her parents' absence. That gave her new confidence in the relation with her daughter. That came as great solace in the times when teenager boys and girls don't care for anyone. They were not even shy of their elders' presence. They could be seen cuddling caressing embracing each other at few feet away in the metro trains or bus stops. Many a times she saw couples smooching in the park nearby. They didn't bother whether it was sunny shiny day or no moon dark in the evening. They wanted to be watched by people as if they acted in movies. That seemed so to Mahima.

Inder switched on the computer. Computer didn't ask for password. "Why did he want to have password when that computer was not his?" he asked himself to validate his intentions. He had not been given that computer to do his work. 'Do it fast' was the motto behind the grant. If he put on password then everyone in the house including Bhumi might feel bad. But if he didn't have password then how he would protect his documents.

With all these thoughts running in his mind, Inder saw Microsoft word on the screen of the computer. He has worked earlier on computer but that was just to writing few words or lines replying to an email. Now got the computer for work so he had to learn how to write and edit documents. He might have to maintain accounts in excel sheets also.

He struggled with Microsoft Word. He wanted to memorize the keyboard so that he could get it handy to write big sentences or paragraphs efficiently as he needed to write a lot. First he took the note pad where he had written a letter to email Mr. Hwaib.

He could see the Microsoft Word had already opened a file with name Document1. He wanted to start writing with greetings. 'Fear Mr. Gwaib' came on the screen when he entered the keys. He looked at the text. He got really feared. Not from Hwaib but his sense of location of the keys on the keyboard. He discovered that he was not used to on the keyboard.

The mistake in the very first initiative was the setback in intended fluency on keyboard. He had pressed the keys of 'f' instead of 'd' in 'dear' and 'g' in place of 'h'. The keys of 'd' and 'f' and 'g' and 'h' were adjacent on the keyboard. So it became 'Fear Mr. Gwaib'.

He laughed at himself. He thought it was not his mistake. It was rather natural expression that came from within him. Mr. Hwaib was a fear for him. It didn't leave him free for a moment.

Also that he keyed 'Gwaib' for 'Hwaib' came from his natural reaction within his subconscious mind. He looked at the meaning of 'Gwaib' then he got tears in his eyes as 'Gwaib' or 'Gaib' in Hindi or Urdu meant to 'disappear' or 'disappeared' from the scene. The tears told the story that he wanted Hwaib to disappear from his mind to set him free. Free from responsibilities which became burden for him. Free from the constraints in which he had to behave like a sophisticated gentleman who fight for a cause. They were responsibilities in a confused sense of the term. They became burden on him.

Tearing watered eyes couldn't see properly 'Fear Mr. Gwaib' on the screen. His miseries were also impediments that didn't let him see clearly what was displayed on the screen. Filth and waste driven miseries and memories laden with rags, sacks, gunny bags and wags around in the landfill area of Ghazipur were also not letting him see clear what could be available to him in the world of promises, responsibilities, and commitments. He couldn't remain the same Inder when he wiped tears from his eyes and cheeks and looked at the screen. He minimized the window. He saw smiling faces of Ishwar Jain and Mahima Jain.

Inder corrected his mistakes from 'Fear Mr. Gwaib' to 'Dear Mr. Hwaib'. Now his fear became dear and what was 'Gwaib' earlier became Hwaib. 'Dear Mr. Hwaib' had endeared him to dream. Before that he couldn't dare to dream improving about himself and his lot. The dreams were taking away his sleep.

"May I help you?" Bhumi asked Inder seeing him struggling with the keyboard of the computer. She came to lock the gate of the house. She just wanted to check if everything was alright with the computer and Inder.

"How many days can you help me out?" Inder answered in question.

"I can help you in your green assignments till you get comfortable with the keyboard." Bhumi extended her helping hands. She first extended her arms around Inder's shoulders to embrace. She stopped herself as she found Inder on different note.

"At this time you want to help me!" Inder looked at the alarm clock and then looked around. "People in neighborhood with your father will throw me out of your house." Inder said. He compromised his dreams to realize the dreams that had taken away his sleep.

"What happened? Why are you talking like this? I really want to help you in your 'green assignments'." Bhumi cleared her stand.

"You also have started to call it my 'green assignments'." Inder smiled. His smile was mixed with pain that he carried since he came to Ghazipur. Miserable smile had to remain miserable.

"Why can't I call them green assignments?" Bhumi asked. She thought her father had called Inder's survey work as green assignment so she also could. She also should rather. Like father like daughter.

"I believe your father calls these assignments as 'green assignments' out of sarcasm." Inder shared what was in his mind. "Green is in currency where elite classes pay lip service to their passion for green if it is not to the environment for which they don't display any commitment to switch to frugal lifestyle" he added as he could not control his anguish over the issues which people label green and forgot as if writing 'green Delhi clean Delhi' will keep away every filth and waste as if that can turn every waste hill into best hill. The best hill on the fossils of the poorest of the poor was to serve picnic spot for the rich.

"You think he calls your assignments as 'green assignments' out of sarcasm." Bhumi came with a bust as she couldn't hear what went against her father or even mother for that matter. "Do you really think so? No Inder it is not like that. You are mistaking" she stood by her father.

"It is already half past eleven O' clock in the night. Please go inside" scared Inder requested Bhumi. "Please teach me your computer and your theories in day time. I want to learn many skills on the computer but in the day time. Bhumi, please try to understand me" he pleaded. He held himself back in holding her with shoulder to show it was time for her to sleep. It was time for her to sleep in her bedroom.

"Ok" Bhumi saw him so serious on that matter that she just came out to go inside.

Inder got busy struggling with keyboard. He first tried headings visible on the home tab of the ribbon on Microsoft word. Many of the heading styles were provided in the option. Inder attempted to learn most of the styles on the document he had opened. He now understood the heading styles to write text on the document. Left to the headings and styles he found some numbers and some other symbol points. He attempted using them and found the text which was written in the document can be numbered in paragraphs.

Inder attempted to insert tab of the menu of the word editor. He got confused with so many unfamiliar options which were there in the menu bar on the ribbon. He found bookmark, hyperlink, cross-reference, header footer, etc. on the ribbon which he did not understand. He came to the left corner showing cover page, blank page and page break and attempted them in writing the document. He got the meaning and significance of items listed in the insert tab of the ribbon.

Inder attempted most of the options provided on the tabs of each ribbon of the editor. He came with improved familiarity with the Microsoft word. He got to feel the cold of the surroundings in the morning. He looked at the alarm clock. It was already five O' clock in the morning. He got up to get ready for the day.

Inder started keying in text that he intended to write to Hwaib in a word document. The challenges he faced on the keyboard were to make him feel that he still needed regular practice. He read the text that he keyed in.

Dear Mr. Hwaib,
Greetings,

This is second installment of my communication to you. This is not reaching you because I am still writhing to reach today's means for communication. I am lucky as my employer and his daughter provided me their computer to write to you. For that I acknowledge Bhumi, daughter of my employer, as she is having powerful intention to this cause. I don't know why. May be women are also not in a promising condition. And she is very much one among them. May be theirs as a lot is not much better than the lot of mine. They are the one in the house who are responsible for all cleaning and gleaning household work. May be she is hoping some empowerment out of this exercise. May be fashion icons inspire them to be in luxuries. For that they need their maids to live in good environment for not to fall sick. May be they would secure consistency in service from maids if the maids are not beaten up by husbands every now and then. May be because of very crude but apparently real reason as wives they would tend to secure their relations as if women in domestic help are empowered to resist their husbands' sleeping lust. May be she is showing that she is sacrificing something for this cause. May be this. May be that. May be so. May be such. May be . . .

But you please don't worry about interfacing and interacting with the people and surroundings here. We want to keep you safe from all infections and diseases we suffer. For that all we have shiny faces of shining India. They are running the shows. They are stopping the show. They are highly educated and running the companies. You may know few *shahs* if not *malikas* in today's enterprising India. You may also know *cochairs* who take interest to increase interest in wealth creation and maintenance for their home and life and their assets which are longer than their life. The company has to be an ongoing concern. So they planned for a time period longer than life and for generations to come.

Yes, coming back to the point that I am still writhing for basic communication needs. You must be thinking that I am lazy or not initiating the project seriously. You may also be thinking that I am a wrong choice for this work.

Frankly speaking I am left with sad experience and not feeling any power in taking up this work. The moment when I touched the Indian land two months back I was full of passion for this work. The shock that I got in converting the dollars with me which I didn't spend in your land is shattering my hopes and me in a progressive manner.

Anyway now I am blessed with a workable computer by my employer for work in his office. If I do the work I am engaged with you would corrupt the practice and break the trust of my employer. So what to do? Luckily my employer knows about this work and supports me as well. He was impressed with the way the opportunity managed by Ms. Veronique for me to attend the conference.

Other than resources, the biggest problem I am facing is related to sampling. The sample includes people I know or with whom I got brought up in the landfill area of Ghazipur. With their support I got educated and earn my living at present. I am not sure what is the scope of my work and that of the entire work.

Inder could have written further if Bhumi had not entered.

"Oh! You are struggling with the word editor on this computer. You could have asked me to key in for you" Bhumi extended her assistance standing by side. She leaned to stand by him.

"Thanks Bhumi. Don't you think I need to be proficient in keying before anything else?" Inder cleared his intentions. "This is what your father also wants" he added.

"I am not saying that you should not get proficiency. But if I can help you in your endeavors and assignments it will give me some confidence to be one with you in your cause." Bhumi came on to impress Inder on a touchy note.

"What happened?" Inder enquired.

"Does everything need a reason?" Bhumi replied.

"I and you are from different worlds. It is not natural to be in other's world. Leaving one's own world to understand other's world is dangerous. It is painful also. If I imitate to be in your world then people would laugh at me. If you behave as if you are in my world it is not allowed by society's rule. People would like to kill you. People would attempt to burn you live. Social stigma fearing parents would attempt to kill their daughters to prove that they couldn't untie their social knot. They regret why they cut daughters' umbilical cord. These are my fears whenever you offer me some help" Inder took a long in explaining why he was shy in taking her help. Bhumi kept quiet for a moment. Perhaps she was thinking an answer as if that was a debate in her college.

"You think you are the only aggrieved in this world. Our conditions are also not very good" Bhumi spoke after framing few thoughts in her mind.

"You people are quite flourishing in India. People from your society are educated, rich and commercially successful." Inder interrupted in disagreement.

"I am not talking about my people or community. I am talking about conditions of women and girls" Bhumi corrected and suggested Inder to overcome his disagreement. "Every now and then the girls are raped. Even at twelve she is raped. She is raped at even ten, nine, eight, seven, six, five, four, three, or two. So the age is no bar in men's society. But at minus one fourth year in her mother's womb she is killed. Her mother is deprived to bring new life" Bhumi wanted to take on Inder who thought he and his lot was the only sufferer in Indian society as if all women were enjoying the luxuries of cars, studios, low and high rise 2/3/4 BHKs, villas, bungalows, studio apartments, etc . . .

Inder kept quiet. He didn't expect that Bhumi had so much pain for women as an entity, social entity.

"Data say every fifth minute a girl is raped in India. In neighboring state we have only eight hundred and fifty girls over a thousand boys. Every minute a girl is killed in mother's womb. We experience death every moment and live a suffocated life, to keeping the social pride. There is very thin line between keeping our lives and death to keep parents' honor and pride" she showed Inder that she was not tired to count on miseries bestowed on womanhood.

Inder got to know more about Bhumi. She was the girl not carried away by TV serials, reality shows, fashion models, or ramp shows even after she joined college.

"People like you only are not the one who suffers inequality. Male focus ranges from eave teasing to rape. A hundred million women are forced into human trafficking. Paid sex is not better than slavery. These women survive on their skin of which every inch may bring some penny or rupees from lusting men's pockets. More than forty out of hundred girls are married before age of eighteen. Most of us have been blowing the fire in the earthen hearth to prepare chapati to feed family members to get asthma or tuberculosis in the gift. Even today five thousand out of each one lac of women have either asthma or tuberculosis because they blow the fire in their hearths to prepare food. Five out of one hundred of us die due to this in every city or village in India." Bhumi spoke in single breathe.

"I got that you are much more informed on women conditions and have your own reasons to stand firm for this cause." Inder admired Bhumi. He accepted the statistics on women and her logic. Inder kept waiting for long as Bhumi spoke vigorous and relentlessly. "Actually, I was thinking you are supporting me out of mercy. I was wrong" he added. He was happy to get an impeccable support for the cause. He got overwhelmed to hold her hand as the character and commitment Bhumi demonstrated was beyond her emotions.

It was beyond physical attraction too. Bhumi noticed his hand raised and went down on the table.

"I came to tell you that you can take my data card whenever you need. You can keep this card plugged in the computer." Bhumi moved data card on her palm.

"That's great! But why I should keep it" he asked. Though the data card brought spark in his eyes.

"This is little device and may get misplaced so keep it inserted in the computer." Bhumi again explained to remind Inder. "Take it" her eye indicated at the data card on her palm.

"Ok" Inder moved his hand to take the data card. Inder's fingers were demonstratively shaking. Bhumi held his hand when his fingers touched the data card.

"*Hum hath na chhodenge toofan ke kinaron tak . . .*" she expressed her stand to be with Inder till his cause was alive.

"Your mother is coming" Inder warned.

"Are you testing my intentions? Or are you teasing me?" Bhumi looked into his eye. "Teasing habit has not gone into you. For that I am sure" she added. She looked once at the door of the room as if she believed him.

"Why are you talking like that?" Inder asked.

"Mother has gone with father to listen discourse from our *Muni*. They will come after completion of the *parv*." Bhumi informed. Her busts expanded with confidence being master of the house. "They will be out like this till *kshamaparv* gets completed" she came closer.

"That's the reason you are recalling Dev Anand" Inder grinned.

"Now I can sing the song in full swing" she garlanded Inder with her hands.

"Then you teach me Microsoft word" Inder demanded.

"That I can teach even when they are at home." Bhumi said. She wanted to teach him the art of love. She knew that she couldn't afford experiment in the science of love.

"But that is my immediate problem" he chose to be innocent. "I am stuck with the word" he added.

"Why are you not getting stuck in anything else? My dear?" she asked. Her hands were still on Inder's shoulder. He also didn't side them away. Inder found it difficult to move his head as his nose rubbed her breasts.

"Stuck is stuck" he said. He intentionally kept his hands down. He would have kept them on her haunches. But stuck was stuck.

"Then, I'll not teach you rather I would coach you" Bhumi got Inder's world. "Alas!" she cried at heart.

"You have been coaching me in my subjects since my school. Now is the time to give you back. Now I am the boss" she laughed. She lifted Inder's chin as if he was a kid of five.

"But I was not bossy" he reminded.

"Now choice is not with you. I'll choose, not you" she laughed. Inder kept his head down below her breasts. She again laughed. She kept laughing. His nose and cheeks pressed her breasts which kept vibrating with her laughter and breaths. She pressed his head into them. "Let me be the boss in this little game. Otherwise every place we are subdued." Bhumi became serious. The game of laughter and love got over.

"For me you are always my boss. You are the daughter of my masters" Inder flared her up. He got her pain.

"I don't want to be the boss on the basis of those masters." Bhumi clarified. She again came closer to show she was reducing the distance between them on her own. He knew temporariness of the pleasure. He feared the permanency of emotions. He stood up to leave the chair. He closed his eyes as her blossoming bosoms were now in his chests to challenge the chastity of his character, personality, and relationship altogether. She tightened the hold over him with her hands to feel him in her breathe. She stamped her budding lips on his chest.

Inder was loosening his hold on the chastity. He also held her torso. He thought why he was always thinking to keep Ishwar and Mahima happy even when they were not there to feel happy. On the other hand hurting and keeping her unhappy every now was also not right. They both experienced each other. Hold on each other got stronger moment by moment. They both closed their eyes to open up each other.

"*Nahin bata hei, nahin batega, mammy daddy ka pyar, ho mummy daddy ka pyar*" louder ringtone on her mobile phone opened the fifth eye in her room. She wanted to rush inside to pick the call immediately before her mother, on calling side, thought something else.

She resolved the dilemma. The dilemma to enjoy the pleasure in each other or to understand the harsh reality was interrelated with controls of physical and socioeconomic survival. She left him silently without any conclusion. She came out of the bosom blossoming world of budding dreams. She ran to pick the call.

Scared Inder started cursing himself. He slapped himself as if he had done something wrong. Why could he not control during the blooming pleasure to keep away the glooming feeling afterward. He just couldn't have luxury of having such pleasure which denied any differences in the society. He couldn't care to enjoy the luxury of such pleasure which had caused those differences in the society. He didn't dare to go inside know the concern of her parents. His fears were his barriers. His fears were his safety. His fears were his life. Inder counseled himself. He looked at the text that he was writing before she entered the room.

He picked the note pad in which he wrote previous text in the context of communications to Mr. Hwaib. He started keying in the text that he had written in the note pad to continue but with slow speed.

Give me some light. Good night.

Sincerely yours,
Inder Jeet.
Landfill Area, Ghazipur,
Inder added to write in the last to move further on the day.

Bottles in a separate plastic bag, polyethene bags in another big plastic bag, rotten eatables in another big plastic bag, paper wastes in separate big plastic bag, packing full intact glass bottles in another plastics bag, broken and used shoes and sandals in another separate plastic bag, a bag for plastic pouches and sachets were being sorted out by Ranchit, Sachi, Maithili, Madan, Mahabi, Jagdish, and others in the group. Ranchit was supervising the team work in a dumping ground of a colony. The dumping ground results out of throwing household garbage everywhere in the surrounding but in a big dumping room built for the purpose. The dumping room was shaded on high walls with shutter doors across.

"The dumping room is so good" Sachi said. "We could not even dream to build our house in the city like that" she wondered. She looked at the dumping room when she collected broken *chappals* in one hand and shoes in the other.

"You know even if we want, we cannot live in this kind of houses." Ranchit explained looking at the dumping room. "We are collecting the wastes almost hundred meters away from the dumping room" he added. He saw a waste corridor spread in more than hundred meters from the dumping room. It was full day work for all of them on the weekend.

"People of this colony are so careless to throw the waste anywhere else on the road than into the dumping room. They leave it on people like us to collect and dump into the dumping room." Sachi lamented covering her nose to avoid the stinking smell.

"You are behaving like the people of this posh colony." Ranchit commented on his wife when he saw she covered her nose. "You are living day and night in the stinking filth to find reusables and recycling items to make your livelihood. How long you can cover your nose like this?" he asked her further.

"We are working like than corporation workers but government never thinks about us." Sachi expanded her wishful expectations.

"Who called you to come here?" Ranchit asked.

"No body. We were starving in village, so we came here for some employment. When nobody gave us any work for weeks we took up this work as we exhausted our saving in surviving for those weeks." Sachi recalled.

"So you are blaming a government here in this state on your conditions while you ran from a village in some other state where you failed to earn your living." Ranchit wanted her to understand complicacies of the governance. "When your own state government and social system failed to provide a living and happy life you are blaming government and system here in Delhi. That is my Delhi for all Delhites" he further continued to make her fully understand the implications of government policies in one place and its aftermath in some other place. "So if you also think that you are Delhite that you also can call it my Delhi. And be happy with that" he laughed for a while to make it lighter for his wife who enjoyed coolness of few houses as maid servant but came out to collect waste with family members on weekly basis.

"Phir bhi is tarah ke ghar mujhe bade faltu lagte hein. Hum kyon nahin reh sakte inmein?" she was still in fascination with the dumping room. She could not see any value in the structure as that was not being used for what it was made for. She wished at the same time as if that house could have been for her.

"You are talking about yourself. Many of the people who live in this colony might also have thought using this dumping room for some other purposes when it was handed over to them." Ranchit explained his own thought.

"Aisa hum nahin bana sakte apne liye" she wandered with her thoughts if she could also have like that. *"Kitna paisa lagta hei ise banane mein?"* she immediately asked how much money that might require.

"Is not like any temple or mosque that people could erect during night and claimed it to be since Mahabharat or Mehmood and come together to gather money much more than required for construction and maintenance. They keep a priest and a committee to run that. Look at yourself who you are where from you have come. They see you as problem only not that you are clearing a niche, a place for their children to play in smell free parks" otherwise sick Ranchit didn't break to manage his gasps.

"Tum to ghoom phir ke dharma par aa jate ho" Sachi said with helpless as she found Ranchit to point out the futility of religion at that level of survival.

"Then you tell what have you got out of your religion?" Ranchit was on the verge of being angry with his wife as she was not listening his enlightenment. "You are here in Delhi you may be taken as Hindu. Had been some other place then you would have been ousted as Bangla desi. In that case you would be taken as Muslim. So tell me what your religion is?" he kept on his enlightening queries to enlighten her. He started panting and spitting after that enlightened conversation.

Sachi kept quiet after that. She also wanted Ranchit to focus on the supervising the team engaged in collection of waste.

Walls of the dumping room with shutter door on two sides were plastered with ceramic tiles on both the sides. Mosaic cemented floor of the dumping room of these posh colonies appeared much better for many of the economically weaker sections houses.

"Most of the people like him thought of living there the day it was prepared and handed over to be used as dumping yard." Ranchit recalled as if he had been a resident of the colony. "Had they gotten the shutter keys from municipal body might have been interesting affairs. Municipal body workers didn't open the doors for week as many people didn't think it was a dumping place" he continued to recall from the past. He had witnessed the construction of many colonies.

"But people of this colony are so careless in throwing their waste bags in dumping room. They throw their waste everywhere far and near but not in this dumping room. Such a big hall with high walls where many of us would have settled down instead of thatched houses" he talked to himself in utter disappointment with the residents of the colony on their waste disposal practices.

"Then where would have been the dumping of the waste in this dumping hall exactly. How come polyethene bags full of wastage thrown everywhere else but exactly not in the room?" Sachi said though she knew that she could not complain to anyone.

"*Are bhaiya!*" Jhihari shouted from the distance. Inder also was sitting on the bench of his rickshaw.

"*Haan* Jhihari, where have you gone?" Ranchit replied back.

"Come Inder, How are you?" Ranchit greeted Inder. "You only can explain Sachi how this dumping room made for waste looks like it is not for dumping the waste" Ranchit handed over the discussion to Inder.

"What's the matter *bhabhi*?" Inder asks Sachi.

"She is saying that this dumping room can be used by people like us for shelter." Ranchit passed the context.

"I am asking your *bhaiya* that people living in this colony throw their waste bags everywhere else in ground surrounding this dumping room but not in this dumping room." Sachi repeated.

"I am saying that it was not like this in the beginning." Ranchit informed his point directing Jagdish to collect pizza boxes in a separate plastic bag meant for all packing papers and wrappers.

"It is not exactly like that. It may have been so shining in the beginning that residents when this was new might not be willing to use it for dumping their wastes." Inder opened his own story. "Then some more posh residents of this posh colony dared with style to throw bags full of kitchen wastes in the evening. As it was neat and clean they probably used to go close to the room to throw the bags in the room" he explained further.

"You are talking like your *bhaiya*" Sachi complained.

"Now let me tell you what could have been the scene when this dumping room was handed over." Inder said. "They may be maintaining the dumping room neat and clean" he added. Sachi looked at him with smile she thought all men put similar logic. "As the ladies of the colony might have been thinking of themselves as national champion Krishna Poonia. They might have thrown the bag full of their kitchen waste in the dumping room in the same style Krishna Poonia throws in discus throw." Inder gave analogy from a sport. "She got the gold for her throw but no one is giving them a medal. Not even their husbands. They probably got disappointed" he added jokingly.

"Who is Krishna Poonia?" Sachi asked.

"Who is Sachin? Who is Dhoni?" Inder answered in question.

"Who doesn't know Sachin or Dhoni?" Sachi answered. "Dhoni is from my area" she added.

"Means you know who Sachin or Dhoni is" Inder said.

"Like them Krishna Poonia is also an Indian sport girl who wins medal in discus throw in Asian games, common wealth games." Inder added to her general knowledge.

"She is national champion in discuss throw." Inder said. Sachi smiled when she came to know how Inder made up an interesting story. She laughed also. She laughed longer to clear her lungs which got filled down to the bottom with bad smell.

"How this is related to dumping? What it has to do with my discussion." Sachi didn't want to lose.

"Do the people of this colony know Krishna Poonia?" Sachi said. She shook the big plastic bag with her both the hands. Jhihari and Maithili put that on rickshaw.

"May be they know as she had won in the last common wealth games." Inder shrugged. "May be many of them don't know" he shrugged again.

Sachi became curious in Inder's Interesting story. She wanted to know the crux of the story.

"Like Krishna Poonia, the gentlemen though not many in number on the evening canvas of the colony were Vikas Gowdas in the beginning when the room was handed over for use." Inder explained.

"Now, who is this Vikas Gowda?" Sachi asked. She smiled. *"Aadmion mein usi khel ka champion hoga"* she threw a stone in the air.

"Bhabhi you are brilliant! I didn't imagine this" Inder praised Sachi. You would have been an officer if you had gone to the school or college.

Words like school and college turned Sachi in cries that Inder didn't realize. Tears rolled down from her eyes.

"What happened *bhabhi"* Inder asked.

Sachi concealed her pain. The pain came from the past when she cried before her parents to send her to school. She kept crying for months when she was eight years old.

"What Brilliant Inder, why are you making fun out of me? I would not have landed in sorting out this waste which people look at with scorn." Sachi shuddered. She feared the past. For her, school and college were put behind high walls which she couldn't jump over, and landed up in living her life as pauper.

Inder forgot the story.

"Without education you just land up in doing this kind of waste collection activities which make you feel like life has gone waste." Inder wanted to improve the story. He took a risk of improvisation which again might hurt Sachi *bhabhi.* "With your kind grace I have been lucky enough to continue my education" he added.

"Everybody wearing good clothes is abusive on us because we are not an educated lot." Sachi shared dirges of her life. Living with that hate and scorn of the people she thought to be lucky for series of miscarriages which failed her to conceive otherwise her children also would have been sorting the waste. She was living a life like dead but a functioning flesh and bones to collect the waste and live in the filth. Functioning bone and flesh to breath rotten air of the fecal stuff in the waste hill. Functioning bone and health to . . . she knew that she was getting died. Getting died or getting killed. To be fossiled. Slowly . . . slowly . . . bonely . . . not lonely . . . not only . . . rusted rot . . . wasted rot . . . her lot . . . his lot . . . millions a lot . . . but to die of breathing poisonous stink generated out of dead animals' and their rotten viscera to plague her lot day and night.

"I didn't have intentions to make you cry" Inder solaced Sachi *bhabhi.*

"My story has broken your narration Inder. Don't stop by my stories. It was interesting for me to know how big people of these posh colonies might have been behaving to create job for people like us." Sachi managed her emotions. Tears in her eyes got dried up with her smile.

Inder resumed his story and thus spake, "Like that weeks passed rotten waste started communicating stinking messages to the residents of colony who might have improved their capabilities in discus throw practicing on their bags."

She nodded for continuation of the story. Sachi looked at the flats of the apartments around the dumping house as if she scolded them with her eyes. She scolded the residents to behave themselves.

"They started throwing the bag from an increased distance to avoid stinking smell stinging their nose and brains adversely." Inder covered his nose in imitation. "Covering their nose caused them lose balance to throw the waste bag around but not in the dumping room" he further added to his narration. He also looked at the flats of the colony to understand what Sachi *bhabhi* might have thought when she gave scolding gaze at their windows.

"Later, may be their attempts might have been going waste in throwing the wastes bags. In beginning they might have cared about the bags not reaching the dumping room. The heroism might have short lived. The sportsman spirit might have died in few weeks of handing over of the dumping room. When you see a couple come out for a walk in the late evening with fear of snatching their chains. They may lose their sleep as his slippers or shoes carry fecal stuff on the sole and toe. Such potential reasons might have caused them to keep a distance in practicing discus throw. Their performance got low" Inder completed the explanation to the present state of affairs.

"What's happening after that?" Sachi retained her curiosity in the story.

"Now, our crickters are new heroes of the residents of the colony who could throw the ball to wicket from any point in the field within the boundary. In cricket, players are at the wicket backup to pick the ball. Here, if the bags don't hit or reach the dumping room, are left to back up for the thrown waste bags in next few days." Inder drew an analogy from the religion of the land.

"Hmm" Sachi and Ranchit took interest in the story. They smiled. They again laughed to clear their lungs.

"As cricket is ruling the culture of the land and there is more cricket now. New type of match has become more popular where players' sixes and four are more than their singles or doubles. These residents also want to hit four and sixes in their life with waste bag from their kitchen and bathroom straight to the dumping room or to waste collecting boy. They throw these bags from a remote place or from other side of the road to the dumping room but bags fell around. So you see there is the corridor of wastes materials close to the dumping room to make it dumping ground." Inder explained. "The residents of these colonies are like us. That's why they convert these dumping rooms into dumping grounds open to communicate diseases. Covered dumping rooms don't appeal them" he added.

"Worst case is witnessed when most of us the waste manager or rag pickers play a role of bad wicket keeper. They collect waste bags and dust bin of the houses in big sacks to keep them in line aligned without dumping room. On the weekend many of us get busy in sorting out the waste. The capacity of the dumping room is not sufficient to match waste generating capacity of the colony after few years." Inder kept explaining the analogy. "Today we are also playing as a good or a bad wicket keeper" he was close to complete the story.

"This is painful for most of the team members engaged in the waste collection. They become sad as their role also is not a good one. But they blame it on their illiteracy, unawareness and ignorance." Inder did not spare their lot for ignorance.

There was silence for minutes as people thought Inder pointed at their mistakes also. Next minutes they all got busy in having their lunch at remote end.

"Inder you have explained it so well, you deserve lunch with us." Sachi invited Inder. He accepted the invitation from the lady who had been serving him food for years. She had been mother to him when she used to wake him up for work and reminded for school in second shift. She had been sister when she used to manage some books from houses in her knowledge where kids have left their old books after passing the classes in the recent past. They ate what she brought and had their lunch together in the shade of a tree.

"What's happening in your assignments?" Ranchit asked.

"I am managing basic things for my work." Inder updated Ranchit on progress of the work.

"Progress is slow. I would not be able to see the impact of your assignment in our life." Ranchit described precariousness of life at his age in the area of waste hill of landfill area.

"*Bhaiya*! Why are you talking like this? You are my inspiration for accepting this work. With your blessing I want to take it to the completion." Inder reemphasized his intentions and responsibility towards society.

Ranchit looked upward in the sky under the sun. Perhaps he was asking where his place was under the sun.

"*Bhaiya* now I would like to go and work on the same." Inder took leave from Ranchit.

The team got back to the work where big plastic bags on few manual rickshaws got swollen with sorted items. Ranchit asked Jagdish to pull the rickshaw with all the polyethene bags which was light in weight to their shelter. Mahabi and two other girls sat down on the bench of the rickshaw. He asked Maithili to pull another rickshaw with pouches and sachets and the bag containing waste papers. Madan and two other boys sat down on the bench of the rickshaw. The bags contained items of bottles, broken shoes, sandals and slippers, and rotten food items all were laden on the Jhihari's rickshaw. Jhihari asked Ranchit and Sachi to sit down on the bench. He kicked the pedal to start the engine of the rickshaw as they settled on the bench.

**Facts do not cease to exist
because they are ignored.**

Aldous Huxley

ðI si:s

The cease

The community building on the highway was famous for its grandeur. Disposal of the waste created everyday in its restaurant was one reason for a person to call Ranchit.

"Leave me here on this road. I will come on the highway when work is complete." Ranchit asked Jhihari to drop him at the gate of the community building in early morning.

"*Theek hei bhaiya*, I will come at nine O' clock." Jhihari assured his brother.

"If discussion doesn't work then I will move out of this place." Ranchit said.

"Ok, in that case tell me where shall I catch you?" Jhihari asked.

"You can't catch me in that case, you should not worry about that. I will come" Ranchit assured Jhihari who kicked the pedal to start the rickshaw. The engine of the rickshaw didn't start. He opened the small tank underneath to check petrol. The petrol was there in the tank. He again kicked the lever but engine didn't start. He then held handle and clutch of the rickshaw and shifted the gear lever and started pushing. The engine got started and Jhihari jumped on the seat to ride the rickshaw towards Ghazipur.

Ranchit saw Jhihari moving towards flyover till the last. He then moved towards the building. The person who called him was present on the gate.

"*Sahab Namaste*" Ranchit folded his hands.

"Come, Ranchit I am waiting for you" he said. "I will introduce you to the manager of the restaurant. You understand what is to be done. Rest all I will see" he added.

"*Sahab*, What will we be getting out of that?" Ranchit asked him out of curiosity.

"What do you want?" he said.

"Some money, so that, my situation will improve" Ranchit said. He avoided the tree of his own height coming over his eyes and followed the person who called up for the job.

"First you stop thinking then only you can focus on the work" he warned Ranchit entering the back door of the restaurant.

"Ok" disappointed Ranchit looked at the person. They both reached the office room of the manager.

"Good morning sir" the person saluted the manager clad in white with unusual sign on his forehead. Ranchit also saluted the manager.

Manager nodded. He folded the sleeves of his shirt.

"Sir he is Ranchit Chhidra lives in Ghazipur area" he introduced.

"*Sahab namaste*, I have greeted you when *babu sahab* greeted you." Ranchit reemphasized. The person pressed Ranchit's hand to keep quiet.

"Have you explained him what is to be done?" the manager asked the person who introduced Ranchit.

"Yes sir" the person said.

"Let him see the area where from he has to collect the food waste to the dumping place. Twice a day" the manager dictated.

The person took Ranchit with him to the rear of the kitchen and washing area of the restaurant. Ranchit saw a big kitchen with many cooking platforms having separate burner from a gas plant. Separate machinery for pizza and burger preparation was also there in the separate part of the kitchen. In the washing area there was a large rectangular sink with many water taps were fitted on all four sides. There was hot water mixed with soap coming from many taps to make it easy for workers to wash the utensils. Outer area was filled with all the wastes that couldn't be reutilized in food preparations. Food waste created in the restaurant was larger than the packing stuff.

"What you have to do is to clear this area twice. Transport the waste to the disposal ground" he explained.

"Where is the disposal ground?" Ranchit asked.

"You decide. You are coming from that area only" he said.

"If Ghazipur area is to be used for disposal you need to have permission from municipality." Ranchit said. "Who is doing it so far?" Ranchit asked.

"No idea, he also has left the job" he cautiously updated Ranchit.

"Then new contractor is to be fixed for transportation through municipality." Ranchit informed the person.

"Suppose you are the person collecting and transporting the waste" the person gave more responsibility indicating Ranchit to move towards the office of the manager.

"I need more persons. What will I get for that?" Ranchit asked.

"You are always worried about money only. You need to show the faith and dedication first to get this work and then to the person who got you this work" he attempted chastise Ranchit. They came back to the manager's office.

"Sir I have shown the area to Ranchit" he said to the manager.

"How will you work? When will you start?" the manager asked.

"What is your name? I forgot" the manager asked.

"Ranchit" Ranchit replied.

"Ranchit Chhidra" the person who called Ranchit completed.

"Ranchit Chhidra from?" the manager asked again.

"Sir, from Ghazipur area" the person replied.

"From" unsatisfied manager asked again.

"Singbhum *Sahab*" Ranchit answered. "Few more persons are required to do this job" he said to the manager further.

"How many persons will work with you? What will you get them for this job? Our contractor might have fixed with you" the manager replied. "Did he not fix everything with Ranchit?" the manager asked the person about the contractor.

"I will manage sir, I will explain him" the person said.

"Oh, this person is the contractor. He is not disclosing anything." Ranchit wondered. He thought that he was getting the contract directly. "He has asked me to show the faith and dedication to get this work" he said. He couldn't manage his disappointment.

"That is the must condition. If you don't have faith then you would not remain happy. If you don't have dedication to your work how can you progress in your career?" the person explained both the terms 'faith' and 'dedication' from his dictionary.

"*Sahab* at the end we have to fill our stomach" Ranchit said.

"Who denies this? You follow our faith show some bhakti see how you progress leaps and bound. This is the power of our faith" the manager explained the mystic power of the faith which he had practiced to achieve the status and peace in his life.

"What about the other fellows who will work with me?" Ranchit clarified his stand and wanted some assurance on how much he would get.

The manager looked at the person who brought Ranchit.

"Sir, I will explain him. You need not worry about that" he showed his commitment to convince Ranchit. He wore the expressions of fear.

The manager opened his eyes wide to look at him and then nodded.

"You bring all your team members in our faith then see the power. You will always be in peace" the manager educated Ranchit. "You will get twenty thousand rupees per month" the manager finalized.

"*Sahab* this amount is not sufficient for diesel of the transport. What about myself, others and the driver?" Ranchit asked.

"This is full and final. You manage with this" the manager ordered. "Who asked you hire trucks? You just manage it with manual rickshaw. You will have all the money" he suggested.

"So when will you start?" the manager asked again.

"I need to ask other two persons." Ranchit said. "They have not met you. They have not seen the power of the faith. They will see their circumstances and their needs. Let me hear from them" he added. "Then I need some time to decide" he excused.

"The master has decided every action for everyone in this world of mortals" the manager said raising his hands up in the air. "He has decided for you also. You will come" he assured Ranchit.

"Ok *Sahab*" Ranchit left the office.

"The person who called Ranchit also came out. Ranchit stood there. He again went inside the office to talk to the manager. Ranchit heard their laughter. Ranchit thought the person who had called was the contractor. As per the manager he also was not the contractor. May be the person was just a middleman. Then who is the contractor?" Ranchit wondered.

"Come Ranchit! Get ready" the person took Ranchit out.

"*Sahab*, tell me the truth" Ranchit requested.

"What do you want to know?" the person asked Ranchit. "Have faith you will have everything." he further assured.

"Was he the manager?" Ranchit asked the person.

The person shook his head in negation. They both came out in the open area.

"Is he the contractor?" Ranchit asked again. He took aside the twig that came before his eyes and face. They were moving to the exit of the community building.

The person again shook his head in negation.

"Are you the contractor?" Ranchit asked him.

The person nodded.

"Why didn't you disclose that before your manager? Why the manager didn't know that you are the contractor?" Ranchit asked.

"That all I will tell later" the person assured. "You just join the work" he said.

"Ok *Sahab*" Ranchit took permission to go back home.

"When are you starting the work? From tomorrow I have given the words to him?" the person who called Ranchit insisted.

"I will tell in the evening" Ranchit said before he left the place.

"How will you tell?" he asked. "I will call you in the evening." he showed his commitment to have Ranchit on the job.

"I have left that mobile at my jhuggi" Ranchit disclosed.

Sunday made it easy for Inder to practice writing to Hwaib because he needed to practice a lot. Ishwar Jain had provided the computer to improve his efficiency in the factory work. To justify the provision of computer, Inder's efficiency had to be visible in the office work. To have utilized the computer for personal communication to Hwaib on green assignments should also be started. But he was far away from the expected comfort level to work on the computer. He kept the key board aside took his note pad which he was used to.

Inder wrote on the note pad to compile it later.

> Dear Mr. Hwaib,
> Greetings,
>
> When I will get smooth communication with you I am not sure. My adversities don't seem to end at any point in coming future. Right now when I have computer and data card I need to maintain balance in my work and this survey. I am not sure what time I would be able to devote when survey under this project will really start. The cases I consider for survey are individuals around me. Sir, I may take few more weeks to get myself well versed in electronic communication.
>
> I want to communicate to you about the progress in teaming with Kul Vilas. I couldn't get any break through. He himself has never called me up so far. The things are stagnated with him because of no communication. In that case it is difficult for me to predict any fulfillment of the promise that I

make. To keep my promises I have to have some time to plan my activities.

By this time I am on the verge of forgetting that I have attended the conference which made me think to take everyone with me and revolutionize the recycling industry. Before I forget that I have attended the conference which made me think to take up the waste management in new dimension. Before I could take this waste management to new heights I fear that my optical nerves may not help my brain to differentiate between useful and wasteful. I want to do my part of the green assignments. It is urgent to reinforce the concept to restructure the recycling in Indian culture and ethos.

We recycle. We don't plan for recycling as such. We are forced in this situation as the last resort. Most of us engaged in this industry are doing this job of picking the rags out of our laziness to take up some other jobs. Other job may require some skill. In our society we are still doing job to fill our tummies. Few people of the rich middle class are able to exercise their choice as their career. This is new trend. They progress on their career in intelligent way while we are stuck up with old idiotic ways. For us trigger may be required to adopt intelligently idiot way of choosing the job as one's passion.

Bollywood has been a magical instrument for stinking rich class. Every dude from that class is doing something filmy whether they are using their muscle power to lift the dancing girdle at the next door or outdoor.

In that case recycling comes at the last for the lazy illiterates who keep busy in cursing themselves. It is my humble duty to grace the work by calling it recycling. In India people call it by various names like waste picking, *kachra binaai*, etc.

Inder had to pay attention to the knocking sound at the door.

"*Thuk thuk*" Bhumi came inside the room. She formally knocked the door as Inder had not noticed her for last ten minutes. Inder looked at Bhumi after he heard the knock.

"Do you need a knock?" Inder smiled at her.

"When I can't understand what's going on. When I can't help you out in this cause which is dear to you then I am stranger only." Bhumi prefaced coming closer to the table where Inder was writing on a note pad.

"Father and mother have gone to the temple. Some preparations for the *kshamaparv* are going on." Bhumi said. She noticed that Inder looked at the timepiece.

"What do you want?" Inder asked.

"Nothing. I am just sharing my opinion." Bhumi complained. She didn't control her snoop in the pad on which Inder was writing.

"Nothing means what?" understanding the intensity of her interest in the work, Inder gave the pad in her hands. "This is what I have noted down so far on what I want to communicate to Hwaib" he added immediately putting the note pad in Bhumi's hand.

"I am not your secretary or assistant. Why are you giving me this note pad?" Bhumi turned her position in the room.

Inder kept quiet.

"You didn't get what I have said" Bhumi smiled. She bent down and closer to Inder's face who was sitting in his chair to look into his eyes.

"I didn't understand" Inder clarified with shy expressions.

"I can take up the role of expediter in managing your project." Bhumi offered her service for the cause.

"Expediter!" Inder exclaimed.

"I can make you work faster. I can make you remind what is to be done. I can point out where you need to decide. But everything you only will be doing." Bhumi explained.

"You are a good decision maker" Inder acclaimed her skills. He could see her role in deciding the shifting of the computer, data card and offer of her mobile phone. "You have decided many things for me which I could not even think to do myself" he was overwhelmed. He got indebted to Bhumi.

"No I am not that also" she denied.

"You want to be my boss. You would have said that if you had been straight." Inder made new meaning.

"Straight? You are not straight? Oh no! I will not waste my life" she dramatized the situation. "Where have I landed up in this law of attraction" she slapped in her right cheek. "He is not straight" she talked to the wall as if she was talking about Inder to amuse Inder.

"Hey! I am tube light. I didn't get you" Inder also laughed as he could understand the different meaning of 'straight' Bhumi hinted at. "I could get only when you said you will not waste your life" he added. "Then I thought what I have said" he laughed at the meaning she drew. He laughed at himself.

"You say that living with those special people is wasting your life." Inder warned Bhumi. "If some happy and gay activists in the state happen to hear saying like that then they may sue you. You are lucky that you are here" he further made his warning intense.

"I hate them. I don't want them to exist. They are creating imbalance for the law of attraction." Bhumi became serious. Inder started laughing. His laughter caused her to be furious.

"Though it should not be the topic of our discussion as we started with green assignments" Inder asked Bhumi leaving everything aside. "Why do you hate them to the extent of making them nonexistent?" Inder posed a question. "Do you know the meaning of nonexistent? To me, it is that doesn't exist on the planet" he provoked her to improve his own knowledge from feminine perspective.

"You just see to find that who are these people? I have noticed that most of them are from the elite class whose parents in the earlier generations have spent their lives in fighting with their spouses either physical or in the legal courts. Most of them fought to be free to enjoy their extramarital relations which they wanted to be the norm of the day. Wives or females among these people spent their life in fighting to assert their freedom to restore monogamy which is not in men's genes." Bhumi explained the basis of her hatred.

"Being female you will never be able to understand them." Inder started trimming his nails with his teeth. He felt jealous with her to be that bold and beautiful to express herself.

"Being girl I can never support their rights. There had been rise in the lesbianism too to prove their stand. If you notice that didn't go long. Why? Because it is against the nature as a hole cannot befit in a hole. They remain incomplete on many aspects. Economy was the major aspect as they couldn't even justify their standalone existence without men." Bhumi explained so categorically.

"I did not get that" Inder surrendered.

"You didn't get or you don't want to get what a girl's experience is all about." Bhumi checked being firmed on her opinion.

Inder kept quiet.

"Lesbianism is not so openly discussed and fought as a right in this men's world. Why? Why it was matter of movies only?" Bhumi took Inder surprised on social matters as she came open on the topics which generally were avoided in discussion among the people of opposite sex. She used to get coaching tips from Inder. She taught him the social dichotomy and nature's stereotypes.

"I thought gay culture is on the rise as solution to combat worse sex ratio in India." Inder pretended as innocent.

"I don't think you are so intelligent to be stupid" she snuffed.

"What happened" he asked.

"O Mr. foreign returned! You have been in a land where gayism is on the rise where male and female enjoy equal degree of freedom. Male in those lands can't misuse females and or can't remain scot free for years or life if he does so. Even a leader apologizes or gets sentence for other relationship" Bhumi educated Inder. "That's the society of equals" she emphasized.

"If you look at the pattern of gay culture on the rise over there is because of male helplessness. Moreover they are innovative people as a pole insert on the hollow side of the pole to enjoy the pleasure of hole to combat the law of attraction" she came with distinction of law of physical attraction. "They wanted to innovate to live standalone life as free from gender dependency also. I hope you understand" she wanted to check Inder whether he was still in the debate.

"Hollow side of a pole means you need to be hollow in some way or other." Inder wanted to confirm from Bhumi.

"I am not sure" she didn't buy Inder's logic. "These people come from the affluent part of elite society. So, they definitely are hollow" she reasoned to disagree with him.

Inder's mouth remained open to say something. He got mesmerized by the bold logic from the beauty. He blushed.

"Are you the same Bhumi, Bhumika Jain whom I used to teach accountancy and book keeping?" Inder asked. He felt the burden of non-essential discussion as she took that on the most essential i.e. the law of attraction.

"You are proving me right Mr. Inder, Inder Jeet." Bhumi got stiff on the stand. "You are showing how a male is not prepared to hear logic and arguments from a female in our society" she took her stand.

"No Bhumi, you are my boss. How can I deny your logic and reasoning?" Inder went defensive.

"You will remain stuck in my being boss, employer's daughter. You can't come out of this" she kept her hand on his shoulder. She wanted to convey some other meaning which he was scared to accept.

"This is the note pad" he said. "I have written down few things which I want to communicate to Mr. Hwaib" he again surrendered to avoid further discussion.

Bhumi took note pad. She flipped through the pages. She read out listed email Ids. List included names of Hwaib, Veronique, Kul Vilas, Inder himself.

Ranchit was feeling giddy over the subject matter. He got puzzled with links in the context. Who was the contractor? The person who was talking to Ranchit was not the contractor. But he claimed to be the contractor. Who was the manager? The person who introduced with the *Sahab* told Ranchit that he was not the manager. Ranchit experienced that more than one hour had gone without any fruitful result in that exercise. Twenty thousand rupees won't be sufficient for diesel. With manual rickshaw all the members would die twenty years earlier. Ranchit moved fast towards highway.

"Does that mean the person who called me was just a middleman? Manager was also a middle man. He may be the real contractor but didn't want to disclose that he was the contractor" Ranchit thought. The person who took him to the office was also a middleman? So many middlemen were involved in that small work? He moved fast on the pavement along the highway where people have come out for morning walk. He was not sure for whom he would work? He was also not sure who would pay those twenty thousand if he works for them? Puzzled with such questions related to his fortune he moved forward to catch a bus to Ghazipur as he didn't expect Jhihari to come before nine O' clock. Engrossed in those puzzles he moved faster. He thought he also could start something new as he had not been able to do any job there in the landfill area for last two years.

He heard humongous thud close to him. Before he could turn to find what happened something hit him in the back and a big cry

"Jhihhaaaaarrrrriiii, Saaaaachiiiii" came out from his mouth and legs flied in the air when something very hard hit him in the waist. That made him falling head down on the ground which clunk.

His head hit the clean rag free red stone of the pavement on which he didn't get the opportunity to pick any rag but to leave many rags of his body and soul. His eyes could see another body was lying on the road. He saw his blood came out of his head, shoulders, waist, thy, knees, and feet. He felt his body was torn apart.

"Achchha bhala saaf tha, mere khoon se farsh ganda ho gaya" new thought was to lengthen his engrossment. Ranchit physically submerged in the streams of his own blood from most of his body parts. His opened eyes were waiting for his brother Jhihari and wife Sachi to take him back to Singbhum. His knees and feet rubbed the ground as if he would go running on his feet to Singbhum. He had come down on his knees acknowledging the might of the world. The might of the harsh world met him with hardness of red stone on the pavement. His body vowed down to the surviving world and gone silent and the chaos huddled him.

A vehicle from Bayerische Motoren Werke in the hands of a showmaker got decontrolled on its speed increased with the decontrol of the petrol price came up on pavement leaving its runway on the highway. The showmaker lost the track to ramp up on the red stone pavement better than the road surface itself but maintained the same speed of the vehicle. The vehicle first hit an octogenarian who attempted to step up on pavement when the vehicle stormed him after huge thud ramp up on the pavement. The vehicle didn't get any jerk or hurdle as the octogenarian was on fringe of the pavement and attempted to step on. He didn't pose any breaking barrier. Then vehicle hit Ranchit to fly him in the air.

Before anybody could understand anything the showmaker wanted to fly it back on the road. He could understand the hangover of the party in the farm house was over with the thud. He decided in fraction of second to fly from the pavement high. He perhaps knew that with the steering in his hand his escape was possible. The vehicle so fantastically landed on the road with huge thud again. It disappeared from its runway on the highway.

People out on the walk in the green belt ran first to the pavement to rescue the bodies of victims. They ran to the octogenarian as many of them knew him. People going out on work on cycles chose to stop near the body in the rags on the pavement. Many of them took a look at the body which didn't resemble with any of their relative and kept on moving away from the spot of the accident. People out on the walk huddled the octogenarian. No body attempted to dial hundred. They talked, talked and talked. Circle of people around the bodies enlarged.

A retired person went close to the fainted octogenarian. The body got bruised with ground he fell down. The retired person recognized him and searched his mobile phone for information to contact his relation. The octogenarian was lying fainted on the ground with mobile in his pocket. He searched for the contacts in his mobile and found a name marked with 'in case of emergency'. He dialed the number.

"Hello" the retired person spoke to the responding person.

"*Beta*, I am not your father. Your father has met an accident" he informed the son of the octogenarian lying fainted on the road.

"He was stepping up on the pavement when a big car hit him" he said.

"It is on the highway near Noida turn" he informed.

"Please come fast, there is lot of hope. You father is fainted" he said.

"Is there anybody who has seen car or number?" the retired person asked the people circled around.

No response . . . He again asked the people. He rather pleaded to the people around.

"Yes uncle, I have seen the car" a teenager boy came forward. "The driver was having his mobile phone in his hand before he lost the direction to ramp up on the pavement" he added.

"Another body is also lying fifty meters ahead" someone voiced.

"Yes" few voiced and people went to look at the other body.

A sedan came fast and stopped near the octogenarian lying fainted on the road. A middle-aged man in blue shirt and black trousers opened the door in hurry to rush towards octogenarian.

"Papa! Papa! What happened? How it has happened?" the middle-aged person cried seeing his father lying fainted on the road. He looked at the people around.

"How long he is lying here?" he asked.

"About half an hour" someone said.

"Why I didn't stop at that time" the middle-aged corporate man busted into tears.

"What happened?" the retired person asked.

"Fifteen minutes back I just passed by this place on the other side of the road. I didn't stop at that time" he regretted among his cries and tears. "I thought someone had met an accident" he again busted into tears.

"It happens in today's world of speed, race, work pressure, and deadlines. You must be rushing to your office" the retired man solaced the middle-aged man. "It's not your mistake" he added.

"Has someone dialed hundred?" the middle-aged man asked.

"I have dialed hundred before I called you up. I found your number in the contact list of your father's mobile phone" the retired person replied. "I think I had done good thing but the police is yet to come. It is good for your father you have come so soon" he added.

"Sir, please rush to the hospital. He is still alive" someone voiced.

"*Koi udhar bhi padha hei bhaiya apne pitaji ke sath unhein bhi hospital le jao*" another person on a cycle requested the son of the octogenarian if he could take other person lying fifty meters away on the pavement to the hospital. He came from the spot where Ranchit's body was lying.

"I think he is no more" the middle-aged man said when looked at the other body lying fifty meters away on the pavement. "There is no use of taking him to the hospital" he judged.

"Uncle, can I request you to come to the hospital? If you don't mind, please" he requested the retired person. "Please" he further insisted again.

"Ok" the retired person agreed.

"Let me take him to the hospital" he asked for help. Some people came forward. They just bent down to lift the fainted octogenarian and took him in the sedan. The police reached the accident site.

"Where are you taking this body?" the policeman asked the men who have lifted the octogenarian to take into the car.

"He is not the body. He is my father" the middle-aged man answered. "Some bastard has driven rash to hit him. My father came out for morning walk" he explained further. "By the way this uncle has rang you up long back" he looked at his wrist watch.

"*Kya batayein sir, aane wale festival ke chakkar mein hamare kuchh sathi lage hue hein. Kuchh doosre sathi pass hi ek park mein VIP movement mein lage hue hein*" fussed in festival and VIP movement in the area the Sub Inspector explained why he was late. "*Peedit ki maut nahin hoti to mera bhi itni jaldi aana mushkil hota*" he added that it would have impossible for to reach the site if the victim had not died.

The middle-aged man kept quiet.

"What is your name?" the Sub Inspector asked.

"Inspector there is no time right now. This is my card" he gave his visiting card to the Sub Inspector. "I will come to the police station to lodge a first information report after I am done with hospital. There is another body lying over there fifty meters away. I believe the driver in the car was mad. He should be booked and should be put behind the bars" he added in a hurry.

"Ok sir, you take your father to the hospital" the Sub Inspector said. He kept the card in his pocket. "When we are here you are taking him to the hospital. There will be problem in lodging first information report. We have to take him to the government hospital in our vehicle" he stated.

"I want to save my father first. I will think later" the middle-aged man said. He wanted to rush to the hospital.

"He can be saved in government hospital also" the Sub Inspector said.

"You know it very well how confident you are in suggesting me" the middle-aged man replied with patience.

"Has anybody seen the car? Its number" the Sub Inspector asked the people around.

"Many people have seen the car and told me the number. I have noted down the number" the retired person said. He gave a piece of paper to the Sub Inspector number written on that.

"How was the car?" the police inspector asked.

"It was big car. Black in color" the retired person again said. No one among the people around voiced any response.

The middle-aged man came to the driving side door of his car. On his request the retired person already seated in the rear seat of the car to hold the octogenarian. A policeman followed him before he fit in the driving seat. After the middle-aged man moved to the hospital most of the people pushed off the site of the accident.

The Sub Inspector then turned to look at the body lying fifty meters away on the pavement. He moved fast towards the body. Policemen followed him. The Sub Inspector looked at details around the body which was losing its warmth. The body of dead Ranchit had turned into a mass of bones and flesh. He asked two policemen to note down the details required for all the formalities.

"Nobody had claimed any relationship with his body. He must be a poor man" the Sub Inspector anticipated when he talked to the head constable noting down the details. Two cars stopped near the spot of accident. The driver of a black car came out to open the rear door for his master. From the other car two ladies came out to reach the Sub Inspector.

"Sir, he is my servant. I will call his relative for final rites" said the man who came out of the black car.

"Sir, your introduction please" the Sub Inspector asked. He pretended as if he didn't listen.

"This is my card" the man possessed highly rich looks gave his visiting card to the Sub Inspector.

"What was he doing here? Where are you living?" the Sub Inspector asked the man in black suit with extremely rich looks.

"Let me tell you after I make a phone call. Can I make a call?" asked the man in black suit who didn't want to answer.

Sub Inspector nodded.

"And, madam why are you standing here?" the Sub Inspector asked the ladies standing close to the body.

"No, he is not our relative. We are from Uttar Daani, the organization works in the field of devising lifesaving mechanism by arranging transplantable body parts of the cadavers of the severe accidents like this" a lady in purple *saree* said. "I am the director of the organization" the lady gave her card to the Sub Inspector.

"How do you know about this accident?" the Sub Inspector asked the lady. He looked at the man in black suit standing around twenty feet away. He looked at the card from the lady but didn't take any interest as everyone had given visiting card since morning. Though he wanted to know the detail but he had another card from the man in black suit also, so, he kept her card in the pocket.

"We have very sophisticated intelligence system integrated with major communication networks. Whenever someone dials hundred to call the police for help and the content of the call contains 'accident', 'road accident' or 'dead body' 'lying fainted' etc. then it prepares a log for us. The details of call like place, voice of male or female, geographical positioning of the calling place, details of the area etc. are reported in the log. Within 15 minutes we need to reach to the accident spot to take the body of the victim whose body parts can save few lives. It is to be done before the body becomes dead" the lady explained the functioning of the intelligent system employed by her non-governmental organization.

"But just before you, that man in black suit is claiming to be the relative of the dead body." Sub Inspector said.

"If you look at the details then you will find him resembling with the rag pickers who live in close vicinity of the landfill area where such people work with the waste and garbage to make their livelihood. He is from there" the lady said. "There are many scars on fingers and hands of the body which are results of working with the waste from garbage which contains chemicals, steel scraps, metal powders etc." she said using the domain knowledge of her field.

"Madam, you seem to be experts of your field. You are explaining like a detective. You can work with us in joint ventures" the Sub Inspector appreciated her. "Working with people like you would make our work easier" he smiled.

"Sir, please first let us complete the formalities fast so that we can take the body to the nearby hospital with facilities of operation on cadavers for extracting body parts which can be transplanted." the other lady in red *saree*. "Your introduction madam" the Sub Inspector asked the lady who spoke all of sudden.

"I am the assistant Director of Uttar Daani" the lady in red *saree* with golden border introduced herself to the Sub Inspector.

"Yes sir, we can appreciate each other at later stage. Let us rush to the hospital" the lady in purple *saree* laid importance to the urgency to take him to the hospital. "You may be surprised to know that a cadaver can save as many as thirty five lives if each of his or her transplantable body parts is transplanted successfully in each patient suffering from ailing body parts. Science has progressed that much" she added to the knowledge of the Sub Inspector. She was sure she had already impressed him.

"Ok that's important" he said. He instructed the policemen in his team to move ahead with the procedure.

"How come the organization's name is Uttar Daani?" the Sub Inspector showed his curiosity in the organization.

"Uttar Daani is taken as an inspiration" the lady in purple *saree* replied. She had to pause as the Sub Inspector's mobile phone rang up.

"Madam, let me take this call?" the Sub Inspector excused.

"O yes" the lady showed her happiness on mannerism expressed by the police Sub Inspector.

"*Jai hind* sir" he stood alert to manage his pitch and tone.

"I am doing inspection for half an hour" the Sub Inspector explained to his higher officer on the call.

"Yes sir, ok sir. *Jai hind* sir" the Sub Inspector said.

"Madam, the dead man is a servant of this rich person only" the Sub Inspector said. He pointed at the man in black suit.

"Perhaps he has the reach to the people who control you" the lady said. Her tone and expression suffered a setback.

"How come he reached here before us?" the lady in purple *saree* asked her assistant.

"May be, someone is tapping the content of our intelligent system" the assistant in red *saree* explained.

"Madam, you are working for a good cause. But he may be in needs to save his relative's life" the Sub Inspector said. Urgency to save his relative's life became priority over what the ladies were up to.

"Sir, this means you know that the person in black suit is not having any relation with the person died in the accident" the lady in purple *saree* caught the Sub Inspector's words for application of her logic and experience earned in running the peculiar kind of organization.

People around the scene started leaving when the Sub Inspector was talking to the ladies.

"We need to hurry up if organs of his body are to be used for any use. Either by us or him" the lady in purple *saree* said to her assistant. "Why can't we both make optimum use of the body parts which can be utilized to save few more lives and his relative" she suggested her assistant. The police Sub Inspector witnessed talks between the two.

"Can I talk to him?" the lady in purple *saree* asked.

"Madam, please" the Sub Inspector agreed. "Madam, hurry up, you are right the body will not be of any use but to be cremated. I understand that you are doing it for a good cause" he added.

"Excuse me sir, we are from Uttar Daani, the organization engaged in facilitation of saving lives of patients who needs organ transplant for their malfunctioning ones to renew their lives" the lady in purple *saree* introduced herself to the man in black suit. "This body of your servant may be a cadaver" she added.

"I am nobody to take this decision as his family members are required to give consent to use well-functioning-body-parts of this body to replace malfunctioning body parts of the patients for whom your organization is working. Let me do my part" the person in black suit spoke in flat tone to the lady with the Uttar Daani.

"Did you inform the family members of your servant?" the lady director of Uttar Daani asked.

"Yes madam, I have informed them. They are living in Bihar. They may take time to come" he said.

"Sir, by the time they come the body will be of no use. What would you do with this body?" the lady director asked him.

"This is none of your business" he moved to anger. "You may go please as I have to arrange for cremation of the deceased" he further claimed.

Listening the answers and his tone, both the ladies came back to the police Sub Inspector.

"Inspector, he is not master of the person in that dead body. I can bet you" the lady director of the Uttar Daani declared.

"What can I do?" the Sub Inspector said.

"He is using the power of the system" the lady director hinted to the Sub Inspector.

"Madam, what are you talking about? How can you talk like that?" the Sub Inspector objected to the lady director.

"Shall I show you my power to claim this body?" the lady director of the organization working for good cause warned the police Sub Inspector. "You know very well that this man is not related to the dead by any means. What do you do in general in this type of situation?" the lady stopped as her talk got interrupted when she saw hundred meters away a man riding a rickshaw fitted with scooter engine stopped and started crying *'bhaiya, bhaiya'* seeing the rag on the dead body. The face of the man in black suit darkens in fury to control the situation. Perhaps Jhihari was running to meet his brother and didn't see what was going on. He snubbed hands of the man in black suit who came to stop him.

"Bhaiya, bhaiya, what happened *bhaiya* I left you on gate of the community building. What happened *bhaiya?"* Jhihari wrapped himself over the dead body of his brother. His tears were washing the face of Ranchit's body. He held the hand. He held the face of the deceased.

"You told me to come at nine O' clock. I came at nine O' clock at the gate of the building. *Bhaiya, bhaiya,* and now you please stand up. *Bhabhi* cannot live without you. I cannot do anything without you. *Bhaiya* you are like my father. I cannot let you go like this" Jhihari kept crying over Ranchit's body. "*Ye sab kisne kiya bhaiya?*" he asked his brother in the dead body.

"*Hum chhote log hein. Humein chhota to rehne do. Jad se khatam kyon kar rahe ho?*" Jhihari cried. "Why big people in big cars don't let us live in our jhuggies peacefully. They kill us the moment we come out on the road only to serve them and keep alive to serve" his cries yelled as he saw the broken backlight lying few feet away on the road. He could make out that brother got died in a road accident. His saliva competed with his tears. His shouting in anger at the rich competed with the cries in sorrow of losing his brother forever.

Ladies with Uttar Daani organization also could not control their emotions. The tears started rolling over their cheeks. The man in black suit kept his arms crossed over chest. He would have thrown Jhihari away from the body if the Sub Inspector were not there. Seeing the emotional burst and cries of younger brother of the dead the police Sub Inspector came forward to stop Jhihari. As Jhihari wrapped himself over the deceased and kept crying, so the Sub Inspector stopped himself.

"*Bhaiya himmat rakho*" the lady director solaced Jhihari.

"Have courage to face the reality" the Sub Inspector kept his hand on Jhihari's shoulder who still wrapped himself over Ranchit's body. The Sub Inspector could notice the relationship and there was no need to verify that person in dead body was his brother. "Who are you? How are you related with the deceased?" still he had to ask the crying man over the dead body to follow the procedure.

"My elder brother" Jhihari replied in his cries.

"What is your name? Sub Inspector asked.

"Jhihari" Jhihari replied.

"What you and your brother do? I mean what was your brother's job when he was alive?" he asked Jhihari who was still not in control of his emotions.

"We pick the rag from the waste and garbage in the landfill area of Ghazipur." Jhihari replied with uncontrollable cries for his brother as if his cries would make his brother alive. The Sub Inspector looked upon the lady director in appreciation as she described the deceased exactly.

Jhihari kept crying and remembering the talks with his brother. Hearing the Jhihari's cries people gathered around the body again.

"Enough is enough. The drama is over. Inspector! Ask this man to leave the body of my servant" said the man in black suit with grim face.

"Sir, it's not your servant's dead body" the Sub Inspector said.

Hearing that from the police the Sub Inspector he again dialed a number. Seeing that, the Sub Inspector rang up his superior but got the busy tone. The Sub Inspector looked at the Jhihari for more information.

"My brother was not doing enough work due to illness. In last few days someone called him up to collect waste from the restaurant in the community building." Jhihari said to the Sub Inspector. His sobs impacted his voice.

Sub Inspector's mobile again rang up. He looked at the man in black suit with scorn. The man in black stood crossing his arms to show the power of the system with him.

"*Jai hind* sir" the Sub Inspector picked the call.

"No sir, it is over. The younger brother of the dead has reached here" the Sub Inspector informed his superior about the dead body. "*Sahab* standing close to me who rang you up again and again is not the master of the dead. The dead person was a rag picker working and living in the landfill area of Ghazipur." the Sub Inspector said. His voice was laden with reporting burden.

"Yes sir" the Sub Inspector replied in mild tone as if his superior scolded him in anger.

"Sir, listen to me for a minute" he collected the courage. "Sir the director and assistant director of a non-government organization Uttar Daani who wants to take the body to remove the functional parts of the body before it is handed to the relative. They take out functional body parts for transplant to the ailing patients with defective body parts. The matter is much more complicated than your imagination. Now the wife and younger brother of the dead will claim dead body" he managed his anger over the matter so trivial but made so complicated by the presence of man in black suit with not so rich looks by then. Grim and mal-intentions cast the dark on his face.

"If this *Sahab* who claims to have the dead body as his servant's body is in some need then ask this man to request the two ladies of the organization working for similar cause. If somehow we commit mistake in this matter next day newspapers will print our photos in connection with cadaver racket. This is what I sense" he cautioned his superior in firm tone being in the field where he had to resolve the complicacy of the matter which was full of greed, grief, education, agitation, commitment, agreements . . . After explaining to his superior on phone he listened to his superior. His superior seemingly got convinced with him.

"Sir, you just talk to him" he said. *"Baat kariye"* he gave mobile phone to the man in black.

The man in black took mobile phone and talked to the Sub Inspector's superior. "Madam, you just save my wife's life, she needs at least one kidney to be transplanted. Both kidneys have gone bad" he begged the lady directors who were in favor of solving his problem earlier.

"That's another thing. You were hiding your problem under false power of buying the entire system" the lady director said. "Your wife can be a beneficiary you just have to behave yourself" she added.

"Let's not waste even a single minute now. We have to talk to Jhihari and the wife of the deceased" the lady in purple *saree* directed her assistant to call up the ambulance of Uttar Daani organization. "Jhihari, I need to talk to you regarding your brother" she said.

Jhihari looked up.

"Look Jhihari, your brother has already gone from this world. The body is still with us" she started explaining in very compassionate voice. "Whoever has done that mistake whether it was the driver or anybody else your brother cannot come back to live in this world again. That is for sure" she further explained.

"But your brother's body parts may get a chance to live in the bodies of other people who are still alive in this beautiful world. But they are also dying because of the failure of their body parts. So when you convince your *bhabhi* to permit us to transplant your brother's body parts which can give new lives to few dying people. This way your brother will get a chance to live in that many patients who will live a healthy life because of your brother's body parts. I know this is very tough time for you and your *bhabhi* to take this decision. For cremation and to upkeep religion or faith there will not be any difference to your brother's body. It will be intact. You and your *bhabhi* will be proud of your decision tomorrow when you see that his body parts have given a new life to other human beings with today's progress in medical science. You please convince her" the lady explained the detail of the purpose to Jhihari. She visualized further course of action for Uttar Daani.

"The ambulance is coming to take the body of your brother to the hospital in case you agree for removing his livable body parts. Meanwhile you bring your *bhabhi* to the hospital to give her final consent" she requested Jhihari and empowered him with good intention to make the world more livable, beautiful, and lovable.

"Mam, *bhabhi* only will tell about that" he said controlling his cry. "I don't have any problem" he added arranging scattered rags on his brother's body.

"If we wait here for your *bhabhi* then it won't help any of us. If someone has mobile phone over there you tell your *bhabhi*" she requested.

"I would request your *bhabhi* to give consent for this good cause" the man in black suit turned to be part of discussion with intentions to save his wife's life.

Jhihari's silence nodded.

Uttar Daani ambulance had reached the spot. The lady director asked the boys. The Sub Inspector asked the head constable in his team to initiate the procedure.

"I would like to take your leave. Let me know if any help is required" the man in black suit spoke to the Sub Inspector. "Mam you are great and living for a good cause. I was behaving very selfish" he turned to the lady director of Uttar Daani. "Forgive me for my behavior. Now, I am for the cause" he pledged himself. "Please take my card for any concern" he gave his card. "Can I have your card?" he asked.

"You're welcome, we do such mistakes when we feel insecure" the lady director accepted his corrected behavior. She gave him her card.

"Which hospital mam that body is being taken?" he asked.

The lady in red *saree* told the name and address of the hospital nearby where the ambulance would rush to. "Now I would take your leave sir" he shook hands with the Sub Inspector. "Madam, I will meet you in the hospital" he folded his hand to honor the lady. He went to his car. He opened the rear door before his driver came.

"What is your brother's name?" the head constable asked Jhihari.

"Ranchit" Jhihari said.

Tattoo on right arm of the dead body confirmed that when ambulance boys straightened the arms and body to put on the stature. The boys kept the body in the ambulance very fast to rush to the hospital. The driver took permission from the lady to move to the nearest hospital with transplant facilities.

"Madam, you were telling about the name of the organization. Why this business?" the Sub Inspector asked. He reminded her about the interruption because of the phone call.

"Sir, I will tell you because you really want to know" the lady said. "There are few literal meanings of the name 'Uttar Daani'. First and foremost is that *'uttar'* in Hindi means later or after and *'daani'* means donor. Uttar daani means 'later donor' which means a person who donates afterwards. This organization manages the organ donation from the cadavers for transplant in the suffering patients. So, *'uttar daani'* means a person who donates something after his or her life that means after being dead. It can be only body parts which a person can donate after his or her brain death. Thus came, the name of Uttar Daani for our organization which is committed to manage donation of organs of the cadavers with consent of its relatives. The other meaning relates to the relatives of the dead as they only can donate the body parts of dead by allowing us to go further to the cause. To make others to live later means *'uttar'* so Jhihari and Ranchit's wife in this case are *uttar daani*" the lady director explained at length. She was proud of her work and the organization committed to better the world which was getting complex day by day with emerging technologies and speed.

"Another reason to name the organization as Uttar Daani is coming from the traditions. In almost all the religions there has been a continuous enquiry about life after death. There are questions like what happens after death? What happens to human body after death? What happens to the life itself after death? Such enquiries are labeled as philosophical enquiries in our educational framework. This makes it a noble work" the lady director opened another direction of the meaning.

The Sub Inspector provided intense listening.

"In this context 'Uttar Daani' provides an *'uttar'* in Hindi means 'answer' or 'an answer' to all such queries by donating his body parts to live in other person. Thus the person who donates body parts secures a life for him or her in another person through his body parts. In this way the person answers or gives *uttar* to the centuries old query of mystery around death and the beyond to continue the momentariness of series which can see beyond life and death. Thus, the cycle gets complete" the lady director got new shine on her face explaining the philosophical perspective.

The Sub Inspector nodded.

"Inspiration behind our organization comes from many quarters. The *munis* in the Jain traditions in the evening of their life start starving to die. Thus they bring down the functional strength of the body parts before death. The body parts live to their full strength when in the absence of any intake of food to the body. Ordinary people can't do that" she said.

The Sub Inspector looked at his wrist watch.

"I will not take much time. You have already given so much time to solve this case for a good cause" she said.

The police Sub Inspector smiled at the lady.

"Another inspiration comes from Persian tradition where body of the deceased is kept at high place called *dakhma* and *vaksh bum* or rising ground in the ancient times to be eaten by the birds like crows and vultures. But organization believes that humanity is suffering in modern times. This suffering is cost of the progress achieved with virtue of the speed of motors, airplanes, sky labs, satellites, etc. The body parts if the human body can be utilized in another body to ease out from this suffering gives value to the body parts for the ailing people like the dead bodies were useful for birds in the tradition of *dakhma*. These are the inspirations behind naming the organization as Uttar Daani" the lady director completed. "Another, but, highly significant reason is at present we don't have culture of volunteer organ donation. At present 1 in around 6 million people donates his or her organ in India. It is pathetic where we have 13 deaths in minute" she added to highlight the necessity of such work or organization.

"Madam you are working for such a great, noble and philosophical cause" he expressed his hearty appreciations.

"You are having great patience and a great listener which is very rare in the police service and that too on duty" she acknowledged him. "Would you like to join us in this great cause?" she invited him.

"I will tell you later" he again looked at his watch.

"Sir, can I have your number?" she requested. She also looked at Jhihari who was waiting for another instruction from the lady before she moved from the spot.

He told his number to the lady. The magnetic personality of the lady director arrested the Sub Inspector so much that he could not leave the spot. He also thought that the case involving one death and a causality of senior citizen would have taken days and weeks which was resolved in two hours or three. So he could afford to be in the company of that beautiful lady with nice talks and high purpose in life.

"How will you reach Ghazipur?" she asked Jhihari. "You have to come back with your *bhabhi*" she added.

"Madam, I don't have courage to tell my *bhabhi* about it. With what face shall I go to her without my brother or his body?" Jhihari again started crying. "*Bhaiya* was telling that there is no need to come if he finished the work before time. He said I can't catch him if he finishes the work early he would move out of this place. He proved that right that I can't catch him now. He has already moved out of this place full of miseries and accidents." Jhihari recalled and linked what Ranchit said before his death.

"Nobody knows what will happen to our life. When will it happen to life? We plan our life and but execute the present moment only" she explained.

"No madam, I can't go home without my brother" Jhihari showed his unpreparedness to face his *bhabhi*. He rubbed the red stone again and again where Ranchit's body was lying.

"I understand the difficulty you have now" she looked at her assistant.

"Madam, if you permit me then I can take him to his place" the assistant lady asked.

"That's great, Chandrika, you take the car. I will manage" she said.

"I think Jhihari has got a *jugaad* rickshaw, how will he manage to come with me?" Chandrika pointed out a difficulty.

"Jhihari! Can you leave your rickshaw somewhere nearby?" she asked Jhihari. She looked at the Sub Inspector who was busy talking with head constable and other policemen.

"I can lock it in the chain with some pillar." Jhihari replied.

"Is there any risk of theft?" she asked the Sub Inspector.

"I have lost most vital support what else I will lose. What someone will do if he takes this rickshaw." Jhihari spoke before the Sub Inspector answered. He looked at the rickshaw in disappointment.

"I don't think there is any risk in day time" the Sub Inspector spoke from his experience.

"Ok Jhihari, mam is with you to come with your *bhabhi* to the hospital" she asked Jhihari to hurry up.

Jhihari nodded. He went to the rickshaw to drag it close to an electric pole and locked the rickshaw.

"Yes mam, I have to go to my friend first before I go to my *bhabhi*." said Jhihari when came back.

"Ok, I understand" she agreed looking at Chandrika. "Where is your friend?" she asked.

"He is in a factory in Ghazipur." Jhihari said. He took control of his emotions. He didn't imagine that he would land up in such a complicated situation in which big people would take decision about his brother.

"No problem. Let's move now." Chandrika moved to the car waving for Jhihari to follow her.

Jhihari stopped few feet away from the car. He looked at himself and his rag ridden clothes smitten in the dust, dirt and blood.

"No problem, you please sit in the car" both the ladies spoke simultaneously. Jhihari sat in the rear seat of the car. Chandrika closed the door after he sat in and opened the door to get into the driving seat. She waved to the lady director, the Sub Inspector, and his team. She started the car to leave the place. The lady director and the Sub Inspector with three team members were left.

"Mam, if you don't mind I can drop you at the hospital" the Sub Inspector requested her.

"Sir, you are very special police officer. The way you treated us makes me feel proud of our police system" she admired the Sub Inspector. "I am coming with you otherwise a lady doesn't feel secure when she lands up dealing with the police" she laughed. "Thanks for the lift" she smiled.

"Thanks madam, it is an honor for me. You are having such a great cause for people. I am very much impressed with your work. And the way you work" he open his heart to praise the lady. He escorted her to the front seat of the Gypsy. "Let me do the honor" he waved for the head constable go to the rear. He fit into the driving seat and looked at the lady. They exchanged smiles. He moved the vehicle heading to the hospital where the ambulance had taken the dead body.

"How did you get to this noble cause and the organization?" he wanted to know more from her.

"It is a long story. I will tell you sometime later" she said. They were silent.

"Ok madam, we have reached the hospital" he said.

"Thank you sir, I am highly obliged. I have your number. I may call you up for the help in future" she moved her hand for handshake.

270

"Any time madam, we are with you. For you always" he shook hand with her. She smiled at him before she got down from the police vehicle to rush to the hospital.

The Sub Inspector looked at the lady leaving the vehicle and then at his hand. He took out her card and looked at that with regret. "Why didn't I see her card when she gave. I could have called the great lady by her name" he thought. He read out her card.

Vasundhara Agrahi
Managing Director
Uttar Daani
Committed to make you live
In the people

Some lives are as white as piece of
paper from birth to decease. Others
are the brilliant colorful pictures.

Kazoronnie Mak

∂Isi:s

Decease

"**P**anic may create some other problem. Don't panic *beta*, don't panic" the retired person comforted the middle-aged man in the driving seat. "One hospital is nearby" he added.

"Ok uncle" the middle-aged man relieved the accelerator of the car for few seconds to slow down.

"The road on the left leads to that hospital" the retired man said.

The middle-aged man drove his car fast to reach a hospital on highway. He took left turn and slowed down the car. Before he could reach the hospital he finds many vehicles, buses, autos, were there on the road. Few vehicles messed up with in absence of the traffic police and the light. Entire traffic at the crossing got choked.

"Let me get out of the car" said the retired man and didn't wait for the nod from the middle-aged son of the wounded octogenarian lying in the back seat of the car. He got out of the car to walk quickly to the hospital which was fifty meters ahead. He contacted at the reception and asked for the ward boys to come for the help. Seeing the agility of the old man the middle-aged son came out of the car and opened rear door. The ward boys came with him to the car to assess the condition of the patient.

"We just bring the stature" a ward boy said. They went back to the hospital to come with a stature.

"Ok" the middle-aged man understood his helplessness and kept quiet. He also assessed that he didn't have other choice in the jam packed road where he couldn't go back.

"Where these ward boys are stuck up? Let me check" the retired person murmured. "One extra-intelligent fellow must have messed up with the whole traffic" he cursed the stupidity of the traffic jam. As the hospital was visible he got more worried to save the fellow of his generation. He behaved like a young person.

"Uncle the ward boys have not come yet. I'll go and check" the middle-aged son requested.

"You be here with the car. You can drive" the retired person replied. "Let me go again" he said and walked fast to the hospital.

The retired person reached fast to the reception. "What is this?" he shouted at the receptionist who came walking slowly to the counter. You people don't have any respect for senior citizens. "The ward boys didn't turn with stature" he added to shout with his frustrations.

"Emergency ward is in the rear and you need to go left" the receptionist pointed to the left. "The ward boys from emergency may reach faster" she added.

"The ward boys from here went with me to the car. What happened to them?" the retired person asked.

"They might have reported to the emergency ward boys. They are on the duty in the wards" she replied.

He came down from the stairs hearing the receptionist murmuring hospital got same payment for senior citizens' dues. Sometimes the payment is jittery in case of senior citizens when more members of the family were sick at the same time. The retired person ignored what he heard. He turned left to the emergency. He contacted the receptionist to send the ward boys to the car. By that time he got tired in the struggle which was unnecessary and unwanted. The ward boys accompanied him.

He came back to the road with the hope the traffic jam would have been cleared. He had lost the hope of any improvement. The jam was as it was and kept choking the entire movement on the road and the pavement which was of negligible width. The movement to fifty meters had become challenge to move fifty miles. He followed the ward boys who rushed to the car he pointed at.

The middle-aged man saw the retired person struggling a lot to save his father and busted into tears. He didn't expect that much from a retired person. He opened the rear doors of the car again. The ward boys took the octogenarian still unconscious on the stature. Two ward boys cleared the way in the side of the road. The middle-aged man ran ahead of the road begging for a passage for the stature.

No one heeded to the begging cries of a son who might have been a powerful officer in some multinational company. The man who might be commanding a team of brilliant engineers and few management professionals from top institutes was helpless in that crowd created by an extra-intelligent guy in a car. The manager whom the clients and corporate customers might be listening for golden words to act upon went unnoticed in a choking jam to paralyze him just fifty meter away from the hospital. He was lucky as the ward boys lifted the stature wherever the people didn't have ears for his begging cries and crossed the traffic. When they reached the hospital they kept the stature down on the floor to push towards the emergency.

The middle-aged man reached the reception of the emergency. The ward boys took the stature to the room.

"What is the patient's name?" the receptionist asked.

"Giridhar Prasad" the middle-aged man answered.

"Age of the patient?" she again asked.

"Eighty one years" he answered.

"Complaint or problem?" she asked.

"Accident, accident on the road" he answered.

"Was the patient driving?" she asked.

"Some bastard had run his car over my father when he was on his morning walk" he shouted.

"Please don't shout, this is hospital" she said. She kept her index finger on her lips to reemphasize.

"What is your name?" she asked.

"Dheerendra Prasad" he answered.

"What is your relationship with the patient?" she asked.

"He is my father" the receptionist entered 'son' on the keyboard. Dheerendra controlled over his anguish.

"You please deposit fifty thousand rupees to start the treatment" she handed over the initial statement for billing to Dheerendra Prasad.

"But you are listed on central government health scheme. You have mentioned on the board" he informed the receptionist.

"You could have told me in the beginning itself" she complained. She thought she also could shout but she didn't. "I have to check it up with the hospital authorities what is to be done now. Please wait" the receptionist left the seat.

Dheerendra Prasad kept patience as he also realized his fault. He could have told in the beginning itself. He requested the retired man to be there with his father in the room. He rang up his wife in her office and informed about the accident. He asked her not to tell his mother about the accident. He remembered his car was on the middle of the road. He wanted to rush to the unattended car but he couldn't rush as he had to be there at the reception to give his nod to start the treatment. He again dialed up another number on his mobile phone as he recalled that he was on the way to his office.

"Hello! Rajiv, Dheerendra this side, you please just cancel the meeting scheduled at eleven. My father has met an accident" he updated his team member.

"I am not sure how long this will take" he controlled his frustrations to maintain his role model image in the team.

"Some bastard has run his car over my father" he didn't hide his anger when it came to point out the nuisance on the road.

"Please calm down. Don't shout. Have patience" the receptionist was back on the counter. "Mr. Prasad, this is hospital" she came out of the counter to reemphasize.

"Sorry!" he regretted. "I will call later" he spoke low.

The receptionist repeated the process again as hospital authorities agreed to cancel the earlier application. Then she asked him about the ministry, department, retiring designation and pay scale which his father enjoyed during service time and he answered them politely.

He rushed to his car which he left unattended in the middle of the road. Traffic jam got cleared by then. He didn't find his car on the road where he left. He then asked people around.

Nobody answered.

"Brother I have left my car here" he asked at a shop.

"Which car" the shop keeper asked.

"One silver grey Honda City" he said.

"Ask the traffic police on the crossing" the shop keeper suggested.

"What happened?" he asked.

"Your car was causing traffic jam so people with cars behind you contacted the traffic police on the crossing nearby" he informed Dheerendra waving his hand to his right. "The traffic police might have towed away your car to clear the traffic jam" he added.

"But I had to leave my car because of traffic jam only" he shared his anger. "I was not getting an inch of space to get my father admitted to this hospital" he recalled the nuisance on the road half an hour ago. "My father has met an accident" he said. He said to inform the shop keeper irrespective of whether it was required or not.

"Boss when jam got cleared your unattended car was causing jam. So people approached the traffic police and got that towed away to clear the jam" he reasoned the action. "It's simple" he added.

Helpless Dheerendra left the idea of locating his car for a while. He bought a dozen bananas from a hawker and ran up in the emergency ward of the hospital.

"Sorry uncle, I have made you landed up in this problem. It is my problem" he folded his hands.

"You are like my son. Your father is like my elder brother" the retired person provided relentless support to him. "I have informed my son and daughter-in-law. Now they know where I am. What I am doing. Only problem is that being diabetic I have to have my meals on time. So, I contacted the canteen of the hospital to have my breakfast" the retired person described.

"I had bought some bananas for you" he handed over the bananas.

"I just had my breakfast. You please keep them on the table" the retired person said. "Hospital people are shifting your father to some other room" the retired person informed.

"Uncle, can I request you to be here? My car has been towed away by the traffic police. I need you" he informed the retired old man. "I have to locate the police station to get my car back" he said. He left the room thanking the retired person who was with his father since morning.

Dheerendra came down on the road crossing. Two policemen on duty were busy in navigating the traffic. Another policeman was standing on the side to control the hawkers. He found it easy to contact him to enquire about his car.

"Excuse me sir, where can I find out my car?" Dheerendra asked the policeman very politely.

The policeman didn't listen because noise of the traffic. He kept talking to the fruit hawkers.

"Excuse me sir, can you please tell where I can get my car?" Dheerendra requested the policeman moving close to him.

"I don't know. Towed vehicles are taken to the police station. You can get it from there" the policeman said. He then scanned Dheerendra.

"Sir, how can I reach the police station?" Dheerendra asked. His voice was very low. All the confidence he might have had when dealing with the tycoons of corporate world was subdued to a police constable on the crossing.

"First you tell me what happened?" the policeman started his enquiry. "Where have you left your vehicle?" he asked his next question before Dheerendra could speak anything.

"Actually my father has met accident on the highway near the community building. His condition is very serious" Dheerendra just controlled his voice broken by the incidents over which he didn't have any control.

"Where were you at the time of accident?" the policeman interrupted.

"I was on the way to my office when I got the bad news that someone ran his car over my father who was on the pavement near the community building for his morning walk. I rushed back to the place where my father was lying unconscious on the road. Then I brought him to this hospital but got stuck in the traffic jam just fifty meters away from the hospital. There was huge traffic jam here in which nobody was listening to anybody." Dheerendra's narration of his story was interrupted by the policeman who wanted to confirm that there was huge traffic jam.

"Yes, traffic jam was there at that time. These nasty jams make our life a big hell. People don't listen without stick" the policeman spoke his experience.

"You are right, they don't listen to anybody other than you" Dheerendra agreed with the policeman. "I was crying and the old man with me ran twice to the hospital to call ward boys to take my father on the stature from there itself." Dheerendra added to prove the policeman's experience in controlling traffic.

"But sir, people in big cars think that we are worthless fellows" the policeman opened box of his complaints against the rich people. "But was that your car which was lying in the middle of the road?" he asked Dheerendra.

"*Haan . . . haan*" Dheerendra interrupted to confirm. "Silver grey Honda City" he said with shine on his face.

"I was there in the middle of the jam at 'tee' of the crossing when I saw two three ward boys of this hospital were taking an old man on the stature. Right" the policeman confirmed what pulled his attention when he was controlling the traffic.

"Yes, yes, it was my car" Dheerendra spoke still about his car. "Yes, yes, he is my father" he corrected himself as the policeman was talking about the old man on stature he saw. "I had to admit my father and I could not move due to traffic jam" he added.

"But sir, you have left vehicle just like that. Unattended vehicle was lying in the middle of the road. Your car was not a problem during the jam" the policeman said.

Dheerendra listened to the policeman patiently.

"The moment traffic jam was cleared people with big cars got mad. Many of them came over to me" the policeman shared his sheer experience caused by Dheerendra's car.

"May be they lost the patience due to that jam as they were already late." Dheerendra convinced himself and the policeman to justify behavior of the people with big car. He appeared to be on the side of people with cars.

"What sir, jam was for thirty minutes they could have tolerated for another five-ten minutes" the policeman said. He knew that time spent in hours didn't matter but minutes or second mattered as their convenience. "What if we could not have cleared the jam for another twenty minute they would have tolerated it. Or what they would do? You tell me" he asked Dheerendra. He felt Dheerendra was on the side with the people owning big cars.

"In that sense you are right, people don't panic during traffic jam in foreign countries." Dheerendra agreed with the policeman.

"They started teaching me what I should do. One smart fellow was not listening to me and told other people also to dial hundred" the policeman said. "They pressurized me to tow away the car. I didn't listen to them. I drove the car to the side instead of towing that" the policeman waved his hand to show his car which he drove to park in safe place.

"Thank you sir! Thank you very much" Dheerendra saluted the policeman. He took policeman's hand in his hand. He took a sigh of relief when he saw his car. He was happy with the policeman he didn't tow away the car which would have added another problem to solve. He might have got that problem to solve for nothing. He might have got nothing.

"No sir, leave this. You are already in trouble" the policeman stopped Dheerendra from putting hand the pocket.

Dheerendra put his hand as if he thought that policeman won't give the keys without taking money.

"I also have parents at home. We should care for senior citizens" the policeman handed over the keys which Dheerendra left in the car. Dheerendra thanked the policeman again and again. He saluted the policeman when drove away his car.

Kul Vilas along with Anang got busy in preparing estimates for the survey. To Kul Vilas that survey was huge and challenging. He knew that was not his domain. Anang was interested in some flow of funds. Anang remained the only one among his friends who had still shown some interest in the work.

"Why is he not having trust in us?" Anang asked Kul Vilas about Hwaib. He put his hand under the table to pull his chair closer.

"I don't think so. People go systematically in those countries." Kul Vilas pulled his drawer to take out some paper. "Before they start any work people generally do most of the initially work which we ignore here. Even if we do then also it is not done on paper" he continued the context.

"Frankly speaking these estimates for survey kind of work are not required." Anang shared his reservations. "They are never accurate" he justified.

"Estimates are not supposed to be accurate. Otherwise why they are estimates." Kul Vilas said. He wanted Anang to have patience to see future course of action. "They require it for their planning and all" he clarified the need.

"I don't know much details of this planning and all." Anang said. He pressed the button of the cordless bell lying on table.

"Why are you worrying much about this all? This work will take its own course" Kul showed his patience.

"Make us two cup of coffee" Anang asked Keshav who came to attend them. "Without taking any drink mind doesn't work" Anang looked at the papers on Kul Vilas' side.

"Any drink? What's the time?" Kul Vilas looked at designer clock on the wall.

"That is why I have asked him to prepare coffee" Anang showed his intelligence.

"Bring something with coffee" Kul Vilas said.

"How many people do we need to start this?" Kul Vilas asked Anang.

"Can we take a particular city in consideration?" Anang came with his logic.

"Yes, Delhi in my mind" Kul Vilas clarified.

"But Delhi is a big city *yaar*, rather it is huge. Many things to be considered" Anang explained.

"You know it very well. You are scared just for nothing. It is great that you take interest" Kul Vilas admired Anang.

"Why are you flying me in the air?" Anang had objection to Kul Vilas' appreciation. "It is simple to take small part of the work to start" he added. He looked for Keshav who was supposed to bring coffee.

"Without drink also your mind has started working. When you will take coffee then it will beat the computer." Kul Vilas complimented Anang.

"I thought your office boy has gone for sowing the coffee beans in the field." Anang took compliment to be comment on Keshav's slow performance to bring him a coffee.

"He has gone to import it. We are in export business we don't need to sow coffee beans, we just import" Kul Vilas replied.

"Come to the point till your coffee comes. You were telling something" Kul Vilas interrupted Anang who pretended to yawn to show the importance of the coffee.

"Dear, if coffee cannot come soon then make it large from the drawer." Anang wanted to drag Kul Vilas from coffee beans' fields to the malt factory.

"Look at your watch! What's time? It is time to work" Kul Vilas ruled out making it large.

"That means you can't make it large" Anang instigated Kul Vilas.

"Don't worry guys! I will make it large for you. You have been waiting for a long" Numi entered in the room with coffee mugs in a tray in her hand. She took the tray from Keshav.

"Wow! What a pleasant surprise! When did you come? Hearing a female voice in the office Anang turned around in the chair. He didn't tell me about you" Anang pointed at Kul Vilas who was also equally surprised.

"Hey! Numi when did you come? You were supposed to come two hour later" Kul Vilas reminded as he wanted to focus on estimates. Numi found that Kul Vilas was looking at her when she entered. That brought her a lot of happiness. Actually Kul Vilas looked at the designer clock on the wall to know she was two hours early.

"Be happy man, your most sexy woman is with you" Anang made Numi's presence to be felt in the office.

"No Anang, most sexy woman is Mimo not me. I am just trying to be Delhi's." Numi wanted to limit herself. She winked to Anang. "I thought I would surprise you coming two hours early. That too, with coffee" she said.

"Thanks for the surprise, please be seated" Anang welcomed Numi.

"So you guys are working on your project" Numi joined the talks. "When are you going to Paris?" she asked Kul Vilas. She wanted to tell that she would like to go with him.

"Next health survey meeting will make it clear . . . and . . . and lot of work is to be done before we start the actual work." Kul Vilas looked anxious.

"What! Are you going on a date?" Numi asked. She pruned her hair after tossing them in the air.

"What? How come you thought like that?" Kul Vilas was surprised. He thought she cracked a joke.

"It is a date only where you need to have lot of other preparatory work to start the 'actual work' to make your date feel that you are going to make it large." Numi flicked her hair and waggled her tongue to have a round trip on her open lips.

Anang appreciated. He laughed like anything. Kul Vilas also had to laugh. All three laughed.

"You are so cool Kul. You don't look nice when you worry." Numi said. That's why I cracked that one liner to make you laugh. She still wanted to divert Kul Vilas to some other topic than the estimate work which she hated since Kul Vilas got a call from Hwaib last time.

"Look at the color of your cheeks. Worrying cheeks don't match with your designer purple" she didn't leave the opportunity to compliment Kul Vilas. "Just now they were pink to make a similar hue with the purple of your shirt" she blandished Kul Vilas who may take her to Paris.

Kul Vilas looked at Numi. Then he sipped his coffee.

"You know even the khan doesn't look that smart." Numi's words kept hitting Kul Vilas in the head. She wanted Kul Vilas to feel the hit below the belt. She kept trying.

"Numi! Kul cannot remain cool if you keep hitting him below the belt. He will become horny hot" Anang warned Numi. He could understand Numi's intentions for Kul Vilas and Kul Vilas' commitment for the work.

"No play, replay, or foreplay, no please, I have to get my estimates ready" Kul Vilas declared. He took a longer sip.

"Anang, please focus on the work" Kul's eyes warned Anang who diverted frequently since Numi entered the office.

"Now, how can my brain work when beauty works?" Anang disclosed that he was already diverted. He looked at the Numi who again tossed her hair in the air to get someone to flare. "Where is your friend Numi?" Anang asked her about Nikki

Numi kept mum. She was in dilemma to continue on her friend. She knew that Nikki was much impressed by Kul Vilas and wanted to try on him rather than Anang. That's the reason Numi came alone.

Anang repeated his question.

"Shall I call her?" Numi asked tossing her hair again. She thought she could afford to call her for Anang.

Kul Vilas looked at Numi.

"Boss wants me to leave now" Anang wanted to excuse for his exit from the scene. He didn't want to be responsible for the great diversion that was due as Numi was in no mood to go unwanted. He looked at the watch; it was already one hour since Numi came and they could not focus on work. He finished his coffee to leave the office.

"How can you leave like that?" Kul Vilas asked Anang. "Estimates are far from being completed" he reminded Anang what they were doing before Numi entered.

"You please continue I will see you later. I need to see the estimates later. Right now I need to receive my father from airport." Anang left the chair to move out. Again he looked at Kul Vilas and Numi. He exhaled from the depth of his lungs. He left for the airport.

"Was that an excuse?" Numi asked Kul Vilas. She pulled her chair to the side which Kul Vilas was sitting.

"I didn't get you" Kul Vilas pretended to be ignorant to understand what Numi wanted. He had already lost the track on the work.

"I mean receiving his father at airport may be an excuse. May be Anang wanted to leave us alone" she trimmed her hair with fingers.

"No, it is not like that. He has to go to the airport to receive his father. His father is coming from Germany." Kul informed Numi.

"Germany?" Numi asked Kul Vilas as if she had lost something. She thought she had underrated Anang. She concealed her feeling of loss.

"Yes his father is running a big export house" Kul Vilas updated Numi about Anang. "His father is coming back from his business tour" he added and got busy with estimates.

Numi took city edition of the newspaper. She got busy in finding out familiar persons in the wedding pictures of Delhi elite on page three of the city edition. She turned the page to find news that she wanted to share with Kul Vilas.

"You know Kul, Mimo is again the sexiest woman of the world" she turned her face to drag attention from Kul Vilas who was busy in applying some formula to prepare the estimates.

"Who?" Kul Vilas showed his ignorance.

"This is very surprising! You don't know Mimo?" Numi asked. She trimmed her heir with fingers. She thought Kul Vilas was not her type.

"Mimo?" Kul was clueless.

"Really! But that day when we met I thought you were very familiar with all these people" she didn't hide her disappointment.

"Are you talking about Minskey Mohan?" Kul Vilas looked at Numi to serve her with one liner which she might like. He again got busy in his laptop.

"That's better" Numi sighed. She sighed as if she was relieved from the pain of investing herself in wrong choice or unwise decision for going below the belt. She finally appreciated Kul Vilas who gave some attention to her. "Yes" she turned herself to Kul Vilas.

"An hour back you were talking about yourself." Kul Vilas reminded her discussion she was enjoying when Anang was in the office.

"So?" she just showed herself clueless. Might be she wanted Kul Vilas to talk more and more. More and more about her. Only about her.

"You were talking something similar about Delhi level" Kul again made that easy for her.

"Oh that, I am the sexiest woman of Delhi. No doubt about that" she bragged.

"You are sexiest woman of the world. What is Delhi?" Kul Vilas attempted at making her happy.

"What do you want?" she was about to leave the chair to be on his shoulders. She pounced upon him with her fronts resting on his shoulders.

"To prepare estimates" he replied. He looked at the screen of his laptop which showed some reference estimates from survey projects.

"That's not possible when your sexiest woman is around" she asserted herself as she placed her haunches on the table and brought face close to Kul Vilas' to look more attractive. She leaned to look more attractive with her open busts.

Kul Vilas still wanted to focus on estimates.

That had irritated Numi.

"If you don't want to be in moods then I can't go unwanted" she reacted to Kul Vilas' intense focus on the estimates. She pretended to leave the office. Kul didn't. She went up to the door. She turned to see if he turned up to stop her or not.

She came back to keep on staring at him till he reacted.

"But I have to finish that to send it urgently" he tried avoiding his frequent attention on leaning Numi's open busts bulging out of her designer top. She again bent down to lean on him. The pendant sagging around her bulging busts got stuck in the deep line. He was not able to keep his eyes away from that as pendant sagged around and got stuck in the deep line again. She bent down further to lean on him and fingered his hair. He didn't get view of his laptop then and she took over his face by her blossoming bosoms and with freshened hair.

"It is my time now!" she pointed out at the clock on the wall to remind him when he wanted to have a look at his laptop. He looked at the clock and made the chair easier. In the moments when he made his chair easier Numi fell on him with her breasts on his face. She let herself lying on revolving moving easy chair. He held her pendant by his teeth to bring it out of the deep line in the busts. His nose got dipped in the deep line and she held his head tightly to make him fit deeper and deeper in her mild blossoming bust. The fire got spread below the belt. He lifted her in the same pose to test the strength of his biceps built up in the gym regularly for years.

"Look I am not the weight. I have weight. You are not in gym. I am whole in your arms. Be careful. I may fall down" she wants him to be cautious.

"Don't worry. You are in safe hands" he took her to the couch.

"Yours Mimo" Numi put metaphor. She opened his designer purple.

They got onto the couch to get into each other. The health penetration survey project for health and wellbeing in healthy environment got aside as healthy penetration took place in healthy bodies to experience the wellbeing.

Inder practiced to improve on keying in on the keyboard of the computer. When he got frequent opportunities to keying in he saw some improvements. For that he thanked Bhumi and his father every time he started the computer. He found that he could write to Mr. Hwaib. He wanted to use the data card to improve his skill on the internet. He looked for the data card that Bhumi gave him other day. He opened cupboard to pick the data card. He didn't find it where he kept. He kept the data card as valuable as those dollars which he got from Ms. Veronique. He found the dollars intact in the cupboard. But the data card was not there.

He kept recalling which could be other place he might keep that data card. He failed to recall. He gave up recalling. He left the chair to go out to have some food in the market. He picked his trousers to change. Suddenly he found something hard in the pocket. That was data card. He wondered how the data card was in the pocket of his trousers. He got the data card. He left the idea of having food outside. He came back to the chair to try on internet. He started the computer. He inserted the data card. He connected the computer to net through data card. He opened his email site to login when internet browser got opened on the screen. He logged on to the email website.

Inder was surprised to see an email from Hwaib. He found it embarrassing that he could not write to Hwaib in time. He opened the mail to read and found that Bhumi had sent a mail to Hwaib. Hwaib got familiar with Inder's situations through Bhumi's mail and sent reply to Inder. But Inder didn't see Bhumi's mail in the inbox. But he found from the mail that Bhumi sent to Hwaib, she sent the same to Inder also. Inder checked his inbox to locate Bhumi's mail. Before Hwaib's mail there were many unsolicited promotion emails ranging from selling three dimension replicas of Rado watches to enlarge the size of male organ were filling the page of inbox so he couldn't find Bhumi's mail which was sent to Hwaib. That got receded into the pages behind.

He finally found one email from Bhumika Jain after clicking another page of inbox. He read the mail in which Bhumi wrote to Hwaib to make him aware what Inder was undergoing. She wrote to Hwaib that Inder was undergoing one or the other hurdle since he came back from the conference. Inder opened the mail to read it out. In which Bhumi wrote

> Dear Mr. Hwaib,
> Good Morning,
>   Let me introduce myself before my identity makes you puzzled and why you are receiving this unsolicited mail. I am Bhumika Jain friend of Inder Jeet who attended one conference which your organization held at Montreal this year. You must be aware of the background and circumstances

that led to his visit in the conference. I believe it is Ms. Veronique who had put her efforts to make his visit a reality. The conference must have got over with many decisions and actions points for the participating representatives. Almost all participants and attendees must be busy in fulfilling the agenda points through performing on their action points. I find Inder's situations very pathetic since he came back from the conference.

He is working for my father's concern and engaged in managing wastes for recycling not as a regular employee but as an attendant whose job varies from maintaining the facility of the concern to managing communication to the vendors and customers to prepare for book-keeping, accountancy and other commercial formality which my father finally manages for the concern. My father runs this small concern to manage our family business and maintains family's wellbeing. Inder also plays crucial role in our household matter as he stays in outer room of our residential house. Being male he also plays the role of security person for the household.

I am witness of how his circumstances are more than sufficient to push him back to the world of poverty and the dark where he was not having any father figure to make his survival meaningful in this world. He was like a homeless orphan who stayed with a family in the landfill area of Ghazipur. He shares bonding relationship with that family which has supported him to survive despite of all the odds.

He could improve upon his life and many others like him from his lot through benevolent efforts by your conference and its measures. However, his circumstances are not letting him to raise his head to look ahead at what to do more than survival. Few steps he had taken to start the work. He collected some information on families in the landfill area of Ghazipur. How good is the information and fits into your work that all I don't have any idea. But I am sure this is always at top of his mind. The project leader that you have fixed for the work is not accessible to him. Rather Inder cannot have any possibility to work with him as they are the classes apart.

I am writing this mail because I want to help him come out of his circumstances. He does not have even mobile phone. He rather cannot afford it. It is a luxury for him. If some communication you can make with him then please feel free to call at my number so and so between nine to ten O' clock in the night here in India. I can make him available to talk to you. I am writing you my number as I am not sure when he will have his own number.

Best regards,
Bhumika Jain.

Inder closed the mail from Bhumi to Hwaib as copy to himself. His eyes could not remain dry after reading her mail. He kept wiping them for minutes. What she was up to was clear to him then. No one other than Jhihari and his brother Ranchit and family had provided that much space to him in the entire Delhi, the great Delhi. When his eyes came back to normalcy he desired to read Hwaib's mail.

He again opened that mail in recent ones and read

Dear Inder,
Greetings,

I am surprised to receive some communication through email from one of your friends but not from you since we departed at Delhi airport. I got to realize why you could not communicate to me only when I had gone through the entire email from your friend. I need to ask you if you know Ms. Bhumika Jain as she has sent a copy of that email to you also. She has opened up communication for you. She wants you to reveal through circumstances which are manifold. Believe me circumstances reveal a person they don't conceal. Your circumstances will reveal who you are and how valuable you are for your lot, for human society. After Bhumika's communication I get the idea what you are dealing with.

Believe me Bhumika's communication has improved the image of Indians in my mind. My general observation about Indians *en masse* was that they start working even when they lack resources. Now I believe that they start working on a project even when they don't have clarity on the subject and

292

strive to bring it out. The objectives themselves make them commit to the work if they are communicated with what would be the end result of the work taken up.

Kul Vilas is taking his own time to give me the estimates for the entire project. His efforts are yet to yield results. I am waiting for the estimates to come from him. I will call you up on Bhumika's number when I receive the same. I am not bothering you about the work because this work cannot be taken and accomplished by any single person.

Regards,
Hwaib,

Inder thanked Bhumi in his self-talk. Inder could not have written few things as clearly as she had written in her communication to Hwaib.

Dheerendra drove his car to the police station of the area. He parked his car at a safe place close to the development authority park. He got down from the car to walk to the police station. He saw a tea stall close the police station. He stopped at the tea stall. He then thought something and decided to meet the police officer first to lodge a first information report of the accident. He read the board at the gate of the police station which prohibited giving and accepting bribe. He entered the gate of the police station to reach a policeman standing in the verandah.

"I want to lodge an FIR" Dheerendra asked the policeman.

"What happened? Tell me" the policeman asked.

"Some bastard has hit my father with his car while he was out for morning walk." Dheerendra complained to the policeman. He told the policeman who wanted to enquire into the reason to lodge a first information report.

"What was the age of your father?" the policeman asked.

"He is around eighty one years" Dheerendra answered.

"How was mood of your father when he left home?" the policeman asked further question keeping one hand on his waist and other in his pocket.

"What do you mean?" Dheerendra asked the policeman. He got puzzled with the question.

"We have seen few cases where old men come out for morning walk. They come down under some vehicle" the policeman took out his hand from the pocket to convince Dheerendra.

"You know some family tension. Problem with daughter-in-law . . ." the policeman started counseling Dheerendra.

"There is no use of talking to you further." Dheerendra concluded. He looked around for some other gentleman in the police station. Then he saw a name plate above a closed door of a room in the police station. The 'Station Officer' sign board was in his line of sight. He left the policeman and moved inside the station.

"Where are you going? What do you want?" Another policeman asked.

"I want to meet the station officer" Dheerendra said. He was not prepared to answer similar questions from another policeman.

"Where from are you coming?" the policeman asked.

"Press!" the policeman said before Dheerendra could say anything.

He found them to be typical policemen about whom he had heard many stories.

"Press statements are released in the evening at nine O' clock" looking at Dheerendra the policeman said.

"You . . ." now Dheerendra got out of control in very scolding tone soon he realized the situation and controlled his outburst.

"Yes, I am here" the policeman asked.

"I want to meet the station officer" he smiled at the policeman.

"*Sahab* has gone for meeting called by the circle officer" the policeman answered.

"When is he supposed to come back?" he asked.

"We can't say. He may come back in an hour. He may take five-six hours if he gets to be on the spot in some event" the policeman replied.

Dheerendra came out of the station. He looked around and went to the tea stall close to the police station.

"Give me an India King" he asked for a cigarette.

The stall keeper looked around, and looked at him top to bottom. He bent down to give him a cigarette.

"What happened sir? Looking very puzzled and sad" the stall keeper asked.

"Some bastard has run his car over my father on the highway. My father's condition is critical" said Dheerendra who got interrupted by the expert speech from stall keeper.

"And you want to lodge an FIR, right? And you must have tough time inside the station in dealing with the policemen? Right?" the stall keeper showed his expertise.

"Yes!" Dheerendra said. He lit up the cigarette with deep inhale of smoke.

"Sir, daily tens of cases I witness like this" the stall keeper said.

Dheerendra did not speak but exhaled the smoke.

"You will be able to lodge an FIR. It will be done" the stall keeper predicted.

"How?" Dheerendra asked.

"You need to spend" the stall keeper hinted.

"How much?" Dheerendra wanted to know.

"Do you want to have tea only?" the stall keeper asked when looked around the stall. Two rickshaw pullers passed by in very slow speed. They were rubbing and dragging their feet on the ground rather than walking.

"This is not the answer to my question" he got irritated.

The stall keeper looked at Dheerendra.

"Yes a tea, sensing his situation" he said.

The stall keeper smiled at him. He couldn't understand anything by offering tea. He had already bought a cigarette if engaging with the shop keeper need to be genuine.

"Can you give me an idea which staff in the station is fair enough to listen to me?" Dheerendra asked. Meanwhile, he dialed his wife's number on his mobile phone and waited for response.

"All are good, everybody will listen to you, your problems" the stall keeper again smiled at him. He had to stop as someone at the other picked up his call.

"Hello! How is mother? Did you tell her about the accident?" he asked his wife.

The stall keeper kept quiet.

"Now we have to tell her" he spoke assessing the situation.

"I have come to the police station. A retired uncle is there with the father in the hospital" he said.

"Office se off le ke aa sakti ho kya? Maa ko ghar se le ke?" he requested his wife to take half day off from her office.

"That uncle has to go back home as he cannot be there with the father infinitely. Try to understand" he pleaded.

The stall keeper poured tea in glass. He stopped the stall keeper from pouring tea in glass. The stall keeper looked at him. He again waived his hand as his call was on. He wanted him to stop pouring tea in the glass tumbler. He kept continued on the call.

The stall keeper kept pan back on the flame. He wiggled the fuel knob to put the stove on simmer.

"Ok I will call later. Please reach hospital with mother as soon as possible" he ended the call assuming his wife would take off.

"Don't you have disposable glasses?" Dheerendra turned his attention to the infrastructure of the stall.

"Sir!" the stall keeper gave full scan on Dheerendra. "The paper of the disposable glasses is laminated with wax which creates ulcers in your intestines. I can give you that disposable glass of paper" he added. "No problem, shall I provide you the source of ulcer in you intestine?" he further asked.

Dheerendra did not appreciated reasoning behind stall keeper for not giving tea in disposable paper glass. But he was not sure that the stall keeper was right or wrong in possessing the information on the health. He thought he wanted to follow cost cutting by preferring washable glasses. He won't wash them properly.

"Ok" he said. He took the tea in glass. "How do you know all that?" he asked the stall keeper. At the back of the mind he accepted the stall keeper's logic.

"My son reads the newspaper for me" the tea stall keeper said. That was a surprise for Dheerendra. "He reads one or two news from every page of the newspaper" the tea stall keeper disclosed the secret of his health awareness.

"Hmm! Good!" he appreciated. He looked around as if everybody was looking at him having tea glass in hand. He finished the tea fast.

"Sir, sir" Dheerendra saw the police inspector whom he met at the accident spot. He was entering the police station. He ran after the police inspector.

"O sir, you have not paid the money for cigarette and tea" the tea stall keeper reminded Dheerendra.

"Sorry!" Dheerendra paid the bill. He was in a hurry to rush inside the police station to follow the Sub Inspector. The stall keeper waved his hand for him not to panic.

"Sir, don't worry, the Sub Inspector whom you have seen is different. He is Prabhat Kumar. You will get your work done" the stall keeper shared his evaluation.

"Thank you" Dheerendra left the tea stall and ran inside the police station to locate the Sub Inspector.

"Yes sir, please come" the Sub Inspector Prabhat welcomed Dheerendra who was out of breath.

"Cool down sir. Take your breath. How is your father?" the Sub Inspector asked Dheerendra relating him to the road accident in the morning.

"Sir, I want to lodge an FIR" Dheerendra urged. He wanted to control over panting. He took few deep breathes to restore it to normal.

"That's what was expected from you" the Sub Inspector said. "Or else what I can expect when I see you here?" he added. "It is for sure that you have not come to ask about my wellbeing" he said as if he reminded Dheerendra to take care of his father first not to get trapped in the matters of an FIR.

"Sir, that rascal should not go un-booked." Dheerendra reacted to rash driving that caused his father to be in hospital. "He should be punished" he added but again lost control over his breathing in excitement over the accident.

"How many eye witnesses are there with you?" the Sub Inspector Prabhat asked Dheerendra. He wanted Dheerendra to maintain cool.

"Sir!" that retired man is with my father since my father got rammed by that bastard. I can request him to become an eye witness." Dheerendra answered to the police inspector with some hope. "He is still there in the hospital with my father" he added as if he had presented a ready eye witness.

"Who else is there?" the Sub Inspector asked.

"No sir, I have not talked to anyone in the morning" he replied.

"What's the number of vehicle?" the Sub Inspector asked.

Dheerendra took out his mobile and read the number of the car on its screen for the Sub Inspector.

"How do you know this is the right number?" the Sub Inspector started enquiry with Dheerendra. "Have you yourself seen the vehicle?" he asked.

"One boy noted me down the number of the vehicle" Dheerendra answered.

"Means you yourself have not seen the number on the vehicle" the Sub Inspector inferred. "How can you see the number and the car? You were on the way to your office. Right?" he applied his logic. "Few more eye witnesses are required to put the driver behind the bar. Lodging the FIR for this will be effective in that condition. Do you have?" the Sub Inspector asked.

Dheerendra looked around in the room and at the picture of Gandhi at one of the wall. He looked beyond the door of the room.

"Look at me sir! Why are you looking here and there?" the Sub Inspector Prabhat asked Dheerendra for his attention.

"Inspector Prabhat you could have told me in the morning itself when we met on the accident site." Dheerendra replied. He expressed his confusion in complaining manner. Later he controlled the bitterness of his expression.

"Sir, can I give you one suggestion?" the Sub Inspector asked Dheerendra in unexpected polite tone. "The retired old man now with your father in the hospital is helping you in the need of your troubled times. What you are planning to give him in reward is 'eye-witness' in this case in which no other eye witness is available. You will make him run under risk for his life just because you have got to know some number of the vehicle. Few years will pass the case will take its own course" the Sub Inspector paused to look at Dheerendra if he was convinced or not.

Dheerendra didn't have any expression on his face.

"During these years your only eye witness of the case that is the retired old man may get retired from life. Then your case will be concluded to end in the dearth of sufficient evidences" the inspector added to convince Dheerendra not to file a case.

"Then what to do?" Dheerendra asked.

"Please go to the hospital and make arrangements for better care and treatment for your father" the Sub Inspector suggested Dheerendra. "You have already taken enough services from the retired old man who is still there with your father in place of you" his tone demonstrated anger when added.

"Sir, that means that rascal, the driver is free to ram some other people also?" Dheerendra concluded on his helplessness.

"No, it is not like that, we have sent an enquiry to the authority to know about owner of the car" the Sub Inspector showed Dheerendra some hope.

"Sir! Some channel people have come to meet you" a constable informed the inspector.

"Ok, you make them comfortable" Prabhat asked the constable. "What's the progress in tracing the vehicle in connection with morning accident on the highway near the community building?" he asked.

"Sir, it is a series three from Bayerische Motoren Werke" the constable informed about make of the car. Grim appeared on Dheerendra's face after hearing that. His jaw bones got to pressed each other. The Sub Inspector looked at Dheerendra's face and understood the anger that Dheerendra instilled with.

"Owner? Address?" Prabhat asked the constable who was still in the room to give desired information. The constable kept quiet.

"Who is the owner?" the Sub Inspector asked the constable.

The constable told the inspector all the information about the car.

"Call him" he instructed the constable to ring up the owner of the car involved in the accident. The constable dialed a number and handed over the receiver of the phone to the Sub Inspector.

"Hello" Prabhat spoke to the owner of the car.

"Where was your car in the morning? Who was driving that car?" the Sub Inspector asked the owner.

"The driver has run over two men walking on the pavement near the community building" the Sub Inspector informed. "How can your driver drive like that?" he asked the owner getting some response from the owner from the other end.

"You please come to the police station" the Sub Inspector asked the owner of the car.

"Mukta *ji*, here two three persons from news channel are taking coverage on our accountability. How can I now ignore this all?" the Sub Inspector said.

"How can I fix the media persons from the news channels when the son of the retired person who is critical in the hospital is sitting in my room in the police station?" the Sub Inspector declined any possibility for car owner not to come in person. "Your car has rammed over two persons and one has already died on the spot" the police inspector said severest part of the news later.

"You please come to the police station" he asked in rough tone.

Dheerendra when listened that the car is from Bayerische Motoren Werke he lost the hope for any fairness in the case. For his solace, the Sub Inspector surprised him by his unique method adopted to solve the case. Dheerendra was satisfied if not happy with the Sub Inspector dealing with the owner in a smart way.

"Sir! I appreciate the way you are handling the case" Dheerendra admired the Sub Inspector Prabhat Kumar.

"Sir! Let me do my duty. You also please do your duty" the Sub Inspector asked Dheerendra in rough manner.

"Ok sir! Now I am sure there will be justice in this case. I am going to the hospital" Dheerendra replied in mild tone to the Sub Inspector Prabhat who spoke to him in not-so-happy tone.

Uttar Daani car was running towards Ghazipur. Chandrika kept talking to Jhihari sitting in the rear seat frequently. Jhihari didn't want to speak even a single word. He was blank. He had no idea on how to face his *bhabhi* when he would reach home. Chandrika perhaps had understood his difficulty. She was also keeping Jhihari engaged in her conversations. She was touched by Jhihari's shyness to take seat in the car. The race among the people to own cars on improved Indian roads was subject of some different planet for Jhihari. She kept an eye on Jhihari's tearing eyes in rear view mirror. Jhihari was sitting in the rear seat of the car.

Jhihari, like most of the servitude, might have been dreaming to get some space into a car someday. He never thought that someday to come like that when someone from his own life loses space in the world to give him space in someone's car. Otherwise he could have enjoyed the cushion that he never even dreamt to see, dare to touch. He was happy when his brother handed over the rickshaw automated with old scooter engine. His brother got that rickshaw automated for himself as he could no longer pull after filling the rags. The rags used to gain weight containing lot of glass waste. Because of repeated lung infections his brother Ranchit was no longer able to ride that rickshaw. That day his brother had handed over his body without life to Jhihari to decide to give life to the dying lives.

"We are reaching Ghazipur crossing. Where to go?" Chandrika asked Jhihari who was looking at his own chest to avoid every other thing that might come to his attention.

"Mam, left side" said Jhihari when he looked up to see where the car was moving.

"Where is your friend?" she asked Jhihari.

After taking left turn we have to come back from flyover. *"mam, wahan hei"* Jhihari waived his hand to indicate the area where Inder stayed. Chandrika looked in Jhihari's eyes in the mirror. She took left turn and kept right to take U turn under the flyover.

"What does your friend do?" Chandrika asked.

"He works for a Jain *sahab*" Jhihari replied looking out from the window. Chandrika took U turn to reach the area where Jhihari pointed out. The car was moving towards underpass. Jhihari again waived his hand to keep left to take left turn in Ghazipur village. Chandrika kept left on the road. Jhihari waived his hand to take left turn on the road heading to Ghazipur village. After the car moved a few hundred meters Jhihari again waived his hand to take a right turn. Chandrika saw a narrow busy road ahead accommodated mix of all types of vehicles. Big trucks and lorries for transporters, cars, bikes, bicycles of the residents, rickshaws, and auto rickshaws of daily earners all were making busy the narrow road.

Chandrika got nervous as she had to face the chaos of the vehicles on the narrow road. Then she took a look around as if she was a master driver. She took charge of the situation and moved car slowly. On the narrow busy road in the area she managed to creep like four-wheel reptile on the narrow road to find it like a tunnel as in many places the upper stories of the houses were bridged as their balcony extensions met each other. Many chemist shops on the road were sufficient to convince Chandrika about health awareness in the area. To Jhihari they indicated major bruises or minor accidents in plenty to make chemists to seek fortunes. Jhihari kept waiving his hand to indicate her to drive ahead on the road till a factory like settlement came in front a triangular area where waste stuff was lying. Jhihari waived his hand to stop the car in front of the factory. She stopped the car.

"Mam, you be here. I am just coming back" Jhihari said. He came out of the car.

Chandrika nodded. She closed the door.

Jhihari moved inside the gate of the factory like settlement where heaps of scraps were lying. Jhihari looked around for Inder and went inside up to the chemical part of the settlement to find Inder working in the register. Inder looked upon Jhihari's face. Jhihari didn't speak anything. Inder left the chair to come out with Jhihari. From Jhihari's face Inder got an idea of some mishappening in their life. Jhihari busted into cries the moment Inder stood in front of him. He held Jhihari by torso to stop from slipping down in the ground and supported to walk along. Inder came out of factory settlement. Jhihari looked out at the car where Chandrika was waiting. He didn't speak anything.

"What has happened mam? Why Jhihari is not speaking anything?" Inder asked Chandrika as Jhihari kept on crying.

"His brother has met an accident near the community building on the highway" Chandrika said. She waved her hand to hurry up.

"Oh no!" Inder also cried. Passing by people also looked at both. Few of them stood by side to understand what was going on.

"*Bhaiya ab nahin rahe*" Jhihari collected his senses to confirm what the lady driving the car had told Inder. "*Wo ek badi si gadi ke pahiyon mein sama gaye*" his broken voice amidst of cries added.

"We don't have time to discuss. You just come in the car with your friend" Chandrika asked. She had already unlocked the rear doors.

"*Kisi ko bata to doon ki Jhihari ke sath ja raha hoon*" Inder ran inside to inform someone.

"You sit down in the car till your friend comes" Chandrika asked Jhihari. She looked at her watch. Inder came back soon and got into the car. Chandrika moved the car ahead on the busy road. Jhihari waived the hand to take right turn to come out on the highway. Chandrika took left turn to drive on the highway. Inder waived hand to take U turn under flyover. Chandrika took U turn and moved ahead and looked for next indication to turn. Inder waived hand to take left turn to enter municipal gate of the landfill area. Inder asked her to stop the car near Jhihari's jhuggi. Jhihari came out of the car to look inside the shelter. He waived his hand to a lady busy in the filth being dumped by the truck in the lower high of mound of the filth in the landfill area. On Jhihari's calling gesture lady got stumbled in her own loose clothes as she rushed to the car.

"Oh Jhihari" cried Sachi clad in loose *salwar* suit. She called up Jhihari with a cry as if she knew about the accident. That might be coincidence. She came close to the car from the filthy heap on the boundary of the landfill area. Many other boys and girls also had come to know what was going on. They were just looking at the car, Jhihari, Inder, and the lady in the car.

"You went with your *bhaiya* on your rickshaw. What happened? Why this car?" Sachi wanted to ask many questions to Jhihari's silence.

"*Bhabhi pehle hamare sath chalo*" Inder hurried up.

"What happened? What happened to your *bhaiya*? He is not in the car" she asked Inder peeping in window.

"*Sab bata denge aapko*" Inder again requested to hurry up.

"You are hiding something" Sachi asked.

"You please come with us we will let you know everything" Chandrika interrupted in the conversation.

"Where I have to come with you?" Sachi took different method to know what has happened to her husband.

"Hospital" Chandrika answered in simple words.

"Hospital! What happened to him?" Sachi asked. She started crying. She rushed inside the shelter and soon she came out to get into the car. Chandrika asked Inder to take front seat. Jhihari and Sachi got seated in the rear.

"You are still hiding something from me" Sachi asked Jhihari as car started moving.

"We will tell you everything. What's your name?" Chandrika wanted to assure Sachi.

"Sachi" Inder said.

"We will tell you everything Sachi. It is just a matter of few minutes" Chandrika reiterated her consolation to Sachi.

Sachi looked at Jhihari.

"*Bhabhi hausla rakhna hoga*" Jhihari said. He didn't have courage to face Sachi's enquiries but helpless eyes. Jhihari broke down and started crying. Inder immediately turned back in front to extend his hand to Jhihari.

"I can understand that your brother had tough time" Sachi anticipated her own. "Inder you must be knowing about what has happened to your brother." Sachi turned to Inder for her queries.

"*Bhabhi*! *Bhaiya* has met an accident on the road." Inder said to Sachi. He looked at Chandrika's face. Chandrika kept looking at the road ahead on the highway to reach the hospital. She took left turn to drive underpass to reach to the hospital right on the highway. She entered the gate of the hospital parking.

"We need to rush to the hospital to save your brother" Chandrika asked Jhihari to come fast. She pretended to Jhihari as if his brother was alive.

"Yes mam" Jhihari got that why she pretended like that.

Chandrika and Jhihari rushed to the emergency of the hospital. She pressed remote to lock the car. Inder and Sachi followed them. Chandrika and Jhihari were so fast to move out of sight of Inder and Sachi. They couldn't follow them and landed up in the canteen of the hospital.

"*Ye to canteen hei*! *Jhihari kahan gaya us mam ke sath?*" Sachi asked Inder.

"They might have gone to the emergency department of the hospital" Inder said.

"*Jaldi se emergency chalein*" Sachi said. She waived her hand towards the doors where from they entered.

"Like me you might not have had your lunch. Before we meet *bhaiya*, would you like to have something to eat?" Inder asked. He was buying time.

"You just eat. I will not" Sachi said. She lost her patience. She wanted to meet her husband as soon as possible.

"If you don't want to eat then I alone will not eat" Inder said.

"Inder you take what you want. You are coming from your office" Sachi gave reason for Inder to eat.

"Same thing may be with you *bhabhi*. You might have been busy doing your job all the afternoon. You also might not have your food" Inder agreed with her reason to convince her to have something to eat.

"What about your *bhaiya*? Where is he?" Sachi reminded Inder why they had come to the hospital.

"We will see him. I will locate Jhihari and that madam first" Inder assured Sachi. She didn't have any clue that Ranchit was no more in his body.

"*Jaldi karo. Lelo jo tumhein theek lage*" Sachi surrendered. She went to table.

Inder went to the counter and bought two patties. He paid at the counter and came back to the table and chair where Sachi was waiting. He gave a patty to Sachi and started eating the other one. They both finished very fast and moved towards emergency of the hospital.

"Is there any patient who met accident on the road?" Inder enquired at the reception of the emergency.

"Sir! Here most of the patients come because of some accident only. This is emergency department of the hospital" the receptionist said. "Tell me the patient's name" she asked Inder.

"Rann . . .ch . . ." Inder could not tell full name to the receptionist as he listened sudden cry just behind himself. He turned up to look at that.

Sachi could not listen what Chandrika was talking to other lady. Chandrika looked upon Vasundhara.

"*Bhabhi*, you have to have to courage" Jhihari held Sachi.

"What happened?" Inder asked. "Where were you?" he asked Jhihari. He looked at the other lady with Chandrika and Jhihari. Chandrika also held Sachi and took her to the chair along with the wall. Jhihari went to take some water from the tap.

"What happened?" Inder asked again.

"We could not save her husband life. He died in the accident" Vasundhara repeated what Chandrika said to Sachi. Sachi already heard some similar when found both the ladies discussing. Jhihari came back with glass of water in his hand. He sprinkled water drops on Sachi's face.

"Oh *bhaiya*! Where have you gone?" Inder also started crying.

"Have courage. This is tough time for you all" Vasundhara solaced Inder.

"You are brave. You can't make your deceased brother to come again but you can do your part so that he lives among us through his body parts after his death." Vasundhara requested Inder. "To give new life to many suffering ones" she added to add pride to the work that she was expecting from Jhihari, Sachi and Inder to do.

"I didn't get you" Inder showed his cluelessness.

"I am Vasundhara, managing director of Uttar Daani, an organization engaged in managing the donation of human organs from cadavers to save the lives of other patients who need transplant for their malfunction or ailed body organs." Vasundhara introduced herself and work together, to Inder. "I think you are Jhihari's friend" she added her anticipation.

"Not friend but brother. I have been with Ranchit *bhaiya* only since my life began in Delhi." Inder said to Vasundhara. He got control over his cries. "*Bhaiya* was like my father and *bhabhi* is like my mother" he added in grieving voice.

"Then you are one of the decision makers. You just convince your *bhabhi* to give her consent as she is wife of the deceased. You please contribute your part to do this great work." Vasundhara said. She wanted to convince Inder so that he could help his *bhabhi* to give consent.

"Decision for what?" Inder again came with his ignorance.

"See your brother is brain dead at present. But his body parts are still alive for some time which can be transplanted to save other lives. They could be transplanted to patients who are dying or on the verge of dying because of diminishing functioning of those organs which can be taken from your brother's body." Vasundhara explained it in simple term to make Inder understand the significance of organ donation.

"You were telling something like cadavers." Inder asked. He looked at *bhabhi* and Chandrika. Chandrika was still busy in solacing her.

"See your brother will not come again to live the same life. His body parts like kidney, eyes, heart, etc. can be taken as donation to save lives of other people through transplants." Vasundhara explained again and again to convince Inder as soon as possible.

"*Bhabhi*! Jhihari! *Bhaiya* cannot live any more in the world but his body parts can live more in the people, not in one but many" shouted Inder as he got convinced so strongly to the concept. He was recyclist. So was Ranchit. So he got that so soon that he saw an analogy of the profession with body of the person also. Ranchit's body organs could be recycled in other bodies to give new life to other people. Death was giving new life. Or lives.

"You talk like an enlightened one" Vasundhara admired Inder as he spoke the same words as she talked about her organization. "He talks like us only" she shared her excitement with Chandrika as she couldn't control her zeal.

After some time Sachi got conscious. "*Bhaiya*, you people decide. Whatever you decide I will follow" Sachi left the decision making for Jhihari and Inder.

"Ok mam, you start your work" Jhihari gave consent to Chandrika and Vasundhara.

"You people are great! Great decision! Great work for good cause" Vasundhara appreciated all of them. "Chandrika is just filling the consent form you just sign it or give your thump impression" she requested Sachi. Chandrika filled the form to start the procedure. Vasundhara rushed to the surgery department.

"You people are doing great work" Chandrika also appreciated.

"Madam, some work if she can take up in your organization?" Inder requested Chandrika. "She has suffered a lot in her life due to the area and its impact on her health. We are still younger than her to bear the tear in our bodies. Let us face that all" he reasoned for Sachi.

"I will ask Vasundhara mam regarding this." Chandrika said to Inder. She caressed Sachi who was sitting helpless in the chair looking outside at the entrance of the emergency department of the hospital.

"Please sign here" Chandrika gave the filled consent form to Sachi for her signature on it. Sachi wanted to put a thumb impression on the consent form to endorse her faith in Jhihari and Inder. Chandrika brought out the stamp and ink pad to take thumb impression on the filled consent form to allow Uttar Daani to arrange for transplant of functioning organs of Ranchit's body to the other patients who were on the verge of dying, or suffering organic dysfunctions.

Dheerendra stepped up the stairs of emergency department of the hospital. He quickly passed the reception to reach the room where his father was being treated. He found the door of the room where he left his father was closed. He knocked at the door. One extremely beautiful lady in her thirties opened the door with astonishment at him. He looked at the lady and then at the patient on the bed in the room. A nurse was measuring blood pressure of the patient and other nurse was hanging drip to the hook. He looked at the patient's face. The patient, in late thirties and much younger than his father, was lying on the bed gasping as if having chest complaints.

Dheerendra struck his hand on his forehead. Finding that all in the room where he left his father. Dheerendra recalled then that his father was to be shifted to some other room. Before that lady could understand anything or get confused he apologized. He came out immediately to rush to the reception.

"Where is my father shifted?" Dheerendra asked the receptionist impatiently. He also looked into the register to find out himself.

"What is the name of your father?" the receptionist asked Dheerendra.

"Giridhar Prasad" he answered.

"Room no 11" she said looking at the screen of the computer. Dheerendra left the reception to rush to the new room.

"Where is the room? How to go?" Dheerendra came back to know the location of the new room.

"This side first room starting from the other end" said the receptionist. She kept looking at Dheerendra till he took few steps.

Dheerendra looked at the number of the rooms as he passed through. He reached at the other end and located room number 11. He knocked the door. The retired person whom he left with his father opened the door.

"Sorry uncle! I am extremely sorry" Dheerendra apologized. He held old man's hands in both of his hands.

"It is Ok. You are like my son. He is like my elder brother" the retired person said. He got worried and looked at his wrist watch.

"Did you have something in your lunch?" Dheerendra asked.

"No" the retired person said.

"Oh no! I have put you in trouble. I will get your lunch" Dheerendra regretted. "Can I make phone call?" he asked the retired person.

The retired person nodded.

He dialed a number and walked to the bed where his father was lying. He looked at the drip running down to the syringe in his father's hand.

"Yes, why didn't you reach hospital with my mother? He asked his wife on the phone.

"Oh no! Why it happens to you whenever some emergency is there? You are not able to leave the office" he complained his wife on the other end.

"Did you tell my mother? She could have come by her own" Dheerendra asked his next question.

"I told you for that time only so that she does not get shocked" he again complained in little irritated voice.

"Look! It is already eight or nine hours are passed. An uncle is still with my father since then" he explained the situation looking at the retired person. "He didn't have his lunch. By this time you could have told to mother about this" he continued.

"Again you are asking the same thing. I was stuck up in the police station." Dheerendra said to his wife in increasingly irritated voice.

"No, I will not ring her up now" he resented. He kept looking at retired person and at his father alternately.

"Why don't you understand? I may have to go home to take her with me" he again spoke with irritation. "I now can't leave the hospital" he added quickly.

"I have not even got the time to ask what is happening to my father in the hospital?" he said.

"How is my father sir?" he asked the retired person.

"Doctor has visited and given some injections but your father is still unconscious" the retired person updated him.

"Situation is not better. Father is still unconscious" he said. His voice got incremental irritation. "Ok I will talk later" he put mobile phone off.

"Don't worry my son, I am here till you take control of your situations" the retired person assured Dheerendra understanding the crisis he was undergoing.

"Thank you uncle. Thank you very much!" he folded his hands before the retired old man.

"Now I have to arrange for your lunch" he walked to the door to leave the room. "I have to talk to the doctor also" he added.

"No problem" the retired person assured him.

The retired person found himself in a weird situation. He was witnessing that younger generations were living in complexity and speed. He had seen in his own life when hospital used to be seen as taboo. Might be in the dearth of medical technologies and facilities, doctors and hospitals were not able to save lives in those times. In the life of the day where people spent entire life in bringing up only or two-only kids to find their kids were not getting time for them in distress.

"Mmm . . ." suddenly there was activity in the bed. The patient was getting back to consciousness. The retired person walked to the bed to know if he was getting conscious. The retired man found that patient winced once.

"Can I meet the doctor who has examined my father in the room number eleven?" Dheerendra asked the receptionist.

"The doctor is on visit. You can just check for him in other rooms" the receptionist replied.

"How can I check every room?" he asked.

"Then, please wait for the doctor to come to your father's room" she replied.

He looked here and there in the corridors for any other person or doctor. He didn't want to talk to the receptionist. He didn't find any doctor. He went to the doctor room only to find out that all the doctors were on visit. He came back to the room number eleven. He lifted his hand to knock the door. He realized that he was missing something. He was not able to recall what he was missing. He finally knocked the door of the room.

"Yes" an old voice from the room.

The voice of the old retired person in the room reminded him to bring lunch. He rushed to the canteen of the hospital. At four O' clock he found no meal in the canteen. He bought some snacks and tea for the retired person attending his father in the room. He heard some voices in the room when he reached at the door of the room. He knocked and opened the door himself. He saw the doctor was talking to retired person.

"Yes doctor! How is my father now?" Dheerendra took charge of the discussion going between doctor and the retired person. He kept snacks and tea pot on the table.

"Oh! The patient is your father? I saw this uncle since morning" the doctor turned to Dheerendra.

"How is my father doctor?" Dheerendra asked looking at his father lying on the bed. "I got stuck in many unwanted problems after I brought him here. Yes, I am thankful to uncle for his impeccable support to me and my father. Uncle is a great man. I can't find a person like him. He came with me from the accident spot. It is very rare. Thank you uncle thank you again and again" he got emotional.

Doctor nodded.

"Your father is lucky he didn't come in any contact directly to collide with the car. There are no direct wounds on his body by the car. But what might have happened is that the car may be coming so fast that your father couldn't maintain balance of his body and fell back on the road" the doctor constructed a probable story based on the injuries. "Does your father walk with walking stick?" the doctor asked.

"Yes" he keeps a walking stick with him to keep the street dogs away. Otherwise he doesn't need that for walking." Dheerendra said.

"Then may be your father was about to step on the pavement. His stick might have come into direct impact of collision with the car. Not he himself" the retired person took part in the reconstruction of scene of the accident.

"He might have fallen on the road because of that" the doctor agreed with the retired person. "Out of fear he might have turned to avoid the head on collision and fell on the road" he said. Hairline fracture in the shoulder that he had seen in the x-rays made him talk like that. "Some more reports are yet to come" he added.

"What is course of treatment?" Dheerendra asked.

"Let's see all the reports then only I will tell you" the doctor answered. He looked at the snacks and tea pot on the table.

Dheerendra nodded.

"I think uncle has not taken his lunch. I saw him here only every time" the doctor wanted to move out. His eyes were at retired person. Perhaps he wanted to admire the retired person. Perhaps he pitied on the retired person being there with the patient whose son was roaming around the police station for petty issues before he focused on the treatment. Or perhaps he found the value of a person in being retired to discover new kind of social value. That was like 'care sitter' in addition to well established role of 'baby sitter'. Whatever it was, it was mixed of admiration too.

"O sure sir" Dheerendra assured the doctor.

"I will come after one hour" the doctor said before he left the room.

"I am sorry uncle. Because of me you could not have your lunch. Even lunch is not there in the canteen of the hospital. Please have some snacks for the time being." Dheerendra requested the retired person with sense of guilt.

"It happens. You also didn't get the time to have your food" the retired person tried to get that normal and came forward without any formality.

"Luckily your father has not been under direct collision with the car. The other person flied few feet high in the air for seconds after collision" the retired person consoled Dheerendra who appeared to be very unhappy with entire episode of the accident as if he had landed up in great miseries.

"Who?" Dheerendra asked.

"The other person that the car hit after your father fell down on the road" the retired person reminded him.

"Oh! I totally forgot" Dheerendra recalled.

"That man got died on the spot. The accident was so lethal for him that he didn't get time to cry for any help" the retired person reproduced the scene as he witnessed. "I believe he was a poor man" he added along with pouring sauce over half eaten samosa. "These potatoes are dangerous for diabetic people like me" he expressed his caution over the content of his lunch. "But was there any choice before him? Being in the service of senior no choice was available" he didn't talk but thought a lot.

"Hmm . . ." Dheerendra kept eating his samosa and cutlet. "I could not make better choice at this odd time" he regretted for bringing potato rich snacks for the retired person.

Before he took another cutlet to eat, he switched his mobile phone and called up his colleague to ensure everything was going smoothly in the office. He finished the call and started eating other cutlet. Again he took mobile in his hand to dial another number. He talked to his wife to find if she was able to leave office before six O' clock. He finished the cutlet very fast and poured the tea in two disposable glasses.

"Uncle, can I request you to be here for some more time?" he pleaded.

"Tell me" the retired person accepted Dheerendra's plea. "*Abhi aur rukna hei*? He said as he anticipated what Dheerendra was going to ask him.

"With what face shall I ask you?" he folded his hands and said. "But what has happened in between is that my wife would have got half day off from her office. She didn't get. Now I have to go home to bring my mother here" he explained his need.

The retired person looked into Dheerendra's eyes without any question in mind. He must be having pity on Dheerendra in that situation.

"Can I expect you to stay here till I come back with my mother?" Dheerendra begged the retired person for his time.

"What time will you come?" the retired person looked at his wrist watch.

"Don't worry uncle. I will drop you when I come back" Dheerendra wanted to assure a drop to the retired person. "We will leave after I come back with my mother" he looked into the retired person's eyes for permission to go home. He didn't think every activity was taking so long. He planned in the office so accurately that its execution might have come with big 'wow' kind of performance. That day he found himself unprepared and helpless. He didn't ring up at home. He left the room of the hospital.

Vasundhara asked Chandrika to drop back Jhihari, Sachi, and Inder at Ghazipur. Chandrika waived her hand for Jhihari, Sachi, and Inder to proceed to the parking of the hospital. Chandrika unlocked the car and opened up all the doors.

"I have got to pick up the rickshaw from the accident site." Jhihari reminded Chandrika. "I came on rickshaw to receive *bhaiya*" his sad tone was out to have Sachi in cries again.

"I will drop you there at the site" Chandrika said. "Sachi you have to have courage" she turned to Sachi who was in tears again.

"My husband was the only cause for me to be here. He was the courage for me to stay here in this world of filth and waste. *Sab kuchh khatam hei ab*" Sachi said. She cried in tears. "Now how will I spend whole of my life? All is finished" she lamented over the loss of her husband and her loneliness in the big city.

Chandrika kept her hand on Sachi's shoulder to cause her move to sit in the car. "Jhihari, Inder, we need to save time, please come" she wanted to hurry up.

"How will your Vasundhara mam go back?" Inder asked Chandrika.

"She has called up to bring another car. The driver must be reaching the hospital any time." Chandrika said to Inder. She sat in the driving seat. She started the ignition and moved the car when all of them got seated. The car moved out of the parking area of the hospital. She stopped the car when passing by Vasundhara's car in the porch of the hospital. She put down glass to talk to Vasundhara. "Madam, I am going to drop them" Chandrika said.

"I am leaving for the day" Vasundhara said.

"I will go back to the office first" Chandrika said.

"We have to be with them tomorrow also. They need to take the body" Vasundhara reminded Chandrika what to be done next. "I am leaving" she said. The driver got the instruction from her intentions. He started the car and moved out of the porch of the hospital. Chandrika also moved out of the hospital.

"What are the rituals in your society for funerals?" Chandrika broke the silence in the car. She looked at Sachi in the rear view mirror.

"What can be the rituals for poor people like us?" Jhihari replied with a question. He also looked at Sachi.

"Madam, can either of them be given some job in your Uttar Daani?" Inder again requested Chandrika.

"Let me see Inder. I can understand how difficult will be the life for her" Chandrika said. "What can she do?" she wanted to know.

"At present she does some cleaning work in few households" Inder said to Chandrika. "Many other things are there on their part. They support their aging family persons in Singbhum" he counted on Sachi's plight and responsibilities.

"Jhihari is a hardworking man. Please arrange some job for him" Inder requested Chandrika.

"Is he educated up to some certification?" Chandrika asked.

"No, he couldn't get education in school" Inder clarified.

"At least matriculation or more than that generally makes you understand writing work." Chandrika said looking ahead on the road.

"He can work as peon in your office" Inder gave idea on behalf Jhihari.

"Inder you are talking about a person whose needs are more than what he may get as a peon. Ours is a nongovernment organization he may not get that much." Chandrika said as she didn't want to discourage at later stage. "For both of them we can't afford at present" she added.

"Whenever, you feel they are the one who can fit in your organization, please arrange that for either of them." Inder again pleaded.

"At present there is not much that can be done" Chandrika replied. "Yes, Vasundhara mam has an idea of expansion in this area" she said.

"Please just give them a chance to serve you" Inder showed his concern.

Chandrika nodded and kept driving the car. She stopped at Noida turn.

"Jhihari need to take his rickshaw first, and then we will go" Chandrika said as she took left for U-turn to drop Jhihari at accident site. She stopped the car after driving it to the place on the road where Jhihari's rickshaw was tied with the pole. "I shall drop him first then I will drop both of you" Chandrika said.

"Shall I also get down?" Inder asked.

"No, you please don't get down here. I will drop you two there in Ghazipur." Chandrika insisted. Inder agreed with her. Jhihari got down at the site to take the rickshaw with him. She then moved ahead on the road heading to Ghazipur. "What kind of work can you do at present Sachi?" she asked Sachi.

"I am doing domestic cleaning in few households." Sachi replied. "It may not be for me to do job outside. Jhihari would take the work with you" she gave her opinion.

"Why can't you?" Chandrika asked Sachi.

"He has entire life ahead, mine is spent, just remain few years without Jhihari's brother. How long I will keep alive?" Sachi replied to Chandrika in disappointed tone.

"Is your life finished? Of course Jhihari's entire life ahead" Chandrika asked Sachi.

"Without husband woman cannot live longer." Sachi shared her view on life of an Indian woman.

"Now it is not the time like that in old days. You can live your life as you wish." Chandrika expounded. "You also have got all the rights to express yourself, your life, your passions, etc." she didn't wait to reach Ghazipur and then talk. "To make your life more and more meaningful, look at me or Vasundhara mam both are running an organization which we are proud of. It is a unique organization" she explained further thinking she might need to rush back to the office sooner.

"No mam, you just manage something for Jhihari first, if he is comfortable then I will join him later with some work fit for me." Sachi said.

"I think she is right" Inder supported, Inder could understand that Jhihari need to have a permanent job like theirs.

"Ok Sachi if you think Jhihari will keep helping you than we will think what can be done to improve your life." Chandrika replied.

"What about you Inder?" Chandrika wanted to know his plan.

"Would you like to open up our office in east Delhi?" Chandrika asked Inder to read his mind in the field which was not yet popular with the people as career option.

"Me?" surprised Inder asked Chandrika.

"Yes! I am talking about you, your plans" Chandrika confirmed to his surprise. "Every organization wants to expand so we also want to expand" she showed her entrepreneurship.

"Right now I am with Jain Disposals and not in condition to leave that" Inder replied.

"We also are thinking of expansion. We have to plan for that" Chandrika said to Inder.

Sachi couldn't understand anything even after she got to hear the entire discussion. She found herself aloof in the entire expansion plan. She might be staying here in near future. She might go back to Singbhum. Ranchit was the only reason for her to be in Delhi. Ranchit had left her in the filth of Ghazipur. Though Ranchit couldn't give her anything else than Ghazipur filth of landfill area but she had spent her life with Ranchit having herself in full Indian tradition as far as being wife was concerned. To Sachi, Ranchit was the first and the last command.

Chandrika drove the car on the narrowed down lanes. The road on the highway was narrowed down to widen the road as other two lanes were taking place in the filling through mud. Two lanes of future's widened highway were being raised to the level of highway. The car was running on the road on which two lanes were left for traffic. She drove straight to pass the Ghazipur crossing to drop Sachi first. She took right turn to the place in the landfill area. She stopped the car on road side close to Ranchit's jhuggi which had frames worked out with plastic sheets wrapped upon semi-circle thatches. Semi-circular structure covered with plastic sheet gave it look of an 'igloo'. A polyethene igloo or poly-igloo.

"Are bhabhi, badi gadi mein ghoom rahi ho koi lottery nikli hei kya?" Niranjan asked. Out of curiosity, he was waiting for the family to come. He didn't know that with few vroooooming zooming seconds had ruined Sachi's life.

Sachi didn't reply. She wanted to cry. Jhihari held her to comfort.

"Kya hua? Mam *badi gadi mein le gayi aur abhi chhodne bhi aayi hein"* Niranjan said. He kept looking at Chandrika and the car in spells. *"Koi naya kaam shuru kiya hei kya? Sab gaye the?"* Niranjan kept asking the same in different versions. "Jhihari was with you. Where is he now? He must be coming with Ranchit *bhaiya?"* said Niranjan. He asked many questions with single purpose in mind.

"Niranjan, now your brother won't come, hearing Ranchit's name Sachi cried. *Wo hamse bahut door chale gaye"* her voice could not come clear as her throat got choked. She wanted to clear the confusion clouded overNiranjan's mind.

"Kya hua? Bhabhi don't talk like that. I thought there must be some urgent work regarding what Inder is doing and that lady in big car" Niranjan said as if someone had poured on all the sorrow on him. Ranchit

to Niranjan was what he was to Inder. The only difference was that Inder took on studies and improved in his life. Niranjan kept bungling here and there since he came out of the innocent childhood. "Oh God! Why did you do this?" he asked looking up in the sky. Few other people huddled them after they heard Sachi's cries.

"A big car has eaten your brother near the community building." Sachi said amidst of her cries.

"Why was he there? What was he doing there?" Niranjan asked. His surprise was not damping out as he was not ready to accept. "That place is so far from here" he reasoned not to believe what he heard.

"Your *bhaiya* went for some new work in the restaurant of the temple." Sachi lamented over the entire episode. "My eye was flickering before he left. I should not have let him go out" she regretted why she couldn't understand her premonition. She cried and claimed that she saw adverse signs were there in the environment.

"A cat also crossed the road when Ranchit *bhaiya* was moving out" another man standing close to Niranjan claimed to have seen. He blew his nose to clear the phlegm out of it. Chandrika moved away to avoid vomiting sensation and nasty feelings. *"Lagta hei uska ant aa gaya tha. Kaal ke gaal mein chala gaya. Honi ko kaun taale"* he shared all his knowledge on omens and fatality over Ranchit's death.

"I would have shot the driver of the big car if I had been there." Niranjan shouted out of fury.

"What you could have done if the big car with high speed rammed and disappeared" that man wanted to teach some lesson to Niranjan on destiny. He explained how everything was pre-decided and nothing could change that. He rubbed his eyes and kept rubbing them. He kept inserting his finger into his nostrils and kept blowing the phlegmy stuff. It was difficult for Chandrika to stay in that surrounding. She felt helpless but she couldn't run away from the responsibilities for Uttar Daani.

"Inder do you want to be with Sachi or shall I drop you at your work place?" Chandrika asked Inder. She wanted to move out. She looked around at the people who were settling to mourn in the area. She thought that she could leave for her office.

"Please let me be here with *Bhabhi* in her bad times" Inder lamented. "They are like parents for me, I want to be here. I don't know whether my parents are there in this world or they flew by a flood, or got killed in rustic feud" he wanted to be free to cry.

"Same is with me madam! In Delhi Ranchit *bhaiya* and Sachi *bhabhi* are my parents." Niranjan also expressed the bond. The bond that got developed amidst of helplessness and miseries got strong in crisis.

"Madam, when will we get the body?" Niranjan asked Chandrika.

"Tomorrow, around three O' clock" Chandrika answered.

Chandrika sensed the degree of sorrow and the impact of Ranchit's death among the people in their life. She was not interested in discussions they had among themselves. Their beliefs and premonitions might have little control over their lives. But she found that premonition was having great significance in their daily life. She wanted to leave but preferred to wait for Jhihari. She kept looking at the entrance gate to the landfill area for Jhihari to come. She didn't imagine that Jhihari would take longer time to reach Ghazipur. She didn't have idea about *Jugaad* rickshaw. She didn't blame that on Jhihari as chaotic and traffic also might have been a factor. She could not wait for Jhihari for longer and left for the office of Uttar Daani.

"My son, your father has not come back since morning walk." Dheerendra's mother asked when tired Dheerendra reached home with gloomy face. "I thought he might have been with his close friend. He could have called up in that case" she added.

"*Maa*, he is in the hospital" he informed mother.

"Hospital! Oh my god! What happened?" his mother got nervous.

"He had met an accident on the road. Some rascal had driven his sedan over him" he explained the accident in hurry. "*Maa* we have to go to the hospital" he hurried up.

"Which hospital? How is he now? What happened?" she asked.

"Hospital is close to the underpass. When I left he was unconscious" Dheerendra said.

"Take me to the hospital beta" she became restless.

"Yes, I will take you to the hospital. Let your *bahu* come from the office" Dheerendra assured his mother. "Otherwise son will keep on waiting after he comes back from coaching classes" he reminded his mother.

"*Beta* I don't know when she will come" his mother said. "You just drop me there" she requested her son.

"Ok *maa*, as you wish" Dheerendra agreed with mother. He looked at his wrist watch. "Let's move fast. Where is the key?" Dheerendra asked his mother.

"It must be somewhere here only" his mother replied.

"It must be on the key hook" he said. He went close to the wall where big key shaped wooden frame studded with brass hooks for hanging the keys. He didn't find the keys of the house. "It must be on the refrigerator then" he kept guessing and moved to the refrigerator with no success. He ran helter-skelter about the entire house of the keys. She also roamed around living room, dining room, bedrooms, balcony, etc. but couldn't find the keys of the house.

"Where are the keys' bunch *maa*?" he asked mother.

"Is it not there on the refrigerator?" his mother said.

"No *maa*, it is not there" he said.

"Where is the key?" his mother grinded her teeth. "We can request our neighbor that we are going out in an emergency. He can take care till *bahu* comes from the office" she suggested as they couldn't find the key.

"Please *maa*! Hurry up do whatever you want" he was on the verge of losing his patience. He exhaled very fast and took a deep breathe. He was not comfortable with the idea of leaving house in the neighbor's control. But he also considered his helplessness.

"What shall we do now? If not this" his mother wanted to retract. She looked at her son and sensed that he didn't like the idea.

"No *maa*, we can do that. No problem" he concealed his anger.

"*Theek hei beta jaisa tum kaho*" she again looked at her son's face and went out to request to the neighbor. She went in for a moment and came back in another.

"What happened? They are also not there?" he asked. He blew up all the air.

She nodded.

"*Maa*! You are here in the house all the time. Where are the keys?" he asked his mother. He also got restless.

"My son, I am all the time here that's fine. But the key are not always with me" she clarified.

"Where can they get disappeared?" he complained.

"*Beta*, can you ring up *bahu* and ask her if she knows about the keys?" she requested her son.

Maa, she goes out even before I leave the house" he said. "How can she tell where the keys are? Moreover she may be driving" he added. He didn't tell that he was not willing to ask his wife.

He looked at mother's face which turned pale with the fear of uncertainty. He forgot his father has got an accident. He suddenly remembered that the retired person was there with the father. He realized the situation. He thought of requesting to the other neighbor. He moved out to the door but came back to give a try to search the keys. Perhaps he was not comfortable with the other neighbor. So, he searched all the almirahs and drawers. He also lost hope to find the keys then. He lost his temper and picked up his son's entrance guide of engineering which was lying on the study table to throw in disgust. The moment he held the book in his hands the keys of the house fell down on the floor. The keys were stuck in the groove formed in the back as the book was lying open on his son's study table.

"*Maa*, here are the keys" he picked up the keys.

"Where have you got them?" she came fast. "May be your son might have been taking them to go out some time when I was sleeping but left them under his book" his mother had her own idea.

"*Maa*, let's move to the hospital" he hurried up and moved to close the interior door to lock after his mother came out.

"*Beta, bahu* has come" his mother stopped him to lock the outer grilled door for safety as she heard *bahu's* stepping sounds from the stairs of the apartments.

"That's good, we can leave now" he rushed down. He met his wife at the stairs.

"It is time for son to come from his coaching classes" he gave the keys to his wife.

Dheerendra came with mother to the parking and fit into the driving to rush to the hospital after his mother got into the car.

"*Beta*, you were out for your office. How did you come to know about the accident?" she asked. She couldn't get time to discuss how that had happened.

"*Maa*, I was on the way to the office. Someone rang me up from papa's mobile phone and told me about the accident" he replied. "I took U turn to come back" he added.

"*Mujhe kyon nahin bataya? Pass mein hi hei main rickshaw le ke chali jati*" she said.

"I thought papa is already in such conditions over which I don't have any control. I know that you are also diabetic and having blood pressure. Disturbed eating also may derail your health. So, *maa* I didn't tell you about the accident" he explained.

"What about you *beta*?" his mother asked clearing the dust on the utility box between front seats. She also turned to look at rear seat for cleanliness.

"Leave it *maa*. Dust might have come in the morning when we were taking papa in the car. The boy will anyway wash the car tomorrow morning. I'll ask him to wash it properly including interior" he reacted to mother's discomfort. "We are close to the hospital" he added looking ahead to take right turn. He then took left turn to enter the emergency ward of the hospital. He stopped the car. They got down from the car. He pressed the remote to lock the car rushing to the stairs. His mother couldn't keep with his pace. He had to come down as she called him for help. He took his mother's hand in his hand to assist her to step up on the stairs. They both walked to reach the room at the end of the corridor. They entered the room to find a doctor and nurse discussing around the patient.

"Mr. Dheerendra we are waiting for you for a long time" the doctor spoke as Dheerendra entered.

"Things are under control. You must be happy to know that your father is responding to the medicines" the doctor updated him. "He is conscious now and sleeping. Please don't disturb him" the doctor advised.

"Thank you doctor" he expressed his gratitude.

"Mr. Dheerendra you should thank that old gentleman who was sitting continuously to support your father. You were busy here and there to make arrangements. He didn't leave the room even for a minute" the doctor spoke about the retired person.

"I am really thankful to that uncle. Where has he gone?" he asked the doctor as he didn't find the retired person in the room.

"Sir, that gentleman has gone with his son ten minutes before you reached here" the nurse replied.

"Oh no! Why did you let him go?" worried Dheerendra asked.

"Sir! How could I stop him? He was here with your father since morning" the nurse reminded Dheerendra. "Moreover, his son was not happy with him. He came with tiffin for his father. Later His son told me that the uncle has high blood pressure and sugar" nurse said.

"Ok dear, take care now" the doctor hinted learning for him and left the room.

"That I know mam" Dheerendra turned to the nurse. "That's why I am saying you could have requested him to wait for some more time. I had promised him to give him a drop" he wanted to clarify.

"He kept waiting for you to come back. He perhaps could have waited for you longer" the nurse replied recalling something. "*Haan*, his son rang him up and came to take him back home" the nurse again said as Dheerendra looked a bit disturbed.

"Oh!" Dheerendra took out his breathe and looked at the mother who was standing closed to the bed his father was lying. She went to look at her husband. She couldn't understand the conversations between his son and the nurse.

"Mr. Dheerendra, his son was not happy as the old uncle was here for entire day" the nurse spoke further.

"What happened *beta*? Who is that old uncle?" Dheerendra's mother could not remain indifferent and wanted to know what had happened.

"I will tell you *maa*" he said to his mother. "Did you take his phone number?" he asked the nurse as if she was responsible to take phone number from the retired person.

"Phone number! Mr. Dheerendra, you would have taken. You kept coming and going out of the room. His number must be already with you. You may have called him up so many times since morning" the nurse surprised him with her answer.

He even didn't try to know the name of the retired person. The phone number was not in his agenda. He couldn't look into his own follies and looked at his mother with many thoughts in his minds. Had his mother been aware of the key he would have met the retired person. Had his wife told his mother about the accident then his mother would have come on her own to the nearby hospital. In the last he thought what he could have done. Had he himself been here in the hospital rather than running to get an FIR lodged in the police station, then he would have been here to thank the retired person. Had it been so . . . had it such . . . had that been that . . . engrossed him in remorse and regret. He sat down with his mother.

Inder went inside semi-circled thatched hut where he has spent years with Ranchit, Sachi, Jhihari, Niranjan and other people destined to live under the filthy hill over the mud to take out big rag of carpet like spread which Sachi might have kept with care for gatherings of few people on some happy occasions. Inder spread that on the ground in front of the door of the hut. Inder, Niranjan and few other people sat down on that rag spread. Sachi went inside the jhuggi to leave them waiting for Jhihari. They saw Jhihari emerged on the gate of the landfill area.

"Has mam gone back?" Jhihari asked loud from the place where he stopped his rickshaw. He got down from the rickshaw to join them.

"Jhihari where have you left *bhaiya*?" Niranjan cried loud with complaint to mourn over the loss of his brother, mentor, and father figure. "Why did you leave him alone there?" he again asked amidst of his cries. He then wrapped himself around Jhihari to cry more and more.

Jhihari didn't reply but cried along with him.

"Who can change someone's end?" a man sitting among them wanted to solace Jhihari.

"Now what is to be done?" Niranjan asked.

"Wait for tomorrow we have to go to the hospital to get *bhaiya's* body." Jhihari answered. He looked into Niranjan's eyes. He found that the sense of responsibility roped into Niranjan which was a surprise to him. He kept quiet but his subconscious mind congratulated Niranjan for being on the right track. Niranjan might be on the right track in the absence of his guard, Ranchit.

"Inder wait for some time. I am just coming back from the grocer" Jhihari said

"Where are you going? You must be tired of riding long distance. Tell me what is to be done?" Niranjan volunteered.

"Jhihari! Let me do. What do you want?" Inder also asked Jhihari to be with the people. "I have to call Jain *Sahab* to inform about *bhaiya*" he added.

"You call Jain *Sahab* later. Let me go" Jhihari replied and moved out to the grocer.

Few women came there and went inside the jhuggi. Suddenly Sachi's cry got high to subdue other voices coming from inside the jhuggi. She was to receive the women from neighborhood who came to mourn over the death of her husband. Sachi's cry was chorused with other mild cries as most of the women contributed to mourning.

Jhihari came back with few bundles of bidis, Gutkha pouches, etc. He went inside the jhuggi to bring some plate. He came out with a plate to place them to welcome the people started coming for mourning. They were expected to sit for some time on the rag spread to mourn over the death of his brother. During that they should be honored with offering of bidis and Gutkha pouches.

Suddenly Jhihari also cried in emotional burst as few new joining women embraced him to show the bond in the time of morning. They then held him with their hands to solace on the calamity, the loss of his brother. The cries inside and outside the jhuggi shrilled the surrounding environment. When Jhihari got inside, the process of mourning got repeated with women inside. After some time the crying voices of women and Jhihari calmed down.

"Inder you were talking about calling your Jain *sahab*" Jhihari reminded Inder when he came out.

"Yes, I have to go to the local call booth." Inder said.

"You take this mobile phone" Jhihari gave a mobile phone to Inder. "Today, *bhaiya* didn't take it with him. May be he knew that his end was approaching him" he said. Hick ups and cries interleaved his voice and were choking his throat. Inder held Jhihari in arms for solace. Other people sitting on rag spread came forward to solace him.

"Perhaps your brother has got his end as written by the almighty" a man with *hina* colored grey beard put his hand on Jhihari's shoulder. "*Hoi wahi jo Ram rachi raakha*" he added.

Stinking smell ridden breeze kept coming from the filthy waste hill of the landfill area. Many of them were habitual to tolerate that while few others covered their nose. They might have thought on displaying that once they had been in good area in their earlier life. Whatever it was but soon they realized covering their nose could not keep them away from the smell, its aura, its impact, its infection, its chemistry on their bodies was at work all the time.

Inder dialed Ishwar Jain's number to inform about the death of his father like brother who brought him up.

Few hours got passed to bring the evening dark. Jhihari took a six-seven feet long bamboo staff with a hook to tangle the end of electric wire to hang on open line to the street light over his jhuggi to light up the bulb one inside and other outside. Women inside the jhuggi had gone out to their jhuggies.

After some time few women came with food in plates.

"No please, we won't eat" Jhihari requested them to take the food back.

"Will you keep hungry till tomorrow?" a man in net like vest and lungi asked. He knew that it was difficult to keep fasting for almost two days as Chandrika told that the body would be handed over to them in the evening.

"No leave it. Don't force them to eat till cremation. *Jab tak dag nahin lag jayega tab tak wo kaise kha sakte hein?*" another man said after he adjusted the thread on his right wrist.

"*To kya inhein bhooke maroge chacha?*" the man in net like vest and lungi asked him.

"*Reet chalan to yahi kehte hein*" he replied. "*Vaise koi apne man ki kare to use kaun rokega?*" he laid emphasis on the tradition over one's own wish.

"*Bada ajeeb sa hisab hei bhai tumhare system mein*" the man in net like vest and lungi waggled his open palm on the other hand.

"These kinds of rites were fixed when distance or complicacy in work was not there" another man in loose raggedy shirt with plenty of pockets explained reason in the genesis of such customs.

Women who came with food plates took them back to their jhuggies as Jhihari insisted to avoid food. Jhihari, Inder, and Niranjan put their heads on the knees to have a nap. Sachi with few women inside the jhuggies also did the same. Two men slept on the rag spread on the ground. The spell of nap and vigil kept continued throughout the night. Those spells were accompanied by the barks of the stray dogs who flourished on the eatables and loaves of meats of different animals thrown out of the butcher stalls of suppliers to the army to keep them strong and fighting fit to survive in the stinking filth. Those chickens who survived from being finger-licking-meal in the hotels, restaurants, *dhabas*, and household kitchens gave morning call to make the people reminded that another day had started. Perhaps it was also that who will make them turn into finger-licking-meal that day or next day. They didn't want to live more in the stinking air of fecal and filth. Rather they won't.

Jhihari raised his head to mark his waking up. He stood up after straightening his legs on the rag spread. Niranjan sitting with his head down on his knees slept by his side to keep his surface area lesser to get covered in single towel size long cloth. Inder also slept on the rag spread where two other men were sleeping to mark the mourning night for them. Light of the dawn triggered Jhihari to take the same bamboo staff again to switch off the light used in the night.

Like other women of the area Sachi also woke up in the dark before the dawn to go to the field to defecate. She needed to bring the milk packet from nearby tea stall to prepare tea for people expected to come for mourning. She shook up a small cylinder to check gas in over which small gas burner fitted on the top to cook food. She couldn't make out whether the cylinder contained gas or not. She struck a match stick to light up the gas stove.

She poured water in the pan on the stove. But its flame died out. The gas in the cylinder was over. She called up Jhihari to inform that there was no gas in the cylinder. Niranjan also went inside as Sachi called up Jhihari.

"Jhihari you should be here more people will come to meet us and mourn. I will get the cylinder refilled." Niranjan took the small cylinder in his hand and moved in the narrow street that was made to have passage to few shopkeepers on the other end where local mechanism to fill the gas from regular size cylinders was provided as service. Service to the servitude. That was invented for survival of the servitude. Niranjan reached the tea stall where he gave the small cylinder to the tea stall owner.

The tea stall owner turned the big cylinder upside down on the small cylinders and fixed up the nozzle to make cooking gas flow from big cylinder to small cylinder through a compatible regulator. Suddenly some sound of spurious pressure spread out and the man closed the big cylinder first. He checked whether the flowing pipe regulator was fitted into the small cylinder or not. He fitted it properly and again he started siphoning the gas into the small cylinder. The small cylinder got filled in around ten minutes. Niranjan paid to the stall keeper for refilling the cylinder.

Niranjan came back with filled cylinder to hand it over to Sachi. Sachi resumed preparing tea for people outside the jhuggi. After some time Sachi again called up Jhihari but Niranjan went inside and came with tea in small disposable glasses in a plate. He kept in the plate to cater tea to the people. It was quiet interesting that family of the deceased could not eat food till they cremated body but tea could be served to the guests who came for mourning over the death. That was the matter of honor so it was to be honored.

Inder wanted to know if there was any news related to Ranchit *bhaiya*. He went to the tea stall to read the newspaper. He picked up the available local edition of Hindi newspaper and turned the page for local news. He did not find any news covering the accident. Inder got disappointed. He turned other pages of the newspaper quickly to look for similar news with some other context or heading. He folded the newspaper to keep back on bench.

As he kept back the newspaper suddenly he gazed at one heading on the lower half of the main page with headline "*Ek badi car mein sawar jawani ek bujurg ko raund gayi*" he took back the newspaper in his hands and read out the news very carefully. He found no mention of Ranchit *bhaiya* in that news. The news talked about how man in his early twenties in a big black car drove and hit an octogenarian and ran away from the site. The car possessed so powerful engine that he could again got hundred kilometers per hour speed in fifteen second to disappear from the scene.

The news didn't mention that Ranchit Chhidra from Singbhum who somehow managed his family against all the odds like poverty and bad environment of Ghazipur near the landfill area was also rammed up by the same car after he hit the octogenarian. The news also mentioned the wounded octogenarian named as Giridhar Prasad.

Inder read out "*Aaj ki mobile technology ke gulam prayog se ek naujawan ne ek bujurg ki jaan ko bahut khatre mein dal diya. Jab ki usi mobile technology ki badaulat us bujurg ke bete, jo ek bahurashtriya company mein naukri karte hein usi raste se apne office ja rahe the, ko jaldi ghatna sthal par pahunchne ka avsar mila. Ghayal bujurg ke phone se kisi madadgar vyakti ne bujurg ke bete ko phone milaya aur accident ke bare mein soochit kiya to Dheerendra Prasad jo Giridhar Prasad ke bete hein ghatna sthal par pahunch kar apne pita ko hospital le gaye jahan bujurg ki halat chintajanak batayi gayi hei.*" Inder got upset after reading the news in full.

Inder held his head as he felt giddy. He sat down for a while. He went to the crossing to look into other newspapers. He found the news on the page for capital region news. One news mentioned similar narration like "The driver engrossed in talk on his mobile phone ran his car on the pavement at high speed. He hit a senior citizen who fell down on the ground. Someone from the crowd called his son from senior citizen's mobile phone to inform about the accident. The victim's son who works in a multinational company just passed by the area around fifteen minutes ago. He came back to rescue his father to a hospital. The condition of the senior citizen is critical." he came back to the tea stall.

"*Chacha* can I take this newspaper?" Inder requested tea staller. "I will send it back soon" he added to have permission from *chacha*.

"Ranchit has met his fate" *chacha* said over Ranchit's death. "What are you looking for? *Chacha* further asked Inder.

"No *chacha*! Nothing" Inder replied. What he was looking for was not related to *chacha* so he didn't tell him anything.

"But you are looking sad and lost" *chacha* spoke. He read many things on Inder's gloomy face.

"What is there to tell you *chacha*? What is there to look for in this newspaper? These newspapers also made us a big joke" Inder shared.

"*Kuchh samjha nahin*" *chacha* said.

"The newspaper has news on the accident in which Ranchit *bhaiya* died but doesn't mention that he died in that." Inder said. Initially unwilling to talk about accident in which Ranchit died but he spoke to make the tea stall owner aware of the mockery of servitude. To Inder, the newspaper appeared to deny a small space to Ranchit who could not get his place under the sun. No wonder that he didn't get the place in the letters not even between the letters. Might be because, he was not the man of letters that mattered a lot, not to his lot, but, to the lot of letters. To the lot of letters.

"This is not first time Inder you know it very well. Poor people are not found in the newspapers, they are found on the newspapers" *chacha* explained to Inder reminding past experiences of the area which could not mention in any newspapers. Inder gasped and took the newspaper to the mourning place.

"Jhihari! Are you sure about the accident? It's place?" Inder asked Jhihari. He wanted to confirm about the place of the accident again to confirm that newspaper didn't really mention about Ranchit's death in the accident.

"Have you gone mad Inder?" Jhihari couldn't hide anger on Inder's question. "You were also with me when I picked up my rickshaw locked in the chain with a pole" he remined Inder.

"Don't get angry my brother. I know that but there is no mention of *bhaiya* in this newspaper or perhaps in other newspapers." Inder explained the ground of his foolish question.

Jhihari became thoughtful on that issue. He was not sure that the news would appear in the newspaper. He didn't bother as he was not aware what difference that would make in his and Sachi's life.

The people got disappointed as they found that nobody listened to the plight of the poor othen than the government. Politics and election times make other people to look into plight only to highlight the dark side. Inder didn't speak much. He just wanted to know what had happened.

"Do you have mam's contact number?" Inder asked Jhihari.

"Yes I have got the number. But it is too early in the morning" Jhihari reminded Inder.

"Niranjan, You need to manage here I will go to mam with Jhihari in day time." Inder turned to Niranjan who was behaving very responsibly since he heard about *bhaiya's* death. Neither Inder nor Jhihari could find any reason for Niranjan's transformation. He didn't take single dose of Gutkha since then.

Inder kept an eye on the time. For him it was very difficult to wait. Around nine O' clock Inder and Jhihari left for the hospital where Ranchit *bhaiya's* body would be handed over to them. Chandrika also told them that she would come there at three. Jhihari found rickshaw handy at that critical juncture. He unlocked the rickshaw to ride.

They reached the hospital at around ten O' clock. They found themselves to wait in the transplant department of the hospital. Chandrika also reached to complete the formalities of the case.

"How are you Jhihari?" Chandrika asked Jhihari. She smiled at Inder.

Jhihari couldn't reply but looked at Chandrika with disappointment in his eyes.

"There is news about the accident in the newspapers. But no newspaper mentions that my brother has died in the accident. Some big man in his big car hit my brother and ran over him." Jhihari said in anguish.

"Is that? How come?" Chandrika also shared her surprise that no newspaper has mentioned Ranchit's death in accident on the road. She rang up Vasundhara to talk on that issue.

"I don't know Jhihari how this has happened?" Chandrika said to Jhihari. Inder gave Hindi newspaper to her.

"There is a mention of an old man and his son in the newspaper." Inder said pointing out on the news in the lower half of the first page of the newspaper.

"I agree with you Inder" Chandrika took on Inder's concern over the issue. "May be that car is owned by some highly rich man who has managed to exclude your brother's death in the news covering the accident on the road" she said reading the news in the paper. "The rascal has escaped clean" she talked to herself.

"Actually one old man was also hit by the car before that mad fellow ran over your brother. His son had taken the old man to the hospital when we reached the accident site" she continued. "People told us about that" she added. "Now no eye witness" she lamented. She cried. She managed her disappointment over the issue.

Jhihari got some solace when he saw her eyes in tears.

"What to do now, if we claim that Ranchit died in that accident we need to prove it first. Then also nothing much can be done. Your *bhabhi* may get few thousands rupees as compensation." Chandrika said. "That too she may have tough time to prove that she is Ranchit's widow" she shared her pessimism. "That rascal may manage his escape" she continued on her pessimism. "I am sorry Jhihari. I am sorry Inder. Not much can be done now" she solaced them. "I have arranged for the ambulance to take your brother's body to your place" she assured.

"Don't worry Jhihari. Don't worry Inder. We will declare here on the board that your brother Ranchit died in an accident on the road but he was reborn in at least in five patients by donating his organs which are still alive. We will make a big hoarding to declare that here in front of this hospital" she assured both of them. Jhihari and Inder agreed with her and left the place to complete the formalities to get Ranchit's body for last rites.

Chandrika led them to the surgery department where Ranchit's body was lying in a rack made for the purpose. The surgeon came to congratulate her as the organs from Ranchit's body which could be donated had successfully been taken out. Few of them had successfully transplanted in to the patients to give them new life.

Ward boy with a stature, led them to the mortuary to take Ranchit's body. Ranchit's body had lot of stitches on many places on his body with sharp cut of the marked area. Inder pulled Jhihari holding his shoulders as he was to cry again. Inder waved for the ward boy to push off to take the body in the ambulance. Jhihari embraced Inder as he could not stop crying. Inder made Jhihari's head comfortable on his shoulder. The ward boy pushed the body to place on the stature fixed in the ambulance. The driver came to Chandrika for instructions. She drew up some lines on a plain paper and wrote some text to make map for the driver of the van. Driver wished if some person could come with him in the ambulance. She looked at Jhihari and Inder. Inder volunteered for the journey to Ghazipur with Ranchit's dead body.

Inder sat on the long seat parallel to the one on which Ranchit's dead body was laid. Inder looked at Jhihari when the ward boy closed the door. Driver took the final nod from the in-charge of the mortuary and Chandrika to move. Jhihari also started to move on his rickshaw.

The ambulance was running towards Ghazipur on the highway. Inder looked at the mark of a ring in the middle finger of Ranchit's right hand. The ring was removed during operations. He remembered that the ring was made up by beating black horse's shoe nail to keep ill effects of the Saturn away from the body. There was no need to have that ring on his body as all the ill effects were there to stay with the deceased. Inder analyzed if any ill effect was kept away from Ranchit. Inder looked at last few years of Ranchit's life. Last four-five years had been very disappointing in Ranchit's life. Ranchit got tuberculosis years back and got treated twice under direct observed treatment.

Black horse shoe nail ring in the middle finger made the situation worse as Ranchit couldn't maintain his health afterwards. If that black horse shoe nail ring had bettered on Ranchit's body then it was Ranchit's death. He got freed him from all the miseries. The Saturn might have impacted Ranchit's life to relieve him from all the miseries of life. The mark left on the finger in Ranchit's hand was there to tell that all story. Little hardness in the finger moved that. Inder thought Ranchit *bhaiya* was getting alive slowly. He looked at his *bhaiya's* face then he got scared as Ranchit's lips got tightened as if his *bhaiya* was smiling. "*Bhaiya*!" Inder shouted in fear. The driver of the ambulance took the vehicle to the side on the road to stop. He turned back and peeped in the window to find Inder was scared as if he had seen some ghost in Ranchit's dead body.

"This is the reason we don't recommend any blood relation with the dead body in the vehicle" driver of the ambulance said. "Don't worry sir, your friend's brother is no more now" he said.

Inder didn't get convinced. He remembered those days when Ranchit used to look like live skeleton due to lack of treatment for his tuberculosis.

It was only after direct observed treatment that helped Ranchit to improve upon his health.

"Inder! *kya hua?*" Jhihari waved his hand peeping from the rear window. He also reached following the ambulance. "*Daro mat. Bhaiya ab kuchh nahin kahenge*" Jhihari assured Inder when he saw Inder was scared. Jhihari wiped his face with his sleeves. He wiped his wet eyes so that Inder shouldn't see.

Inder kept quiet. The driver started the ambulance to move fast. Jhihari also rode his rickshaw. The ambulance reached at the gate of the landfill area. Seeing the vehicle the entry in-charge got alerted to wait for the vehicle to enter in the landfill area. He then realized that it was an ambulance not the municipality vehicle. Women in the jhuggi started crying as one boy went inside to inform them about the arrival of Ranchit's dead body. Inder got down from the ambulance to wait for Jhihari.

Inder went inside the jhuggi to look for some more sheets to spread on the ground. The rag spread on the ground was not sufficient to accommodate more people. More people than previous day were expected to join them for cremation. Children including Madan, Maithili, etc., who assembled around the ambulance went to different jhuggies to inform their elders about arrival of Ranchit's dead body.

Niranjan also came from other jhuggi with a big bundle of old carpet like sheets. With the help of children he rolled out rags to make more space for people to mourn.

The driver of the ambulance looked at the gate where from Jhihari would come. He then looked at his wrist watch. He looked at the waste hill of Delhi's filth in the landfill area and covered his nose with his hanky. He could afford to do that as he would be out of its influence in few minutes otherwise in worst case of carrying rotten dead might have been more stinking ones. He showed signs of impatience which Inder had to ignore as the only option. Jhihari appeared on the gate to the landfill area. He sighed of relief. He came to the backside to open the rear door of the ambulance.

"Jhihari *bhai*, let's get the body from the ambulance" the driver opened his arms.

"*Haan*" Jhihari replied. He got down from the rickshaw.

The driver, Inder, Jhihari, Niranjan all held Ranchit's body to bring down on the ground. They walked few steps to keep the body on the rag spread. Once again, the women's cries inside the jhuggi went high. The women came out. The cries were on the peak when Sachi wrapped herself over Ranchit's body. Other women huddled the body. Later they all sat to mourn with Sachi over her husband's death.

Jhihari thanked the driver with folded hands for the cooperation so far.

The driver went to the driving seat. He could understand that they were the people who lived on low level of hand-to-mouth survival. He didn't expect any reward or tip from Jhihari that he gets from the rich people. He gave a hundred rupees note to Jhihari to mark his funeral contribution to Ranchit's unwanted and uncalled end. *"Dena to humein aapko chahiye tha bhaiya hamare pass kuchh hein nahin hamari majboori ke siva"* Jhihari hesitated to take the note from him. First it appeared to Jhihari that he was hinting for tip for ambulance service. Later Jhihari could understand that it was not the case.

"Chandrika mam had given me three thousand rupees for funeral rites." Jhihari told the driver.

"Please take this to honor your brother with a shawl on my behalf" the driver insisted. He got down from the driving seat and came stood at the feet of Ranchit body with folded hands to pay the last honor.

Jhihari took the note as the matter of last honor paid to his brother.

"Tumhare bhaiya and tumne mil ke bahut bada kaam kiya hei" he complimented Jhihari's for his great decision to go for Ranchit's organ donation. Nobody could expect that he would have donated his organs to make dying patients to live more. He praised Jhihari and took driving seat in the ambulance to leave for the hospital. Inder and Niranjan joined Jhihari to sendoff the driver.

Jhihari took his place on the ground to mourn with the people. He handed over the one thousand rupees to Inder which he got from Chandrika after they left with the body in the ambulance.

Inder took rupees and handed over the money to an elderly man who wanted to accompany Inder to buy things which were required for funeral rites according to traditions. If something specific to their village or region that was desired to follow the traditions of their region Inder was willing to bring that to give full respect as part of the last rites. With few other willing persons, they both left for buying them from the market close to Ghazipur.

"This was the worst thing that has happened in my life since my childhood." Niranjan said. He was talking to Jhihari who hosted morning people came from different jhuggies in the area.

"May be you are right Niranjan. But bad things happen to us ten times in our daily life." Jhihari agreed and explained deep sense of disappointment that was taking roots in him.

Niranjan accumulated lot of anger since previous day, could control himself. *"Kal se mera khoon khaul raha hei"* he said as if he wanted to take revenge.

"Nothing will happen if your blood boils" Jhihari counseled Niranjan on futility of the poor's anger. "One day your blood will boil you to your end" he cautioned Niranjan.

"That means we will keep on doing all these menial work of picking up from the waste and to clean the debris and waste that people create. People will keep running their vehicle over us" Niranjan said in utter anger.

"I have just said your anger would not yield anything" Jhihari again scolded him.

Inder with other people came back with things required for Ranchit's cremation. Other people waiting for them took charge to make a bier for Ranchit's body to be tied with. One man kept two six feet long bamboos parallel to each other at distance of one and half feet. Other man placed across two feet long six pieces of bamboo on the bamboos kept in parallel. Third man picked a hammer to fix a nail crossing point of each piece. Husk was placed on the structure over which a sheet was spread. So carrier for Ranchit was ready for his last journey.

Mourning women once again gone high on their cries as elder people were waiting to place Ranchit's body on the bier. Sachi cried at the peak of her voice as Jhihari held the feet of Ranchit's body in his hands. Sachi once again wrapped herself with Ranchit's body to resist his departure from her life. Other women got the communication and held Sachi's hands and dragged her, so that, Ranchit's body could be placed on the bier. Jhihari, Inder, Niranjan and elder people lifted the body to get that cleaned with milky water. They tore down the clothes off Ranchit's body and wrap that in new white cotton cloth. Then they lifted and placed Ranchit's white clad body on the bier.

Next they wrapped the body in with shawl and tied that with thread of yellow and red colors. They tied every small piece of bamboo tied with these threads. Now other men came one by one to cover Ranchit's body with a shawl to mark their last honor with folded hands at Ranchit's feet. In the midst of women's cries all the males lifted Ranchit's body tied on the bier for the last journey to cremation ground in Ghazipur.

All the boys of the jhuggies of the area took one or two twigs to follow the elders who were taking Ranchit's body on their shoulders. When they reached the cremation ground Jhihari gave another thousand and five hundred rupees to buy the wooden logs for funeral pyre. They cleaned the platform to prepare funeral pyre by stacking the wooden logs. Ranchit's body was placed on the logs to be covered by other logs.

Finally the funeral pyre was ready for Ranchit's body to be cremated with rites. The funeral pyre caught fire as Jhihari touched the burning charcoal pieces wrapped in husk. They all kept waiting for the body to burn to ashes completely. All people including Jhihari, Inder, Niranjan, etc. left the place after Ranchit's body got burnt completely. They went to water taps to clean their hands and faces to come back to their jhuggies in the landfill area.

At home, people came with simple food of dal and chapatis for Jhihari, Sachi, Inder, Niranjan and other close ones to the family.

"Niranjan! Take this key and chain for rickshaw. Now you take this rickshaw to make your living" Jhihari gave chain, lock, and key to Niranjan.

"What will you do?" Niranjan asked before taking them.

"I am not sure what I will do" Jhihari said in sad tone.

"Has the madam assured you about any other job?" Inder asked Jhihari finishing his grub.

"That also I don't know" he replied with deep disappointment set in him as if his life was also over.

Inder didn't ask Jhihari. Perhaps Inder knew that when someone lost some relation which one was not prepared to lose, then disillusionment from life might come as its effect. Though Ranchit was not that young that Jhihari's life would be dependent on Ranchit's existence. Ranchit was also not that old too that Jhihari could accept his sudden and cruel demise. Niranjan also didn't disappoint Jhihari and took the key, lock and chain. That was the rickshaw which Ranchit got prepared. Tears had washed Niranjan eyes. He continuously looked at the rickshaw for minutes perhaps with new eyes with new outlook towards his life.

Inder was sitting next to Sachi to discuss out what family should take on as future course. Jhihari was also sitting in front of Sachi to participate in the discussion. Ranchit's phone which Jhihari gave to Inder rang up.

"Hello" Inder picked the call.

"Hello, who is speaking?" voice from the other side asked.

"I am Ishwar Jain speaking from Ghazipur colony. Inder spoke to me from this number" Ishwar Jain said from the other end of the call.

"Sir, I am Inder only, this is *bhaiya's* phone which Jhihari has left with me" Inder said.

"That's very unfortunate what has happened to your brother" Ishwar Jain said. "Will this number remain with you or what?" he wanted to know.

"I am not sure whether this number will be with me or not" Inder clarified.

"Today children have not reached yet. What has happened?" Ishwar asked Inder about the children who work in his scrap factory. "When are you joining us back?" he asked.

Jhihari wanted to know whether Inder had to go to Ishwar Jain's scrap factory or not.

Inder didn't want to leave Jhihari alone.

"You join Jain *Sahab* in the factory" Jhihari requested Inder.

"*Sahab*, Inder and other children are coming in one hour." Jhihari replied taking mobile phone from Inder's hand. He could hear in feeble voice what Ishwar was talking to Inder.

"Are you Jhihari?" Ishwar Jain asked as he differentiated the voice from Inder's.

"*Haan Sahab*" Jhihari answered.

"*Bahut bura hua tumhare bhai ke sath*" he sympathized Jhihari on his brother's death. Ishwar Jain talked for few more minutes mourning over Ranchit's death before he ended the call.

"I think I am here with Niranjan. You should go to Jain *sahab's* place" Jhihari suggested looking at Niranjan and the jhuggi.

"Poor people don't have any choice" Inder agreed with Jhihari.

"Take Madan, Maithili, Mahabi and Uttar with you" Jhihari asked Inder.

Inder nodded.

"Niranjan, can you call these children?" Jhihari asked.

Niranjan left the mourning place to call them.

"Madan . . . Maithili . . . Uttar . . ." Niranjan shouted at a turn twenty meters away from the mourning place. Madan and Maithili came running to Niranjan.

"Just call Mahabi and Uttar also" Niranjan asked Madan coming out with Maithili. Madan went back to other jhuggies to call Mahabi and Uttar.

"What is there? What will I do?" Maithili asked Niranjan.

"Inder will tell you" Niranjan said. He joined them back.

"Maithili, you go to Jain *Sahab*" Jhihari replied as Inder kept quiet. "All of you have to go there" he said.

"*Theek hei* Jhihari *bhaiya*" Maithili said in sad tone. He wanted to make off. He looked at Inder for agreement. He thought that Inder also didn't want to go that day.

"Get ready! Come here to go with Inder" Jhihari instructed Maithili. He was getting molded in Ranchit's character. He felt responsible to keep the routine after Ranchit.

"Ok" Maithili agreed with same sadness turned back to come prepared. Madan also came with Mahabi, and Uttar.

"Get ready! Come here to go with Inder" Maithili asked children facing all children coming to the mourning place. All children became sad.

"What's going on Jhihari? Why these children come and go?" Sachi asked. She came out hearing many voices.

"Nothing, Jain *Sahab* called up Inder for work" Jhihari said.

"Mourning goes at least for three-four days for everyone" Sachi said. "Inder, didn't you tell Jain *Sahab*?" she turned to Inder.

"*Bhabhi*, poor people don't have choices" Jhihari replied. "They need to do what they are ordered to do" he added to complete his opinion. "Jain *Sahab* asked for the children to come but they will not go without Inder. He didn't ask for Inder" he explained.

Sachi looked at Inder who kept quiet.

"*Bhabhi*, otherwise also these children and Inder have to go for work in a day or two" Jhihari said.

The children had come back. Inder took them with him and walked out towards colony in Ghazipur village. The children looked at cars, trucks, lorries, autos, bikes passing them under bridge of the highway. After crossing the highway holding Uttar's hand in his hand he chose the way to factory. Inder opened the gate reaching the scrap factory where Jain was waiting for them.

"*Namaste* sir" Inder greeted Jain standing at the gate. The children followed.

"*Namaste*" Jain replied Inder and smiled at children entering in the working area.

"That has been very bad Inder" Jain expressed his condolence over Ranchit's death. "He was much younger than me would have lived longer life if the driver had not been mad." Ishwar Jain sympathized.

"Sir, poor people get older in their middle age for many reasons." Inder agreed and presented his own explanation. He had joined to resume his work and went inside the room where account books were kept.

"License must be cancelled for these boys who drive big cars so fast for nothing but to lose control and take others' lives." Ishwar Jain paid his critic part on rash driving by the youth of the day.

Ishwar's sympathy brought tears in Inder's eyes.

"I understand how sad it is for you" Ishwar Jain further sympathized "He was like your father figure who guided you reaching at this age and success" he added.

Inder thought Ishwar held him successful while that money changer and those policemen in the night on the way back from the Airport had held him simply a rag picker. Might be Jain thought him to be a rag picker but he could see how he had gone to an international conference. That might be a success from Ishwar's perspective.

"Inder there is no hurry. You go to the room, take bath, and come for work" Ishwar Jain stopped Inder who was going inside the factory. Death and mourning taboos might be few reasons for Ishwar to behave like that.

"Ok sir" Inder looked at his clothes and got what Ishwar Jain was asking. He left the factory and took shorter path in the streets to reach his room faster. He knocked the gate of Jain's house. Bhumi opened the gate. She got surprised to see him. She felt like hugging him at the gate itself. She looked around in the street and restrained herself.

"Papa talked to *maa* about the road accident in which your brother had died." Bhumi said in sad tone. "I felt very bad. I am very sad about whole of the episode" she grieved to experience that she was one with him.

Inder didn't say anything.

"Where is Jhihari? I think he has to be there at home" Bhumi asked Inder.

She followed him when he moved to the room and opened to settle on the folding. She put her hand on Inder's shoulder to convey deep communication of her grief. Inder saw a waterline in her eyes which was sufficient to bring him in tears. She held his head in her bosoms to sooth him in his sobs. They moved apart after feeling each other's beats. He picked his clothes from almirah to take bath.

"Bhumi, Bhumi" her mother also came out to meet Inder.

"Yes *maa*! I am here in the room" she replied.

"Inder, it is very bad. I feel very bad about sudden demise of your brother in the road accident." her mother also sympathized with him. "The driver who ran his car over your brother will meet his fate one day" her mother cursed the driver of the car.

"Aunty *ji*, worst thing is that no newspaper has mentioned that *bhaiya* died in car accident on the road." Inder said in acceptance of her grieving message. "The newspapers mention about another casualty of an old man but not about *bhaiya*" he sobbed again.

"May be car fellow is highly rich and must have managed with the police to hide this fact" her mother solaced Inder. "By revealing your brother's death the driver of the car may be tried for ignorance murder and to pay compensation to your *bhabhi*. *Beta* rich people manage to hide these facts of their uncaught and undeclared crimes which let them run scot free" her mother added to extend her sympathy to him.

"I heard some knock at the gate. Bhumi came out to open the gate to find you coming after one day. Bhumi's father told me about the accident and your brother's death in the accident. I felt very bad" Bhumi's mother explained in detailed what was discussed in the house previous day. "I have to bring vegetables from the market" she added. "Bhumi, *beta* Inder may have to go for work. Please leave him to get ready for work" her mother reminded her to leave the room. "Come with me to buy vegetables" her mother called again and moved out.

"Yes *maa*, I am coming in few minutes" she assured her mother.

"Inder, some Surya Shekhar from America rang up on my phone. He wanted to talk to you" she said. She updated Inder about a phone call from a stranger.

"From America? How come?" surprised Inder asked her after her mother left. "I remember him very well" he recalled the name. "He is the same person who has a house in Mayur Vihar. I am using the same address in my passport" he added.

"How come he got my number Inder?" she asked.

"I don't know" Inder squinted brows.

"I don't know Inder. Might be possible that I wrote my number in the email to Mr. Hwaib" she recalled. "How come Hwaib gave my number to him?" she wanted to solve that puzzle.

"May be he has taken your number from Mr. Hwaib himself" he anticipated.

"He was in a hurry he didn't listen what I told him" she said.

Inder shrugged as he didn't have any idea.

"It was my mistake. I wrote my number to Mr. Hwaib to call you up between nine and ten O' clock if he needs to talk to you" she regretted. "Inder, you are running with bad luck nowadays. I wish this person should not ask you the price of providing you address for your passport" she looked contrite.

"Bhumi, you please don't talk like that" he pleaded. "People over there are not that mean. Moreover, they earn in dollars so they can afford to be big hearted" he said what he wanted to believe about Indians abroad.

"This is what strikes to my mind at the moment" she said. She appeared not to be convinced with Inder's logic as she had attended the call and knew how that man talked to her. "I wish what you are saying should be true" she solaced Inder.

"Did you tell her about the accident?" Inder asked Bhumi.

"No, I didn't know about the accident at that time" she said. "He may call you up today evening" she informed him.

"Your mother is right. She might have talked to your father" Inder said to Bhumi. "I have to go for work" he added on cautious note. He took his clothes to the bathroom. She looked at him, smiled. She left the room before her mother might call again to go for buying vegetables. Inder went into bathroom to get ready for work. Bhumi's smile instilled a sense of happiness in him even in that sad moment of loss. The loss of his brother. The loss of his father figure.

Kul Vilas made it large with Maker's Mark in his one hand having a hundred mm Dunhill International embedded in his fingers and cap of the bottle in the other hand. He didn't come to the office with intentions to keep his hands busy to make it large at eleven in the forenoon. Last week he sent project estimates which he prepared over two weeks to Hwaib. He prepared estimates with Anang's assistance. That day he expected a reply after review of his estimates for the survey project. Hwaib had replied to his estimates with properly analyzed review feedback. He gulped from the large to light up another hundred mm Dunhill International. He again opened up the inbox of his mail account and read every word of Hwaib's mail carefully. His concentration got disturbed by Anang's coughing in a chair with smoke passing by.

Anang sitting in front was in no mood to have hundred mm Dunhill International so he coughed as naïve for smoke and drink, perhaps to draw Kul Vilas' attention.

"When did you come?" Kul Vilas asked Anang who was still coughing. Anang looked at hundred mm Dunhill International between his fingers which got over. He threw it in designer dust bin under his table.

"Well! I came when you were so engrossedly focused on the screen of your laptop." Anang updated Kul Vilas on his arrival in the room. "The hundred mm long stick had been showering welcome smoke over my body for last few minutes." Anang pointed at Kul Vilas' fingers where a hundred mm Dunhill International was stuck in between. "Stuck was stuck" he thought and preferred waiting for Kul's attention.

Kul Vilas looked at his hand. He took a tissue paper to wipe the embers lying near his hand on the table into the bin. They reminded him about the cinders that Vaibhav caused flaking on his shirt. He was happy they were not hot like that day nor they fell on his designer denim which had bullet burnt bruises.

"What happened?" Anang worried for Kul Vilas. "Is there some dying-hard sweetheart on the screen of the laptop?" he immediately completed the question to make Kul speak.

"He is not sweet heart" Kul Vilas said. "He wants us to sweat hard and harder and hardest in this project" he added immediately.

"That's why he is capable to make you *devdas* at eleven in the noon?" Anang asked. "May be me too, so soon" he laughed. "Are you OK?" his laughter asked as he raised his brows. "I didn't know that you have changed your gender preferences?" he again cracked a joke to make Kul laugh. He himself laughed without knowing that project took Kul's head if not his heart. Dollars mattered. Travel mattered. Champagne mattered. Same plane mattered. Same plane of the domain expertise was the matter.

"This is not the time to joke" Kul Vilas wanted Anang's focus to get the project in their control.

"What happened? Is matter that serious?" Anang asked.

"This is an email from Hwaib" Kul Vilas turned the laptop so that Anang also could read. He gulped from the large in his hand.

"Thanks to the French people they didn't make your Maker's Mark like cigarette in your hand. You felt like a man" Anang commented looking at the glass in Kul hand.

"Who says?" Kul Vilas answered in question.

"Have they made it like that?" Anang took it as surprise.

"Yes, all the wines are volatile in nature" Kul Vilas replied.

"Is that?" Anang kept his curiosity on.

"All the alcoholic drinks are more or less volatile in nature" Kul took sipped from his large.

"That's the reason our courts are not accepting the statement under the influence of alcohol. It makes memory volatile." Anang concluded. "System also boot by nonvolatile memory" he laughed.

"That I am not sure why our court here or elsewhere in the world don't accept that all." Kul Vilas stated indifferently.

"Wanna yo large?" Kul asked. He took another sip before keeping back his glass.

"Thanks my dear! You have not forgotten the etiquette class of your school teacher" Anang commented on late offer from Kul to make a large from Maker's Mark for him. "Remember our manners teacher? She was . . . aah she was . . . she was . . ." his lower lip got curved. He was preparing his horn till his large was served.

"I am much bothered about the survey and project" Kul got apologetic in the context of manners' teacher.

"No dear" Anang made his comment light for Kul Vilas. "I said it just like that. Otherwise also I don't want to take it at eleven in the noon" he excused holding Kul right.

Kul Vilas still made him a large.

"Why are you so much bothered about the project?" Anang asked. He looked at Kul's laptop. "What makes you bothered so much about this project?" he wanted to know why Kul was so disappointed by that mail from Hwaib.

"Did you read the mail?" Kul asked Anang. He gulped from the glass. He finished his large.

"Honestly speaking, I haven't read it yet" Anang disclosed.
"I know that" Kul accepted.
Then, Anang read the email.

Dear Kul,
Greetings!

Thanks for your communication on the project estimates. I have referred them to the domain experts here. They will mail me review feedback in couple of days. I also have gone through the estimates that you have prepared. I have observed that estimates prepared need improvements as they lack many of the activities which are specific to the logistic parts of the survey work.

Of course problems of coordination are ignored in preparation of estimates. Problems and challenges of coordination in Indian context are quite considerable factors which most of us ignore while preparing project plan or estimates. Never mind I also would have not considered them had I not been challenged by coordination issues in my earlier projects.

The list counting on work packages and activities that you include is not exhaustive. Up to some extent I agree with you that they cannot be so exhaustive like not leaving any activity or part of it. It need not be exhaustive up to that extent. At the same time that should not lack sufficiency. That is to be improved in this case.

Where I want to draw your attention in the estimates is to the activities listed in the work packages are not reflecting domain expertise required in the project. My observation is that you have not engaged any domain expert while preparing the project estimates for this survey. It would have been better to engage domain expert who would have prepared proper list of work packages and activities that are to be performed when survey is actually conducted.

Next observation I wish to share with you is that the estimates mentioned for fifty percent of the activities are highly inflated. Magnitude of overall estimates also reflects fifty percent inflation. This is alarming for us to take the project as many activities are yet to be included in your list. In that case overall estimates may again be inflated up to hundred and fifty percent. This is what appeared to me. Fifty percent or more as buffers may not be acceptable to take up this project. When you improve upon your estimates by the time it would have been too late to take up a project. The estimates that you have furnished in last week were supposed to be done two months back. In that case it will be difficult for me to convince other members of the group to take up this survey as per your estimates and planning.

I hope Mr. Sharma is doing well in Delhi. I met him three weeks back when he came here in Washington. Please convey my regards to him.

Warm regards,
Hwaib,
Asia Head,
PHO.

"Hmm, that's really shocking" Anang shook his head to come out of his head.

"This is not the only shock" Kul Vilas brought in another context.

"What is the other part of the shock?" Anang asked. He scratched on the table glass with his glass. He forgot to sip from his large of Maker's Mark.

"Hwaib talked to my Uncle on phone day before yesterday" Kul Vilas updated Anang with new developments. "Hwaib already met my uncle in Washington where he was on official visit" he informed.

"Who? Why to your Uncle?" Anang asked. He asked as if he had forgotten everything of the past story about the project.

"I told you that my uncle works with PHO. He referred my name to Hwaib when considering a project in India" Kul re-informed Anang.

"Why you?" Anang asked.

"Once my uncle visited us at our home then I shared with him in light discussion that I wanted to diversify my portfolio." Kul Vilas said.

"Your uncle is highly sincere *yaar*. You desired about something and he acted upon that so fast." Anang appreciated. He changed his position in the chair.

"He said in that discussion that I must go for international assignments." Kul Vilas recreated the story for Anang.

"Why are you looking so worried about that now?" Anang asked.

"I had expected some international assignment in the fashion industry." Kul Vilas opened up what kept puzzled him. "Not in this" he added looking at the screen of the laptop.

"Then, my dear, why are you worrying?" Anang wanted to relieve him. "You leave this health survey. I have an idea" he came ready with suggestion.

"What idea?" Kul Vilas asked.

"We will open a software company" Anang proposed a new plan.

"*Sala* another unknown domain" Kul Vilas reacted at the idea. "Why software?" he asked. "Neither you nor I know anything about software nor even how software industry works" he added to reinforce the validity of his question.

"To run a company we need to know how to run a company" Anang educated Kul.

"That's it" Kul attempted to get it.

"Why software company then?" Kul Vilas asked. "You can run any company. Why not shoot a porn or roast popcorn for people with their horn in the Dolby where you run that porn" Kul Vilas took his suggestion to the extent of mockery. "That would be a good business" he added further compliment.

"India is having lot of software skill" Anang ignored his mockery to focus on the topic. "If you are able to open an office in the States then you can mint millions of dollars" he added more to Kul Vilas' education. "Another good thing with software is that only effort is the cost" Anang opened up the channel of knowledge.

"*Saale third party software kaun kharidega*, your father?" Kul came again to snub Anang to point out another grey area as they didn't know anything about that all.

"Open source" Anang showed great degree of tolerance to ignore Kul Vilas' rebuffs and snubs.

"*Abe open source ke bhi maintenance source hote hein. Jo bahut paise lete hein*" Kul frowned at Anang. He pointed out another challenge on maintaining open source software. He was not ready to appreciate Anang's hasty and sketchy idea.

"*Kitna kuchh janta hei yaar tu software ke bare mein?*" Anang's wittiness replied. "So, now we have another reason to open a software company" he added to reinforce his reason.

"To have an office in the States, you need to invest in millions first" Kul Vilas wanted to remind him as if Anang had forgotten. "My dear, that too in dollars" he added. He rubbed his ears again and again.

"Once you have good software then you can really mint money. Rather you mint dollars" Anang deduced.

"You want to start from the States itself?" Kul Vilas asked.

"No, not that way" Anang wanted to make it real for Kul Vilas.

"Then what way it is if it is not that way?" Kul Vilas attempt to puzzle him.

"You know when you have some idea on which if you develop software then you can really mint money" Anang said.

"Boss I don't have such idea on which we can mint money." Kul Vilas said cynically.

"You don't have I have" Anang declared thumping the table with right fist.

"Tell me, what's that idea?" Kul Vilas asked him.

"The idea is so great that you will jump out from your chair" Anang claimed.

"Is that?" Kul Vilas was surprised with Anang's confidence. He jumped from his chair to make a mockery and added "*Aise.*"

"Yes boss" Anang voiced his confidence ignoring Kul Vilas' mockery part again.

"What is that idea?" Kul Vilas didn't want to suppress curiosity.

"First you promise that you are going to float a software company to develop the software based on this idea." Anang wanted to secure his future for his idea if not the future of his idea. That was opening a software company.

"Why don't you ask your father to open a software company for you for developing that idea?" Kul Vilas said.

"My father doesn't understand me" Anang revealed beating his left palm with his right fist. "He says I must focus on exports business only" he added further pushing a nail of his finger into the nail of another finger. "You also don't believe me?" he asked Kul Vilas looking for his 'yes' to explain his idea.

"No Anang! It is not like that" Kul Vilas assured him of his confidence. "However, business has its own rules and ethics, friendship can help understanding of business but cannot guarantee of partnership." he explained what was there in his mind. He looked at the screen of his laptop.

"Are you reading something" Anang asked Kul Vilas who was still staring at the screen of his laptop.

"No, I am not reading on the screen" Kul replied. He came back into the talk in the blank of the mind from blank of the mind. Anang tokk him as reading on the laptop.

"Tell me, what is your idea?" Kul Vilas asked Anang.

"Shall I tell you my idea before the deal?" Anang raised his collar.

"Smart boy" Kul Vilas joked.

"My dear Kul, my idea focuses on the solution for today's traffic in Indian cities like Delhi where vehicles are growing at the pace faster than our population growth. It is to establish a warning system of communication by dialing registration number of the vehicle. People in vehicles can ease out themselves by dialing registration number of the other vehicles to communicate warning like messages." Anang delivered first installment of his idea. He looked for Kul Vilas to gasp with surprise or jumping from the chair. But it didn't happen.

"Are you listening?" Anang checked with Kul Vilas who maintained pin drop silence. Kul Vilas remained still. He didn't wow in excitement over the idea. That discouraged Anang.

"I'm" Kul Vilas responded.

"At present it is the traffic police who are responsible to interrupt and control the vehicle when they see that as violation of the traffic rules. My system is to provide some autonomy to the car owners on the road stuck in traffic" he explained genuine need of such system in his second installment of wow kind of idea.

"What do you want to communicate to the other vehicle ahead or in side with yours in the traffic?" Kul Vilas asked him doubting the need of the solution.

"Like 'You are not driving with traffic', 'You are disturbing the traffic', 'The tyre of your vehicle is punctured', 'Your vehicle is creating hell lot of pollution', 'Mind your own lane', 'You are interfering ahead on in my lane' are few examples." Anang explained that without any pen and paper.

"You are assuming that warning system by blowing horn is likely to go away?" Kul Vilas shared his ideas.

"In coming future, horn of vehicles on the roads will be banned as people will be fed up with noise pollution. In that case we will be contributing to make India a great state" he presented n^{th} installment of his idea.

Kul Vilas yawned. He pretended as if his head fell on the table.

"Is it not interesting you?" Anang asked.

"How will that work?" Kul Vilas replied a question to keep awake.

"Your mobile phone will be enabled to dial vehicle's registration number." Anang said as if he came with an ultimate solution. "Solution of the age that needed cutting edge technology to cut the pockets of the consumers to cut the traffic apart to avoid cut to skin, cut to bone, cut to bonnet, cut to . . . The call is to land up at the registered mobiles number with the vehicle" he continued the explanation.

"*Yaar*, your assumption is dangerous that vehicle is driven by owner ready with the phone in the car." Kul Vilas warned Anang about the basic premises of the research to be taken up. "What about the taxi drivers? Chauffeur-driven car, relative's car, Borrowed car" Kul Vilas had many questions.

"There will also be a car phone to receive warning messages" Anang suggested a solution in answering the question.

"Where will the call land, on mobile phone or car phone?" Kul Vilas asked.

"The call will land up at car phone and mobile phone with number registered with transport office. Both" Anang explained complexity of the system network.

"What about vehicle registered in other cities in India?" Kul Vilas asked further clarifications.

"There will be centralized database connecting all the transport offices. Registration numbers of the vehicles registered in other cities will have connectivity through transport offices." Anang came ready with details of the transport network.

"What about the consulate vehicles?" Kul Vilas asked.

"In all such cases car phone will be instrumental to communicate the messages." Anang said. He started to get puzzled as he did not think much about it when he took up to develop as a solution.

"In that scenario all existing vehicles will not be able to communicate these messages." Kul Vilas clarified. "They may hit these vehicles. What will you do in that case? We have largest number of vehicles in our Delhi" he posed another aspect.

"Existing vehicles may get fitted this car phone as additional accessory" Anang came with n^{th} solution. He thought to appreciate Kul Vilas as he did not think so many cons of the idea before. He devised many answers on the fly.

"What about motor bikes where you will install the system?" Kul Vilas asked Anang. "Many times we have difficulty because of bikers. Being in their own world they expect you to drive keeping them safe on the road" Kul Vilas added another questions to make Anang to work properly on requirements in the problem domains.

"You are having many doubts" Anang got irritated and surprised too. He was surprised on queries put forward. "Are you not promoting my idea?" Anang asked. His tolerance to ignore Kul Vilas' mockery was also on the verge of being disappeared.

"It is not that I am against the idea" Kul Vilas clarified.

"A solution can work only when there is really a problem. In this case it is may be a solution but there is no problem perceived as such. And perception is the reality. And the reality is to be presented from popular perspective to make money. To mint money" Kul Vilas took his turn to educate Anang.

"Your idea is rather a future not the solution" Kul Vilas commented on Anang's idea and named it as transport network phone.

"Whatever you want to call it you call it" Anang agreed.

"You are proposing transport network phone without having transport network or transport phone network" Kul Vilas concluded Anang's idea on the phone. "Shall I call it 'transphone' or what?" he became enthusiastic about the future of the idea.

"That means you are not supporting my idea" Anang concluded on Kul Vilas' questions and doubts.

"No it is not that way" Kul Vilas clarified.

"I can see its possibility only when there will be fiber connectivity among the transport offices of India. The last mile of the network is to be wireless for physical interface for car phone or mobile phone." Kul Vilas added value to the solution. "The last mile would also be hierarchical" he added.

"At present I don't have a 'go ahead' for your idea as we alone cannot have transport network. India needs to have all the data centralized to have such kind of dedicated network for specific purposes." Kul Vilas concluded on the idea.

"Why not present?" Anang asked.

"Ok! Tell me, where is the need for this solution?" Kul Vilas asked.

"At present you cannot tell the person ahead you in the car to mind his speed or driving style or vehicles health as you don't have the number of person who is driving a car ahead on the road." Anang advocated for the present need of the system.

"For that you have horn in the vehicle" Kul reminded Anang. "For that, why should so humongous investment be there?" he wanted to close the analysis part of the idea.

"Why are you bringing the entire discussion back to square one?" Anang wanted to blame Kul Vilas in disappointment.

"I think your father really could not understand you" Kul sympathized with Anang.

"I did not get you" Anang asked. He expressed as if he was confused.

"You live in future and your father loves the legacy and luxuries of past and his privileged position in the exports. So he doesn't believe in you" Kul Vilas extended his sympathy to Anang.

"Means you are reminding me that my father is right?" Anang asked.

"No, I didn't say that" Kul said.

"Then please make another large for me now. The entire discussion on the idea has frustrated me" Anang took the bottle of Maker's Mark to mark the present fiasco of the futuristic idea development workshop of the two. Kul Vilas asked Keshav to bring another set of two glasses. Anang made two large of Maker's Mark one for him and other for his master who had mastered the sense developing business requirements.

Inder found the kids were sorting out the scrap which got accumulated for two days when came back to resume the work. They were not looking happy in the factory. Ishwar Jain was out for dealing with market customers for scraps.

"*Bachcho yahan aao*" he called them.

"Maithili you are elder" Inder said when they came.

"*Haan, par ye sunte hi nahin*" Maithili replied with complaint that they didn't listen him. He anticipated some complaints from Jain *Sahab* about the work or absence on previous day.

"I am not talking about any complaint" he clarified. "What I see is that you all are sad, right?" he said.

"This is a place where you need to lift some heavy piece of scrap which may fall on your feet" he explained. He wanted to apply what he experienced from Bhumi's smile which instilled happiness.

"*Wo to hei, tab kya karna hei?*" Maithili accepted. "*Hamara kaam ka sharirik kasht se lena dena hei*" he thought on unavoidable physical work.

"If you all are not happy then you may get injuries. For your safety, attention is required. You will be happy only when don't get injuries" he expressed his concerns over their safety. "If your attention is not on your work then you may get hurt in your foot or leg during your work" he explained.

"*Wo to hei*" they agreed. Mahabi and Uttar looked at Inder.

"Few acidic chemicals are also there as part of our work" Inder related the other work to their safety. He was obsessed with safety as he had lost his brother in the road accident. The concept that accidents could take place anywhere any place was driving his action of training the children. Five lives. Mix of adolescents to innocents. "*Kya samjhe*" he intended to confirm what he has imparted to those kids.

"*Apna dhyaan rakhenge*" they spoke simultaneously.

"You cannot take care of yourself if you worry. That can never happen if you are not happy" Inder warned. He wanted them to understand the significance of happiness in their performance.

"Why are you so concerned about happiness today?" Maithili and Mahabi found that strange.

"We take care of these things in day to day work in this factory." Mahabi spoke her mind on safety at work.

"I am telling these things today to you as you got hurt last time" he looked at Uttar.

"Uttar got injured last month" Madan said. He also looked at Uttar who looked burdened with scrap work as if he would go to play if allowed.

"Where is Jagdish?" Inder asked Maithili. "Today he wanted to start working with you" he asked. "Last week I talked to Jain sahab about him" he further added.

"He has spoiled his stomach. He is resting at home. He will come tomorrow" Maithili described about Jagdish's health. "Niranjan didn't call him as he was not part of the team so far" he added.

"No problem he can join from tomorrow" Inder said.

"Why I am saying all this is because I have lost Ranchit *bhaiya* in car accident so we all are sad." Inder disclosed his own state of emotions. "We didn't want to come today so we are not happy" he said in sad tone. He shared his own displeasure and his own unhappiness to train them.

"We also didn't want to come" they said.

"But we are here for work today. Right?" Inder asked them.

They nodded.

"That's why I am telling you about this all. Now, we are landed up in doing our work as normal routine." Inder revealed. They were not happy to come on the next day after cremation.

"Now I can understand why you are telling that all" Madan, Mahabi, and Maithili replied. Uttar smiled.

"We are here for work whether we want to come or not" he deduced to what was their destiny. Destiny of the destitute. "So we need to be happy to carry out our work safely" he added. "If we are sad and thinking about those things which are making us sad may interfere in our work to get it wrong or unsafe to make us wrong or injured" he re-emphasized.

"Ok Inder *bhaiya* we have got that. How caring you are. Now we all are happy" they all assured him. They caressed Uttar who was smiling at them. Their conscious mind became happy by programming. The subconscious mind of theirs was avoiding unanticipated sadness. Sadness that might be an outcome of their bruises with scraps. The sadness that might be brought by an acidic chemical poured on any part of their body.

"Now! Please take care of your work" Inder programmed them to be happy. He was not sure about his own happiness. But he understood the significance of Bhumi's smile recalling of which instilled the sense of happiness in him. Hour passed. They were busy in their work of sorting scraps to keep at their marked place.

Inder opened the gate when Niranjan knocked the gate. Niranjan looked at Jhihari's rickshaw on which Jagdish was sitting on the bench.

"Who is there?" Inder came out of the gate to know Niranjan was looking at whom.

"Jagdish! Are you OK?" Inder asked. "You were having stomach ache. How are you now?" he wanted to know.

"Nothing happened, I had stomach ache" said Jagdish and looked at Niranjan.

"Tell him the truth" Niranjan asked.

"What happened?" Inder wanted to know.

"Jagdish, Shall I tell Inder?" Niranjan looked at Jagdish with big eyes to scold him.

Jagdish didn't speak. He put his head down.

"His mother came in the evening when I was coming here" Niranjan said. "She told that Jagdish was pretending of having stomach ache. When he knew that all other children are here then he told his mother that he was pretending to have stomach ache. Then his mother brought him with stick in her hand" he narrated the story.

"Now, you are here. Are you Ok?" Inder asked Jagdish. "If you keep pretending then nobody will give you work. Like your previous master Jain Sahab may also not allow if you keep bungling" he cautioned Jagdish.

"Theek hei bhaiya, aage dhyaan rakhoonga" Jagdish assured. *"Wahan par paise kam kar diye the to man nahin lag raha tha"* he informed Inder about his previous job.

Inder asked Niranjan to come inside. Niranjan locked the rickshaw to come inside the gate of the factory. Inder noticed Niranjan for last two days that he was not shouting at people not chewing Gutkha not any other nasty act was on his part. His arrogance was also not present as if he had never moved to anger. What the secret for that change was Inder could not understand fully. He could get an idea on the basis of loss. Other reason might be taking responsibilities in the vacuum created by sudden demise of his brother.

Now Niranjan appeared to be more responsible in any work he took up. Niranjan came to take back these boys to the landfill area as Jhihari was busy at home. Jhihari used to come to take back these children earlier.

"Niranjan, you were building another jhuggi nearby" Inder reminded Niranjan. "What happened? Is there any progress?" Inder further asked.

"Had building a jhuggi been that easy then I would have built it much earlier." Niranjan said in sad tone. "Now I realized when Ranchit *bhaiya* is no more to counsel me. He used to take my side against all the odds in most of the matters of livelihood and household. Now I know who he was to me" he revealed. He was aggrieved over Ranchit's death with his cries and sighs and tears in his eyes.

"I am not closely related with him then also he let me live in his jhuggi for years." Niranjan expressed his gratitude towards Ranchit. What was the paradox of life when Ranchit was live Niranjan spent all the time to curse him for taking him to a big city like Delhi from Singbhum. Now Niranjan expressed his gratitude and homage towards Ranchit.

"It is good Niranjan that you have realized that" Inder said.

"It is over for today" the kids came to Inder.

"*Chalein ghar?*" Niranjan asked. Their homes didn't have any houses. They were homes not made of concrete, lintel, or girder house doors, almirah, or fridge or television. Homes of theirs had their parents who might support them or get supported by their might but they also had homes.

Inder looked at the chemical side of the factory. "I will also move after half an hour" he said sending off Niranjan and the kids.

"Will you come home or stay at your room?" Niranjan asked.

"Someone from America would call me up on Bhumi's mobile phone." Inder reminded himself when Niranjan asked. "I have to go to the room today" he said.

Niranjan came out with Maithili, Madan, Mahabi, Jagdish and Uttar to go home. Inder also prepared to close the office. He reached the room following the same street. He knocked at the gate. He expected Bhumi would again come to open the gate with same smile to make him feel live.

"Inder, come?" Ishwar Jain opened the gate. "Have you closed the office properly?" he asked further.

"Yes, thank you sir" Inder moved towards the room.

"Inder" Ishwar Jain called.

"Yes sir" Inder responded.

"Would you go again to the landfill area as mourning days are still on?" Ishwar Jain asked Inder a relevant question from traditional perspective.

"No sir, I will go tomorrow" he replied. Ishwar went inside. Inder got into the outer room.

"After nine O' clock" Bhumi's phone rang up. She looked at the calling number before picking up the call. The call was from same number. Bhumi called up Inder to attend his call. Inder took her mobile to talk.

"Hello" Inder said.

"Sir, how are you sir?" Inder answered.

"How can I forget you? Surya Shekhar Sir" he replied him with humbleness and gratitude. "Because of your permission only I could get your address on my passport" he mentioned the contribution of the person in his life.

"Is that? I have not gone to your house after that" Inder said.

"How can the Board disconnect power supply of your house? You are a non-resident Indian. A non-resident Indian in India is honored everywhere. Otherwise also you are very rich person sir. *Bade aadmi hein*" he said.

"What can I do?" Inder asked.

"I didn't get you, sir" he said. "Rather I got confused" he added.

"Bill! I have to pay the electricity bill?" he got surprised. His surprise came as a burden when he came to know from the non-resident Indian to pay electricity bill for the house in Mayur Vihar address of which he had mentioned in his passport. The house was owned by the non-resident Indian.

"Why are you joking sir? I am extremely poor man" he begged.

"However low is the amount It is huge for me. I would not be able to pay it. Sir, you know it all that I am extremely poor man" he kept begging.

"Sir, may I clear that I did not visit Canada for fun" he got defensive as the other person on the call talked abusive. "Why are you talking like that?" he resisted. "Sir you are confused with some wrong information" he added in hurry to convince him.

"Do you think I should pay electricity bills? When I am not staying there" he put forth his logic.

"Sir, can I talk to Ms. Veronique regarding this?" he asked.

"Why should I not talk to Ms. Veronique about this?" he wanted to know.

"Tell me why should I not talk to Ms. Veronique about this all? It is that great lady who asked you to provide a working address for my passport" he reminded. Where from I will get that amount sir? I don't have money with me" he shared his helplessness.

"The dollars she sent me through you were to meet my expenses there in Canada" he moved into anger. But he didn't want to express his anger to a man who had helped though it was under Veronique's influence.

"Sir, I will change my address in my passport. Don't worry! Who knows? Now I may not be able to go to any foreign country" he replied.

"Sir, why are you talking like that? Why do you want to send me in jail?" he spoke louder.

"Sir, sir, your all savings are going to contribute for community building that is fine. That will not make my pocket filled with money to pay your electricity bill of your house." Inder clarified that he was not going to pay his electricity bills.

"On the passport I am shown as your care-taker in India. For that I must get some salary. Sir, do you know that?" he talked with confidence. Bhumi came back in the verandah outside the room.

"Sir, if I am talking rubbish then do you think you are talking meaningful?" Inder asked Surya Shekhar from America.

"Sir! You are running in financial crisis over there is one thing and I must pay your electricity bill in India is another." Inder showed his resistance to pay the electricity bill.

"Sir, it is not a deal and it is not America. Have mercy on me I am extremely poor man. Even if I agree with you to pay your electricity bill, then also I would not be able to pay that in this life." Inder again begged.

"I would ask Ms. Veronique for monetary help if you are forcing me to pay your electricity bills" he said further.

"Why should I not mention that you have asked me to pay your electricity bill?" Inder stated to Surya Shekhar on the other end of the call. "Sir, you are asking me to pay the price for allowing me to mention your address on my passport" he added.

"Sir, Sir . . . I will talk to Ms. Veronique about this all" Inder said.

"I am not in the capacity to relieve you from your financial crisis there" he stated on his helplessness. "Your financial crisis is in dollars and I am begging here in Ghazipur for paisa not even rupees." Inder explained further so that Surya Shekhar could get sense of his condition.

"Sir, why don't you understand the fact that I am not in a condition to pay your electricity bills? Believe me, day before yesterday my elder brother with whom I had stayed in the landfill area of Ghazipur slum had died in a car accident on the road." Inder disclosed his own calamities and casualties in the family to Surya Shekhar who perhaps was not ready to listen to any of Inder's logic and kept begging in the name of his financial crises.

"What! Compensation! Because he died in the car accident on road!" Inder was surprised the way Surya Shekhar was talking. Surya Shekhar thought Inder might be getting good compensation for Ranchit's death. "Sir, no newspaper has mentioned that fact the big car ran over my brother on the pavement." Inder said. He started crying as he could not control his emotional outburst triggered by talks on the accident. He thought even if compensation had been there then it would be for Sachi *bhabhi* and Jhihari not for him.

"I am telling you the truth. The truth of Indian realities" he cried.

"Sir, six thousand? I am not getting it even working for three months" he disclosed. "Why are you talking like that? How small may be the amount for you. For me it is huge" he expressed his own helplessness. "If I sell myself then also I won't get six thousand rupees to pay your electricity bills" he clarified his worthlessness as the last resort.

Ishwar Jain, who heard entire conversation, also came out in the verandah as Inder was almost shouting. Bhumi was already in the verandah walking restlessly. She was cursing herself why she had mentioned her number in Hwaib email.

"Sir, please have pity on my conditions. I am not able to pay your electricity bills. I will surrender my passport. I don't want any passport. I don't want any visit to foreign country" he busted into tears. He cried for mercy as Surya Shekhar threatened him to complain in the passport office.

To Bhumi and her father, Inder's facial expressions didn't communicate that he was talking to right person. Rather he appeared to be talking to some cheap trader like Shylock from The Merchant of Venice times.

"It is enough, Mister." Ishwar Jain spoke. He took mobile from Inder to deal with the non-resident Indian as he saw Inder's miserable conditions.

"I am Ishwar Jain and Inder works for me" Ishwar briefed about himself. "I came out from my room to see who that powerful person is?" he added.

"Yes, you are powerful to pressurize Inder from such a long distance of fifteen thousand kilometers." Ishwar Jain took a pause. "And I see Inder is begging for his mental peace at this juncture in his life when his brother has died in a car accident" he took control on the discussion.

"You can't claim that you are not pressurizing Inder" Ishwar Jain said.

"Instead of helping a poor man to come up in his life you are extorting money from him. Shame on you" Ishwar Jain warned Surya

Shekhar. "Inder is right when you have shown him as housekeeper providing address for his passport. You must give him salary for housekeeping job at your palace in Delhi" he scolded him in harsh tone.

"No, You can't talk to Inder now. With Inder it is over. You have to talk to me" Ishwar Jain took over. "This is my daughter's mobile phone number. How did you get this number? Inder is simple and honest man that he is talking to you" he warned Surya Shekhar.

"I will teach you the lesson if you keep on pressurizing Inder to pay your electricity bill. Shame on you! Don't you think your house is your house and you should pay the electricity bill even if it is lying vacant?" Ishwar kept continuing the scolding.

"If you keep talking like that Mr. Surya Shekhar I will lodge a complaint with police that you are stalking my daughter on her number which you have got from Internet. You will get the taste of life over there" Ishwar had to talk tough. To Ishwar, Surya Shekhar appeared to be some extortionist sitting in some city infamous for underworld activities.

"Hello! Hello! What happened?" Ishwar Jain asked. "I believe he has ended the call" he said to Inder and handed over the mobile phone to Bhumi.

"Don't worry Inder, you inform the change of address at our address in your passport record" he suggested Inder.

"You have solved this problem. Thank you sir" Inder expressed his gratitude.

"You just change your address in passport" Ishwar directed him.

"Sir, that all is fine. A fresh passport is issued after inquiry and verification on the new address" Inder stated.

"Why are you afraid of that?" Ishwar asked. "If you keep getting afraid, people will take you for a ride" he counseled Inder. "People like Surya Shekhar have only one thing in mind that is dollar and its current value in rupees. That drives them throughout their life. That fellow might have provided you with an address under some compulsion from his colleague. That much I can guess. May be he wanted to show that he was concerned for Indians' wellbeing to get benefited in some way or other. Why he was avoiding informing Ms. Veronique. My anticipation is that he might have taken the number from her or your Mr. Hwaib by promising some further help. Otherwise those people would not have given Bhumi's number to that cheap fellow" he gave long conclusion to complete the counseling. He went inside to his bedroom to sleep. Inder also could sleep because of Ishwar Jain's prowess.

Niranjan rode the rickshaw to ferry the garbage from neighboring colonies to the dumping houses. After Ranchit's death his life got changed a lot. Previously he could afford to be irresponsible as he expected Ranchit to manage for his follies. That privilege was no more available to him. He got to learn that it was difficult for him to take the people on ride for petty gains. That was too dangerous when he did not have any one to back up him in his bad times.

He started to wake up early in the morning to collect the waste sorted out by his fellow pickers. He started taking his meals on time in some local stall where cheap food was available so that he could save some money.

Bhutti's stall was situated close to the institute in a big colony. The delicacies available there were not what people enjoy by their taste buds. Their pockets enjoyed the bucks they retain in comparison to others. Students, shopkeepers, salesmen, counter boys, daily wagers, rickshaw pullers all enjoyed the easy-to-afford ease-of-food at Bhutti's stall.

The stall owner Bhutti had many policemen also as daily visitors. Bhutti might not be enjoying the quality but quantity of his customers.

Bhutti certainly enjoyed un-questionability from most of his customers. His customers were with vulnerable earnings or savings. Students had to manage expensive mobile phones, cock and hen parties, bike and its maintenance, girlfriend and expenses etc. In the youth their stomach could handle any kind of food but they could not cut on those essential things of their life in the age of erotic ads on almost all the channels of family TV and peer pressure.

Shopkeepers got the time to just fill their tummies. They relied on early morning yoga classes in the park nearby to manage ill-effects of Bhutti's food. But they worried to tell the doctor what they ate in case yoga failed.

Salesmen were like birds they eat here and excrete there. So no one was responsible for rot of their lot. Counter boys at shops were busy in managing the shop and imbibing the scold of the shopkeeper and shoppers to digest what they ate.

Daily wagers were compromised with routine and accepted their present as their destiny. Rickshaw pullers also comprised of the same lot as they had accepted that they were born to rot. They focused on some food item like milk and other nutrients to keep themselves under the impression they were healthy and to keep them strong enough to pull their rickshaw to pick and drop not-so-rich customers and liquor in the night to sleep in peace with their plight. Most of the Bhutti's customers comprised those who were struggling to coming out under the sun as they knew they were far from fun.

Other than those all, policemen were honorable guests at Bhutti's stall. They enjoyed whatever they were catered with honor to the guest might be free of cost. Bhutti enjoyed popularity in the area with grace and blessings from his wide clientele.

After two ferries to the dumping house Niranjan wanted to have food at Bhutti's stall. He sat on a chair in the stall.

"O rickshaw. Come here" the policeman, Chhavi Ram, shouted in a direction where a rickshaw puller was standing.

"Ji *sahab*" rickshaw puller said in submissive tone.

"Give me a drop to Sabji Mandi" Chhavi Ram asked.

"*Sahab abhi roti kha loon, tab chhod doonga*" he begged a respite from Chhavi Ram's to have food first. "I have already ordered for chapatis and milk" the puller said that he was stuck with the order. He kept his hand on his empty stomach assuming some mercy from Chhavi Ram.

Chhavi Ram was not that kind of policeman and got amused when he had tussles with rickshaw pullers and auto drivers. He felt like all-powerful among those pullers and auto drivers.

"*Baad mein kha lena*" Chhavi Ram ordered the puller to eat later. He did not want to entertain puller's order of chapattis and milk to take over his order to drop him at Sabji Mandi. He assumed himself to be *sarkar* like powerful man of the locality. The bugger rickshaw puller's dared to deny moved policeman's anger high. Out of fear, the rickshaw pullers used to pay standing ovation in salutation to him.

"*Sahab*, I didn't have dinner last night" the rickshaw puller pleaded for respite. He had already ordered for six chapatis and a glass of milk. Chapatis with milk were required to give him the protein to repair building blocks in his body which were bound to be broken in the toiling ferries. The rickshaw puller thought his *sarkar* would let him have food first. He used to salute him wherever he saw the policeman. The rickshaw puller didn't know any other government in surrounding area.

The rickshaw puller was pushed from the Samastipur. The rickshaw puller was pulled by the lure of the big buildings, smooth roads where he could ride a rickshaw smoothly so that he could earn some money. The puller had tough time not only on rough roads but to plough the fields of his *maai-baap* in the village in Samastipur.

"You will not fall from rickshaw. Drop me at Sabji Mandi crossing first" Chhavi Ram decided to enjoy the priority.

"*Mere* sarkar, please leave me to have food first" the rickshaw puller requested the policeman in meek voice.

"What you will do first and what second that I will decide not you" Chhavi Ram gave impeccable logic that his command was the last word. The puller's hunger had some challenge for Chhavi Ram.

"*Sarkar*, the food is ready, let me have it first" the rickshaw puller requested again looking at Chhotu who stacked chapatis for him.

"You will not be seen in this area. You just understand this" Chhavi Ram warned the puller of ills if the puller didn't heed to his wills.

"Sir, Chhotu has stacked chapatis" the puller again requested him to wait for few minutes. "Let him prepare milk for chapatis" he added.

"How dare you do like that?" Chhavi Ram shouted at Chhotu who got scared and stopped to serve the puller. How Chhotu could serve the servitude before the drop at Sabji Mandi crossing. Terribly scared Chhotu stopped pouring milk for the puller. The rickshaw puller's plea didn't land into Chhavi Ram's ears as if stuffed with wax and molten lead. Chhavi Ram took it as an attack on his ego. How he could let the puller go.

"Sir, why are you taking on a poor man?" Niranjan could not tolerate that for long. "He is poor rickshaw puller. You are great person who run the traffic" he further requested policeman to wait for the puller to finish his food. He forgot that Chhotu, the boy at Bhutti's stall, stopped the serving for the puller.

"*Kaun hei be tu?*" Chhavi Ram asked Niranjan. "I saw you dropping the waste at the dumping house" he could recall Niranjan's face.

"Yes sir" Niranjan showed his happiness as the policeman recognized him.

"*Tu apni tang kyon ada raha hei?*" Chhavi Ram rebuffed Niranjan for interfering.

"I have been watching this all" Niranjan folded his hands before policeman.

"Chhavi Ram didn't leave when someone folded his hands" the policeman declared ill fate for Niranjan. He took the nail lying in the stall which was used in breaking ice slabs.

Chhavi Ram warned Niranjan. How a waste picker like 'no entity' could challenge him.

"Sir, I am sorry. I don't want to stop you" Niranjan begged for his life seeing ice breaking nail in Chhavi Ram's hand. You please do whatever you want to do with that rickshaw puller" he further begged before Chhavi Ram for mercy.

"Now you cannot escape the ire of mine" Chhavi Ram took on Niranjan leaving the rickshaw puller spare.

"*Sarkar*, I am ready to drop you at the crossing" the rickshaw puller pleaded with Chhavi Ram. He surrendered as he saw a foot long nail in Chhavi Ram's hands to deal with Niranjan.

"You keep away the bastard. How did this rag picker dare to challenge me?" Chhavi Ram stopped hearing voice raised in the stall. He ignored Bhutti's resistance too.

"No *sarkar*, no please spare his life" rickshaw puller fell in Chhavi Ram's feet to beg for Niranjan's life. The rickshaw puller looked contrite. He filled with guilt to put Niranjan's life in danger by denying him free ride to the road crossing.

"You bastard got intelligence very late" Chhavi Ram held rickshaw puller's head by hair to lift him to push out of the scene. The rickshaw puller's head struck at the iron pole which supported the tent structure of the Bhutti's stall. The rickshaw puller got fainted. Chhavi Ram didn't care. "Let me see this new rascal" Chhavi Ram talked to himself in accepting the challenge none other than from his own ego.

Niranjan saw Chhavi Ram in fury and got scared. Toe to temple whole of his body got great trembling. Niranjan also fell in Chhavi Ram's feet and begged for his life.

It was too late for Chhavi Ram to forgive. He kicked Niranjan who lied in his feet begging for life. Chhavi Ram had gone deaf earlier. He then went blind also. He couldn't hear any plea. He couldn't see any pleading creature lying in his feet begging to live. Chhavi Ram could see Niranjan's *jugaad* rickshaw. He went close to one of the front wheel of the rickshaw and punctured that.

"You don't know me. How can a rag picker take on me?" Chhavi Ram kept shouting. He went close to the other wheel punctured that also. Chhavi Ram's fury was on the extreme. He kept on freaking with fucking words. He flattened all the tyres of Niranjan's rickshaw. Intimidated Niranjan was still Ok as he thought that Chhavi Ram had damaged his rickshaw only not his body.

Niranjan couldn't do anything else than cursing the cruel policeman but only in his mind as he didn't dare to bring the cursing words on his lips. Throat couldn't afford to give voice to the lips trembling in sheer fear. And, the throat could open only to request, to have mercy to leave him free.

Chhavi Ram started labeling Niranjan as Bangla desi. He asked what Niranjan's real name was. Hearing that kind of words and Chhavi Ram's intentions Bhutti left the stall pretending home delivery for students of the institute.

"*Sahab* leave me to live I will not come again in this locality" Niranjan pleaded as he didn't understand why Chhavi Ram was asking his name.

"*Wakar tujhe bekar kar doonga*" Chhavi Ram continued on his fury.

"Spare my life, *Sahab* I am also a poor man like the other rickshaw puller" Niranjan still begged for his life.

Chhavi Ram moved towards Niranjan with nail in his hand. Chhavi Ram moved the nail to attack in Niranjan's head but Niranjan stepped back to run and save his life. The nail in Chhavi Ram's hand moved in the air. He also ran to pounce upon Niranjan. He held Niranjan by neck.

Niranjan trembled in fear finding his neck in Chhavi Ram's one hand and nail in the other. Niranjan again bent down in Chhavi Ram's knees to beg for his life. Niranjan had not seen such a cruelty by a policeman. So far he had not even heard of such cruelty by policeman.

Niranjan got the first blow back in the shoulder. The nail started its work from the scratch on the back. Chhavi Ram continued with fury. The fury seemed to be neverlasting.

Niranjan's breathes went short. His breathes would go shorter. Seeing the end of his life, he collected all the courage to side with pole with which the rickshaw puller lying fainted on the stall.

"Tunnn . . ." the blow came to Niranjan's head. All the hope that he had lost as his life was to meet its unwanted and unnecessary end. But, the nail hit the pole to get a flight from Chhavi Ram's mighty hand. That had given great respite to Niranjan. Within fraction of seconds his brain collected all the information from the entire body which commanded the damaged parts not to communicate the pain. The brain commanded the body to move to the nail.

He could see few feet away the nail was lying and Chhavi Ram got trembling jerk in his hand with the strike to the pole of the stall.

Chhavi Ram's brain didn't understand the map of Niranjan's movement. He also couldn't expect Niranjan to move so fast after getting beaten to blue and red. Not blue and red, but beating Niranjan to red and red.

Within, no time a foot long nail was in Niranjan's hand. Chhavi Ram pounced upon Niranjan to take back the nail. Niranjan collected all his strength from his brain, heart, lungs, stomach, pancreas, kidneys, etc. over to the hand holding the nail. Niranjan got to escape from Chhavi Ram's grip to move in opposite direction. Niranjan took side of the pole to shield himself from Chhavi Ram.

Chhavi Ram again pounced upon Niranjan. "Tunnn . . " his head struck with the pole to make a metallic sound. He banged into the pole and got to see the stars in the mid of the sun.

Chhavi Ram would have proved him Bangla desi if he was left free.

Niranjan wrapped up all his courage on that nail and hit Chhavi Ram in the head which was not in Chhavi Ram's dream. Chhavi Ram yelled at Niranjan.

Niranjan's brain again collected all the strength information from all the parts of the body and handed over to the hand to have hands-on the Chhavi Ram's back.

"Kkkrrr . . . . . . kkrrr . . ." that time on Chhavi Ram's back Niranjan moved the nail. The khaki got long wound on the back. The khaki got wounds long back. Blood then had stopped flowing to Niranjan's brain.

Chhavi Ram begged for his life. Then . . . Niranjan knew that few breathes in his body were to last anytime. He knew that his end anyway was there either in Chhavi Ram's hands or executioner's hand after judgment.

Niranjan used his hands with full of strength to sprocket a foot long nail on the strongest links of vertebrae of Chhavi Ram's spine. "Kktt kattrr kttt kttttt kkkkttttttttt . . ." like the sprocket on the chain in the rickshaw did when he pulled in the summer with loose chain drive to give the drop to eighty kilogram Chhavi Ram at the crossing for free. He didn't spare Chhavi Ram to command a drop to the crossing in life anymore, any longer. He stamped Chhavi Ram with nail again and again . . . and again . . . again . . . gain . . . gain . . . ain . . . ain . . . in . . . in . . . n . . . n . . .

Blood from Chhavi Ram's mouth sprinkled out competing with his bleeding lungs and stomach beneath the chest and from the back. Chhavi Ram attempted to rise but to fell down again. He raised his head. He fell down again. He fell down forever.

Seeing much, suffering much, and studying much, are the three pillars of learning.
Benjamin Disraeli

ðeI si: Iz

They see is

Blood got dried up and the platelets pleated the wounds in Niranjan's back. Below his left cheek above neck was a deep digging scratch of the nail where big blood clot dried up. People from the locality huddled Niranjan in the stall. They looked at Niranjan as if he had done something which was not expected from him. Few of them commented on Niranjan's act. Others whispered to their immediate neighbors in the crowd.

"*Bhai* for me you have put your own life in danger. Why did you do that?" so far lying fainted rickshaw puller asked Niranjan when he got into consciousness. "The policeman might have spared me after beating me up" he said. He looked at chapatis which he couldn't eat. Now he didn't feel like eating.

"I didn't think that it would end in this" Niranjan looked at Chhavi Ram's body and cried. He wept in tears. He didn't run out to escape. He knew that he couldn't run out. Nobody was there to offer him a shelter to hide. How long he could hide himself. He didn't know how big people with infrastructure to hide in the world wide hid themselves for years.

"Now the police will not leave you" the rickshaw puller advised Niranjan to surrender in nearby police station. "You can avoid the police wrath" he added.

"Perhaps you are right" Niranjan agreed with the rickshaw puller. "*Bhai,* I am going to surrender in the police station. Let me go" Niranjan requested people huddled him. He stood up to go to the police station.

Niranjan reached the police station, "*Sahab,* I have killed a policeman. I want to surrender" he said to a policeman. The policeman looked at Niranjan with surprise. A man with normal height and meager built claimed to have killed a policeman. He might have thought Niranjan not to be in the balance of mind.

"*Maine sipahi ko mara hei*" the policeman imitated Niranjan in mockery. "Look at yourself" he rebuffed Niranjan.

Niranjan found the same place to be safe. He ran back to the stall where he had killed Chhavi Ram. People huddled Chhavi Ram's body in the stall started disappearing. Someone among them when Niranjan left for surrender dialed hundred to call the police.

The police had reached Bhutti's stall after half an hour. Niranjan was lucky as he came back in time. The rickshaw puller's advice did not work. The rickshaw puller ran away from the stall to save his life.

"This is the man who has killed the policeman" said a man among the people. He told the Sub Inspector who leaned on Chhavi Ram's body to confirm whether he was still alive or not. Niranjan was sitting by the side as if he wanted to claim that he had killed a policeman. To the people around he appeared to have hunted the policeman. They had seen the pictures of hunters standing with the dead animal by side. Hunting got banned. The Sub Inspector stood up and looked at Niranjan. The rags on his body with wounds between neck and left cheek and in the back, the left shoulder was left without any rag as that got torn apart.

"Can he kill a policeman?" the Sub Inspector asked the people who huddled them. People looked at each other and then few people confirmed that Niranjan had killed Chhavi Ram.

"Have you killed this policeman?" the Sub Inspector asked Niranjan. Niranjan nodded.

"How dare you?" the Sub Inspector slapped and thrashed Niranjan on the ground. He was not ready to accept that a rag ridden poor man had killed a policeman.

"Ah" Niranjan winced. Lying on the ground Niranjan looked at the Sub Inspector. He didn't speak.

Two other policemen also wanted to have their hands-on on Niranjan. The policemen rubbed their hands as they had to restrain when the Sub Inspector stopped them from doing so. He communicated to them that it was not the time to show cruelty in public when the culprit accepted the crime.

"What happened?" the Sub Inspector asked Niranjan. "Yes boss, now I have to call you boss. *Bhai*, you can kill a policeman" he went sarcastic.

Niranjan narrated the entire story to the Sub Inspector and his team of two policemen. A vehicle from a television news channel came on the spot. They prepared their footage shooting out on the Sub Inspector, the policemen in his team and Niranjan with Chhavi Ram's dead body and the people around. The vehicle went back as channel people didn't find any rating point in the news. The channel journalists with cameraman made face at each other as if they were cheated by the person who informed them about the incident. They were afraid that the dump prepared would be dumped forever as that was not worthy become a breaking news as who got killed was merely a policeman or who had killed the policeman was a rag ridden hunger stricken waste smitten rag picker.

They discussed the matter with the Sub Inspector in detail before they went away. Perhaps the Sub Inspector had told them about futility of the news and its poor saleability. The sociability of the killer and killed capably reduced the image building face lifting opportunity for both the dutiful and the dirtful.

"*Naam kya hei tera?*" the Sub Inspector asked.

"Niranjan" Niranjan replied.

"*Kahan rehta hei?*" the Sub Inspector asked.

"Landfill area" he answered. He didn't want to speak much.

Chhavi Ram's body was identified by investigation of the Sub Inspector as Chhavi Ram. Chhavi Ram was posted in the same police station. Niranjan sat with policemen in the rear side of the vehicle. They reached the police station where the policemen brought Niranjan down by dragging and beating. He didn't react. Perhaps he was prepared to meet his fate. Niranjan's wish was that the police wrath should not ruin Jhihari and Sachi.

He prayed that police would spare Inder who was the only hope for them to improve their lot from the rot.

The Sub Inspector prepared occurrence report of the case and that with the station officer.

In the evening two policemen went to the jhuggies of the rag pickers in the landfill area. They searched for Niranjan. They reached Ranchit's jhuggi. They didn't find Jhihari or Sachi in the jhuggi. Sachi had gone for housekeeping work. Jhihari had gone to meet Chandrika as she promised to arrange some job for him.

The fury of the policemen triggered them to revenge on the loss of their colleague Chhavi Ram. They wanted to throw everything out of the jhuggi. One policeman found a bundle wrapped in a bed sheet thinking them as quilts. He dragged the bundle of quilts to throw them out of the jhuggi in fury. He could caught merely bed sheet that came in his hand under which pieces of rags of different colors were layered and bundled to give that a shape of a quilt. He threw the bed sheet over it. The bundles of rags got covered again in the thrown bed sheet. He looked for something else.

Other policeman kicked of the utensils which were not many in number. Two plates, three tumblers and two bowls with cracks were lying here and there in the jhuggi. The policeman shook the outer thatching's wall to dissipate his rancorous energy. He got blinding curtain of few raggedy *sarees*, shirts, *salwar* suits, and lungi hanging over a wire going to other end of the thatching's wall. He came out of that mesh cursing the inhabitants of the jhuggies.

Two policemen came out of the jhuggi as they didn't find much to vent out their fury over the stuff. They looked around at the other jhuggies in the neighborhood. What was use of looking into other jhuggies if they didn't find anything over there? They left raggdy clothes and utensils scattered helter-skelter about the jhuggi. They came back to the police station. They didn't tell that they went to the waste nation where they didn't get anything other than few over used utensils and raggedy clothes in the jhuggies down the waste hill of the landfill area. The waste nation was not their destination. So, they spared that and didn't dust that in the nation.

Niranjan was on the floor in the custody room of the police station. Many things he then reminded himself. His entire life in Ghazipur spent on the mercy of the policemen. Also he could have successfully avoided face to face situations with them in the past. But he didn't have any remorse on what he had done to Chhavi Ram as he didn't have any control over that. He still believed all the benevolence showed by the khaki.

Supporting the rickshaw puller who had requested a respite to have his lunch before dropping him to the crossing had changed the entire life for Niranjan. He was also a rickshaw puller. He pulled a *jugaad* rickshaw for waste collection. The rickshaw puller might have got all the reasons to think higher on social rank than him. Though Niranjan was working with waste but he thought himself as puller and identified with the rickshaw puller. He couldn't control as no one from the surrounding came forward to rescue him.

He had realized his responsibilities towards Jhihari and Sachi. Ranchit's death had taught him about them. Society's ignorance over Ranchit's death had taught him great lessons on sociability of his lot which got destined to rot. The accident taught him lessons on precariousness of a miserable life that gets controlled by those who had the control over means to live a measurable life.

What would happen to him was not clear to Niranjan. He was clear that he would not give any trouble to Jhihari, Sachi, or Inder. Unwanted but drastic and devastating turn in his life had turned him to be in custody room of the police which was bound to lead to the jail. That should not have any adverse impact on their life. For that, he didn't want them to come to the police station.

The Sub Inspector checked if the occurrence report was sent to the magistrate or not. With the team he completed the formalities with Chhavi Ram's dead body which was sent for postmortem. He had prepared *panchnama*. He had been assigned with investigation of the case.

Other two persons brought to the custody room were restless while Niranjan was peacefully sleeping on the floor. The charge of murder was an honor for Niranjan in the custody room to make him feel like life was valuable. The policemen had to forget that he had killed one of their colleagues if they could not forgive him. The Sub Inspector asked if food was given or not.

"*Sahab* you are bothered about his hunger. He has killed a policeman" a head constable of investigation team asked the Sub Inspector sharing his surprise.

"Your question is quite right" the Sub Inspector said. He looked at the head constable to hand over the case file. "We should not care for him. But he doesn't have any relation to be taken care of" the Sub Inspector informed as Niranjan didn't tell about any relation in Ghazipur. "If he dies in your custody then many of us would be suspended for months. Do you know that?" he reminded the head constable about some of the cases from past few years. He could hide his good intentions for Niranjan as Chhavi Ram lived a life of a spot on the police lot. He got rotten in the system much more than the system rot.

"Do you know why he had killed Chhavi Ram?" the Sub Inspector asked head constable. He took the file again to have attention from the head constable who wrapped the red tape on finger.

The head constable nodded.

"Then?" he said.

"*Wo to hei sir*" the head constable said. "This person is hero if we believe his story why he has killed Chhavi Ram" he added.

The head constable looked at the Sub Inspector's face and then he looked at the custody room where Niranjan was sleeping.

"Chhavi Ram didn't let a rickshaw puller to finish his food at the stall just for his free drop at Sabji Mandi crossing" the Sub Inspector said.

The head constable kept quiet.

"Chhavi Ram was another extreme case" the Sub Inspector continued explaining his view on Chhavi Ram's end. Listening to the Sub Inspector's view the head constable got a shift in his opinion. He got a lesson that if you lose being human then a sub-human like Niranjan, so meek and docile, might bring an end which was not so meek but cruel and ugly to highlight the ugliness of the society and rotten lot.

When Inspector was preparing *panchnama* he came to know what Niranjan had stated in his version of story was true. Chhavi Ram didn't let a poor rickshaw puller to eat chapatis with milk and insisted for the drop to the Sabji Mandi. Owner of the stall Bhutti told the Sub Inspector the same story on the condition of not being witness in the case.

"Why Bhutti was avoiding being a witness in the case?" the head constable asked Sub Inspector.

"Bhutti is not the only one who avoids being witness in this case" the Sub Inspector kept sharing his opinion as the head constable took interest in talking more on Niranjan's story. The head constable took interest as if he had similar experience in his village before he joined the police.

"Moreover, Bhutti didn't want to take on other side that may go against the police" the Sub Inspector threw light from his insight on the case. "People like Bhutti who run business with the help from police cannot go against" he added.

"*Maine bhi Chhavi Ram ko kai bar samjhaya tha ki gusse aur lalach ko control mein rakha kare*" the head constable also shared his own experience with Chhavi Ram with conseling suggestions to control anger and greed. Knowingly or unknowingly he was also on the Sub Inspector's side as he also had counseled Chhavi Ram many times in the past to avoid misusing his police position. A petty position to rule over empty stomachs. Disgusting . . .

"Chhavi Ram would not have understood what you taught" the Sub Inspector said. He agreed with the head constable. "Everyone has his own fate. Many of us die in encounters genuine or fake. He got his end met like that" he added.

"Chhavi Ram used to say that there must be someone in the common public over whom a small rank of government machinery like policeman should also get some opportunity to rule. He also used to say when big people in power were using them to rule over the public. Chhavi Ram got changed to that extreme only after his experience during his posting at Lodhi Road. He used to watch policemen in personal security of our leaders who used to come for walk in the Garden. He had seen his fellows being used. Then he also determined using people in similar manner" the head constable described about Chhavi Ram. *"Duniyan aisi hi hei. Unmein main akela nahin hoon. Wo kaha karta tha"* he added more on what Chhavi Ram was in his stories.

"I am leaving for the day, tomorrow morning we have to take Niranjan before the magistrate" the Sub Inspector instructed. The head constable went into another room for record keeping.

The Sub Inspector came out of the police station where he found two persons were standing at the gate of the police station.

"Who are you? Why are you standing here at the gate?" the Sub Inspector asked. First he gave casual look at them then he stopped to enquire.

"Sir, we wanted to meet our friend. But now it is too late" one of them said to the Sub Inspector.

"Is your friend in this police station?" he asked. "What is your name? Where from you have come?" he further asked though he was in a hurry to leave the station.

"Inder" Inder said. "His name is Jhihari" he said further.

"Our friend is in custody" Inder said.

"Who is your friend?" the Sub Inspector asked them.

"Niranjan" Inder answered.

The Sub Inspector turned in fury as he knew Niranjan didn't have any relation. He controlled himself as they told that they were friends. He then pacified with his own anger. "He is sleeping in the custody room, he is fine?" he was in a hurry to leave. He denied.

They pleaded.

Then he thought Niranjan had accepted his crime. So, he would be sent to the jail next morning after case was presented before a judge. Moreover, he was in hurry. He was already late to meet his wife who was waiting for him at home. He didn't want to stay longer in the police station. He called same head constable to deal with them.

"These two men are Niranjan's friends. They want to meet Niranjan. *Mila dena, dare hue hein*" the Sub Inspector instructed the head constable. *"Kal Niranjan jail bhej diya jayega to inhein aaj mil lene do"* he further said.

"Ok sir!" the head constable said.

"In par nazar rakhna" he instructed and moved.

"So you are Niranjan's friends?" the head constable turned to Inder and Jhihari after the Sub Inspector left.

"Yes sir" Inder said.

"Do you know what Niranjan has done?" head constable asked.

"Yes sir, we are sorry for that" Inder replied to the head constable. They were afraid being in the police station. *"Nahin to rehne dijiye sir"* he added. They were ready to go back.

"What do you do?" the head constable asked.

"I am working with Jain Disposals" Inder said.

"I collect and sort out the waste from waste houses and public dust bins" Jhihari said.

"What does Niranjan do?" the head constable enquired.

"Same work as I do" Jhihari answered.

"When did you come to know about this incident?" the head constable asked. He would have not talked to them if the Sub Inspector had not discussed the matter at length. They were lucky that he talked to them with niceties not expected from the policemen.

"When I came back to my jhuggi in the landfill area I found everything was lying here and there." Jhihari answered. "I enquired in the neighboring jhuggies to find out what happened. My *bhabhi* also could not reach from the household work as there was a party in one of the house. She works as maid" he narrated what happened previous evening after Niranjan's arrest.

"Phir?" he asked.

"I came to know from the people in neighboring jhuggies that Niranjan had killed a policeman in a stall where he was on the work in a colony." Jhihari said further. He told the story under fear. "People in neighboring jhuggies told me that two policeman came to my jhuggi in search for Niranjan" he added.

"When he doesn't have anything and any place to live then also he can kill us. *Sala,* if he had some means and resources then he would have been dangerous for all of us" the head constable scolded Jhihari. *"Jinke paas dhan daulat aur power hei wo humein nachate phirte hein. Iske paas hoti to roz ek marta kya?"* he added in exclamation.

"Then I went to Inder's place to inform him about what Niranjan had done" Jhihari said.

"Ye donon kaun hein?" asked another head constable who passed by.

"*Niranjan jisne hamare constable sathi ka khoon kar diya hei uske parichit hein. Milne aayen hein*" the first head constable said.

"*Inko bhi kar do andar*" other head constable gave his verdict to put them in the custody along with Niranjan.

"*Nahin* sir, *hamne kuchh nahin kiya hei.* We are poor men" they folded their hands in plea on the ground that they were innocent.

"*Milna nahin hei?*" he asked as if he had taken charge of the situation.

"Where is Niranjan?" other head constable asked.

"In the custody room?" the first head constable answered.

"Put them also in the custody. Take them on third degree. They will come to know what the meaning of killing a policeman is" other head constable suggested the first one.

"*Sahab* they want same thing" the first head constable said to other. "That's why they have come here. They know that police custody is more comfortable than their jhuggies in landfill area" first constable shared his perspective with the other.

"Really! They are so bare handed!" other one shared his surprise.

"That's why they dare like this kind of acts" other head constable added. "See at what time they have come to meet their friend" he said and looked at his watch to confirm what he said.

"*Sahab* just look at Niranjan who is sleeping in the custody room. Other two men are sulking for this or that. They are cursing their relatives for not turning up" first head constable explained. "That is why I am not putting them in custody room" he added.

"*Duniyan badi ajeeb hei*" other head constable commented.

The first head constable smiled.

"We live on your mercy only" Jhihari his folded hands to the head constable.

"We were also scared about the same before coming here" Inder said.

"Then why have you come here?" the head constable asked.

"I told Jhihari that it is not always like that. We want to know what will happen" Inder asked the head constable.

"What is there to happen now?" Niranjan has accepted that he has murdered Chhavi Ram" the head constable answered. "Tomorrow morning, Niranjan will be presented before the magistrate for prosecution" he said. Indirectly he hinted that they could meet Niranjan.

"Don't you want to meet Niranjan?" the head constable showed all the signs of mercy.

They got happy to listen that.

"Wake him up. He is sleeping" the head constable said.

"Ok sir, with your mercy" Jhihari looked at Inder for the support to have courage to meet Niranjan in the custody room of the police station.

The head constable took them inside the station and pointed out the custody room where Niranjan was sleeping. Inder and Jhihari went close to the custody room.

"Niranjan" Jhihari called.

Niranjan didn't buzz on the call. One of the other two men in the custody room woke him up by shaking up his body.

"Niranjan, Inder has come to meet you" Jhihari spoke in low voice.

"Who? I don't know anybody by this name" Niranjan replied.

"Who are you?" Niranjan declined to recognize Jhihari also.

"What Niranjan! Don't do that. The head constable here has been very kind to us" Jhihari said.

Niranjan looked at other two men in the custody room.

"He has allowed us to meet you" Jhihari said.

"I heard that two policemen went to the landfill area for searching me when I was here in the police station." Niranjan said. He came close to the bars of the iron door of the custody room and spoke in low voice.

"You are right! Luckily neither I nor *bhabhi* was there at that time" Jhihari confirmed what Niranjan said.

"I got scared that they would catch you to put behind the bars" Niranjan shared his fear.

"One head constable has been very nice to us. He allowed us to meet you" Inder said. Other two men in the custody room looked up at Inder hearing that.

"What happened? How come you did such an unthinkable job of murder?" Inder asked.

"I was having food at Bhutti's stall. A rickshaw puller ordered for food. Chhavi Ram also was having his food in the stall. Chhavi Ram asked the rickshaw puller for a drop at the Sabji Mandi. Chhavi Ram *Sahab* wanted the drop before that puller could have his food." Niranjan stated what happened at the stall which made him to be in that lock up room.

"Then?" Jhihari asks.

"My mistake was that I asked policeman to wait for the rickshaw puller to finish his food then he would drop you at the Sabji Mandi crossing. That was my crime for Chhavi Ram was not ready to leave me alive. Leaving the rickshaw puller free the policeman started beating me like anything. I got many wounds" Niranjan showed few of the wounds.

"Then, what happened? How come? That all got reversed" Inder asked. He looked here and there in the police station where few staff members on duty were busy and others in having their dinner.

"Policeman got struck with the iron pole of the stall and a foot long nail from his hand fled to the place where I was lying wounded. He pounced upon me to beat me. I had picked up the same nail and I replied back. Then I thought I would not be saved even if I leave him free. So I stabbed him with the nail till he died. Then I came here to surrender. Nobody believed me in this police station when I told them that I had killed a policeman. So, I went back to the stall" Niranjan completed the story.

"Now what will happen? Have you ever thought?" Jhihari asked Niranjan who looked comfortable in the custody room.

"What will happen? I will get punishment. I am ready to go to jail. No problem" Niranjan declared acceptance of his fate.

"Niranjan, you got changed. So fast" Jhihari asked. He expressed his surprise over the entire development.

"Ranchit *bhaiya's* death in the road accident has changed me to this stand. And up to this extent" Niranjan said. He recalled Ranchit's importance in his life. Jhihari got into tears hearing that. Inder took him aside.

"Have you taken some food?" Inder came back to ask Niranjan.

"I don't feel hungry now" Niranjan said.

"Shall I bring food?" Inder asked.

"They will not allow food from outside" Niranjan clarified.

"I don't want to disclose any relation with you. Otherwise you will have tough time" Niranjan reasoned for their safety. "You would have seen that two policemen went to the landfill area and put the entire jhuggi at chaos and ruin" he added emphasis to his reason.

"*Chalo* then, tomorrow the court will send me to the jail for remand" Niranjan said. He shook hand with Inder and Jhihari to sendoff.

One of the other two persons in the custody called Inder when they both started to move out. "Can you call up at this number?" he asked Inder showing his palm with a number written on that.

"Sir, I don't have mobile phone" Inder wanted to move. "Please forgive us, we won't be able to help you out" he clarified.

He waved hundred rupees note to pay the price.

"Please ask them. They will definitely help out" Inder said. He pointed at the police staff on duty.

"What happened? Talks become never ending" said the head constable who allowed them to meet Niranjan. He asked them to leave the station immediately. "Shall I put both of you with Niranjan in the custody room to carry on your talks?" he cautioned them to know where they were.

"No sir, it's over" Inder dragged Jhihari to the gate of the police station.

"Thank you sir!" Inder and Jhihari thanked head constable for his permission.

Lawyers' chambers in the compound of the session court in east Delhi started witnessing their masters' presence with assistants who were running here and there. They were busy with their clients and sometimes clients roamed around to photocopy the documents. Sometimes lawyers themselves got busy in taking notary papers or getting their cases enrolled for the call in the court.

The Sub Inspector with his team of two policemen and Niranjan in handcuffs in control of one policeman in the team came down from the police van. They proceeded to the session judge before whom the team would make Niranjan to appear for case proceedings. They all came under the verandah of the court room where the session judge was to hear the case.

Court room was waiting for its regular and spurious occupiers. The Sub Inspector and his team members knew that there was nothing pending on the inquiry as Niranjan had admitted that he had killed Chhavi Ram. The court counsel had prepared the case as the team had initiated the proceeding.

The Sub Inspector had submitted the charge sheet to the court authority. The hearing of the case was scheduled at nine O' clock in the morning court. The session judge had taken his seat in the court room.

The cases scheduled for the day were being presented before the session judge. Niranjan's case was second to be heard.

There was no chance that Niranjan might escape as he had accepted that he had killed Chhavi Ram. One of the two policemen however held tightly the rope of handcuffs in Niranjan's hands. Because it was the duty of policemen to assume that human mind may change any time. Because Niranjan might change his mind at any point of time to run away. Because . . . all that was sufficient to make Niranjan in handcuffs. People involved in normal cases of petty crimes were brought in handcuffs while Niranjan was charged with murder that too the murder of a policeman.

"Sir, Niranjan is asking to make water" the policeman having handcuffs rope in his hand asked the Sub Inspector.

"Be with him, though he won't run away. But, be on safer side. Be with him" the Sub Inspector instructed the policeman holding the rope of handcuffs in Niranjan's hands.

Niranjan went with the policeman who had rope of his handcuffs. Nobody had cared up to that extent since Niranjan's juvenile days. Even in early childhood days in Singbhum he was not accompanied by elders for such things. That day he was making water in one cubicle with hands in handcuffsrope of which was in the policeman's hand in the next cubicle. They both came back to the verandah of the court room.

The Sub Inspector went inside the court room to submit few more documents. Finally the call came sometime after nine O' clock. Niranjan was presented in the court.

Niranjan was brought in the accused box to begin the proceedings. Niranjan found everything in the court room appeared to be unfamiliar. The session judge in the chair asked the court counsel to present the case.

"Me lord! The cases brought to you might have been presented before which include culprit's emotions to kill someone in relation or strangers for some consideration or other. Today the case being presented before you is beyond emotions to kill someone just like that" the counsel of the court stated before the session judge to present the case in which Niranjan was to be tried for a policeman's murder. "If not just like that it is to be taken as the act of terror. Even by mistake that should not be taken as the act of error" the court counsel gave a glimpse of his judgment before the session judge could get a glimpse of the accused and the case.

"Me lord! This will bring light on an inhuman face of a killer who has killed a brave policeman on duty just for nothing but his whim and fancies" the counsel of the court stated further.

Session judge raised his hand to communicate to proceed further.

"What is your name?" the counsel of the court asked Niranjan standing in the accused box.

"Niranjan" Niranjan answered. He looked at the people around. His eyes searched for someone familiar in the court. He had categorically asked them not to come to the court. None of Sachi, Jhihari, or Inder was present in the audience in the court. His gaze came back after riding over the heads and faces of the people present in the court to stay at the face of the counsel who asked his name.

"What do you do for your living?" the counsel asked Niranjan.

"I collect waste materials for recycling" Niranjan answered.

"What do you get out of this job?" the counsel of the court asked next question to Niranjan.

"Just to keep myself alive" Niranjan replied.

"Which area you collect waste materials?" the counsel of the court asked Niranjan.

"Few colonies in Ghazipur area" Niranjan answered.

"Did you see Chhavi Ram before the day of incident?" the counsel of the court asked.

"Only two or three times" he answered.

"Did Chhavi Ram know you earlier? I mean like had Chhavi Ram also seen you or knew before the day of incident?" the counsel of the court asked Niranjan. He took out his specs in hand.

"Whether he has seen me before I don't know that" Niranjan replied.

"Me lord! The accused didn't know Chhavi Ram earlier and brave policeman who got killed in the incident also didn't know the accused" the counsel of the court argued. He tapped the wooden railing of the accused box. He again put on specs. "What happened that day? What was a trigger that got into this man? Nobody can know other than accused himself. But the brave policeman on duty had lost his life?" he narrated the case came out in the light and asked to put his perspective before the court. He again proceeded with Niranjan in the accused box.

"*Sahab* I was eating food at Bhutti's stall near institute. Chhavi Ram *Sahab* was also having food over there in the stall. I had just finished my food and waiting for my tea. Chhavi Ram *Sahab* also finished his food and was looking for some rickshaw puller to drop him at the Sabji Mandi crossing. At the same time a rickshaw puller came to the stall with firing hunger in his stomach. The rickshaw puller ordered milk and chapatis to eat" Niranjan narrated the niceties so far.

"Chhavi Ram *Sahab* asked the rickshaw puller to drop him at the Sabji Mandi crossing. That rickshaw puller wanted to eat chapatis first so that he could get strength to pull his rickshaw to give a drop to Chhavi Ram *Sahab*. Chhavi Ram *Sahab* was not allowing him to eat food first. He wanted him to go for the drop at the Sabji Mandi crossing first" Niranjan took a pause.

"Then, what happened?" the court counsel prompted.

"When the rickshaw puller declined to drop Chhavi Ram *Sahab* at Sabji Mandi crossing. Chhavi Ram *Sahab* didn't like that. According to Chhavi Ram *Sahab* the rickshaw puller should not deny for what Chhavi Ram *Sahab* had asked. Chhavi Ram *Sahab* wanted to teach him a lesson so that he could not deny for a task that Chhavi Ram *Sahab* asked to do. Chhavi Ram *Sahab* held the rickshaw puller by his hair that time to thrash him in the ground" Niranjan paused to take breath.

"*Phir kya hua?*" the court counsel asked.

"I just could not see the miserability of the rickshaw puller. I asked Chhavi Ram *Sahab* to leave the rickshaw puller to eat his food. My point was that if rickshaw puller had food then he would have dropped Chhavi Ram *Sahab* at the crossing happily. Chhavi Ram didn't like me. He took it as intervention. He did not like a rag picker like me could interfere in the matter. Nobody else also came forward to mediate to pacify furious Chhavi Ram *Sahab* and the rickshaw puller. He threw the rickshaw puller holding head by hair. The rickshaw puller hit the iron pole of Bhutti's stall" Niranjan took a pause.

The session judge kept looking at Niranjan. He was so keen in the case that he spared less time to look into the paper evidences and other people.

"Chhavi Ram *Sahab* took it on ego and pounced upon me to teach me lesson. I begged Chhavi Ram *Sahab* for mercy. I begged him for my life. He had been high with keeping ego on the sky had beaten me like anything. He was not satisfied beating me by hands. He picked up a foot long nail. He attacked me many times with that nail" Niranjan narrated what had happened before he got the chance to reverse the situation.

The session judge looked at Niranjan. Many of the spectators in the court watched Niranjan with open mouth. They perhaps were left with surprise that no one could come for rescue. First to rescue Niranjan then obviously Chhavi Ram's life also could have been spared by the destiny. Destiny of the attitude got severed by the servitude.

"Chhavi Ram *Sahab* could not mind the pole that supported Bhutti's stall and missed the attack on my head and his hand struck with pole. His head also hit the pole with momentum resulted in the loss of balance and the foot long nail in his hand flew in the air" narrating that, Niranjan looked at the spectators sitting in the court to know whether they believed him or not.

"Then what happened?" the court counsel asked.

"The nail fell on the ground where I was lying beaten and broken. Collecting all the courage and strength then remained in my body I picked the nail to save myself. I couldn't run as I was wounded. So, I decided to fight back as I couldn't be spared. I had to die in any condition whether it was in Chhavi Ram *Sahab's* hand or at the hands of executioner for killing him" Niranjan explained the turning point of the story.

The judge noted down something in his papers.

"I jumped at Chhavi Ram *Sahab* who was not able to manage the wound on his head that he had given himself by hitting the pole. I hit him in the arm with the same nail. Then I didn't stop and kept hitting him on the back. I kept hitting him at the same spot till he had any strength in his body. When he became almost dead I sat aside in the stall. People started looking at me having various points of view" Niranjan completed the narration.

Many of the voiced emerged in the audience in the court.

"Order, Order" the session judge in the chair reminded.

"I ran to the police station to surrender. In order to surrender I told a policeman in the police station that I had killed Chhavi Ram *Sahab*. He didn't believe me. I came back to Bhutti's stall till someone dialed hundred to inform the police about the incident. Then the Inspector *Sahab* came to the stall with his team" Niranjan narrated the part on how his surrender failed or caught on the spot.

The court counsel took his turn.

"Do you know the rickshaw puller?" the counsel of the court asked.

"No, I saw him there only" Niranjan replied.

"You fought for him without knowing him" the counsel of the court asked.

"When you don't know the rickshaw puller but you fought for him till the brave policeman on the duty died" the counsel of the court argued to seek agreement or disagreement from Niranjan.

Niranjan didn't understand what the counsel of the court stated. He kept quiet.

"Me lord! Now I would request you to grant witness opportunity to the investigation officer of this case" the court counsel took permission to call witness in the box.

"Granted" the session judge said.

The court counsel called the investigation officer of the case to come to the witness box. The Sub Inspector who had brought Niranjan came to the witness box.

"Officer, what did you see when you reached the place of incident?" the counsel of the court asked the investigation officer after getting introduction of the Sub Inspector to the court.

"Sir, I got a call from the station officer to respond to an information about the incident where a policeman got killed" the Sub Inspector stated standing in the witness box of the court. He looked at Niranjan in the accused box.

"What did you see when you reached the spot?" the counsel of the court asked the Sub Inspector. He looked at the judge alternately.

"Sir when I reached the venue I saw that Niranjan was sitting on the ground by an iron pole of the stall. The body of Mr. Chhavi Ram, our policeman on the duty was lying close to him. Niranjan was surrounded by local people and few students of the institute" the Sub Inspector stated in the witness box.

"Was there any rickshaw puller?" the counsel of the court asked the investigation officer.

"No sir, the rickshaw puller was not there" the Sub Inspector replied to the counsel of the court.

"Point to be noted me lord" the court counsel raised his hand.

"I asked Niranjan about the rickshaw puller during my interrogation when I came to know. According to Niranjan the rickshaw puller got fainted when his head hit the iron pole after Chhavi Ram thrashed him. Niranjan said that he ran away from the spot when he was back into consciousness" the Sub Inspector stated in the witness of the court.

"Thank you officer, you may please go back to your seat" the court counsel said.

"Me lord, this person who claims to be a rag picker is a rag on the society who does not see people who are better than him with equality. In that spirit of nourishing inequality he killed a government servant who was on the duty. He interrupted a government servant doing his duty. When he found the opportunity to revenge for some past experience of enmity he killed Chhavi Ram, a brave policeman on duty. Chhavi Ram got educated and recruited in the police service. People like Niranjan roam happily during their education days to avoid any responsibility. When they grow up and realize that they need to do some work for their livelihood then they take on small or big crimes as easy path like this. In guise of waste collector or rag picker a killer is before you in this box" the counsel of the court said.

"He should be given harsh punishment for murdering a policeman on the duty he is a dangerous person though he looks weak, poor, and meek. Me Lord, I request you please not to go by his looks. His looks are deceptive. Please take a deep look onto his killing outlook. He kills people just like that to enjoy himself. He is a killer. He is a living danger for society. He is not a rag picker. He is a rag on the society" the counsel of the court put forward his arguments.

"As he has committed this crime he should not be given any bail. But prosecution may also not be required as arrogance is evident in accepting that he has killed the policeman. He should be executed without wasting court's valuable time in prosecution" said loud the counsel not to leave any of his arguments go unheard. He wanted to make it fit case for Niranjan to get at least life sentence if not death sentence. He looked as if he could not let Niranjan apply for bail.

"Is there any defense counsel for the accused to present the case from the accused side?" the session judge enquired.

There was silence in the court.

"Do you have any advocate to fight the case for you?" the session judge asked Niranjan.

Niranjan kept quiet. He shook his head in negation.

The session judge asked same question again.

"No judge *Sahab*, I don't have any money to eat or live in sheltered place. Wherefrom I will get money for advocate?" Niranjan replied to the session judge.

"Give me the punishment. I deserve that only" Niranjan said leaning on the railing of the accused box in the court room. *"Main samaj par kalank hoon"* Niranjan didn't negate the stand posed by the court counsel and accepted that he was a big blot on the social fabric.

"Seeing the presentation from police and witness of the case, this court decides that a counsel should be assigned to defend the case for the accused. The accused shall be on remand of fourteen days to further investigate why he had killed the cop. This court advises the assignment of a counsel to the defense of the accused in this period" the session judge adjourned the case to the next hearing after fourteen days.

There were many voices in the court room to make the court chaotic and noisy.

"Order, order" the session judge called. He waved his orderly to call for next case.

Niranjan came out of the accused box with the policeman who held the rope of his handcuffs. With investigation team he moved towards the big door of the court room to come out. He saw Inder and Jhihari who were standing in the rear part of the court room. Inder and Jhihari saluted the Sub Inspector who allowed them to meet Niranjan in the custody room. They came along with the investigation team. Niranjan didn't talk to Inder or Jhihari. Inder wanted to talk to Niranjan but he shook his head not to meet him.

The greatest value is what you are having
at this moment, this time, this life!
                                    Kazeronnie Mak

ðIs Iz

This is

Niranjan got seated in the police vehicle again. Inder and Jhihari watched him going to the jail. What they could do, they did. They watched him going to the jail. It was not even in their dream for them to hire a lawyer to defend his case in the court. The Sub Inspector also got settled in the front seat while the policemen went inside the vehicle along with Niranjan. Jhihari raised his hand to say something but the police vehicle started moving out of the court premises.

Niranjan saw them walking behind the police vehicle. The world outside the police vehicle appeared different to him. The people on the road in the court premises might be looking at him with reprimand. His solace was that he was not a known social figure or business tycoon to feel embarrassed. Also that he didn't have any identity so he didn't feel any need to cover his face. He didn't have face first of all. But the counsel of the court was proving him a rag on the society, not a raggedy face of the society.

Niranjan also thought about the prosecution lawyer saying people like him cannot see an eye to eye with the people from civic society. Niranjan's whole life might be shorter to find it the way that was advocated by the prosecution lawyer. Life so far, he spent accepting people's eye on him with hate and scorn wherever he went for waste collection. He found the otherwise true.

The vehicle ran on the Vikas Marg and Niranjan's eyes were on the buildings and houses which were housing markets on the wide road. His eyes were getting dried on the hoarding of connecting people.

Niranjan got connected with a waste picker close to a public dust bin when the vehicle stopped at red light of Laxmi Nagar. Topless boy in early teens covered his waist with rag shorts with torn bag might have been used for packing wheat. He smiled at Niranjan when he realized Niranjan was continuously watching him. Plastic bag in his hands which once might have contained wheat was full of paper and packing waste sorted out from the dust bin.

Communicating eyes of the boy looked into Niranjan's eyes moved with the move of the vehicle on green light on the road. Niranjan also kept looking at the boy till the metro line high on the road just overtook his view. The skyline of the metro rail in the foreground got converted into a checkered railing over the river bridge. Casing checks on the window glasses of the police vehicle presented parallaxes to his eyes.

Vikas Minar removed the parallax as the vehicle kept moving ahead. He turned his head on other side when he could not watch full height of Vikas Minar. The talks of policemen about the building of their headquarters got him interested to look at the building. The police building, police uniform, the policemen appeared to scare him before he really got worried seeing huge Hanuman statue.

He closed his eyes not to take a nap but to see pictures of barred doors and big Iron Gate of the jail. He couldn't keep his eyes closed for long time as the policemen discussed about names of the soldiers on the walls of the India Gate who died fighting in the world wars. Niranjan opened his eyes to look at the Gate and couldn't see any engravings from that distance. He could see only couples, girls, boys, teenagers, kids, enjoying the picnic environment at the memorial of the war martyrs. Many boys of his lot were busy in picking ice cream wrappers, waste paper plates, to have clean Delhi and green Delhi, the Delhi.

As the vehicles kept moving he again attempted for a nap. He saw a huge man in police uniform with two feet long iron nail rather than baton in his hand to welcome him at the big gate of the jail. He thought that huge man might be the jailor. Later, he saw that the jailor didn't let him have food during lunch time in the jail. He was asked to collect the waste created at the kitchen and the Jailor's office. He was collecting the waste in the kitchen where cook was creating waste out of cutting the vegetables for inmates of the jail. Niranjan took a basket filled with pumpkin peels to dump into the dumping house at the jail boundary. He slipped down on the ground after stumbling at leg hurdles by the policeman who sat in a chair with stretching legs across the door of the kitchen. Slipped in his dream, he opened his eyes in the vehicle which was passing a flyover reaching the mess of flyovers. The vehicle was now running on the ring road faster than it was running around the India Gate.

"Jai hind sir" the Sub Inspector saluted his station officer on his mobile phone.

"We are yet to reach the jail" he replied.

"We are passing by the corporation godown" the Sub Inspector again replied to the question from his station officer.

"No sir, here they have grains only. Otherwise, I would have brought a crate for you" the Sub Inspector laughed while answering to his senior. The talks were audible as the window in rear of the driving cabin was opened. "That's not this go down but somewhere else in the country.

If I go there then I will bring one crate for you" he laughed. Both the policemen also laughed hearing the jokes the Sub Inspector cracked with his senior on the phone. The vehicle kept moving towards the jail.

"Sir, there is no guarantee in this job that I don't get chance to go there" he commented on the nature of his job. "So sir, we should not lose hope" he became a bit witty. Faces of the policemen listening to the Sub Inspector on service conditions got a dim.

Niranjan could understand what was going on but he could not relate the discussion of the Sub Inspector to anything. He could understand the senior asked the Sub Inspector where he was at that point of time if he had not reached the destination, the jail.

Thinking of the jail as his destination had brought water line in his eyes before turning to the jail road. The junk market made him surprised to see lot of scope for big business on waste collection. He mistook resalable machinery with salable waste of daily life not from the household but commerce hold. Opportunity to work with machinery junk would have brought luck and prosperity for Niranjan to have strong foothold. But that could not happen. And, that would not happen.

Niranjan got a strong jerk in rope chained handcuffs in his hands. The policeman asked him to get down as the vehicle had reached the jail. That was the first time he came to the jail which was to house him physically otherwise he had been in the open jail of waste hill full of fecal filth for years and years together. That day the investigating team had brought him to the jail where he had to have his destination semi-permanent or permanent. External and eternal. It might be eternal for him for the gravity of his crime.

"*Tumhari manzil aa gayi bhai*" one of the policemen said to Niranjan who was looking down at the bottom of the big iron gate of the jail. The police vehicle went inside the big iron gate of the jail and the vehicle stopped in the side closed to the Jailor's office.

"Nothing would help, come" the policeman asked Niranjan looked at the small door of the big iron gate. The Sub Inspector called the policemen to hurry up and entered the Jailor's office for completing the formalities. Niranjan didn't speak anything but stepped down from the vehicle. He walked few steps and stopped to look at the jail.

"*Jaldi karo*" the policeman asked Niranjan to move swiftly following the instruction from his superior. Niranjan's feet got frozen in front of the Jailor's office. He then thought he was prepared to face any consequences as Chhavi Ram got killed at his hands accidentally or intentionally. How did that matter.

But at that time when he had been brought to the jail he thought why he was being tried he had not killed Chhavi Ram but Chhavi Ram got killed during the struggle to save his life. He thought then that he didn't have the right to live how could he got the right to save his life. Though Niranjan had not gone inside the jail and had not seen or heard anything about the jail but he realized that jail was not good place for him.

Niranjan saw huge open area surrounded by barracks and the cells for the prisoners. He again got stuck with the openness of that close boundary walls so high that no one could dare to run away. With policeman he went to the office of the jailor where the Sub Inspector was waiting for him. His feet dragged when he moved to the jailor's office. His feet dragged as his body was not where his head was.

Another policeman asked Niranjan to give his finger prints for the record. Niranjan rubbed his fives on the pad to print on a paper. The team with the Sub Inspector moved out of the jail after completing the formalities.

The cell number was given to him along with a uniform. Niranjan was charged with murder. That too, the murder of a policeman, so he was going to get harsh punishment. He looked at the uniform in his hands and then looked at his own raggedy clothes. He put on the uniform and handed over his rag ridden blood smitten wounded clothes like him for his deposits. Two policemen on the staff of the jail escorted him to the cell when other prisoners of similar crimes were kept in the other cells of the barrack.

"Are you coming for the first time?" the inmate in the neighboring cell asked when Niranjan reached his cell.

"*Haan*" Niranjan answered. He looked at the policemen escorting him.

"What have you done?" the inmate asked Niranjan looking at the policemen who was taking him to the next cell.

Niranjan didn't answer. He thought he was saving his life but advocate and people in society called that a murder.

"Murder?" the policeman replied as Niranjan kept quiet.

"Hmm" the inmate got surprised. He looked at Niranjan from head to toe. "Brave boy" he murmured.

The policeman tapped Niranjan on his shoulder to move ahead. He was at the door of the cell. Thoughts running into his head were chaining his feet to move ahead. He finally entered into the cell. One of the policemen locked the door.

Niranjan looked on things in the cell. He didn't have any choice but to settle in the corner of the cell. He looked outside the cell. He looked in the ground. Suddenly Niranjan started crying like a kid. He saw a rope hanging with the rod of the ventilator in the cell with loop for head ready for execution. A policeman came running from the Jailor's office.

"What happened?" the policeman asked rushing to the cell. But Niranjan didn't answer and kept on crying.

"What happened?" the policeman asked him again. Another policeman came to the cell with the keys to open the cell.

Niranjan still didn't speak but pointed out at the loop of the rope hanging with the ventilator of the cell. The policeman also looked at that. He looked at the other policeman then both the policemen laughed. When they laughed he stopped crying.

"This is a painting by an inmate in this cell" the policeman informed him.

Niranjan didn't understand anything from the information. He looked at the policemen with surprise.

"Ok, why did you cry?" the policeman attempted to understand what had gone into Niranjan's head.

"I thought someone will hang me with the rope in the night" Niranjan disclosed his fears.

"Are you fooling us or what?" the other policeman asked him.

Niranjan didn't understand.

"You have killed a policeman and you are scared of painting of the rope in a hanging loop?" the policeman shouted at him.

"This is a painting not the real rope" the policeman shouted again. "Previous inmate living in this cell was good painter and made great paintings on the walls here and there" he added.

"Take him out as it is going to be time for lunch" the other policeman said.

"Come out in the ground" both the policemen called Niranjan. Niranjan started moving towards the door of the cell. He kept looking at the loop of the rope hanging with the ventilator. He managed to take steps to the door with turning his head to look at the painting.

"The inmate of this cell used to say that if you want to run away from this cell through this ventilator then this ventilator itself would execute you" the policeman explained the theme of the painting.

"So there is no escape in life, only escape from the life" the other policeman stamped the intention of the painter.

"How come? So real appearing rope! How come a prisoner painted so well? So real!" Niranjan wondered. He came out of the cell looking at paintings again and again.

"This is your first day. You will come to know that this is not a jail" the policeman assured Niranjan.

Niranjan was overwhelmed by the treatment that he received from the police staff of the jail. The treatment Niranjan could not even imagine when he was out in the streets or on the roads. He used to get a strong snub from everyone in the streets. Engrossed in thoughts from the past Niranjan stood in the queue for lunch.

"Come, welcome" an inmate turned to Niranjan to greet him.

Niranjan didn't respond.

"By age you look like as if you have been booked for Eve-teasing. Right?" the inmate standing ahead in the queue asked him. Niranjan was in uniform so no one could make out who he was or what he did for living. Apparent equality of the economic status was the first benefit that Niranjan could feel as the inmate in the jail.

"No" Niranjan answered.

"That's what I am saying the boys of your age come here for molestation. But you speak less that says you have come here for some serious crime" the inmate gave full reading on Niranjan.

"Did you rape some girl?" the inmate asked looking at the other inmate standing just behind Niranjan in the queue.

Niranjan again didn't reply.

"No rape!" said the inmate who had just come to stand behind Niranjan slapped in his face. "There is no place for a rapist in this jail" he supported the first inmate immediately. He heard 'rape' in the talk and concluded that Niranjan had been booked for rape.

"What is the matter?" A police staff came to the queue when heard slapping and spate of the inmate in the queue for lunch.

"Nothing sir! We were just telling him that there is no place for a rapist in this jail" the inmate standing just behind Niranjan who slapped him answered to the police staff of the prison.

"Do you want to know what he has done?" the staff asked the inmate behind Niranjan.

"Yes sir" the inmate wondered.

"Murder!" the policeman said.

"Oh!" the prison inmates around Niranjan in the queue said at once. They created space for Niranjan to stand in the queue comfortably.

"All of you cannot even think whom he has murdered" the staff said.

"May be some girl? At this age boys have boiling blood for everything and libido decontrolled" a middle aged prison inmate joined the queue interrupted the talks as if he got the context of ongoing discussion.

"By physique he looked like pick pocket" other inmate guessed looking at Niranjan.

"By appearance he looks like a poor man, so, may be, he was traveling without ticket. He didn't have money to pay the penalty" said another inmate who didn't hear about the murder. He gave x-raying gaze at Niranjan from head to toe to reach that conclusion.

"Like our archers from his state a policeman have sent to the jail for shelter. The helpless policeman was unable to give them shelter at his rented small room. So, best solution he thought for them to commit such crime that ensured that they were in this jail" said an inmate standing much ahead in the queue. "They were lucky they were under trial for a long time. They learnt music and painting along with participating in archery events" he added to complete.

"No, it is not that, you are comparing it with some exceptional case where the archers were really sincere to their archery. They couldn't attend the competition event in north east even after mortgaging their paternal land in their village" another inmate in the queue presented another perspective.

"We are diverting from the topic" still another inmate standing at the end of the queue commented.

The policeman enjoyed the gravity of the discussion and concern of the people involved. "I didn't get what did you say?" the police staff said.

"Sir! You may know better than us that the head constable in your department couldn't arrange shelter for archers from his state who came to earn money to repay the debt taken for their flights" the same inmate informed the police staff of the prison. "The policeman couldn't make them stay longer in Delhi even in a rented place as they didn't have money to pay the rent" he added.

"Then what he did is very pathetic. He booked them under theft in his own house to get them sentence for one year" the staff on the prison answered further. "They used to teach archery to other inmates. They themselves learnt music and painting during their stay" he further added with grim face. He was not happy that he had to share the story of other person's helplessness. But what to do then?. There was nothing for him to be sad.

"Sir! You know everything! You may know him" the first inmate said.

"Any other idea?" the staff asked all the inmates after managing his grimace. He asked them in entertaining spirit.

"Sir *ab bata bhi dijiye*" said the inmate standing just ahead of Niranjan.

"He has killed a policeman!" the policeman shared as if he created surprise to the inmates in the queue. That brought pin drop silence among the inmates in the queue.

"How dare you?" the inmate standing just behind Niranjan in the queue again slapped in Niranjan's head. Perhaps he did so to please the staff.

"Why are you showing this much fury now" the policeman scolded the inmate who slapped Niranjan. "Why didn't you slap the witness who could have proven you innocent?" the policeman pressed the paining nerve of that inmate.

The inmate standing behind Niranjan kept quiet. Inmates responsible for kitchen started serving lunch.

Silence prevailed in the queue. The inmates took their lunch one by one. Niranjan also took his lunch. He looked at the food. He took a piece of chapati in his hand. He looked at the other chapati in the plate. That reminde him the chapatis the puller ordered in the Bhutti's stall. His interruption in the matter with Chhavi Ram Sahab had landed him to be behind the bars with high wall.

One senior inmate came to Niranjan and whispered in his ears. He looked at the senior inmate and nodded. He was new to the place so he didn't dare to deny. One of the senior most inmates wanted to meet him. That was an honor for him.

"Where I have to come to meet him?" Niranjan asked the inmate. He finished his food fast to reach in his cell. The policeman also moved to the office as all the inmates had finished their lunch. He moved towards his cell. The senior inmate followed him.

"Don't you listen? I said our head wants to meet you" the senior inmate asked Niranjan.

Niranjan nodded. He didn't dare to speak.

Niranjan entered his cell and stared at the wall painting of the rope loop for hanging and came out of the cell to follow the senior inmate. The senior inmate moved to a verandah where Iron Gate was closing the cells. The Iron Gate had thick bars efficiently communicated scaring messages that not to dare an escape. The senior inmate entered another cell with big gate. Niranjan followed him.

"Welcome Niranjan! Welcome" the elder inmate greeted.

Niranjan couldn't dare to respond to his greetings.

"It is good! *Himmat wale ho. Kisi ki jaan lena aasaan kaam nahin. Jaan lene mein jaan chali jati hei*" he said as if he was appraising Niranjan's work. "Had you been with stigma of raping a girl we would have beaten you till death. This is a jail. It is an *ashram* for improving life. This is not your aunty's place or road where you can do anything you want. If you were charged with raping a girl we would have brought you close to your end" the elder inmate cited some rules of the jail that they set for every inmate to follow to a peaceful person-developing life where a criminal could grow his or her talent to the extent that he could get handsome package up to three lakh rupees annually in the placement annually arranged by the management of the prison.

"Boss, Niranjan had killed a policeman in a *dhaba*" inmate who went to call upon Niranjan spoke about Niranjan. He gave a careful look at Niranjan.

"*Maine pehle hi maan liya. Ye kaam ki cheej hei*" the elder inmate had accepted the value of being Niranjan. He kept his praising eyes fixed on Niranjan's face. "Have you been convicted?" the elder inmate asked.

Niranjan kept quiet as he didn't understand what elder asked about.

"Has the judge pronounced you a sentence?" he again asked Niranjan.

"No" Niranjan answered.

"That means you will keep going out to the court during your trial. Can you keep giving our messages to people from our lot to go on crimes like murder, loot, plunder, burglary, theft or that could ensure a guaranteed punishment for years in the jail" he talked on very serious note putting lot of emphasis on the mission. His face was glowing when he was imparting the training to Niranjan with powerful clarion call. "But whatever one does to come to the jail should not be a rapist, molestation, or even Eve-teasing for that matter" thus stated the elder inmate of the prison.

"Why?" Niranjan dared to ask the elder.

"Good. You have opened your mouth at last" the elder inmate appreciated Niranjan to break his silence.

Niranjan didn't dare to speak after the acknowledgement from the elder.

"You have asked 'why' so let me answer to your 'why' otherwise you won't disseminate my message to the people" the elder inmate showed his intense intentions on the role of the people of his lot in the mission. "My dear Niranjan people of our lot are getting rotten in the dust bin near dumping grounds of the big cities and around big industries" he added to Niranjan's knowledge. "Lakhs of people in this country have to eat rats to fill their stomach to meet both the ends to see the light of the next day" he continued. Grimace which took place of the glow on his face was capable enough to give an idea about the gravity of his message that he wanted to disseminate among his lot. He expected Niranjan to disseminate his message to the lot rotten in the waste hills and around the dumping heaps and to all those who had to meet both the ends in being smitten, smashed, and clashed with waste and fecal filth and rotten or dangerous chemicals every now and then.

Niranjan didn't ask any other question. He also didn't dare to interrupt what the elderly inmate spoke.

"Have you ever seen your slums in detail?" the elderly inmate asked Niranjan.

Niranjan kept quiet. The elderly inmate looked at the person who brought Niranjan on his command.

"Don't get afraid, sir is very gentleman and a literate person" the senior inmate said. "Have you seen details of your jhuggi in the landfill area? Don't worry. Sir knows everything about you" he added.

"Yes" Niranjan answered.

"What is there inside the slum? What is there outside the slum?" the elderly inmate asked further.

"Few clothes, few utensils, one broken box inside the slum" Niranjan replied. Niranjan's eyes dare to meet with the elder inmate's.

Niranjan kept quiet. That moved the elder inmate in anger. The elder inmate looked at Niranjan with his eyes broadened to their maximum as if the eyes themselves would finish Niranjan.

"*Sahab*, outside it is dumping ground for the wastes from the lakhs and lakhs of the people of the cities and it includes molasses, fecal heaps, drainage dirt, lots and lots of plastic wastage, wastage of rotten vegetables, wastage of rotten flesh from butcher's house, and mountains of wastes of all kinds" Niranjan had to collect all his courage to reply to the anger of the elder inmate. He quickly counted on the things as if he was a waiter like Chhotu who counted menu items in a Bhutti's stall.

"Most of the waste hills in big or small cities are to house the fecal wastes that get generated around by every sewage system. They are to house fecal waste from the facility gutters of unorganized unstructured colonies where newly rich generate lots and lots of semi-solid fecal waste as they don't have proper water supply which could have diluted that to have less dangerous impact on our skin and health" he said interrupting Niranjan. "Can I conclude like that what you had seen outside area" he immediately reinforced Niranjan's observation.

"What is here?" the elderly inmate of the prison asked Niranjan commanding the discussion in convincing way.

"Big building, big rooms, big lawn, good food, good uniform, many good things which I cannot get in a jhuggi in the slum" Niranjan answered getting the gravity of talk by the elder inmate of the prison. Beauty of the prison became clear to Niranjan then. That brought a spark in his eyes. His face lit up. His skin started glowing in the day light of the sun casting its spell through a high window on the wall.

"My dear, you are still missing to count on something very important" the elder said looking into Niranjan's eyes with sparkle of the goodness of life at that time. Perhaps he was more than happy with that much.

"I don't have any idea of what I am missing to count on" Niranjan said still having the same shine in his eyes.

"Many of the inmates got placed in good companies for last few years" the inmate who accompanied Niranjan to reach the elder reminded what Niranjan missed out. "Last year forty five inmates were placed in different companies. Furniture that the inmate make here is having turnover of tens of crores and always remains in short supply to ever increasing demand for prison inmates' made furniture" he added to

Niranjan's knowledge on institutional significance of the jail. Also that Niranjan was luckily being sent in.

"Other inmates who are not placed also can work like artisans, like artists, like painters, like weavers, like . . ." the elder inmate further educated Niranjan on all the virtues of the prison which was weighing against worst situations outside for his rotten lot.

Niranjan couldn't say anything but nodded. He was mesmerized under the magical influence of the elder inmate of the jail.

"What else you are missing to count on?" the elder inmate again asked.

"No idea" Niranjan surrendered. He looked at the elder inmate and the one who accompanied him to the cell.

"Get an idea from the boss" said the senior inmate who accompanied Niranjan to the cell.

Niranjan didn't break his silence.

"Security!" the elder inmate spoke to wake up Niranjan who was in deep slumber.

Niranjan got puzzled at that time. Security was never his concern rather he didn't know what security was from the conceptual perspective. But when got the concept then it brought great enthusiasm to bring another sparkle in his eyes.

"Can someone kill you on the road out there?" the elder inmate of the prison asked Niranjan to answer.

"Yes, anyone can" Niranjan replied.

"Can someone kill you in this fortified high walled city with big building and rooms?" the elderly inmate of the prison asked Niranjan insisting an answer.

Niranjan kept quiet for while. "No" he replied then.

"Exactly, no one kills you here, neither like vehicle on the road, nor like sickle in the field, nor like fire of the blast furnace, nor like bare wire near transformer to light up the riches' life" he educated Niranjan on the unique feature of the prisons, 'security' the jail provided to the inmates. "If someone kills you here then you become big news. You are martyrs for some and victim for others to be in the headlines of the big newspapers" he completed his education on prison, its significance to improve life of the rotten lot.

Niranjan got intiated into the education on the virtues of the prison to the level of his satisfaction. The 'security' of the jail he never dreamt of himself and people like him. He bent down to touch the feet of the elder inmate of the prison to show respect for him. He got blessed by the elder inmate. Niranjan moved towards his cell. Leaving both the inmates discussing out solution to the problems before the inmates. He entered the cell and looked at every detail of the painting on the wall of the cell showing the loop of the rope hanging with the ventilator of the cell. That time it did not scare him. Not a lot. Not the less. Not the least. Not at all. Not at all . . .

At eight O' clock in the morning Inder heard the knock at the gate of Jain's House. He guessed it could be Jhihari but he didn't have the key of the lock at the gate. He heard the knock again. Bhumi came out to open the gate. Inder chose to be in the room. He wanted to avoid facing Bhumi as he might not be able to hide the impact left on him by Niranjan's killing of a cop.

"Jhihari? You?" Bhumi expressed her surprise. She didn't expect him to come at that time.

"Some urgency" Jhihari replied. He looked at the door of the outer room.

"What happened?" Bhumi asked. She looked at Jhihari from head to toe. Jhihari looked contrite.

"*Baad mein*" Jhihari wanted to avoid telling her about the urgency.

"Inder also was out of the office and house yesterday" Bhumi expressed that she knew about misfortunes that Jhihari was not willing to talk about.

"I have to wake up Inder" Jhihari stepped towards Inder's room. Bhumi went inside the house.

"Inder, O Inder" Jhihari called.

"What happened?" Inder opened the door of the room.

"Yesterday late night some leader type people came searching you in the landfill area" Jhihari said.

"Leader type? *Samjha nahin*" Inder looked up at Jhihari's face.

"*Main bhi nahin samajh paya*" Jhihari replied. He shared his confusion about the topic, man, and his intentions.

"Today one of them came in the morning. He has come with me to meet you" Jhihari informed Inder.

"Where is he?" Inder asked.

"He is standing outside" Jhihari looked at the order of the things inside the room. He picked up the bed spread and sheets on the folding bed to fold them properly. Jhihari ordered the table chair in the room.

"Let him come here" Inder moved out of the room to receive him. Jhihari also came out to follow Inder. He ran to overtake Inder as he had to introduce the leader type person to Inder.

"*Sahab, ye Inder hei*" Jhihari introduced Inder to a white clad man who was waiting outside Jain's House.

"Inder! *Sahab ko tumse kuchh baat karni hei*" said Jhihari turning to the leader type person.

"Are you same Inder who had attended the PHO conference on health and wellbeing combined with Green Environment's?" the white clad man asked Inder. His index pointed at Inder's chest.

Inder nodded.

"Great! *Shabbaas*" he said. He touched Inder's shoulder. He patted Inder's back to demonstrate his appreciation.

"Thank you sir" Inder acknowledged his appreciation.

"We are an organization working for people like you" he took out his visiting card from the pocket. "I am Managing Director of 'Eco Fighter', the organization winning the battles of the war that it had waged to improve lives of all the people of the planet including people like you" he said. He raised his collars to feel proud with what his organization worked for.

"Please come" Inder requested him to come to the room. They came to the room. Inder arranged the chair nicely to make him feel comfortable.

"Inder, you are living very luxurious life!" he exclaimed. "You don't seem to come from people of that background. How come, you happened to attend the conference?" he asked. He was surprised to see Inder had gone to the conference. He wanted to know the details how Inder had managed his journey.

"Sir, you are doing great job" Inder praised him. He offered him a glass of water.

"Inder, I don't feel thirsty my dear. Rather I am hungry for bringing people like you to the daylight" he spoke to Inder and kept the water glass aside on the corner of the table. "'Eco Fighter' has sent two participants in the conference each year. That you attended was the third one" he put forward his fives intending to stop Inder not to offer anything else.

"Sir, you are great! Your organization is also great!" Inder felt need to praise him.

"Which organization managed your visit to the conference" he looked here and there in the room. He could not find anything interesting or impressive. His gaze came back to Inder to continue the talks.

"Sir, it is not an organization it is one or two individuals" Inder answered honestly.

Shine on his beaming gleaming face got reduced. He managed that in next few seconds. Perhaps he expected some international organization which he also could approach for funds and visits.

"Who are they?" he asked after he managed the shock from an unanticipated reply.

"You are already doing great! I read many praises for 'Eco Fighter' and you personally" Inder wanted to change the topic.

"I want to fight on many fronts, if person like you can work for me then nothing like it. I can show you where we can take your living from present dismal pattern to the luxuries of the life available in the world" he offered. He proposed a dream to Inder.

"What kind of struggle? 'Eco Fighter' is already in advance stage of having a say in the public decision making over the issues of recycling, controlling the uncontrollable habitat and biosphere" Inder opened up with him. "Moreover, it is able to garner the funds from governmental sources from different ministries." he added to make the white clad domain expert to experience the impact on him after he attended the conference.

"Lot many things I am fighting for you" he attempted to win Inder's heart. He got another setback Inder knew a lot about 'Eco Fighter' and its role and say in government decision making and funding sources.

"What are those things that you are fighting through your 'Eco Fighter'?" Inder became curious.

"Lot many! My dear lot many. You will not understand that all in entirety" he claimed. "Massification of smart dust bins for every five houses in a posh colony, for every ten houses in an approved colony, and every twenty houses in a recognized colony, every hundred houses in an unauthorized colony so that those people also taste good life" he quipped.

"What about the slums?" Inder asked him.

"One highly revolutionary idea in the area of education to be implemented if I succeed in winning the bureaucracy for its implementation in primary education" he bragged of his new ambitious plan for people like Inder. He didn't answer directly to Inder's question on what he was doing for the slums.

"What's that?" Inder's curiosity went on new height. He held his face in both of his hands. Jhihari was so cooperative to provide pin drop silence in the room.

"We are fighting for waste collector to be included in the chapter on occupations under our primary education" he again bragged.

"I didn't get you?" Inder shook his head.

"May be, it's not easy to understand. Let me make it simple for you" he started explaining the new revolutionary idea. "You must have seen in the environmental studies books for children" he looked at Jhihari's face. He turned to Inder as no quick response or appreciative reaction came from Jhihari.

"You must have seen a chapter in environmental studies books for children in their schools" he reminded Inder about his childhood days.

Inder kept quiet. He did not have books on his own during childhood.

"That chapter on 'Persons who help us' includes driver, carpainter, plumber, postman, watchman, gardener, etc. at present" he wanted to give a glimpse of his education plan to Inder. "Waste picker or rag picker will also be part of the chapter as 'waste collector' under the chapter 'Person who help us' in the books of the children" he added to his brags.

"What way will it benefit people like us?" Inder had a question.

"At last but not the least it will help people like you who are living under the scourge of hate and scornful behavior from all the quarters. For that much I am sure" he wanted to assure Inder. "The children studying with those books will accept you as part of the society when they are grown up as responsible citizen of tomorrow's India" he added his social vision on future equality to his brags.

"What I need to do for that?" Inder asked.

"You just join 'Eco Fighter'. Get aligned with the organization's ideology to live with, this is what is demanded from the members of the organization" he commanded Inder to join. "I got to see you during Niranjan's trial in the court. You are closely related to Niranjan who killed the policeman in Bhutti's stall." he disclosed the source of his knowledge about Jhihari and Inder.

"What will I get for my involvement in this?" Inder asked.

"Your whole society will get benefited, not only you" he assured.

"Can I carry my current job?" Inder enquired.

"In that case you may have to spare few hours in the evening" he came with a new possibility. "But that may not get you any remuneration. In that case we have to keep you as volunteer" he clarified.

"Let me have some time to think over it whether I would be joining your organization as volunteer or full-timer" Inder replied.

"You have my card. Please come. Anytime, you're welcome" he left the chair to move out of the room. Inder and Jhihari accompanied him to the gate of the house. He moved fast when he came out of the gate of the Jain's House.

"What was this person explaining? He claimed a lot of betterment to our lot. I could not understand many things when he was explaining" Jhihari shared his confusion.

"It is better that you didn't understand. I have read news regarding his organization. What they do is they catch someone from our lot to show as if they are fighting for our cause to improve our life. Actually they improve that individual's life. Thus, may be few members from our lot might have bettered their lives. This helps them raising funds here and abroad. Of course there is substance in the work by such organizations. The society moves ahead as those individuals got bettered their life and living conditions" Inder explained to Jhihari what probably was behind the tall claims of the organization and his brags. "The greatest difficulty with people from such organizations is that they want to fight for us but not to make us fight for ourselves" he shared his observation.

"That means people will look upon us also with respect as the leader was claiming?" Jhihari expected miraculous happening for his rotten lot that it will not further rot.

"I am not sure about that. We are plenty in number so no one wants to plan any jobs of this kind. Every rich person is a job provider for us. In Mumbai we are the largest slum of the world. Has any one cared for us? I think, it is not that encouraging" Inder educated Jhihari on the unsociological paradigms of sociology. Rather he explained on sociology for nonsocial.

Jhihari nodded.

"Do you know why? Why people don't care for us" Inder wanted to wake up Jhihari.

"No idea" Jhihari said.

"Just because we are plenty. We are plenty with no choices to exercise in life but only to fill our stomach and as if we come to make the rich to improve on their luxuries and way to achieve them" Inder showed the plight of being plenty.

"But people generally come and ask for vote when some elections are there" Jhihari said. He knuckled his fingers.

"They come where they guess that we have votes. The moment they come to know that most of us don't have votes or voter Ids, they don't care. Yes you might have seen few grass root workers in arranging voter ids for few of us if possible" Inder talked on politics driven administration in the slums. He shook his head in disappointment. "That too is rare as most of such people are busy in colonies to update the voter lists. Our's lot is not a community in their eyes so no one will come even for the sake of democracy. Many of us are nomads or homeless so we cannot help anyone getting weight on the ballot" he further educated Jhihari.

"That means nothing better can happen to us" Jhihari lamented.

"Being plenty is our problem" Inder gave his own logic.

"How come being plenty and no one cares for you" Jhihari wanted to solve the puzzle for himself. His self on that matter was changing state from dormant to vigil one.

"You must have seen a tiger on the poster mentioning a number. That number of one thousand four hundred and eleven had worked as magic. Everywhere tigers are being protected and new jungles were being grown for them" Inder gave an example on how the magic of few had worked successfully. "Why? I think just because they are only one thousand four hundred and eleven in the entire country when the 'project tiger' highlighted it on the hoardings in mass communication for awareness and care. And the number got improved to the order of one thousand eight hundred" Inder elucidated. He looked at Jhihari with hope by that example he would definitely get the idea. "So if we improve our lot then many of us won't be considered what we are seen as today" he further continued. "Otherwise there is no end to our miseries and miserabilities" he opened up his thesis on his lot.

"One thing I forgot to ask you. Did you go to madam Chandrika for some job in Uttar Daani?" Inder asked Jhihari as if something was missing in the debate.

Jhihari shook his head.

"Then you please go today, let's see what she does in the light of the news that a policeman got killed by a waste picker" Inder suggested Jhihari. "Sorry, not waste picker, waste collector if they look upon us like 'Eco Fighter'. Or was it to look down by making waste collector as permanent" Inder apprehended the impact of Niranjan's case on Jhihari's fortune in Uttar Daani.

"What a paradox of rich suppression of the poor's loss and rich expression of the poor's job. The poor's job of killing the cop. Ranchit's death in a car ramming on the road went unnoticed went as the rich committed the crime and suppressed the news. Niranjan's role in killing the cop got a good space in the newspapers." Inder thought. He thought a lot.

"We need to go to meet Niranjan also" Inder puzzled himself on what was to be done.

"Tomorrow is trial date for Niranjan's case. We can meet him in court itself." Jhihari said. He removed his hand from Inder's shoulder.

"Then you meet Chandrika madam today and make sure you are there in Uttar Daani's staff in coming days as she promised" Inder asked Jhihari in demanding tone. He could observe that demanding like capability was developed within him. "Was that the trait of leadership?" he was not sure.

"Inder, your confidence has gone up. You are talking like an educated successful man who gets things done with confidence and also by other people" Jhihari evaluated Inder on leadership of the society.

"I am also noting that my tone has changed. Is this an infection from that leader's presence in this room?" Inder agreed with Jhihari.

"I need to go to work" Inder rose from the folding bed to move into the washroom. Jhihari kept waiting for Inder to get ready for the work.

"You also can take bath here itself. Put on my clothes to go to Chandrika madam." Inder asked Jhihari to make it a quick. Jhihari got into the bathroom and came out immediately.

"What happened?" Inder worried.

"In such a clean bathroom I take bath then it will not remain clean. I am feeling one smell in the bathroom" Jhihari appreciated and complained simultaneously.

"You just take bath with care that you are not slipped on the floor" Inder warned Jhihari. "The smell is nothing in comparison of what you have during defecating in an open area where you pollute the environment for others also. Flush it out if you feel if that smell is too much" Inder prescribed Jhihari on toiletries.

"Ok Inder *Sahab*" Jhihari smiled. He got amused with training from Inder. He again went into the bathroom and closed it. After half an hour he came out, bathed with combed hair. Now they both were ready for their work. They came out to latch the door and heard the knock at the gate.

"*Chacha*! How come you are here?" Inder came fast to open the gate but only to get surprised. He found one far relation of Niranjan knocked the gate.

"Let's sit in the room as *chacha* has come here first time" Inder wanted to turn to the room.

"No Inder, at the corner we will have our food in the stall" *chacha* said. "We will talk there. May be Jain *Sahab* would not scold you for being late but he may think that you are taking liberty of the situation" Jhihari suggested Inder to keep moving ahead.

"What do you say *chacha*? Shall we have something in the food stall at the corner" Inder asked *chacha*.

"We will talk at the stall" *chacha* replied. They all moved to the food stall. Jhihari ordered food for two and tea for three.

"What happened *chacha*? *Yahan kaise*?" Jhihari asked *chacha* about the purpose to be at Inder's place of stay.

"Yesterday I went to meet Niranjan in the Jail" *chacha* updated Inder and Jhihari.

"You! You went to the jail, to meet Niranjan!" surprised Jhihari asked. Inder was equally surprised. *Chacha* didn't like Niranjan because of Niranjan's irresponsible conduct before Ranchit's death.

"Yes, Niranjan has gone mad" *chacha* concluded.

"Why? What happened?" Inder asked.

"He talks about some '*Jail Raho Aandolan*' where each one of us must commit some crime with gravity to ensure imprisonment for himself or herself" *chacha* updated.

"What? *Jail Raho Aandolan*? Has he gone mad?" Inder asked.

"That's what I have said that he has gone mad" *chacha* recreated.

"He said he met with a big man from our lot in the jail. That big man was talking like that. And Niranjan says that big man is right" *chacha* became red in fury.

"What else he told you?" Inder enquired.

"Niranjan told me that we should live in the jails because the jails are better place for us. He has accepted the big man in the jail as his 'guru'. That big man is guiding him to take more people from our lot to the jail so that they can live healthy and peaceful life in the protected cell of well-constructed jails in the country. He has gone mad" *chacha* said all that in single breathe. He looked at the stove on which the stall keeper was preparing tea for them.

"You just listened to Niranjan or you attempted to convince him that what he thinks is not right" Inder asked.

"I said that" *chacha* said. He asked the Chhotu of the stall to bring a glass of water.

"What Niranjan said on this?" Inder and Jhihari asked simultaneously.

"Inder, what he said is also not wrong but we cannot do what he wants us to do" *chacha* lamented.

"What he says that also is not wrong? What is that?" Inder enquired from *chacha*.

"He says that places where we live in the cities are worse than the jails and in that sense they are also like jail. So the Jails are to be made dwelling place for our lot" *chacha* replied.

"Worse than the jail! I did not get anything" Jhihari told.

"That is what I also said when he kept telling that all time. Then he said look at our places in the cities they are surrounded by low and high rise building to make boundaries of big and open jails where we live among these people defecate in open where even rich people living in big house or flats are also exposed to the excreta we created in the pockets of negligence and dirt. Those are also jail only" *chacha* gasped in telling the story. "He further said that's why we can go out of this loop because we have to earn our livelihood by sorting out the waste they create. We tolerate every kind of insults and reproach at the hands of the residents of the colonies which we keep clean for them" *chacha* kept telling to enlighten Inder.

"Then what?" Inder asked.

"He said, in the jails particularly in Delhi, people don't call them jail. They call them '*aashram*' a place for *sanyasis*, a place of old education system where disciple used to get a job in some *darbar* of a king after completing their education in an '*aashram*'. Similarly here in the jail, Niranjan said, prisoners who are learning some artistic work earn a good amount which we can't think of earning with that respect in these places filled with dirt, filth and fecal stuff" *chacha* again recreated what Niranjan told, as if he got convinced with Niranjan in explaining the concept to Inder. Perhaps he himself was not willing to act as Niranjan but wished for the young ones of the lot to follow Niranjan. "Many of well-behaved prisoners have got their placement in the good companies with good salaries of one to two lakhs for a year. Here we can't think of the salary for few months continuously where they get like rich people get salary package for year" he gave idea of what Niranjan shared with him and predicted that if the members of our lot who were capable of committing some serious crime to ensure rigorous punishment for a good length of time to live in the jail. One can also learn some great art to improve.

"Inder, Niranjan, in twelve days, knows about many persons who have got the placements this year" *chacha* updated Inder and Jhihari.

"He is quite right when he talks like that" Jhihari opened his eyes wide after listening thoughtful descriptions from *chacha*. Jhihari got Niranjan's stand. He also got convinced with the idea of committing serious crime to flourish with *'Jail Raho Aandolan.'*

"It is not like that Jhihari. Look at me! Education has improved my life" Inder countered Jhihari who got convinced with what Niranjan told about. He grinded his teeth to express his anger.

"Inder, how many are educated in our lot? And in what way the education has improved your life? You are at the mercy of your Jain *Sahab*" *chacha* said. He looked at the pieces of chapati that Inder and Jhihari started eating after they were served by Chhotu of the food stall.

Inder kept quiet. He never thought from that perspective.

"But whoever is not educated is qualified to do some act that can ensure imprisonment for months if not years." *chacha* said. "When you come out of the jail then again you commit the crime to ensure your continuous stay in the jail" *chacha* was ready to convince the people of his lot. "So one can improve his life by living in the jails. That's why he calls it *'Jail Raho Aandolan'*" he added.

"Then why are you telling us that Niranjan has gone mad? Rather Niranjan has got enlightened in the jail" said Jhihari. He looked at the face of Inder who gulped water from his glass to avoid coughing.

"There is one problem" *chacha* said.

"What is that?" Inder asked.

"Most of us do such petty crimes where policemen catch us, beat us, and throw us out of police stations with broken ribs and limbs but they don't send us to the jails. Niranjan is charged with murder so he has been sent to the jail. So, the jail cannot be a possibility for each one of us" *chacha* concluded. He looked at Inder and Jhihari with the hope to continue the *Jail Raho Aandolan.*

"There you are! That's what I am saying" Inder reclaimed his right to the right way of education to better the life and living conditions.

"Why do small crimes I can also kill someone to get a sentence in jail" Jhihari came with new enlightenment. "In which types of crimes I can get imprisonment for years?" he immediately enquired with *chacha* who came enlightened after meeting with Niranjan.

"Why?" Inder swatted on the back of Jhihari's head.

"Is this the only way to improve life?" Inder asked Jhihari. "I don't think so" he answered before Jhihari could reply. In that discussion they finished his food. They came out of the stall. *Chacha's* enlightenment after meeting with Niranjan had been passed to Jhihari. Jhihari was ready to take some action to fulfill the mission on *'Jail Raho Aandolan.'* Jhihari thought Inder had improved his conditions by education. It is his time to improve his life by following the path shown by Niranjan. That was *'Jail Raho Aandolan.'*

Bhumi was restless in the verandah waiting for Inder to come from the scrap factory. She was roaming in verandah to pretend as if she was on evening walk. Otherwise also it was true she could not come out in the evening as eve-teasing was on the rise in the street. Her mother was also not spared by libido ridden liquor licking lips of the young or old men out in the streets.

"I was waiting for you" she opened the gate hearing Inder's steps on the road. Inder looked at her face and came inside the house to enter the room.

"I wanted to talk to you Inder" Bhumi followed Inder in the room.

"What happened? Where is your mom?" Inder wanted to know.

"*Maa* has been fighting with father since he came to know Niranjan killed the cop. Today the fight has gone to the peak" Bhumi disclosed what was going on in her family. "Father has taken her to the *Muni* in the temple" she added.

"Fighting with father! You didn't tell me" Inder asked. That triggered him to worry.

"She is pressurizing father to make you leave this house" Bhumi informed.

"Oh" shocked Inder couldn't say anything else.

"She has created panic, and asked my father to make you shift to some other place" Bhumi said. "Even if he keeps you engaged with the scrap work" she added another big shock to Inder's disappointment. Now it was clear from her updates that Inder might lose his job with Ishwar Jain.

"What happened exactly?" Inder enquired. He wanted to know what could be the reason to throw him out of the house.

"Mother in the morning asked father that nowadays you cannot believe someone like Inder who is a stranger for us. He should not be allowed to stay in our house. She is triggered by the news and reports of the crimes on the girls and the rapes going rampant in the capital. She wanted me to be safe at least if she can't make every girl safe in Delhi, the Delhi" Bhumi unleashed her energy to update Inder on what was going on since morning. Her eyes got wet as she didn't want to lose Inder and not even to lose his job with her father. She was not ready to lose him from her house also. If everything didn't work then her father would not be able to manage Inder's stay in the house.

"What happened in this matter then?" Inder got worried. He found prediction by *chacha* came to be true to him. He really found himself on Ishwar Jain's mercy. Not Ishwar Jain's mercy. Mrs. Ishwar Jain's rather. Not even Mrs. Ishwar Jain's even. It was Mahima Jain's. Might be woman in her identity shaped and brought under the fears of her own society and preconceived notions against the destitute of the society. Her attitude got shaped to de-shape Inder's destiny. The destiny of the destitute.

"My father says you have been with us for last five years for the job. So you are not a stranger. Safety is a concern but you should not be doubted too much" Bhumi familiarized him with her father's view point also. She looked worried for Inder as if she wanted to take promise to be true on father's assumption if her father could convince her mother to let Inder continue.

Inder didn't tell anything. He could see how *chacha's* prediction was going to be true if he was to lose the job and the house. Jhihari might choose to follow the path shown by Niranjan.

"Where are they now?" Inder asked. His worries were on the rise.

"I told you that they have gone to the temple" Bhumi re-informed Inder who might have forgotten because that triggered lot of worries for him. "My father has taken her to the *Muni* for counseling. My father says shifting you is a costly affair. He wanted you to be in this house. Like him I also don't have any doubts on your intentions for my family. But you have to be true to my father's expectation. So that, my father is right" she described things from her perspective.

"Your father or you being 'right' or 'wrong' that doesn't matter much. What matters is the peace in the house" Inder replied. His worries brought wrinkles on his forehead. He held his forehead in both of his hands.

"Inder, do one thing, you write to Mr. Hwaib about every detail that is going with you. Please" she pleaded Inder to communicate to Hwaib on his green assignments if that all could be continued in the hour of turmoil in his life. In her life too.

Inder didn't say anything. He seemed to agree with Bhumi.

"Convince him for some job or other opportunity like your green assignments. Under my mother's pressure, father may ask you leave this place as well as the job. Though that may be the worst case" Bhumi cried. Her cries carried warning for him to continue his stay in the room.

"Taking cue from reporting of the rapes on the channels your mother is concluding everything. This is highly disappointing. At least for me" Inder said.

"That's what my father said" Bhumi said.

"You please write down to Mr. Hwaib to make some arrangements for you" Bhumi suggested.

"Don't be so childish Bhumi, Mr. Hwaib is not my employer or he is not anyway responsible for my well being or security. He wanted me to be part of his green assignments and reporting. That's all" Inder wanted to show her what his reality was in the context of survey project.

"I don't think so" Bhumi assured. "When Ms. Veronique and he had shown some interest in your work they must be interested in making you perform. They may think that work would improve upon your career and life" she added to show new hope for Inder.

"That's fine but they cannot go beyond their constraints of being foreigners" Inder negated Bhumi's assurance.

"Why can't they, I have heard about many of the rich people serving in lucrative jobs to get assignments with the international organizations like Hwaib's. Why can't you get a job of your level in that kind of organizations?" Bhumi's optimism though at another extreme wanted to see the same in Inder's eyes.

"It doesn't work that way Bhumi" Inder declined to develop that level of optimism. He found Bhumi's optimism would not be a reality for him.

"Why it cannot be like that when many of the graduates from the rich families get scholarship on recommendation of their superiors or professors here or abroad. These rich people are from such families that they themselves could afford to have their kids study abroad even if they don't get scholarships. But they fight for it and they get it" Bhumi argued. "You fight to get that for yourself and get that for your lot if possible" she added to her fight to get what she wanted from Inder.

"In that all, the richness of the background is required to make sure they are not the burden on their nation" Inder put his logic.

"But few of them become burden on theirs" Bhumi dared to beat Inder.

Inder grinded his teeth. He didn't want to react to disappoint Bhumi.

"Or you can make a point for help from Mr. Hwaib to arrange something like joining the campaign on green environment and awareness education" Inder wanted to say something but she stopped him. She reminded herself about a new hope regarding ongoing recycling campaign on effective management of recyclable items collected from the waste.

"Are you talking about world wide known environmentalist who had been on both the poles of the planet in the past and his recent campaign in India on recycling methodologies to keep the environment healthy?" Inder asked.

"Exactly" she confirmed.

"Now you have experience of one international conference and domain experience. You can request for that. Nothing wrong in that" she showed another ray of hope. "I believe you can be utilized for educating people on recycling of the items and how management of recycled items of the waste that is generated in the process of development. I want to see you like that" she said. She wanted to utilize her own expertise gained so far, to convince Inder to see his future beyond the scraps lying in her father's settlement. So that, he can really improve upon his life and career beyond what he got as destiny since he was brought up in the landfill area. The destiny of the destitute.

"I think you should go inside as your parents may be back anytime. Your mother may get concerned about you" Inder opined.

Bhumi's burning eyes stared at Inder's. She didn't say anything and went inside. Her sandals struck on the ground with sound at every step she took. Inder came into the room to act on Bhumi's suggestions. He sent Bhumi back inside the house as he was scared that even if her mother came convinced to let him stay in the house might revert back if Mahima would happen to see Bhumi with him. That too in her parents' absence. Then all effort put forth by his father and the *Muni* together would go waste. That also he couldn't afford. Bhumi might not think that way. At the same time he recalled what *chacha* said in the morning. *Chacha* was saying that he was living here in Jain's house out of their mercy.

He switched on the computer. By the time, the computer started he collected his writing pad, papers, and diary. He inserted the data card that Bhumi gave him for the internet connection.

He opened up his email account after the computer got connected to the Internet through the data card. He wanted to compose a communication to Mr. Hwaib. Before he sent email he wanted to write it properly so he closed his email account to write in the word document.

> Dear Mr. Hwaib,
> Greetings!
>
> You must have a received a communication from Bhumika Jain about what I am undergoing these days. My elder brother, a father figure to me, here in this city where I did not have anyone else, had died in a car accident on the road. Now brother Jhihari, one of the great aides of mine, and earning hand in the family I am indebted to is also dealing with the loss. The worst thing has happened is that his cousin has been charged with some serious crime which earned him to be in the police custody and then in the jail. Rest of things, in my life, are going as usual as they were. Now I understand why companies or people like you choose a person who must be free from unnecessary burden of life so that he or she can perform. This is the reason people from the destitute remain the destitute till they are burdened with life or throughout their life.
>
> I am not able to get some breathing space and time even as being amongst the situations what many a times are called

circumstances in any language with rich vocabulary. I am realizing, rather, living through many of such things. I am not sure whether I would be able to contribute to the survey project or not. In future I may be. At present I am having tough time. I don't want to disappoint you regarding the project. I believe Kul Vilas and his team must have taken up the project to the next stage by this time. I wish all the success for him, all of you, and the project if I am not a part of it. I am commited to the the project to make it a grand success if I am part of it. I pledge for the environment, health, and wellbeing through healthy practices of recycling and waste management.

Yours sincerely,

Inder Jeet.

Landfill Area, Ghazipur,

India.

After completing the communication Inder opened his email account to compose a letter to Mr. Hwaib. He copied the text from the word document and pasted in the text portion in text window created by reply link of the mail from Mr. Hwaib. He read it once before clicking the 'send' button on the screen.

Acknowledgements

To my brothers Govind Singh, and Shiv Prakash and sisters Nirmala, and Meena who provide me the space that my parents Sh. Garib Das and Smt. Kalavati who created before they abode above which is shaping who I am today. To my elder brother late Om Prakash and sister Vimla who deserve mention as they had provided me the space of responsibilities during my childhood to share with my parents.

To Krishna, my wife, daughter Mohini, and son Prashant have inspired me to take up this book. They have taken away a lot of my pain and responsibilities of daily routine to enable me to take up and complete this work that deserves to be in your hands. Prashant being eight was more concerned about the book to be seen in your hands and managed many of the tasks on his own for which he needed me most. In a sense he had sacrificed a lot in the process of writing this work of fiction.

To my friends Nikhil, Vishwajeet, Saurabh, Vikas and Anubha who have provided proof reading for the entire book along with their editing skills as gift to this work. Nikhil has been a sincere companion since he came to know that I have taken up this work. Throughout the publishing process, Vishwajeet, being a friend, has been in many shoes including content editing to make this possible to be in your hands. Saurabh pointed out rare mistakes which I could not notice. Mohini provided another level of refinement when she gone through the book.

To the cool of pool where Avinash, Praveen, Jai, Raja, Rajesh, Pankaj, and Arvind have provided the wonderful mobile space congenial to reading and writing passion. This space enabled me continue writing work just after reaching home after commuting for longer than an hour. Pankaj and Raja have been of great help in information gathering.

To my friends, Manish, Pramod, Tanay, Ajay, Rahul, and Vishwajeet were always there to keep me high to see this work in hands for kind and keen reading.

To Murari, my special friend, being with whom many triggers and contexts became available to me to develop in the work. Such a powerful company he is.

To Sanjay who has assisted me in realization of preliminary version of cover design which was provided as prototype for the AuthorHouse team who had designed the cover of the book.

To the team of Partridge India involved at different stages of the publishing process. Right from the beginning with Ben Roslind under whose persona the process was initiated to undergo the production with Ann Minoza and cover and interior designers. All have provided untiring support to realize the work deserving to be in your hands.

Some of the events worked out in this purely fiction work turned into partial or full reality during writing journey, finalization, and published and reached your hands. Few events which carried pure imagination where they were first written down but turned into partial or exact reality deserve to be mentioned. Few of these events like Inder's breakfast in Mahima's living room, like wall paintings hanging loop in the ventilator of the prison, and the initiative of cadaver organ donation taken by Uttar Daani which a leading daily started as movement to mobilize volunteer for organ donaton are few to count on. For that kind of premonition I acknowledge myself.

To you, for being with me so interestingly and committed to the cause that made me undergone the pain that inspired me to take up the work that you have read the book thoroughly.